1-800-Henchmen
The Complete Series

By Katherine C. Wielechowski

Cover art by SelfPubBookCovers.com/ Viergacht

Author photo by Geist Photography. Used with permission.

Edited by Jessi Miller

Table of Contents

Dedicated to my friends and family who have supported this insane idea of mine to be a writer. I don't know if you guys fully understood what you were getting yourselves into when I started, but I'm sure glad you decided to stick around! I would not have been able to do this without your support, advice, and inspiration.

Jessi, thank you for being my best friend. You have provided countless laughs, quotes, and experiences and my life wouldn't be the same without you.
Oh, and thanks for the editing expertise!

First Shot

Alfie looked up from the ad he had clipped out of the classifieds to the large, futuristic looking building in front of him in disbelief and back down to the ad. Its lettering was tiny, minuscule in fact, and left much to be desired. He couldn't help but wonder why it was such a cheap, obscure ad when the offices looked like they were in George Jetson's building.

"Ah hell, whatever. I need the job," he muttered and walked through the glass door into the sunlit entry way.

"Welcome to Resources, Inc.! How can I help you?" A cheerful, pretty blond receptionist greeted him from her place behind a stainless steel and glass counter. She was wearing a Bluetooth headset and was typing on her keyboard without looking at the monitor that was recessed into the desk.

"Uh, hi. I'm Alfie Vihar. I-"

"Yes, Mr. Vihar. Take the elevators to the fifty-third floor. Misha will meet you there." With a smile and not another word, the receptionist answered the phone with the same cheery tone as she had addressed Alfie.

He stared at her for a long second, unsure what to do. She jerked her head to the hallway behind her without looking at him and he leaned over so he could see the elevators around the corner. He nodded his thanks and walked around the desk toward the polished steel doors. One opened as he approached so he stepped inside and pressed the button for floor 53. The doors closed and opened mere seconds later. Alfie stared in surprise at the different floor and glanced up at the digital screen above the door to make sure he was where he was supposed to be.

1

"Mr. Vihar? I'm Misha." Another pretty blond in a pantsuit waited just outside of the elevator for him to disembark.

"Yeah, sorry." Alfie finally stepped onto the floor and looked around. There were rows of glass-walled cubicles filled with suited people working at their desks. He felt very underdressed in his khakis and polo as he followed Misha down the aisle between the glass cubicles and the floor-to-ceiling plate glass windows that illuminated the floor. He looked out the windows and could see half the city laid out below him and the ocean beyond.

"That's a pretty prime view. There are people who would pay a fortune for it."

"Oh, yes. It is quite lovely."

Alfie frowned at her back, confused. It was seriously the best view he had seen in the city and she acted like it was just a solid wall in a nice color.

"Mr. Kadish is waiting for you."

"Oh, sorry. Am I late?" Alfie silently cursed himself. He needed the job and didn't want to be counted out because he was late for the interview.

"No. You are early, actually. He is simply waiting for you."

"Oh." Alfie bit his tongue so he wouldn't say how weird that was.

"Here we are!" Misha announced cheerfully as she stopped in front of the door to the corner office. Alfie looked through the glass wall with trepidation. He could see a man with steel-gray hair sitting with his back to the door looking out the window. The man's glass-topped desk was empty except for a large flat-screen monitor that sat on the corner and a moving Newton's cradle front and center.

Misha knocked gently before pushing open the door. She motioned for Alfie to follow her in. "Mr. Kadish, Mr. Vihar is here for his interview." She said cheerfully.

The man suddenly swung his chair around. Alfie's jaw dropped. James Bond was sitting there with a welcoming smile on his face.

"Thank you, Misha. Mr. Vihar, would you like anything to drink while Misha's here?"

"What? Oh, no. Thank you." Alfie barely sputtered out. He cringed to himself. Nothing like making a good first impression. At least he had spoken in passable English. The last interview he had, he got nervous and started throwing random insults out in different languages. He obviously didn't get the job when the interviewer coldly told him that she spoke German and didn't appreciate being called a 'malformed trout biscuit'.

"All right. That will be all, Misha. Thank you." Mr. Kadish dismissed the woman and motioned to the empty chairs in front of his desk.

Alfie finally remembered his minimal interview skills and walked forward with his hand out. Mr. Kadish's smile broadened as he stood to shake Alfie's hand. "Welcome to Resources, Inc. Mr. Vihar," Kadish started as they both settled into their chairs. "I see on your resume that you are fluent in four languages? That's very impressive for somebody just about to graduate high school."

Alfie felt the blood rush to his face. "I know three languages but I am not fluent in any but English and German, sir. I am fairly adept at conversational French and have just started studying Chinese."

"Well." Kadish's smile dimmed slightly. "That is still impressive for an eighteen year old. What do you plan on studying in college?"

"I am planning on majoring in international business with a minor in human resources and foreign policy. That is why I applied here for a summer job. I thought I would learn a lot that would help me in the future." Alfie finished his canned response, hoping it came out naturally rather than rehearsed.

Kadish studied him for a long minute with an unreadable expression on his face. "No."

Alfie felt his heart plummet. "Excuse me, sir?"

Kadish smiled and rested his elbows on the arms of his chair with his fingers steepled in front of his mouth. "The business experience is not why you're here. Now give me the real reason."

Alfie struggled to swallow the panic before he decided to throw caution to the wind. He slouched back in his chair in defeat. "I just need a job that pays more than fifty bucks a week like my last one. I want to backpack around Europe for the next few years and need the funds."

"Okay."

"Uh, okay?"

"Yes. Okay." Kadish grinned at Alfie's stunned expression. "Tell me about yourself. The real you. Not the you who wants to major in international business."

Alfie sighed. He knew he already blew the interview, he figured he might as well be honest. "Mr. Kadish, I don't want to major in international business. In fact, that sounds like the second most boring major possible. I want to write, which isn't consistent1` enough work for my parents so they and I are at an impasse right now. I figured a few years traveling on my own might help us get over that. I have spent my entire life in this corner of California and San Luca is beginning to feel like a prison. I played football and lacrosse in high school and I wasn't half bad. I learned German because a foreign language was required. I learned French to impress a girl. I'm learning Chinese because it is used a lot in a T.V show that I like. I like shooting guns when I have the time, which scared off the girl I learned French for. My best friend is a girl who is nerdier and scarier with a gun than I am. And you look like James Bond which is freaking me out a bit."

Mr. Kadish leaned forward, a gleam in his eyes. Alfie felt his stomach drop.

"What do you write?"

"I dabble in most genres. Haven't really found my niche. I've-"

"Where in Europe?"

"All over, focusing on Central Europe and the Mediterranean."

"Get seasick?"

"Not that I know of."

"Why German?"

"Hot German foreign exchange student sophomore year."

"Sight of blood make you sick?"

"Not yet."

"What T.V. show?"

"Firefly."

"Siblings?"

"Two brothers and a sister."

"Parents?"

"Two of them."

"Favorite gun?"

"1911."

"She wasn't worth it."

"I know."

"Friend?"

"Almost sister."

"Shame."

Alfie shrugged, breaking the rapid-fire Q&A Kadish had just thrown at him.

"What's the first?"

Alfie frowned. "What?"

Kadish chuckled. "What's the most boring major possible?"

"Oh." Alfie laughed softly. "Anything involving math."

"I agree." Kadish stood up and came around his desk to lean against it right in front of Alfie. "Well, Mr. Vihar, I don't think you are quite right for the summer internship program" he began with a small smile. "But I think I have a better job for you. Show up at that address on Saturday at 10am." Kadish handed Alfie a business card that simply had the company name and an address printed on it. "Thank you for coming in and being refreshingly honest. Most people don't do that, even when I tell them to. They just say what they think I want to hear."

Alfie slowly go to his feet. "Are you seriously giving me a job?"

Kadish laughed. "Yes, and it pays a little more than 50 dollars a week. It won't be what you were expecting but I want you to give it a shot. Stay as long as you need to and then you can head to Europe."

"Thank you!" Alfie sputtered as he grasped Kadish's hand.

"You're welcome." Kadish motioned to someone behind Alfie. He turned to find Misha just opening the door to escort him out. "Oh, Mr. Vihar? Which Bond?"

"Uhh... does it matter?" Alfie stuttered.

"Well, I very much doubt I look like Daniel Craig. He's a little too blond." Kadish said with a chuckle.

Alfie laughed. "True. If I had to pick, I'd go with a cross between Sean Connery and Pierce Brosnan."

Kadish thought about it for a long second and nodded. "I'll take it." Kadish shook Alfie's hand one more time. "Don't forget, Saturday at 10."

"I won't. Thank you!"

"This way, Mr. Vihar." Misha guided Alfie out the door and back to the elevator. "Welcome to Resources, Inc., Mr. Vihar," she said with a smile as the doors closed.

******

If the main offices of Resources, Inc. were in George Jetson's building, the address Kadish had given Alfie led to a building that was Fred Flintstone's. He stood on the curb of a bad neighborhood in front of a dilapidated warehouse that looked like it had not been used in fifty years. He pulled the wrinkled card out of his pocket one more time and compared the address on it to the one spray painted above the door. It still matched.

"He sent me on a wild goose chase," Alfie muttered, angrily crumpling up the card and tossing it into the gutter. He turned to walk back to the main road when the door opened behind him.

7

"Boy, you going to come in or stand out here all day?"

Alfie turned back around to see a large black man standing in the doorway with his hands on his hips and a frown on his face. "You talking to me?" Alfie managed to spit out.

"Oh, you a wise guy now? Get your ass inside." He walked back into the building, leaving Alfie no option but to follow.

"Is this another office for Resources, Inc?" Alfie asked as he followed the man down a dim hallway. "Mr. Kadish told me to be here at 10."

"And it is now 10:04. You are late."

"So, I'm in the right spot?"

"You are Alfred Louis Vihar, eighteen year old son of Vivian and George Vihar. You go by Alfie. You have two older brothers and a younger sister. You are graduating in three weeks from West Central High School. You speak four languages at varying skill levels. You play football and lacrosse. You were accepted to three different colleges on lacrosse scholarships but did not accept any. You applied for the summer internship in the business division of Resources, Inc. but did not get it. You are now employed by a different division of Resources, Inc. I am now your boss. Did I miss anything?" the man barked out.

Alfie stared at the back of his head for a long moment then shook his head. "Nope. You pretty much covered it all."

"Good. Now, come on." The man pushed through a set of double metal doors and led Alfie into a huge open room. It looked like a gym from the 1930s. There was a boxing ring in one corner, large canvas punching bags hanging from a catwalk that served as a running track five feet above their heads, a huge padded area took up the middle of the floor, and treadmills, multiple benches, and free weights took up the far wall. A climbing wall filled the far corner from ceiling to floor, hiding part of the track.

Alfie looked around in amazement at the people who were using the equipment in the gym. They were predominantly male, but there were a few women holding their own in the boxing ring and on the grappling floor. A few of them, Alfie knew for sure that he would never want to meet in a dark alley.

"This way." The man turned left and led Alfie to another hallway. This one was brightly lit and would not be out of place at a hospital. Alfie wrinkled his nose at the disinfectant smell as he peered into rooms that held the most modern medical equipment he had ever seen.

"We go from Sugar Ray Robinson's gym to a New New York's hospital? Where's Boe?" Alfie wondered out loud. The man turned to glare at him over his shoulder but did not respond. Apparently, the man was not a Doctor Who fan. Alfie was thoroughly chastised and held his tongue until the man led him into an exam room at the end of the hall. "Is this where I get probed?"

"Would you stop the chatter?!" The man practically bellowed.

Alfie shrank back from the anger he saw on the man's face. "Sorry. I tend to talk when I'm nervous."

"You'll have to get over that. You're not getting paid to chatter and where you're going, being loud will get you killed." The man nodded in approval as Alfie kept silent and proved his understanding. He relaxed and ran a hand over his shaved scalp. "Get undressed and put this on." He threw a hospital gown at Alfie. "Stay here."

9

The man left the small room and Alfie stared at the closed door a long moment. "What the hell did I get myself into?" Alfie wondered as he pulled his shirt over his head and dropped his jeans to the floor.

"Sorry about the wait, Mr. Vihar. Brutus did not tell me you were here. I am Dr. Olafson."

"AH!" The doctor's arrival startled a scream out of Alfie. He spun around, trying to cover his nakedness with the robe while tripping on his jeans that were still bunched around his ankles. He hit the floor with a thud.

The doctor finally looked over the edge of the file she was reading with a raised eyebrow. "Problem?"

"Umm... No. I'm good." As Alfie struggled to his feet, he could feel half of his blood rush to his face while the other half rushed to another part of his anatomy. The doctor was HOT. Like just stepped off the cover of a magazine- hot.

"Do you need help?" She asked with an expression that said 'you better not say yes'.

"Uh, no. I'm good," Alfie stammered.

"Is that all you can say?" She asked as she brushed her long blond hair back over her shoulder. "Never mind. Put on the robe and hop onto the table," she ordered, setting the folder on the counter and pulling a pair of rubber gloves out of a box on the wall.

"Uh, yeah. Sure." Alfie quickly pulled on the robe and climbed onto the table, the cold steel was akin to being doused with cold water, freezing his embarrassment among other things.

"All right. First, we'll do a standard physical, then immunizations, and finally stress tests."

"Stress tests? I'm up to date on my immunizations. I had to be to play sports."

The doctor's eyebrow went up as she grabbed her folder off the counter and read. "You are good on Meningitis, MMR, and Hepatitis A and B. Your flu shot ran out two months ago. You need a tetanus booster. You've already had chickenpox so we don't need to worry about that, but I will give you the shot for smallpox to be on the safe side. You will also need the vaccine for Anthrax, Diphtheria, Syphilis, Malaria, Typhoid, Typhus, TB, Polio, Rabies, and the Plague."

Alfie finally picked his chin up off the floor. "The Plague?! What will I be doing? Time traveling to the Dark Ages?"

Dr. Olafson looked down her nose at Alfie as she put her folder back and pulled up a tongue depressor and a penlight from her coat pocket. "Just covering our bases, Mr. Vihar. We don't know where you will be going and would rather you not get sick when you are there."

"You don't know- What the hell did I sign up for?" Alfie exclaimed, all caution gone out the window. "What do I need stress tests for?"

The doctor sighed and leaned a hip against the counter. "The stress tests are to make sure you are healthy enough to work here. As for what you signed up for, shouldn't you know? You took the job."

"I was told to be here today at 10 a.m. by Mr. Kadish for a job, so I came here at 10 a.m.. I have no idea what this job is! I expected to be here in time for some sort of orientation, not to be shot full of drugs!" Alfie's shoulders slumped and he stared at his hands where they lay in his lap, all of the frustrated anger slowly draining from him.

The doctor looked at his defeated form for a long minute before picking up a phone the wall by the door. "Send Brutus in here."

"Great. He's coming back. Yay," Alfie mumbled.

Dr. Olafson turned toward the wall to hide her grin.

"What did you need, doctor?" Brutus walked into the room without knocking.

"Please tell Mr. Vihar what his new job is. He seems to think he needs orientation."

Brutus frowned. "Boy, you are here as help-for-hire."

Alfie rolled his eyes. "Yeah, and what does that mean?"

"Somebody needs help doing what they are doing, they call us. We send them people who are trained in fighting, technology, thievery, intel-gathering, and sabotage."

"Am I training to be a spy?" Alfie asked, excited for the first time that morning.

Doctor Olafson smirked and Brutus laughed. "No, boy. What you're doing, you will be working in a unit under close supervision of your employer. Most of the time you will be standing around waiting for orders but once the action starts, you have to be ready."

"Am I a mercenary?" Alfie asked hesitantly.

"Kind of. Is that all, doctor?"

"Yes, thank you, Brutus." She closed the door behind him and picked up the tongue depressor and penlight again.

"How can I "kind of" be a mercenary?"

"Mercenaries fight wars. You will be support, mostly against one particular person- like an arch-nemesis- or small group of people- like a police force."

"Arch-nemesis? Am I training to be a... Henchman?"

"Yes, now open up and say 'ah'."

******

Alfie collapsed onto his bed, exhausted from his first day at his new job. The last eight hours had felt like a bad movie montage of being poked, prodded, stuck, stabbed, and judged by lab-coated people with no senses of humor. Obviously, it was not directed by Howard Hughes, nor was the soundtrack by John Williams.

Which would have been awesome.

Alfie felt like they had drained half of his blood for their tests and he had sweated the other half out during his time on the treadmill.

"Alfie! Tessa is here!" Alfie heard his mom yell up the stairs. He groaned and rolled onto his back hoping that if he didn't answer, his mom would make an excuse for him and send Tessa home.

"Well, you look like shit."

Alfie opened one eye to see his best friend, Contessa Pellegrini, standing in the doorway with her hands on her hips. "Go away," he mumbled and put an arm over his eyes.

"Not gonna happen." Tessa laughed and jumped onto the bed, making Alfie groan in pain. "How's the new job?"

Alfie groaned and mumbled nonsense as he wiggled around on the bed so he could prop his feet against Tessa's hip and suddenly pushed.

"Ah! You ass!" Tessa laughed as she rolled forward onto his legs, pinning him in place. "You didn't think that would work did you?"

Alfie sighed and shook his head. "It was worth a shot, though."

13

Tessa propped an elbow on Alfie's chest and put her chin on her hand. "What did you do at work that you're this beat?"

"Lots of testing. Now, leave me to die."

Tessa laughed again. "Not likely. We have finals to study for and your mom invited me to stay for supper. Which, she told me sternly, is almost ready." Tessa paused to sniff the air. "You stink. Go shower and I'll convince Vivian to not kill you for being late to eat." Tessa got up, using Alfie as a prop. He groaned in pain. "Hurry, you pansy!"

"Woman... always trying to kill me," Alfie grumbled as he got painfully to his feet to get cleaned up.

******

Alfie's first week with Resources, Inc. flew by faster than he thought possible. He finally got the orientation that he was expecting, complete with a training video featuring laughing villains, victorious heroes, and picturesque henchmen doing their job perfectly. He learned that he would be taught at least two different forms of hand-to-hand combat (Jujitsu and Krav Maga sounded most interesting to him), weapons training, climbing and rappelling, extraction of both humans and valuable items, and a course that Alfie nicknamed "MacGyverness." It was a class on how to turn everyday objects into anything a henchman might need.

Alfie also learned about the clientele that contracted with Resources, Inc. and with that, came the realization that many of the "natural disasters, training accidents, and terrorist attacks" that the world had been subjected to over the last half century were the work of those same clients.

He was floored to find out that the insane man who tried to bomb the Golden Gate Bridge during rush hour the previous year was not the next Timothy McVeigh but was actually a rising supervillain named Heinrich von Wolff, creatively nicknamed the Wolf. The destruction of the Golden Gate was going to the be his first large-scale declaration of villiany after many small bombings but his plans were foiled by the Alliance of Justice, a group of five superheroes who worked in secret to keep supervillains from taking over the world.

The AOJ was led by Gil "Crux" Farris. Crux could control the four elements with deadly precision. His brother, Luther "Force Field" Farris could, as his name suggested, create force fields around objects and people. He could also send out a blast of energy that worked effectively at disarming the enemy. Sidney Powel also known as Warp had the ability to change herself into anything, living, fictional, or inanimate. Daniel "Bullet" Zenkle had unbelievable accuracy with anything that he could shoot. Hazel Moonbeam Sunray (obviously not her real name) aka Earth Child could control plants and animals.

Oddly enough, both the AOJ and the Wolf had units from Resources, Inc. working for them. Something the company tried to keep from happening because of the Human Resources department's dislike of the extra paperwork that comes with employees killing each other while working with different sides of the law.

Resources, Inc.'s Henchmen Division rented out units of five members to whomever could pay the exorbitant fee. Which, surprisingly, a lot of people could. The unit as a whole was expected to be well trained in hand-to-hand combat, extraction techniques, marksmanship, and keeping their mouths shut.

And Resources, Inc. had the best henchmen in the business.

Alfie's first day that he wasn't filling out paperwork, being fingerprinted, giving blood or urine samples, or being subjected to any other form of medical torture, he was introduced to the other members of his unit.

"Vihar, follow me." Brutus met Alfie at the front door and led him down a hallway he had never been in before to a small conference room. Three men and a woman sat around the large table in the middle talking, but they trailed off when Brutus entered with Alfie on his heels.

"Team 9, this is your newest member, Alfred Vihar," Brutus said without preamble. "Vihar, this is your team."

"Hi," Alfie said quietly with a small wave, earning a glare from Brutus. One of the men stood. "Vihar, this is your team leader, Jeremiah Gibson." The team leader put out his cigarette in a half-full coffee cup and held out his hand. He was a six foot tall silver fox who Alfie thought looked like he should be featured in Marines Weekly, if there was such a magazine. His steel-blue eyes saw everything and his active past was painted across his face in wrinkles and scars. He wore black cargo pants, black boots, and a desert khaki tee shirt.

"Welcome to 9, Vihar. You can call me 'sir' or 'captain'." Alfie was surprised at the captain's quiet, husky voice. He was expecting him to bark like the drill sergeants he had seen in movies.

"The number two in command of Team 9 is Nikolai Maklakov," Brutus continued.

Alfie almost peed his pants when a man who looked like a forty-year-old Ivan Drago stood up to shake his hand. The man was 6'7" if he was an inch, was built like an ox, and his blond hair was in a crew cut. Alfie had no doubt that Rocky would lose very quickly to the huge Russian staring at him like he was something he scraped off the bottom of his shoe. Nikolai wore all black: cargo pants, belt, boots, and painted-on tee-shirt. He also wore a dark red leather cuff on his left wrist that Alfie swore had the Communist hammer and sickle on it in gold.

"Then we have Evelyn Green."

"Hey Alfred! You can call me Ray. Everybody else does," She said as she shook Alfie's hand."

"You can call me Alfie," Alfie barely stuttered out.

Evelyn "Ray" Green proved Alfie's theory that Resources, Inc. did not employ women unless they were drop-dead gorgeous (aside from the scary ones he had seen training in the gym). She was younger than the rest and a few inches shorter than Alfie's 5'10", slim but muscular, had sparkling brown eyes, and her long, curly brown hair was pulled back in a fluffy ponytail. She looked like a spokeswoman for Under Armour in black work-out pants, bright orange and green sneakers, green headband, and a lime green spandex top.

"And finally, LeRoy Monte-Pierre."

"It's Le*Roy*, emphasis on the 'Roy,' not the 'Le'. Good to meet you, Alfie." LeRoy's New Orleans drawl thickened as he shook Alfie's hand and sauntered back to his seat.

Alfie couldn't help but wonder if the short, thirty-something, Cajan batted for the other team. His sleeveless tee shirt and gym shorts were tighter than Ray's spandex, his short dirty-blond hair was perfectly gelled, and Alfie was fairly certain LeRoy was wearing mascara.

"Now that you know everybody, I'll leave you. Gibson." Brutus shook the team leader's hand briefly and left the room.

Alfie didn't realize that he could feel any more awkward than he did before but he proved himself wrong. The team stared at him, studied him, trying to read him. He must have passed some test because Gibson kicked a chair out from the table across from him for Alfie to sit down.

"Talk," Nikolai barked.

Alfie jumped a little and tried to cover it with a quick adjustment in his seat. "About what?"

"You," Gibson answered. "Tell us why you are on my team."

Alfie frowned a little. "I'm on your team because Brutus said that when he dropped me off." He shrank back a little from the dead stares he got from the captain and second in command, wishing he could melt into the floor. Alfie turned to eye LeRoy when he heard the smaller man scoff. Alfie wasn't sure if he had actually ever heard somebody scoff before. That was the last straw and Alfie was done with the BS and non-answers he had been putting up with all week. He put his arms on the table and leaned forward.

"Why don't you ask me a real freaking question and you will get a real freaking answer? Enough of the evasive crap that everybody else in this place has been feeding me all week. I'm on your team because this is where I was told to go. I don't know any other reason. Be straight with me and I will do all that I can to prove that I deserve to be on this team." He never raised his voice during his speech. If anything, he got quieter, surprising himself at how controlled he sounded.

"Captain, if you don't think I will work here, tell me now and I will request to be transferred to another team. There's no reason to waste everybody's time if you don't want me." Alfie didn't even know if he could request a transfer but he was on a roll and couldn't stop until he said what needed to be said. When he finished, he sat back and waited while the others stared at him again.

Gibson studied Alfie with an unreadable expression on his face until he smiled slightly. "All right, Vihar. Glad to see you have a little spine. I want to know what you will bring to the team. Everybody here has a set of skills that the team needs and they are valuable for those skills. For example: Nikolai here is an expert in hand-to-hand combat. He was also trained by ex KGB agents before he moved to the US from Russia. He knows surveillance and espionage. Ray is a crack shot. She was on the Olympic shooting team, is a trick shooter, and a hell of a sniper in addition to holding the highest ranks in four different forms of martial arts. LeRoy is our brains and thief. He holds a doctorate in theoretical astro-physics, a masters in nuclear engineering, can break into almost any vault, and can get into almost any building. I am the leader. I know how to use the skills you bring to complete our missions. I am the one who deals with our employers, and I will keep you from getting kills if it is within my abilities. I am also the resident computer hacker. Now, what can you do?"

"Shit," Alfie breathed, all of his bravado gone. "Nothing like that. Looks like I'm just a body to fill out your team."

Gibson smiled coolly. "That's to be determined. Talk."

"I'm about to graduate high school. I am fluent in English and German, am passable in French, and am learning Chinese. I play football and lacrosse so I know how to take a hit as well as give them. I'm decent with pistols, and know more about pop culture than is probably good for me."

"That is all?" Nikolai finally spoke, disdain dripping from every accented word. "Send him back, Gibson. We get another."

"Uh, I'm still here," Alfie said quietly, raising his hand to get their attention, but they just ignored him.

"I do believe I am still the team leader," Gibson said quietly, but all were blistered by the acid in his tone.

"Let's see what he can do, sir." Ray leaned forward so she could see the team leader. "Brutus gave him to us for a reason."

Alfie smiled in appreciation as Ray stood up for him, although, watching the dynamics between the two in charge, he was not sure if he wanted to be caught between them.

"I agree. I don't think we are still so far down on Brutus's shit list that he would give us somebody who was absolutely worthless." Gibson studied Alfie thoughtfully.

"You can see me right?" Alfie fidgeted in his chair. "I didn't get hit with an invisibility ray or something, did I?"

"Oh isn't he just adorable. Invisibility ray." LeRoy's condescending tone emphasized his southern drawl. He chuckled. "Boy, invisibility rays belong in comic books. With our technology, we can make invisibility suits!"

Alfie frowned at the man, earning himself a long perusal that made him uncomfortable and a knowing chuckle. Alfie shrugged. "At least he can see me."

******

"No, no no! You talentless boy! I give in!" Nikolai threw up his hands and stalked away from the mats where he was training Alfie the very basics of hand-to-hand combat.

Alfie watched him leave from his back on the mat where the large Russian had thrown him seconds before. Nikolai stormed down one of the many hallways that lead away from the main training area, muttering in Russian. Alfie rolled his head to the other side when he heard Ray laughing from where she sat on the sidelines. "What did I do?"

Ray jumped up and walked over to pull Alfie to his feet. "He's tired of you not listening to him, Alfie. When he tells you to do something, you do something different."

"How do you know that?"

Ray raised an eyebrow. "I speak Russian and you don't want to know what all he said in his mutterings."

"Shit. Well, can you explain what I'm doing wrong? Ivan sure isn't helping with his 'No! No! No!' and nothing else."

Ray bodily moved Alfie into a fighting stance, kicking his feet to the right position and adjusted where he held his hands and head. "Ivan?"

"Oops. I meant Nikolai." Alfie colored slightly when Ray stopped in front of him and stared until he explained. "He is a dead ringer for Ivan Drago from Rocky IV!"

"Dude, you're totally right!" Ray threw her head back and laughed.

"None of you have noticed that before?" Alfie asked, surprised.

"I hadn't and the guys haven't said anything before. Now, you've been training for almost a week. Have you ever actually punched someone before?" Ray stepped back with her hand on her chin, studying how awkward Alfie seemed in the fighting stance.

"Punched, no. Not intentionally, at least. I have hit plenty of people with a lacrosse stick and I have tackled even more people playing football."

"Well, that's a start, I guess. So-"

"Good." Ray and Alfie turned when they heard Gibson's voice. "Ray, I was going to ask you to take over for Nikolai. He seems to have thrown in the towel with Vihar here."

Ray laughed. "I saw, sir. That's why I stepped in when Nikolai left."

"Thank you. As for you, Vihar, I have to congratulate you." Gibson said with false cheer as he swatted Alfie on the back, making him stumble forward with the force of it.

"Why, sir?"

"Because in the fifteen years that I have been working with Nikolai, I have never seen him give up training somebody. Threaten them with death, beat them senseless, and almost kill them, yes. But give up? Never. How did you do it?"

Alfie tried to smile but it looked more like a grimace. "I'm just talented, I guess."

Gibson sobered instantly, scaring Alfie a little with the intensity of his stare. "Well, try to not use that talent on Ray. She's your last chance to become at least adept at fighting by our next assignment."

"Yes, sir."

Ray chuckled. "I'm not worried. We'll get him fighting in no time. Plus, he's decent with pistols so he's not completely helpless."

"Good." Gibson nodded at them before leaving the training floor.

"Did I really break Ivan?"

Ray shrugged. "Eh, he'll get over it. Now for you. Let's see if we can give you enough skills to at least win a slapping contest with a twelve year old girl."

After two hours of struggling, Ray was about ready to throw in the towel, too. After beating Alfie's head into the ground, of course. "How the hell did you survive lacrosse and football when you trip over your own feet walking three paces?" Ray exclaimed as she threw a water bottle at Alfie's head.

He snatched it out of the air without looking and shrugged as he took a huge gulp. "I don't know. Maybe-"

Alfie was cut off by a motherly voice over the PA system. *"Team 9, report to your den. Team 9, to your den."*

"We have a den?"

Ray rolled her eyes. "What do you think that room is that you've been leaving your clothes and stuff in?"

"Oh, I just thought it was a locker room. It's really a room just for Team 9?"

"Yeah, all the teams have them. The better the team, the nicer the den."

Alfie backhanded Ray in the shoulder as a sudden thought popped into his head.

She quickly grabbed his wrist, spun, and tossed him over her shoulder onto the mat.

He landed with a thud and a gasp as he tried to pull air into his lungs. "I don't think that was called for but question: we're Team 9. Is that like nine out of ten as in almost the best?"

Ray frowned down at him with her hands on her hips. When he didn't notice and kept talking, her frown slowly faded into a smile and she shook her head. "On your feet, man."

"Easy for you to say," Alfie groaned as Ray pulled him to his feet once again. "Who's the best team here?"

"Team 1 is the best. They are the elite of the henchmen here at Resources, Inc. which means they're the best in the world." She nudged Alfie with her shoulder and nodded her head at a group running in sync on the suspended track. "Team 1. Don't talk to them, don't touch them, don't even breathe the same air as them."

"Why? They're not contagious, are they?" Alfie asked in false terror.

Ray laughed, despite herself as she nudged Alfie to get walking back to their den. "No. They're just the best with egos to match. They'll squash you like a bug if you step out of line around them. Team 9 has been down a man for nearly a year. We don't really want to lose you already, even if you are incompetent."

"You say the nicest things to me," Alfie said dryly. "So we're Team 9 out of how many teams?"

"Right now, 25. Teams 18-25 are all brute squads, while the rest of us have something to offer, like a scientist, a sharp shooter, or an expert thief."

"So we're pretty good!"

"*We're* pretty good. You still suck."

"There you go again, being all sweet and shit."

Ray laughed again.

"Can you move teams?"

"Like be promoted to a better team or dropped to a worse team?" Ray asked. Alfie nodded. "Yeah, you can. Team 1 wasn't born that way, it was built. One of the guys started on Team 15 and worked his way up. One of the guys was actually put there to begin with, so it depends on your skills when you start. There was also a man who was dropped from Team 4 to Team 10 after he broke his hand and lost a lot of mobility in it. We are all kind of surprised that Brutus would put you with us considering your lack of skills."

"Seriously, you guys know I'm human and can bleed, right?"

Ray punched his shoulder. "Gotta toughen up, Vihar. Team 9 doesn't allow little girls on it."

"So how do you explain you?" Alfie asked with the most innocent expression he had at his disposal. Ray turned to him with her teeth bared and fist raised but as soon as she caught his eye-lash batting, she rolled her eyes with a laugh. "Who was the woman on the intercom?"

"Esther. Now sit down, shut up," Nikolai ordered as Ray and Alfie walked into the den. They quickly sat on one of the couches as Gibson stood up with a folder in his hand.

"Who's Esther?" Alfie whispered to Ray. She elbowed him in the ribs and shushed him as Gibson started talking.

"We got our next assignment. We are headed to Beijing. Looks like Hun-xang is trying to take Beijing hostage again."

Alfie felt himself begin to panic as he raised his hand. Gibson paused and turned a pointed look at Alfie. "Sir, Beijing? I don't have a passport and it takes forever to get one."

25

Alfie looked around as the others started to snicker. Gibson frowned at Alfie before walking to his desk in the corner and pulled a small blue book from the top drawer. "Now you do." He tossed the passport at Alfie, who was surprised to see his picture and information already inside when he flipped it open. "Now, Hun-xang has been pretty quiet for that last year or so, so he is wanting to make a huge splash with this attempt... which is probably just so people don't forget that he was once an actual threat."

Alfie frowned, trying to translate the 'hun-xang' Gibson mentioned. He had never come across a word that sounded like that but he admitted that he was still learning.

"We on the good side or the bad side this time, boss?" LeRoy asked, taking notes at the table.

"We're with Hun-xang on this one-" Alfie looked around as the others groaned. "But his plan looks a little more ridiculous than usual so it should be a fast trip."

"Sir, can I see how his name is spelled?" Alfie asked suddenly.

"No. What? Why?" Gibson frowned at Alfie.

"I haven't come across 'Hun-xang' before and was wondering if I would recognize it in writing."

"Oh. Right. You're learning Chinese. Well, we might finally have a use for you."

Alfie rolled his eyes as the others chuckled. "Thanks." Gibson handed Alfie the file and pointed out the name of the villain they were being sent to assist. "Oh! Huánxiáng!"

"Isn't that what I said?" Gibson asked quietly. The others picked up on the warning in their leader's tone but Alfie was still too new to notice.

"No! It's said '*wone she ow,*' not whatever you were saying. It means Phantom."

"Wonderful," Gibson gritted out from behind clenched teeth. "Now *wan she oo-*"

"*Wone she ow,*" Alfie interjected.

"*One sh-* oh screw it! The Phantom has plans for some sort of nuclear device to be dropped into the city center. LeRoy, you are why we were picked for this job. You will work with the Phantom on his weapon, the rest of us will run support and protection, along with teams 20 and 22."

Alfie watched in surprise as his teammates all stood and shouted their anger about the other teams assigned to join them in Beijing. Gibson let them shout for a minute then whistled. Loudly. Everybody shut their mouths and retook their seats.

"What's wrong with 20 and 22?" Alfie asked.

"I'll tell you what is wrong with 20 and 22!" LeRoy put down his pen and stood up in one fluid movement. He sauntered over to the couch where Alfie and Ray sat with a hand on his hip, his other hand clenched in a fist and raised in the air. "They are brainless Neanderthals who couldn't pour piss out of a boot with directions on the heel! They have no subtlety, no intelligence! They just go in and Hit! Crush! Maim! Kill!" The small Cajun was so worked up, Alfie thought he was going to hyperventilate.

"All right, LeRoy. Go sit down." Gibson cut LeRoy off before he could hurt something.

"Vihar!" Alfie jumped when Gibson barked his name. "Do you still have school?"

"Uh, yes sir." Alfie paused as he figured out what day it was. "Tomorrow is my last day of classes and then graduation is next Saturday."

27

"Good. We leave tomorrow evening for Beijing and should be back the middle of next week."

"Why we work around him?" Nikolai grumbled.

"Because he is the only one still in school and we don't officially have to be there until Sunday. Get your go-bags together. We leave HQ at 6. Uniforms will be waiting for us when we arrive."

"Ugh. I hate when they provide uniforms. They never fit right." Ray complained. "Does The Phantom know I'll be there? Last time he was kind of pissed about a woman being on a team."

Gibson sighed. "Yes, Ray, he knows. Brutus and I discussed it when he assigned us this job and we did all we could to prevent the mess that happened last time from happening again."

"Thanks, cap."

"Ray," Gibson said warningly.

"Captain, sir. Sorry, captain, sir." Ray saluted with a grin.

Gibson sighed again and shook his head. "If there aren't any more questions, you guys can head home. Vihar, hang back a moment."

Alfie swallowed his nerves and stood as the others headed for their lockers. "Yes, sir?"

"Here." Gibson handed Alfie a plain white envelope and a small booklet. "The first is always paper, after that, it'll be deposited directly into the account you gave HR. Read the book before you get here tomorrow. It tells you what you need to bring and how you're expected to act on the job."

"Thank you, sir." Alfie had butterflies in his stomach as he took the envelope and book and went to his locker to grab his gear. With his back to the others, he tucked the book into his bag before slowly opening the envelope to see more digits on a paycheck than he had ever seen before. He nosily let out the breath he was holding.

"Good one, eh?" LeRoy grinned as he pulled his coat out his locker next to Alfie's. He peeked into the envelope. "Oh boy, that's beans compared to your next one. Checks with jobs on them are easily twice to three times what a normal check is. Hazard pay and all that. And just wait until you get your year-end bonus." The short man whistled.

"Are you serious?" Alfie whispered.

"Of course. Just wait until you put in a few years and actually know how to do something useful. The pay goes up. Oh, and if you get moved to a better team!" He whistled again. "Major pay day. See ya tomorrow, newb."

"Yeah, see ya, LeRoy," Alfie said, distractedly.

"Hey, Alfie. Want to go grab something to eat?" Ray asked, leaning against LeRoy's locker door.

"What? Oh, no. I can't. I have homework." He showed her the booklet that Gibson had given him. "Plus, I've never packed a go-bag before so I have to get that sorted and I'll have to run out to get anything I'm missing."

"I can help, you know," she said with a warm smile.

"I appreciate it, Ray. But I have to take a rain check. Maybe when we get back?" Alfie asked, trying to dispel the disappointment he saw in her face.

"Sure." She shrugged.

"Cool. Hey! Come to my graduation party next Saturday. Food, music, everybody worshiping me," he said with a grin.

She laughed. "Sure. Just let me know when and where." Ray punched him lightly in the shoulder before

29

slinging her coat over her shoulder and sauntering out of the den.

******

"Hey! Mom! Dad!" Alfie yelled as he walked into his house. He knew 100% that he couldn't tell his parents that he was going to Beijing. There was no way they would let him and there would be too many questions about the passport. His mind raced, trying to come up with a story that would explain why he wasn't at home yet something that his parents would go along with.

"In here, Alfie!" He heard his mom call from the living room.

He kicked off his shoes at the door and dropped his bag at the bottom of the stairs before heading to the living room, where he stopped short just inside the doorway. Tessa and his mom were in gym clothes working out to something that looked like it was from the 1980s if the bejeweled Richard Simmons prancing across the screen was any indicator. "Dude, what're you doing here?"

Tessa stopped swinging her arms around with a laugh and wiped her forehead with the hem of her tee shirt. "Sweatin' to the oldies with your mom."

Vivian chuckled and stopped the VHS. "You hungry, honey?" She asked as she passed Alfie, dropping a quick kiss on his cheek.

"Yeah, sure. Wait, I have something to tell you. Where's dad?" He asked as he followed her to the kitchen. Tessa brought up the rear and headed straight to the fridge for some water.

"He's puttering in the garage. GEORGE!" She yelled as she started pulling food from cupboards and the fridge.

"WHAT?!" Alfie cringed as his dad yelled back from the garage. George Vihar never did figure out his volume controls.

"YOUR SON'S HOME!" Vivian hollered. "Tessa, dear, are you staying for supper?"

"WHICH ONE?!" George yelled back.

"ALFIE!" Vivian yelled, rolling her eyes.

Tessa waited a heartbeat, to see if George would yell anything else before answering. "Hell yeah, if you don't mind. It's clean-out-the-fridge night at the Pellegrini house and it usually ends in my brothers having a fist fight over the last meatball."

"We don't mind at all! Supper will be about an hour. Alfie, you probably want to shower," Vivian said with a pointed look at his work-out clothes. "Tessa, you can get cleaned up in the downstairs bathroom if you want."

"Ok, mom," they answered in unison. Vivian rolled her eyes again and laughed as they left the kitchen.

"How was work, man?" Tessa asked, racing Alfie up the stairs.

"Good. Got my shit handed to me by a girl your size." Alfie said with a sigh.

"You would think all the years of fighting me, you'd be better." Tessa said as she leaned against his dresser. She turned to look in the mirror as she pulled her curly black hair out of the pony tail and rubbed her scalp with her fingers before putting her hair back up. She leaned forward to get a better look. "Are my freckles getting worse?"

"You would think." Alfie mumbled. "And no, for the millionth time, your freckles are not getting worse." He dug

31

his paycheck and the booklet that Gibson had given him out of his bag. The check went into his wallet, then he plopped down on his bed to flip through the book.

"What're you reading?" Tessa walked over to plop down next to him.

"Something for work."

"Why do you have to know how to make a go-bag if you work at a gym?" Tessa asked, reading over his shoulder. He snapped the book shut.

"They like us to be prepared for everything. Now, I have to shower, and you smell like you really were sweating to the oldies."

Tessa lifted an arm and took a deep breath, then wrinkled her nose. "Yep. I was definitely sweating to the oldies." She laughed as she stood up, her brown eyes sparkling. "Got any clothes I can borrow so I don't have to put these back on?"

Alfie rolled his eyes. "How about you just pick from the pile of crap you left here?" He pointed to an over-flowing tub sitting in the corner of his room full of clothes, books, CDs, DVDs and miscellaneous things Tessa has left at his house during the ten or so years that they had been friends.

"Look at you, using your brain!" She laughed and rifled through the pile until she found a pair of jean shorts and a tank top that smelled cleanish. "Get cleaned up stinky! See ya downstairs."

"Yeah." Alfie responded, distractedly. He waited until he heard Tessa's footsteps on the stairs, shut his door, and flipped open the book again. He ran a finger down the list of things he would need and was surprised at how many he already had. He would have to make a Wal-Mart run to get the rest. He jotted down what he needed, stuffed the note into his wallet, making a mental note to deposit the check on his way to the store, then headed for the shower.

He was just pulling on a pair of jeans when he heard his mother's voice echo up the stairs calling his sister and him to supper.

"Your mom has a set of lungs on her," he said to his sister as he stepped out behind her into the hall.

"You think that's loud, you should hear my dad!" Ruth responded with a laugh. The inside joke had developed years ago between the youngest of the Vihar children when they realized that their older two brothers and their parents were always shouting over each other to be heard.

They ran down the stairs and followed the sound of shouting to the kitchen only to stop in the doorway as Vivian ran by with George hot on her heels. Alfie quickly slapped his hand over his sister's eyes just as George caught Vivian around the waist and pulled her into his arms. Alfie slapped his other hand over his own eyes as the shouting was cut off by the sound of kissing.

"Your parents making out again?" Tessa whispered from behind Alfie. Both Vihar children nodded and the trio slowly backed up into the hall so they wouldn't see what was happening in the kitchen. They loitered awkwardly in the hall until they heard pots and pans banging around on the stove.

"Mom! Dad! Is it safe?" Ruth yelled, fingers crossed that the answer was yes.

"Yes, you damn kids!" George yelled back with a laugh. "Get in here and set the table!"

All three heaved a sigh of relief. Out of all the Vihar kids and their close friends, Tessa was the only one who hadn't made the mistake of walking in on Vivian and George doing anything more than holding hands and she very much wanted to keep it that way.

Alfie's nerves grew exponentially during the meal and he about choked on his water when his mom asked him about what he had wanted to talk to her and George about earlier.

"Well, you know my new job?"

"The gym, yes." Vivian prodded gently.

"Well, they're also having me work with the business side of it," Alfie said slowly, pulling the lie out of thin air, hoping it would hold water. "Well, they think I have been doing really well so they want to send me with four of the managers on a business trip this weekend."

"That's amazing!" Vivian jumped out of her chair and ran around the table to hug Alfie. "I knew you would do so well in business!"

Alfie felt his smile tighten into what he imagined was more of a grimace.

"Congratulations son! Where are you going?" George asked.

"What?" Alfie felt sweat dot his forehead and lip. His mom finally let go of him but it was just so she could step back to look down at him.

"Where are they sending you on this business trip?" George asked again.

"Oh, umm Albany."

"New York?" Vivian nearly screeched.

"Yeah, it's where Health Universe's main office is." Alfie added a name and a place to the lie using the name from a letterhead he had happened to see tacked to the bulletin board in Team 9's den.

"That's quite a trip, Alfie," George said slowly, studying his son.

Alfie felt Tessa and Ruth's eyes alternate between his parents and himself. "Dad, they think I have a lot of potential and want me to get a grasp of what the corporate side of the operation is. I will be with four adults over the age of 40 the entire time," Alfie pleaded while mentally begging Ray and LeRoy's forgiveness at his exaggeration of their ages. He knew 100% that if that part of the lie got back to them, they would have no qualms about murdering him in his sleep and he knew they could do it with very little trouble.

"It would be a good opportunity for him, George," Vivian said slowly, squeezing Alfie's shoulder.

"Albany? Alfie hasn't really even been out of California." George shook his head.

"What better time, Dad?" Ruth jumped in. "It's for his job! They will make sure he doesn't do anything stupid, not that Alfie would act up anyway. He's not Nathan."

George sighed. "True. All right, Alfie, you can go. When do you leave?"

"Tomorrow night. I have to be at the gym at 6 and they'll take us all to the airport in a company car."

"Wonderful! I'll take you! I've been wanting to see where you work!" Vivian declared as she retook her seat.

"What? Mom, no!" Alfie about came out of his chair at his mother's suggestion. He couldn't let them see where he worked. The decrepit old warehouse would never pass for a modern gym owned by a multimillion dollar company.

"Oh, Vi, don't do that. He would never live down being dropped off by his mom like it's his first day of kindergarten," George argued as he finished his dinner.

"But..." Vivian looked around at four faces telling her to not do it. "Fine. But you can bet I will be waiting, hidden, down the street to pick you up when you get back!"

35

Alfie laughed and sighed in relief. "It's a deal, Mom."

******

"Ow!" Alfie flinched as Nikolai pulled the needle from his shoulder. Every Resources, Inc. henchmen were marked with a small GPS chip in their shoulder so if they happen to get kidnapped, buried, or in any other situation where they could not be found, the chip would allow them to be located. Usually this was done at HQ but since nobody seemed to think Alfie would be on any missions so soon, it was missed. Nikolai, who usually had a few extra in his go-bag, volunteered to get Alfie set up. The Russian roughly slapped a band-aid over the puncture mark and finished getting dressed.

"Hey, what do you tell people who ask what you do?" Alfie asked hesitantly.

"CEO," LeRoy said simply with a shrug.

"Henchman," Nikolai answered seriously.

"Really? And your families believe you?"

"No, but it makes them happy to think that I'm earning all the money they take from me doing something respectful." LeRoy laughed. Nikolai didn't answer.

"I told my parents that Health Universe, the 'gym' I work for, sent me to the corporate offices in Albany."

"How you know that?" Nikolai demanded.

"What? No, I didn't! I just saw the names on a piece of paper in the den and when I was telling them, they popped into my head. I just went with it."

LeRoy threw a bare arm around Alfie's shoulders. Alfie tried to squirm away from the Cajun's nakedness, but the shorter man was very strong. "You have a good eye, kid.

'Health Universe' is our cover and it's 'corporate offices' are in Albany. We have shit at the den that you can give as souvenirs from Albany along with a packet of papers you would get from a gym's corporate offices like contacts, growth numbers, quarterly goals, etc."

"That's awesome! Can I grab those when we get back?" Alfie's enthusiasm wafted off of him like bad cologne as he got dressed.

"Yeah, it's why we have it. You just have to talk to Esther."

"Who is Esther, anyway?"

"Receptionist on the Health Universe side," Nikolai answered.

"We actually have a Health Universe side?"

"Duh." LeRoy smirked as he stepped into his provided uniform. "Why can't these villains ever use fashion when they decide on their uniforms?" LeRoy complained as he zipped up his nylon onesie.

"This can't be our uniform..." Alfie looked down at himself in doubt. The charcoal colored leotard covered him from his head to his ankles, ending in stirrup straps so the legs stayed down in the soft-soled, black boots he was given. The gray was accented by a black strip that ran from shoulders to wrists and from armpits to ankles. The addition of a black utility belt and goggles completed the outfit. "I feel like a cartoon character."

"You get used to it," Ray said walking into the room and pulling the hood up over her braided hair.

Alfie felt his jaw drop at the sight of her in the skin-tight outfit. It left nothing to the imagination and with her standing there like a supermodel, he just hoped he didn't look like a skinless zombie.

37

"This is special material. Is not bullet proof, but will slow it down. Is also good in knife fight." Nikolai said as he pulled on his boots.

"Really? That will come in handy if I slip on the ice when I'm-" Alfie pulled up his hood and struck a pose. "Speed skating."

Ray and LeRoy laughed. Nikolai even cracked a slight smile. They agreed with how ridiculous the uniform was but, as seasoned henchmen, they were used to the crazy outfits employers wanted them to wear.

"Funny."

They all turned to see Gibson standing in the doorway with his arms crossed, looking anything but amused. He was in battle mode and would tolerate nothing less from his team.

"Team 20 and 22 are already out there. We move, now."

"Yes sir." They all responded in unison. They quickly finished dressing, grabbed their gear, and headed out the door.

"First, Hun-" Gibson paused with a slight growl. "The Phantom wants to address us, give us our orders, then we get to work," Gibson explained as they followed him down the hall.

Alfie barely heard him as he was busy examining his surroundings. If there was a stereotypical super villain lair, he was in it. Everything was unpainted steel, grated catwalks, gray walls, florescent lighting, and exposed pipes. There were people all over on the balconies and catwalks, doing whatever Huánxiáng ordered them to do. Some wore lab coats, some carried equipment or weapons, most were dressed the same way Team 9 was.

When they had arrived, they all had loaded into an elevator and dropped 200 feet below the surface to reach Huánxiáng's secret base. Alfie felt buried. Even with the 60 foot tall ceilings in the main part of the base, he could not stop thinking about the tons of dirt on top of them, waiting to crush them alive.

"Dude, you need to breath," Ray whispered.

Alfie gasped. He hadn't even realized that he was holding his breath. "Thanks. I just can't get over the feeling that the ceiling is going to collapse and we are all going to die."

"Wow. Claustrophobic much?"

"Wasn't until now."

"You have to get over that, man. If things get exciting, being buried alive is the least of your worries," LeRoy said with an evil grin.

"Seriously?" Ray punched LeRoy in the shoulder but it did nothing to squelch the glee coming from the small Cajun nor damper the rising panic in Alfie.

"Yes! What if the nuclear weapon isn't properly contained? What if there is mutiny of the Phantom's personal staff? An earthquake could destroy the structural integrity of this bunker! The police could find us. Oh! What if the AOJ shows up?" LeRoy cackled and rubbed his hands together.

"You are so dead." Ray gritted out from behind clenched teeth.

Alfie surrendered to panic. "What's going to happen? Am I going to get shot? Stabbed? Melted? Die?"

Ray pulled Alfie to a stop with a hand on his shoulder. LeRoy whistled quietly to get Gibson and Nikolai's attention. They turned back and the three formed a half circle around Ray and Alfie.

Ray grabbed Alfie's chin and forced him to look her in the eye. "Alfie, you need to control that panic. It will only get you, and possibly someone else, killed. The chances of any of us seeing action in the next few days are slim. More than likely this will all fail horribly and we will just go home. If, by some miracle, something does happen, we will look out for you and keep you safe. But being a henchman, you will be a target. You have a gun. Use it if you need to. Try to keep at a distance. That's where you're more effective. Let us handle the close-up stuff. Okay?"

Alfie heaved a huge sigh and nodded slowly. "Keep at a distance. Keep my head. Don't die. Got it."

"We done with touchy-feely stuff?" Nikolai grumbled.

"Yeah," Ray said quietly, still holding Alfie's eye.

"Good. Come on." Gibson turned back around and led them to Huánxiáng.

******

"I thought you said nothing would happen!" Alfie shouted as he ducked behind a golf cart as a round of bullets that were trying their hardest to aerate his innards imbedded themselves in the cement wall behind him.

"I said that *probably* nothing would happen!" Ray shouted back as she dodged a clumsy punch aimed at her face and elbowed the man hard in the gut before sweeping his feet out from underneath him. "Some UN soldier you are." She glared at the man at her feet for a second before she was off to take out the next.

After Alfie's panic attack, all of the henchmen and other staff were gathered in a large room to be addressed by

Huánxiáng. To Alfie's surprise, Huánxiáng was not some mad Chinese mastermind bent on taking over the world. He was actually just a pissed off white guy from Utah who thought Beijing would look better melted.

But as henchmen, it was their job to follow orders and see that the job got done if it was within their power.

When Huánxiáng was done with his pep-talk, LeRoy was quickly ushered to the lab to help with the weapon that Huánxiáng planned on setting off in downtown Beijing. The others were led to their area of operation, aka the hallway outside of the lab. Team 9 would be in charge of close-quarter protection of Huánxiáng and the weapon while 20 and 22 with the support of Huánxiáng's personal staff would spread out throughout the base now, and later, the city, to thwart any attempt to stop the attack.

They spent six hours at their posts and were just preparing to move the weapon out of the base when the AOJ and UN military forces burst in.

"Screw your 'probably'!" Alfie yelled after her, quickly realizing that yelling was not the best way to stay hidden in a fight. He dropped flat to the floor a heartbeat before a .50 cal bullet buried itself in the wall behind where his head was. "Shit!" He army-crawled to the edge of the golf cart and peeked around it. The henchmen and Huánxiáng's team were holding their own against the UN soldiers but nobody was really coming close to touching the AOJ. Since four of the five could do damage from a distance, they hung back and helped where they were needed.

"Vihar! Get out here!" Gibson ordered.

Alfie's heart attempted to jump out of his chest. "I think I'm good here, captain."

"Now!" Gibson bellowed as he nearly ripped a guy's head from his shoulders.

Alfie swallowed nervously as he looked around for another good spot to hide. Part of the wall had been destroyed when Force Field had blown into Huánxiáng's bunker and there were large piles of rubble that looked safe from the fighting. Alfie quickly got to his feet, making sure he stayed covered by the cart. He glanced up once and waited for most of the fighting to be focused away from him before darting to a large pile of rubble. He dove for it when a hail of bullets swept his way, pulling his forgotten .45 from the holster at his hip on the way to the ground. He rolled up into a crouching position with his back to the pile, gun at the ready. "That was freaking sweet!" He chuckled, the 10 year old boy in his head in awe of the action star move he just completed.

"ALFIE!" Ray screamed.

Alfie jumped at the sound of his name and looked over the edge of the pile. Team 9 was getting backed against a wall by UN troops and what looked like a mini transformer with guns out. They kept fighting but Alfie could see that Ray had blood running down the side of her face, Gibson had been shot in the shoulder, LeRoy had a bloody nose and a limp, and Nikolai was pretty much just covered in blood, making Alfie unsure how injured he was.

"Now or never, newb," Alfie mumbled under his breath. He braced his elbow against the rubble, aimed his gun and fired once before ducking. He heard a scream, terrified and elated at the thought that his bullet found its mark. He crawled to a different position in the pile and carefully aimed again. He watched his second shot take out a soldier's knee, dropping the man to the floor next to the first. Alfie decided to risk another shot from his position and felled a third before his sniping was noticed by the AOJ. He crawled to a third position, aimed and fired a fourth time. He ducked quickly as people headed for him.

"Shit!" Alfie crawled further into the piles of rubble, coming face-to-face with a snarling cheetah. He froze, trying to not even breath, his mind was blank, unable to even process what a cheetah was even doing in the bunker.

"Hello." Alfie glanced up to see a girl, probably around 15 years old standing next to the cheetah with a hand on its shoulder. She wore a flowy, off-white dress of rough material, had green vines wrapped around her arms and legs, her feet were bare, and she had a wreath of flowers sitting atop her short brown hair.

"Hello," Alfie answered, unsure what else to do. When he started to ease back, the cheetah growled again, making him freeze.

"Don't move or Darla will get you," the girl said with a giggle.

"Darla? You named it Darla?" Alfie asked, surprised and unimpressed at the name. He would have gone with Speedy or Rip-you-from-limb-to-limb-in-two-seconds. Maybe not the second one, it was a little too long to yell when the cheetah threw up on the carpet.

"No," She answered, her sweet smile fading from her face to be replaced with a snarl that matched the big cat's. "*She* named herself Darla."

"Oh. Well, nice to meet you Darla." Alfie felt sweat drip down his face and between his shoulder blades. "And you are Earth Child?"

Earth Child nodded with a giggle, delighted to be recognized.

43

"VIHAR!"

Alfie heard Gibson yell his name and he spun around toward the noise, unheeding the growls coming from the cheetah and girl behind him.

"I wouldn't move," Earth Child whispered coldly. Darla growled again and padded forward a foot.

Alfie sighed, tired of everybody ordering him around when he knew he was so out of his element. He felt something in his brain snap as he stood. He turned partially toward Earth Child and Darla as he raised his .45, pointing it directly at the cat's head. "She shouldn't move."

Earth Child gasped and put a hand on Darla's shoulder, stopping the cheetah from going further.

"Back up and get out of my way," Alfie whispered. Earth Child snapped her fingers and Darla followed her as she quickly backed away from Alfie. He watched until he felt they were safe enough away before he turned back to his team. The soldiers he had injured were replaced by twice as many as before.

Alfie felt like he was in a dream, or maybe an action movie, when he calmly walked around the pile he had hidden behind, raised his gun, and fired rapidly into the legs of the men who were surrounding his team. He felt his slide lock back and pulled another magazine from his utility belt as he dropped the spent one. He had the new one loaded and the slide closed by the time anybody knew who exactly was firing. He fired four more times before he realized that somebody was returning fire. He looked up and spotted Bullet shooting full-auto from a catwalk, the line of bullets hitting the ground in front of him and getting closer.

"Shit!" Alfie yelled, the spell broken, he fired off one more erratic shot and dove for cover, but his appearance had done what his team needed. They were able to subdue the few soldiers left standing before rushing to help the rest of their side.

"ENOUGH!"

All action in the bunker ceased at the shouted word and all heads swiveled up where Crux hung suspended in the air on a platform of air he had created. He had Huánxiáng in handcuffs in front of him while Force Field protected them with a wall of energy from the ground to the ceiling. Warp and Earth Child walked over to stand on either side of him. Alfie eyed Darla where she stood glued to the little hippie's side. Bullet stood up from his nest on the catwalk but kept his sights on the enemy.

"Huánxiáng has been captured! Surrender!" Crux yelled.

Alfie slowly stood up, suddenly feeling all the bumps and bruises he had gotten from diving for cover. His teammates slowly released the soldiers they were fighting and dropped their weapons as they raised their hands. He thought it would probably be safer if he did the same.

"See Captain, he can say it right," Alfie mumbled.

"Vihar," Gibson growled quietly, subtly ordering Alfie to keep his mouth shut.

Team 9, 20, and 22 were rounded up and lead away from Huánxiáng's personal staff by UN soldiers while the AOJ kept a tight hold on the evil mastermind.

They were led to a large room that had previously been the home of Huánxiáng's lab equipment but it had been hastily cleared out. The door shut behind them.

"Seriously? At least give us some first aid kits if you're going to lock us in here!" Ray yelled through the door.

LeRoy let her yell and beat against the door for a minute, then tapped her on the shoulder.

"*Chére*, over there." He pointed at a table against the far wall that had all they could need for tending to their wounds.

"Great. Malcolm." Ray took over the situation and recruited the team leader of 20 who had been a doctor before he lost his license and became a henchman. "I'll help you with whatever you need."

"Thanks, Ray." He grinned at her, his adoration shining from his round, flat face. It didn't matter that he was close to 30 years older than Ray, he still loved her, although his affection for her probably ran closer to that of a daughter or prized hamster rather than romantic.

"Everybody! Amputations and gunshot wounds here!" She pointed to a spot closest to the table. "Other severe wounds here! Everybody else over there!" She first pointed to the other side of the table, then vaguely around the room.

Alfie found an abandoned stool in the middle of the room to collapse on, while he watched the others get their medical attention. He didn't spend much time in the fight and wasn't concerned by his minor injuries. He was concerned by Nikolai's wounds though. The man had simply picked up a large bucket of, what Alfie hoped was water, and dumped it over his head, washing most of the blood away. While it showed that a lot of it was not his, it did show that his injuries were far worse than he let on. Alfie adjusted his seat on the stool, taking note of a scrape on his left side that seemed to burn more than the others, but shrugged it off as Ray grabbed Nikolai and bodily dragged him to Malcolm for medical attention.

"She's not going to come get you."

Alfie jumped as LeRoy spoke softly next to him. "I'm just trying to stay out of the way, man." Alfie shrugged and hissed as the scrape in his side burned more.

"Why? You should be up there in that line." LeRoy put a hand to Alfie's back and shoved him off the stool.

"What the hell man?! Leave me alone! I just want to sit over here and process what happened. No talking!"

"All right, all right. I've got a deal for ya." LeRoy stepped closer to Alfie so he could speak quietly. "You go get that gunshot wound tended to, and I'll leave you alone."

"Gunshot wound? I was shot?" Alfie nearly screeched.

All the others turned to look at the newbie and laughed as Alfie lost his mind.

"When was I shot?!"

"Probably when you were out in the open shooting at people. Always find cover, man." One of the men from 22 shouted out his advice with a laugh.

"Oh, great! Thanks! Just trying to help my team and I get shot!" Alfie gently touched the burning hole in his side with his hand with a grimace. "I've-I've never been shot before," he said weakly to LeRoy. He looked at the blood on his hand.

LeRoy chuckled. "Didn't imagine you had, boy." LeRoy cursed in French when Alfie hit the floor.

******

"Alfie? Can you hear me?" Ray asked gently, leaning over Alfie's crumpled form, looking for signs of life.

Katherine Wielechowski

"How am I going to tell my mom I was shot? I'm supposed to be in Albany with gym executives," Alfie groaned as he opened his eyes to see Team 9 and parts of 20 and 22 standing over him.

"Oh poor baby has to run and tell his mommy," a man from 20 whined as he mimed rubbing his eyes and crying.

"He is an 18 year old boy and you will treat him as such!" Alfie barked Gibson's favorite line from training before Gibson himself could get the chance. Team 9 laughed-except Alfie, he groaned because Nikolai chose that moment to pull him to his feet.

"It's not as bad as I thought," Ray said to comfort Alfie before she turned wide eyes to Gibson. The team leader bent to check the wound, a through-and-through and something that should have brought a newbie like Alfie to his knees long ago.

Gibson stood up again and looked Alfie in the eye. Alfie tried to not cringe back as Gibson raised a hand and set it on Alfie's shoulder with an approving nod. Alfie's eyes widened and he looked at Nikolai and LeRoy, hoping to find answers but they looked as shocked as he felt. "Am I dying?"

"You're free to go!" A UN soldier yelled from the door, startling all the henchmen who had gathered around Alfie as Ray and Malcolm tended to his wounds.

Gibson recovered first. "Thanks," he yelled back before turning to the henchmen. "All right, everybody get changed and gather your gear. Take off in 30. Ray, just get it covered so he doesn't bleed to death. You can finish on the plane."

"Yes sir," Ray said, pulling gauze and tape from a bag before slapping them over the wound in Alfie's side. He tried really hard to not cry but when her finger slipped and actually went into his side, he had to sit down before he collapsed.

"Shit! Sorry Alfie." Ray cringed as she apologized, then slowed down her work so she wouldn't cause him any more pain. "Okay, let's get out of here."

"So why are they just letting us go?" Alfie asked as Ray pulled his arm around her shoulders and she helped him walk from the room.

"We did our job but got beat. Now we go home."

"Why aren't we being arrested?"

Ray laughed lightly. "We're for hire, Alfie. We fight, we go home. That's it."

"We don't get punished for hurting, possibly killing, soldiers?" Alfie was shocked, to say the least.

"Nope. We work for the company. We can't be punished for the company's actions... Just don't try to go into corporate America with that attitude. They'll hang you. In this game, we are just pawns- unpunishable pawns. The Phantom and his personal staff- people who chose to be here- will be arrested and imprisoned. We go home-"

"You're Evelyn, right?"

"Ray."

Alfie turned to see Bullet walking on the other side of Ray with puppy love on his face.

"No, I'm actually Daniel," he answered with a sweet smile, his green eyes sparkling.

Ray chuckled lightly. "No, I'm Ray. That's what everybody calls me and that's what I answer to."

"Well that's too bad," Bullet responded softly.

Ray pulled Alfie to a short stop and turned to the superhero with her hands on her hips and eyes blazing. "What the hell does that mean?"

Bullet leaned close with a flirty smile on his face, not deterred by the angry woman in the slightest. "Because I think Evelyn is a beautiful name... Just like you," he whispered the last in her ear before walking off.

"Damn," Alfie breathed, his eyes wide.

Ray turned to glare at him. "What?!"

"Nothing, Ray. But the man's got game. I might be a little in love with him," Alfie said, laughing at the confused look on Ray's face before remembering how painful laughing actually was.

"Stuck up superheros think they can take their pick. Then they get all pissy when they realize that you are not interested and they think it's your problem, not that they're assholes that you would never date in your life," Ray muttered angrily.

"Ray, chill, please," Alfie surrendered with a laugh.

"Sorry. I've just been around superheros and super villains and everything in between for four years. Men think you have a problem when you're not interested. It gets old."

"Not all men think that, Ray," Alfie mumbled, trying to calm his teammate down. His breath caught in his throat at the sight of the smile she gave him.

"Thanks, Alfie," She whispered, briefly kissing him on the cheek before dropping him off at the men's locker room and heading to hers.

"No. Thank you," he whispered at the empty hallway.

"Vihar! Pack up!" Gibson yelled, breaking Alfie out of his dream.

******

1-800-Henchmen

Alfie spotted his mother's car two blocks away from HQ partially hidden by a dumpster just like she promised. He tried to choke back the tears that formed in his eyes, repeatedly thinking that henchmen don't cry because their moms are awesome. He straightened his back with a grimace, trying to hide how much his wound hurt. Malcolm had shot it full of local anesthetic and stitched it up on the plane but the drugs were wearing off and Alfie's whole side was on fire.

Vivian started waving as soon as she caught sight of Alfie and quickly jumped out of the car, which hit a snag when she suddenly realized she still had her seat belt on. Once she got it unhooked and the door open, Alfie was waiting. Vivian threw herself into her youngest son's arms, separation anxiety oozing out of her every pore. Alfie broke out in a cold sweat when her arm brushed the skin just above his wound.

"Mom, I'm alive but if you don't let me go, I won't be." Alfie laughed as Vivian quickly let him go.

"I'm so sorry! I'm just happy to see you! You look tired! Didn't you get any sleep?! Are you hungry? We can stop for something on our way home."

"I'm good, mom. A little tired but not hungry. Let's just go home. Dad off work?" Alfie asked, throwing his bag in the back seat of the car and climbing into the front. He pulled a tissue from the glove box and handed it to his mom to help control her leaking eyes and nose.

"He should be just getting home now. He wanted to be there when you got there."

"Awesome. Let's go." He gave her a dubious look. "Should I drive?"

51

"Oh hush. I'm fine!" Vivian sniffed once more, checked her makeup in the mirror quickly then put the car into drive.

Alfie walked in the front door in time to be tackled by Ruth, her little arm hitting his injury almost brought him to his knees. "Hey sis!" His voice cracked and he hoped he didn't look as nauseated as he felt.

"You bring me anything?" she asked, letting him go.

Alfie took in a huge gulp, then noticed Tessa leaning against the wall across from the door, studying him with a concerned look on her face. "Of course! I got everybody something."

"You can pass them out after supper, it's almost done," George said, walking into the entry way from the kitchen, wiping his hands on a towel. He pulled Alfie in for a hug. "Glad you're home, son. There are too many women around here for me to be alone!"

"Love you too, dear." Vivian backhanded her husband in the stomach while trying to keep a straight face. "Alfie, why don't you run your bag up to your room and get cleaned up. We will get the table set."

"All right." Alfie tried to hide his relief. With all the abuse, he wanted to check his side to make sure he hadn't torn his stitches or bled through the bandages. He took the stairs two at a time and jogged down the hall to his room, tossed his bag on his bed and swung the door shut before he pulled his polo over his head in front of the mirror. The bandages were mostly clean but the back one was just starting to show blood. He pulled the extra supplies Ray had pushed on him out of his bag and gently pulled the back bandage off to check his stitches.

"Holy shit!"

Alfie spun around to find Tessa standing in his doorway. "What're you doing here?!"

"What the hell happened?!"

"Shush!" Alfie gestured for her to be quiet as he pulled her further into his room and shut and locked the door.

"You can't tell anyone!" he whispered forcefully.

"Tell me what happened, Alfie," she begged quietly.

He shrugged, trying to brush off her concern. "I hurt myself at the gym. It's nothing serious, I just don't want them to know or they might make me quit. It's the best job I've ever had."

Tessa slowly turned Alfie so she could get a closer look as his injury. "Alfie, this looks like a gunshot wound."

"Oh come on, Tessa! Why would I have a gunshot wound?!" Alfie forced a laugh as he went back to the mirror to work on re-dressing his side.

"Alfie, two of my brothers are cops and one is a Marine, remember. I've seen gunshot wounds," She said, her tone daring Alfie to argue with her or lie to her again.

"Shit, okay." Alfie grabbed her by the shoulders and dipped his head so he could look her in the eye. "You seriously can't tell anybody what I'm about to tell you. No one, Tessa! Not even the brother who's a priest!"

"Are you doing something illegal, Alfie?!" Her concerned expression morphed into an incredulous one.

"God, no! I did get hurt on the job. I just don't work for a gym." Alfie took a deep breath. He knew he could trust Tessa, he just wasn't sure he wanted her to be in this position. "I work for Resources, Inc. I'm a henchman."

Tessa stared at him for a long moment before punching him in the shoulder, right where a bright purple bruise painted his skin. He groaned. "I thought we were

53

friends but I guess we're not if you can't even tell me the truth!"

"Ow! Tess, I am telling you the truth!" He grabbed her hand so she wouldn't walk out and pulled her over to his bag where he pulled out the informational booklet Gibson had given him before the trip and handed it to her. 'Resources, Inc.: Henchmen Division' was blazed across the cover. She slowly flipped through it, reading about how to fix up a broken leg with chopsticks and a lamp cord, what goes into the perfect go-bag, and how to turn yourself into the ideal henchman.

"Shit man, you weren't kidding." Tessa sat on the bed, unsure what to say.

Alfie took the opportunity to bandage up his wound and pulled a clean tee shirt over his head. "You going to be okay?"

Tessa shook her head. "Yeah. No. I don't know. How did *you*, of all people, become a henchman?"

"Thanks for that vote of confidence, man."

"No! I mean, why are you doing this?"

Alfie shrugged. "It's not business, it pays really well, and I get to travel. Plus, I work with some interesting people and get paid to go shooting."

"Where do I sign up?"

Alfie smiled and shook his head. "You are better than this. You're going to be a doctor. And I'm going to need you to put my ass back together after a job." He gestured to his side with a laugh.

Tessa carefully hugged Alfie with a sad laugh. "Deal."

Double Lives, Double the Fun

"Everybody healed up?" Gibson asked as he walked into Team 9's den.

It was the Monday after Alfie's graduation and nine days since the Huánxiáng job in Beijing. It was also the first time they had all been together due to the company's "mandatory seven-day leave due to injuries" policy and Gibson's unofficial "I don't come in on the damn weekend unless it's for a mission" policy. Alfie glanced around to check out the condition of his teammates. In the short time he had been working as a henchman for Resources, Inc., the four people around him had quickly become friends and comrades in arms, but being put into mortal danger tended to knit a group together pretty quickly.

Gibson, team leader and hacker extraordinaire, had a black sling supporting his left arm, but, by the way he moved, Alfie could tell he wouldn't be wearing it much longer. LeRoy, resident scientist and thief, had a brace around his right ankle and two black eyes from his broken nose. Ray, shooter and martial artist, was sporting a neat row of stitches in her hairline above her left temple.

"Nikolai actually looks worse. How is that possible, son?" LeRoy struck a pensive pose with a hand on his hip as he examined the large Russian.

Nikolai, the former spy and combat expert, had a black eye, swollen jaw, and a bandage around his upper arm, but he barely tolerated the perusal. He glared at LeRoy. "Call me son one more time," he growled, making the smaller man lose some of his swagger.

"Nikolai," Gibson warned, quietly.

"Bar fight," Nikolai said as an explanation.

55

"No means no, man!" Ray slapped him on the shoulder. He turned a bland stare at her but didn't speak.

"Nikolai, I told you that you couldn't do that after the Chicago incident," Gibson rebuked, the bored tone of his voice telling them all that he said it merely because his position required it.

"What happened in Chicago?" Alfie asked, his interest piqued, but nobody paid him any attention.

Nikolai bristled at the teasing he was getting from his teammates. "I was bouncing."

"Oh shit," Alfie muttered. He couldn't imagine anybody getting drunk enough to take on Nikolai, especially if he was working as a bouncer. He nudged LeRoy. "What happened in Chicago?"

"If you look this bad, how does the other guy look?" LeRoy laughed.

Nikolai slowly turned to LeRoy with a wicked smile. "Worse."

"As we expected," Gibson said, coming around his desk to lean against the front. "Take a seat, gentlemen." Gibson winked at Ray when she pointedly cleared her throat. "And Ray. Now, I just got our performance report back from the Phantom job. He, of course, rated us 'below satisfactory,' but that's nothing abnormal from a villain who lost."

"Well surprise, surprise," LeRoy drawled. "They always seem to think it's the henchmen's fault when their harebrained ideas – like melting Beijing – fall apart."

"We took bullets for that lunatic and he rates us 'below satisfactory?!'" Alfie jumped to his feet, incredulous.

"Calm your tits, kid." LeRoy put a hand on Alfie's shoulder and forced the younger man back to his seat on the couch with a smirk. "You pull your stitches and your mama will be upset."

"You guys aren't mad about this?"

Ray shrugged. "No, Alfie. It's all part of the job."

"I am," Nikolai grumbled.

"When aren't you mad?" Ray laughed.

"Someday, they let me kill one." Nikolai cracked his knuckles and somehow looked more threatening than usual.

"Don't hold your breath. Now, for my evaluation." Gibson turned a pointed look at Alfie, who immediately tried to crawl inside the couch.

"Yes!" Ray punched the air. "Not the newest member of the team anymore, not the first with the eval!"

"Now, Vihar." Gibson pushed away from his desk and slowly walked around the room, pausing behind the couch where Alfie and Ray were sitting. "It is not... customary for henchmen to hide behind things when the fighting starts." Gibson leaned close to Alfie and spoke in his ear. "Is it?"

"I'm going to go with... no." Alfie flinched when Gibson's hand made contact with the back of his head.

"Correct. But I do have to commend you. Once you pulled your head out of your ass, you actually did some good. The four or five kneecaps you shot will ruin the careers of the soldiers they belong to, but it kept them from kicking our asses even more, so it is acceptable. I do have a question," Gibson said as he sat on his desk, picked up a file, and glanced at it. "Did you actually threaten to shoot Earth Child's cheetah?"

They all watched as Alfie's eyes widened. "Yes."

"Why?"

Alfie couldn't believe the tiny smile on Gibson's face. "You were yelling at me to get out and help, she and her stupid cheetah, Darla, were threatening me. It pissed me off. I needed to help you guys and I figured a big cat was easier to bully than you."

"Ok. I'll accept that, but from now on, please don't threaten something that can run 60 miles per hour and eat you."

"Yeah, especially when it's controlled by a brat like Earth Child," LeRoy smirked.

Alfie nodded while the others chuckled.

"Other than the hiding and the little actual fighting, you did pretty well for your first job, Vihar," Gibson continued as he settled back on his desk. "I don't think we need to focus much more on your handgun use, but let's see if Ray can beat some more hand-to-hand skills into you. You won't be able to avoid it in many more fights. Eventually, you'll need to know how to defend yourself without a gun. Nikolai, you willing to work with him on rifle shooting?"

"I know how to use a rifle," Alfie jumped in. "My dad has taken my brothers and I hunting since we were little."

"Not your sister?" Ray asked quietly.

"Ruth wasn't interested until this year. We're taking her out this fall."

"Aww, that's nice. Is she excited?"

"If you two are done?" Gibson sharply cut off their side conversation. "Vihar, shooting an animal is a lot different than shooting a person. Plus, there is an art to being a sniper. Nikolai?"

Nikolai glared at Alfie for a long, tense moment. He nodded. "I try."

"Good. Now, everybody else did well as far as I could tell. LeRoy, try to remember situational awareness. We've been working on it for long enough that you should be better at it."

"What'd you do this time?" Ray asked.

LeRoy looked ashamed as he pointed at his wrapped ankle. "Tripped over a cinderblock right after Force Field blew the wall."

Ray started laughing but sobered when Gibson turned his eye on her.

"Ray, take one more shot to the head and you are wearing a helmet on all missions."

"Captain!" Ray jumped to her feet, indignation pouring off her in waves.

Gibson held up a hand, silencing her. "No, Ray. You have more concussions than anybody else in the top ten teams. Doctor Olafson has warned you, and it took a lot of fancy talking to keep you active after this one. Just try to not get knocked out again or she will pull you."

Ray dropped back into her seat. "Yes, sir," she mumbled.

"And Nikolai, I'm getting complaints that you're being too brutal again."

"They don't want henchmen to be brutal?" Alfie's words were colored by surprise.

"Not excessively so," Ray explained. "We're supposed to protect the boss and his job while keeping ourselves alive. Nothing more."

"Always complaining," Nikolai grumbled. "Pencil-pushers are too soft. Get paper cut, cry and sue paper company. Should be happy I don't kill them." Gibson gave him a pointed look. "Well, kill them all."

"All I ask," Gibson conceded.

"You could always try to not act like you're having fun when you're beating the crap out of people," LeRoy suggested.

"Yeah, I'm sure the smiling doesn't help," Ray added.

"Or the laughing." Alfie grinned. Nikolai glared at him and he shrank back into the couch. "Too soon?"

"Later, Nikolai. Just don't kill him," Gibson warned dryly as he looked back at his folder. "Our team had the least number of injuries of the mission and tied with Team 4 for the least number of injuries of the week, so that was good. We also had the least severe injuries of the week and the fewest enemies killed. Brutus hasn't been this happy with Team 9 for a few months, so keep up the good work."

"Yay, us." Ray lifted a fist in the air. LeRoy leaned over and bumped it with his own.

Alfie raised a hand. "Can I ask a stupid question?"

"Better than anybody on this team," LeRoy sighed.

Alfie frowned at the Cajun. "Thanks man. Anyway, you've mentioned a few times how they don't want us killing people – or just kill if necessary..."

Gibson raised an eyebrow. "Is there a question there, Vihar?"

"Yes. They sure felt like they were trying to kill us. How are there any henchmen left if we're not supposed to kill them?"

"We're just that good," LeRoy boasted.

"Heyoh!" Ray cheered and held up a hand for LeRoy to slap.

"If there are no serious questions, let's get to work. The schedule for the week: Ray, work with Vihar on his fighting. Try different styles and see if something will sink in. Vihar, when you're not working with Ray, get with Nikolai and learn how to snipe. LeRoy, Brutus said he got in those new safe doors you wanted. They're in the tech room whenever you want to tackle them."

"*Fabuleux!*"

"Hey, LeRoy, wanna teach me how to crack a vault?" Ray asked.

LeRoy winked at her. "Of course, *Chère*."

Gibson looked at them with a raised eyebrow.

"I'll train anybody who wants to learn, *le Capitaine*."

"When did we get on a boat?" Alfie asked, confused by LeRoy's incorrect noun.

"Good. Whoever wants to learn to open a safe, get with him this week, and LeRoy, Brutus gave me some files that were pulled from the DOD's research department over the last few weeks. He wants you to take a look and see what would be appealing or valuable to steal."

"Will do, captain."

"Are we stealing stuff from the Department of Defense?" Alfie couldn't contain himself any longer.

"No, *we* are not stealing stuff from the DOD. It was procured so we could have an idea of what a villain might go after so we have a heads up," Gibson explained dryly.

"Isn't that illegal?"

"You're a henchman, Alfie," Ray laughed.

"You shot UN soldiers and are not in jail. Why you ask about files from DOD?" Nikolai set down the knife he was sharpening, awaiting Alfie's answer.

"It just seemed odd to be stealing from the government when we could be working with them tomorrow," Alfie mumbled.

61

"Being proactive makes us good henchmen. If we know what the big new weapon or science breakthrough is, we can create options to either: A) protect it, or B) steal it. We also have informants at the largest research and development companies in the world. If something big happens, we know about it almost immediately."

"Isn't that dangerous?" Alfie asked, utterly appalled that one company could have that power.

"Yes." Gibson picked up a stack of files from his desk and handed them to LeRoy. "Back to work, everybody. Let's see if the new guy can work through the pain."

******

"Nope. I can't," Alfie mumbled into his pillow four hours later.

"You can't what?" Ruth asked, plopping down next to her brother on his bed.

"Work through the pain."

"What?"

"Nothing." Alfie painfully rolled over and sat up. "What's up, kid?"

"What's your IQ?"

"No idea. Our mother never had me tested." Alfie grinned and nudged his sister with a shoulder. "Why?"

"Sue and I took a test online today."

"And Sue is?"

"New girl in my class at school. She's pretty cool."

"School's been out for like a week and a half."

"I can't have friends?"

"Of course you can." Alfie laughed. "Okay. So what about the IQ test?"

Ruth concentrated on tracing a finger over the pattern on Alfie's bedspread for a long moment. "I scored a 133."

Alfie frowned. "Isn't that really good?"

"Smart person is 80-115. Einstein got 160."

"So yes, it is." Alfie studied Ruth, trying to figure out what was going on in her newly discovered beautiful mind. "What now? Should I find you a Mensa application?"

"No!"

Alfie raised an eyebrow at her alarm.

Ruth sighed. "No. I just wanted to tell someone and I knew you wouldn't tell mom and dad."

Alfie put an arm around her shoulders. "Why don't you want them to know? They could set up something to get an official test taken for you to see if the results are real. This could open a lot of doors for you."

"Yeah, in medicine or law or astrophysics," Ruth spit out with a bitterness that belied her 15 years.

"So none of the boring stuff for you, either?" Alfie squeezed her shoulders in understanding. "What do you want to do?"

"Well... I'm good at art stuff."

"No, you're amazing at art stuff," Alfie smiled. "Do that."

"Mom and dad aren't going to like it."

"They want us to be happy. They'll learn to live with it."

Ruth finally perked up. "You think?"

"Why do you think they didn't disown Robert when he decided to drop out of law school to be a costume designer? And they still talk to Nathan even though he became a gym teacher instead of playing pro football."

"You're totally right!"

"I totally am!" The siblings shared a laugh.

"So, how are you going to disappoint mom and dad?" Ruth asked, inadvertently elbowing Alfie in his injured side.

"Instead of going into business, I'm going to become a superhero and save the world," he said with a grin.

"Oh, dude. I wouldn't." Ruth could barely hang on to a serious expression. "That's too far. They will disown you for sure."

Alfie jumped to his feet and struck a Superman pose. "I must do what I have to do! The world depends on me!"

Alfie and Ruth spun around in surprise when they heard laughing from the open door.

George stood in the doorway doubled over. He stood upright when he finally caught his breath. "Come on Superman and Wonder Woman. Supper's ready."

******

"Am I getting *any* better?" Alfie whined from where he lay on the floor. He and Ray had been working on different styles of combat all week, and he was getting really tired of eating mat.

"No. You're really not." Ray was looking at him, but her mind was dissecting what they had gone over, trying to figure out what went wrong. By Wednesday, Ray had gotten frustrated and asked a martial arts expert from Team 4 to help. Thursday, she got one from Team 2. By Friday morning, she was desperate and asked Gibson to help. Even with all of that, Alfie couldn't retain anything but the basics. He could punch, he could block a punch, and he could do basic boxing footwork, but that was it. "Take a break for a few minutes. I need to talk to Gibson."

"Thank God," Alfie breathed. He army-crawled over to his water bottle and took a swig before stretching a little to work out some of the aches he was already getting. His mind was busy going over what Ray and the others had been trying to teach him all week. He could name most of the moves. He could picture them in his head. He could describe what a properly executed one should look like. He just couldn't make his body do what his mind knew. Even with all the training, the only person he was a threat to right now was himself. And judging from the black eye and bruised shin he felt developing and the bloody nose from earlier, he should be arrested for assault.

"Alfie," Ray started as she sat down next to him as Gibson towered over them. "Gibson and I can't figure out what's going on. With the amount of time we've been spending on this and who you have training you, you should be miles further than you are. We're stumped."

"Awesome. I'm broken and the best in the biz don't know how to fix me." Alfie screwed the top of his bottle back on and dropped it between his knees. It hit the mat with a thud.

Ray put a hand on his arm. "We don't think you're broken, Alfie. We just need to find the key to unlock your abilities."

"I've seen some of your lacrosse game film, Vihar," Gibson broke in. "You weren't nearly this self-destructive on the field. And that was with a stick in your hands."

"Right?" Alfie mumbled.

"We'll figure it out, Alfie," Ray reassured him.

"My turn. You know how to use this?" Nikolai walked over and dropped a standard AR-15 rifle in Alfie's lap.

"What? No M4?" As Alfie got to his feet, he dropped the mag and tucked it into the waistband of his shorts, checked to make sure the chamber was clear, pulled the pin to flip the upper from the lower, quickly checked to make sure all was clean and lubricated, closed it back up and put the pin back in, pulled the charging handle back, let it slam shut, shouldered it, and pulled the trigger to hear the click. "Yep."

Nikolai nodded and took the rifle and magazine back. "Go change gear and meet me in back hallway." Nikolai walked away without another word.

"Aye, comrade!" Alfie muttered, earning himself a smack in the back of the head from Gibson and a giggle from Ray.

"Go practice with Nikolai. Ray and I are going to see if we can figure something out for you," Gibson ordered.

"Yes sir!" Alfie saluted and just managed to dodge Gibson's fist heading for his stomach. "See ya," he called to Ray as he ran for the den.

Alfie was excited to start something new with Nikolai. They had been practicing with bolt-action rifles all week, and, while Alfie had been stoked to learn what he needed to be a sniper, he had been shooting bolt-actions since he was eight years old. ARs were something that Alfie had just started shooting, and he was looking forward to getting some more experience. Back in the den, he quickly changed into cargo pants, boots, and a tight-fitting T-shirt. He grabbed his shooting glasses and ear plugs from the shelf in his locker, tucked his gloves into his belt and headed for the back hallway.

Alfie had only been halfway down the hall to the door that led to the rooftop long-distance range. They had it set up so the henchmen shot rooftop to rooftop, all different distances and different targets. Nikolai was waiting and silently led Alfie down the rest of the hall through a thick double door at the end. They walked into a small prep area that was set up with both practice rifles and real ones. There were crates of paintballs on one wall and cases of live rounds on the other with dozens of different kinds of rifles on racks in the middle.

"You know how to clear room?"

Alfie ran his hands over the different rifles, amazed at being allowed to use them. "Only what I've learned from movies and Call of Duty."

Nikolai snorted in disgust. "We work on that next. First, we see how you handle rifle in combat situation." Nikolai shook his head when Alfie gleefully picked up a Ruger SR-556 from the rack. "Paintball first."

"Still fun," Alfie grinned. He picked up one that looked about right, shouldered it and checked the sights. He quickly adjusted the stock and moved the rear sight back a notch. He pulled on the plastic torso plates and goggles that Nikolai handed him. "No helmet?"

Nikolai frowned at him. "Only gets in way." He flipped a switch on the wall and pointed out the window.

Alfie could see the practice range in a huge room below him. To the left were three lanes of obstacles for people to work their way through. To the right were areas for close combat shooting practice. Three areas were set up like houses of varying sizes, complete with mannequin bad guys and hostages. At the very back was a larger area that was two stories, the first was an office building with cubicles, and the second was a warehouse with heavy equipment and lots of debris on the floor. A seven-foot-high wall separated the two and was peppered with paint splatter and bullet holes.

"We start with course first. Let's go."

******

Alfie groaned as he heard his gun click. His magazine was empty. He ducked behind a box and checked his pockets, searching for another full one he knew wasn't there. He caught movement out of the corner of his eye and quickly ducked as Nikolai's shot splattered against the plywood behind him. "I surrender! I surrender!" he yelled as he tossed his rifle at Nikolai's feet.

"In war, there is no surrender," Nikolai growled and pointed his rifle barrel directly at Alfie's chest.

"Goddammit!" Alfie groaned as the paintball splattered against his chest plate, covering his entire torso, neck, and face with red paint. The force of the point-blank shot knocked the wind out of him. "Shit man! Seriously?!" Alfie wheezed.

Nikolai reached a hand down to help Alfie to his feet. "No blood. You will be fine," he laughed.

Alfie froze when he was reaching for Nikolai's hand. "Dude. I didn't know you could laugh."

The large Russian growled at Alfie as he pulled him to his feet and right into a headlock. "You impress me with AR. Maybe tomorrow we use my gun. AK-47. See how you do then."

Alfie was amazed that he could possibly impress the former spy. He stumbled as Nikolai started dragging him to the stairs. "Yeah! I've always wanted to shoot one. We using live rounds?"

"Of course."

"Awesome!"

"*Team 9 to conference room Whiskey. Team 9 to conference room Whiskey.*"

"Esther calls. Get cleaned up." Nikolai released Alfie at the bottom of the stairs, leaving Alfie to run after him.

"Where's conference room Whiskey?" Alfie asked as they returned their equipment to the prep area.

"End of hallway where den is," Nikolai called over his shoulder as he left the area.

"Great." Alfie headed to the den to change and wash off as much of the paint as he could.

"What the hell happened to you?" Ray asked when she caught sight of Alfie's paint-covered form.

Alfie stopped just inside the doorway of the den with his arms crossed and his feet apart, trying to channel Batman. "Paintball warfare. It's not for the faint of heart," he said with the deepest, gravelliest voice he could muster.

Ray chuckled and rolled her eyes. "Boys. Hurry and get cleaned up. They called us to-"

"Conference room Whiskey. I know. Nikolai headed straight there." Alfie grabbed a washcloth, ran it under hot water, and scrubbed at the paint on his face and neck as he dug around in his locker for a clean shirt.

"How did rifle training go?" Ray leaned against the back of the couch and watched Alfie trying to get cleaned up.

"It went really well. Nikolai said we would work with AK-47s tomorrow. I'm pretty stoked. I've always wanted to shoot one." Alfie finally gave up and dropped the rag on the bench so he could pull off his painted shirt.

"Damn."

"What?"

"He's very protective of his Kalashnikovs. He doesn't let just anybody use them. You must've impressed the hell out of him today."

Alfie nodded as he turned to face Ray with a clean shirt in his hands. "He even laughed."

"No shit? Congrats man. It took me like three months to see him smile and I came here from the Olympic shooting team." She took in the large red spot on Alfie's chest as he pulled the shirt over his head. "Who hit you with a baseball bat?"

"What?" Alfie exclaimed.

"Here." Ray walked over and pulled his shirt up so he could see for himself. "What happened? I didn't do that in training, did I?" she asked, worry evident in her tone.

"Oh! No, it wasn't you," Alfie reassured her as he pulled his shirt back down. "Nikolai shot me in the chest. Point-blank."

"Well, that was stupid."

"Hurt, too. But I'll be fine." Alfie wiped a little more paint off of his face and gave up on the rest. "Let's go. We're late as it is." Ray nodded her agreement and led the way to conference room Whiskey.

"God, what're they doing here?!" Ray exclaimed as she walked into the dim room with Alfie a step behind her. Alfie peered around her to see Crux, Bullet, and Warp of the Alliance of Justice sitting across from Gibson and Nikolai.

"Green, Vihar. Shut up and sit down," Gibson ordered.

They hustled to their seats with their heads down, not saying a word, but their curiosity was evident. After a few tense minutes, the silence was oppressive. Alfie started rocking his chair forward and back as boredom took over. He glanced around, studying the superheroes and trying to figure out what they were doing there. "So... Anybody catch the game last night?"

"Vihar," Gibson's tone was enough to shut Alfie up again.

"What game?" Bullet asked, interested.

"Sorry for making you wait!" LeRoy gushed as he waltzed into the room with stacks of papers and books in his arms. He walked straight to the head of the table and dropped everything, scattering papers all down its length.

"What did you find?" Crux asked, leaning forward in his chair.

"Oh, lots! Lots! But nothing that has to do with this guy in Canada," LeRoy frowned as he pulled over a chair and sat down. He shuffled some things around, pulled a sheet from Alfie's curious perusal before slapping his hand for touching something that wasn't his, and finally found the paper near the bottom of the pile that he was looking for.

"I actually had to get info from a secret research and development company that the Canadian government is contracting out to survey the entire area. Thanks to Gibson, we were able to access what we needed. Here." He handed the paper to Bullet to pass to Crux.

"He hacked them?" Crux asked with a disgusted tone in his voice.

"How else do you think we got them?" Gibson's temper flared a little. There was no love lost between the two leaders, and everybody in the room knew it.

LeRoy quickly took control of the conversation again. "Looks like your guy wants uranium for something big he's building."

"What would require that much?" Warp asked, reading the sheet over Crux's shoulder.

"Either he is actually a nice guy who is building a nuclear power plant in Saskatchewan, or he wants a really big boom." LeRoy grinned, enjoying the thought of the explosion.

"Is uranium used in power plants?" Alfie whispered to Ray. She shrugged, unsure of the answer herself.

"Oh, honey," LeRoy drawled as he patted Alfie on the head like a pet.

"We kill him now." Nikolai got to his feet and pulled his pistol from the holster and checked the magazine.

"Not yet. Sit down," Gibson ordered gently.

"I will not stand by and let another Chernobyl happen, sir," Nikolai growled from behind clenched teeth.

"We won't let it come to that," Crux said. "But right now, he hasn't done anything. We are keeping a close eye on him. We will stop him if he acts. I talked it over with Brutus. We need Dr. Monte-Piere on this, so we have contracted Team 9. I will let you know when we need to head north."

"All right." Gibson's usual unflappable calm was being flapped. He had final say on missions for Team 9. Brutus and Crux left him out of the loop, and he did not appreciate it.

"Good. Dr. Monte-Piere, please let me know directly if he does anything big. We will need to know ASAP in order to stop him before he does something irreversible."

LeRoy subtly glanced at Gibson before nodding. "Of course." His loyalty to Gibson outweighed any pull the AOJ had, so he would be going through his team leader if he discovered anything.

"Good. I think we're done here." Crux, Warp, and Bullet stood at the same time and all three leaned across the table to shake Team 9's hands.

Bullet lingered with Ray, making her grimace. She leaned over to Alfie and took his hand. "Pretend to be my boyfriend."

"What?" he whispered back. He noticed her distress and Bullet walking purposefully around the table toward them. The pieces fell together in his mind, but they didn't make sense. Bullet was good looking – tall and built like a rugby player, wide through the chest and shoulders, trim waist, and heavily muscled legs. He had African-American features, but his skin tone and hazel eyes suggested a Caucasian ancestor.

"Evelyn. How are you doing?" Bullet asked, leaning uncomfortably close to Ray.

Alfie had the unfortunate position of being between them, and he was very uncomfortable.

"Fine, Bullet. Thanks."

Bullet grinned. "*You* can call me Daniel, you know."

Ray grimaced. "And you can call me Ray."

"Why?" Bullet's grin widened, oozing charm. "Evelyn is such a beautiful name for a beautiful woman."

"Hi, I'm Alfie... and you can call me Alfie," Alfie blurted when he felt Ray's elbow dig into his ribs. He held out his hand.

Bullet slowly pulled his eyes from Ray to examine the shorter man in front of him. "You were the one who got shot in Beijing and didn't know it, right?"

"Yeah. That was me," Alfie chuckled awkwardly as Ray squeezed his hand harder.

Katherine Wielechowski

"I'm impressed." Bullet slapped Alfie's shoulder.
"The last time I got shot, I couldn't move, it hurt so bad...
then again, the round did shatter my femur, so I couldn't have
moved if I wanted to."

Alfie nodded, acting like an expert on the subject.
"Ah. Yeah, that was your problem. Mine was just through my
side. Didn't even hit anything important."

"Still, though, that's impressive that it didn't drop
you. You're new here, aren't you?"

"Yeah, that was my first mission. First gunshot
wound, too."

"Cool," Bullet nodded and turned his attention back
to Ray. "Evelyn, can I buy you dinner tonight?"

"Sorry, Bullet. I have plans."

Bullet's smile faded a little. "You do? Doing what?"

"Alfie is going to take me to a play at the Play Box."

"Alfie?" Bullet looked at the wiry redhead standing
between Ray and himself, confused that someone like Ray
would date someone like Alfie when someone like himself
was there.

"I was?"

Ray stared at Alfie, praying he would figure it out.

"Oh, no... I told you yesterday that the play is next
week. We were going to see the new Ryan Reynolds movie
tonight," Alfie bluffed.

"Oh, that's right!" Ray forced a smile as she leaned
into Alfie.

"All right..." Bullet drawled, looking back and forth
between the two, trying to decide if they were faking or not.
"Well, Evelyn, if it doesn't work out with him, give me a
call. The offer still stands."

"Thanks," Ray gritted out as Bullet stepped around them to the door with the rest of the AOJ following. Team 9 fell silent as they left, trying to process everything.

"You going to explain that, *Chère?*" LeRoy asked, pointedly looking at Alfie and Ray's still-clasped hands.

Ray let go of Alfie and dropped into a chair with a sigh. "No, *Chère*, I don't think I will."

******

"Hey, do you want to go grab a drink or something? I need one after today." Ray leaned against Alfie's locker as he got ready to head home.

Alfie grinned and pointed at his chest. "Eighteen, remember?"

"Damn, I keep forgetting that you're a young 'un. Well, how about that movie you were talking about earlier? I haven't heard much about it, but I like Ryan Reynolds."

Alfie felt his jaw drop and quickly looked down in his bag to cover his amazement. "Yeah, sure. I think the next show is at 7:30 at Center 8."

"Sounds good. Oh, and you're paying," Ray said with a grin.

"Yes, ma'am."

Ray shoved Alfie back into his locker with a laugh, then pointed at herself. "Twenty-two, remember? You don't get to 'ma'am' me until I'm like 45!"

"Roger that!" Alfie laughed.

"Good. See you at Center 8 at 7:15," Ray called over her shoulder as she left the den.

"That's going to end badly," LeRoy observed as he stepped out of the bathroom attached to the den.

"Probably, but it's going to be a hell of a ride," Alfie grinned, then turned beet red when he realized what he had said. "Not that there will be any riding... I just meant..."

"Yeah, I know what you meant. Go." LeRoy made a shooing motion with his hand, excusing Alfie before he said anything else stupid.

Alfie raced home as fast as he could. He wanted to get home as quickly as possible to tell his family about his date so they could finish their torment of him before he had to meet Ray. He ran into the house, slamming the door behind him. "Mom? Dad?"

"In here, Alfie!" his mom called from the living room.

Alfie paused in the entryway to kick off his shoes before heading that way. "Hey, can I borrow the car? I've got a date..." He trailed off as he entered the living room and saw the back of a tall man standing by his mom. "What- Ah!" Alfie yelled as he felt himself being tackled from behind. He grabbed his assailant's wrist and spun around, wrenching the man's arm around behind him. Alfie then kicked the man's feet out from under him and fell with him, pinning him to the ground.

The man groaned. "Shit, Alf! What the hell, man?!"

"Alfie! Let Nathan up!" Vivian screeched.

Alfie looked around in confusion before he realized that the man who had attacked him was his brother, Nathan, and the man who had his back to the door was his other brother, Robert.

"What the hell is all the commotion?!" George walked in to find his family up in arms. He whistled shrilly until they all quieted. "Can someone explain what is going on here?"

"Nathan tried to get the jump on Alf and sometime since the last time we were home, the guy turned into a ninja," Robert explained with a laugh, settling onto the couch.

"Alfie, you can let your brother up now," George said, calmly pulling Alfie off Nathan and to his feet.

"Alfie try to kill Nathan again?" Ruth asked, walking in with her sketch pad up in front of her face. She plopped down on the ottoman and spared them a glance before going back to her drawing.

"Yeah, and did a pretty good job of it." Nathan laughed as he rolled his shoulder, trying to work the ache out of it.

"Did you say you had a date?" Vivian suddenly blurted out.

"Awesome timing as usual, mom," Alfie sighed. "Yeah, can I borrow the car?"

"Oooo, little brother has a date!" Nathan grabbed Alfie and gave him a noogie.

Alfie punched his brother in the kidney, and Nathan suddenly found himself on the floor again. He quickly jumped back up to his feet.

"Shit, Alf! What have you been doing?" Nathan rubbed his back.

"Helping teach Tae Bo at the gym," Alfie answered distractedly. He turned back to his mom. "So, can I?"

"There is no way trophy wives are learning to do that," Robert exclaimed.

"Fine, kickboxing, whatever. Mom?"

"You don't even know?" Robert laughed. "You must be an awesome teacher."

77

"Since when have you been going to a gym?" Nathan asked.

"I work at Health Universe. Mostly business stuff, but they've been training me to teach classes."

"Alfie went with his supervisors to their corporate offices in Albany a couple of weeks ago for a business meeting." Vivian's pride was evident.

"You have a date?" Ruth gaped.

"Who with? Do we know her?" George asked, dropping next to Robert on the couch.

"It's totally Tessa. Nathan, you owe me $50!" Robert cheered.

"*Verdammt!*" Alfie growled. "It's not Tessa!"

Vivian motioned for her brood to quiet down as she walked over and put an arm around Alfie's shoulders. "Who is it, dear? Do we know her? Or... him? Which of course would be fine, too!"

"Nothing wrong with a him!" Robert grinned.

"Speaking of which, how's Lawrence?" George asked his oldest.

"He's good. He's sorry he couldn't come with me, but his mom is in the hospital."

"Oh no!" Vivian gasped.

"No, it's okay," Robert reassured his family. "Nothing serious. Just some liposuction and collagen injections. He sends his love and a present for mom."

Alfie sighed. Keeping his family on topic was like herding chickens, and he needed to get the chickens back to coop soon so he would have enough time to shower before meeting Ray. "It's a her."

"Ok, who is she?" George prodded.

"She's a girl I work with. Evelyn, Ray for short."

"How is Ray short for Evelyn?" Ruth frowned in confusion.

"Yeah, no idea. I'll let you know when I find out. So can I use the car, mom?"

"Well, of course! What are you kids doing tonight?"

"We're going to see a movie."

"Original, brother," Nathan criticized dryly.

"Her idea, brother," Alfie responded just as dryly.

"Did she do the asking, too?" Robert teased.

"Yes. Are you guys done?" Alfie growled.

"Hmmm." Robert and Nathan locked eyes for a long moment before both turned to look at Ruth. She simply shrugged. "We'll see," they all answered in unison.

"Wonderful. What are you guys doing home, anyway?"

"Mom's birthday is next week and neither of us could make it then."

"They came down to surprise me!" Vivian gushed, dropping a kiss on her two oldest sons' heads.

"Awesome." Alfie sighed at the thought of an extended visit from his brothers. He loved them and would do anything for them, but they were exhausting to be around 24/7. Alfie was silently praying that Gibson would call and say they had a job that weekend. "Well, I'm going to go shower."

"Be quick, honey. Supper is almost ready. What time is the movie?" Vivian asked, walking with her youngest son to the living room door.

"I'm meeting Ray at 7:15."

Vivian glanced at her watch. "Perfect! It's six. Gives you an hour to shower and have supper with us before you leave."

79

"Awesome," Alfie grumbled again as he headed for his room.

******

"Get the duck!" Alfie quoted loudly, then burst out laughing for the third time since they left the theater.

"Don't tell me that you actually liked that movie," Ray laughed.

Alfie's jaw dropped dramatically as he stared at her. "You didn't? How could you not?"

Ray rolled her eyes. "Alfie, it was all fart jokes and innuendos."

Alfie couldn't believe the perfect set up for his favorite line from the movie. "I'll in your endo."

"God," Ray laughed and shoved Alfie. He dramatically threw himself up against the restaurant window they were passing, startling the people inside. Ray ran over and waved apologetically as she grabbed Alfie's arm and dragged him away. "You are so weird," she giggled.

"Hell yeah, and proud of it," Alfie grinned. "But seriously, you didn't like the movie? It was hilarious!"

Ray glanced over Alfie's shoulder and her whole demeanor changed. "No," she whispered.

"What? Are you dead inside?" he laughed.

Ray shushed him with a hand on his mouth. "Here comes Bullet. Act like a boyfriend," Ray hissed as she pulled Alfie's arms around her waist.

"What-what are you doing?" Alfie whispered. He could feel himself blush as Ray pulled him closer. He was attracted to Ray. A man had to be dead or gay to not be, although Alfie was pretty sure most gay men would seriously consider her if they were given the chance. He was also a thousand percent clear on how bad of an idea it was.

"Just act like a boyfriend," Ray hissed again.

Alfie held onto Ray and backed up until he felt the wall behind him and leaned close to whisper in her ear. "Where is he?"

"My three heading this way. He saw us right before I saw him," Ray whispered back.

Alfie threw back his head and laughed, the sound echoing down the street. "I love a woman with a sense of humor." He dropped a quick kiss on her cheek. Ray gave him a confused look. "Play along, girlfriend."

Ray grinned. She wrapped her arms around Alfie's neck and rested her cheek against his shoulder. "The movie was fine."

"Better than fine," he growled quietly. Ray giggled.

"So it is true." Bullet's voice cut through their pretend moment.

Ray tried to jump away from Alfie, but he tightened his hold on her, figuring her reaction would ruin the facade. "Hey man. What're you doing downtown? I thought you guys were heading back to your secret lair or something." Ray choked on a laugh and buried her face in Alfie's shirt.

"We have lives outside of the AOJ, you know." Bullet leaned against the wall next to them and crossed his arms. "How was the movie?"

"Hilarious," Alfie responded enthusiastically.

"Fine," Ray mumbled. She moved so she stood to the side but kept an arm wrapped around Alfie's waist while he had one around her shoulders.

"She didn't like the fart jokes," Alfie explained, shaking his head sadly.

"Girls just don't understand the value of a good fart joke," Bullet lamented.

"My friend Tessa does, but she's more of a guy than a lot of guys I know."

"Really? She straight? Single?" Bullet's interest was evident.

"Yeah, yeah, and yeah. But she's like a sister to me, so I have to say this." Alfie cleared his throat and puffed his chest a little. "She has a mind of her own. If she wants to date you, she can. But if you hurt her, I'll kill you."

Bullet snorted at the thought of Alfie trying to kill him.

Ray giggled a little and leaned against Alfie.

"What? I thought it was good." Alfie looked to Ray for confirmation.

Ray smiled. "It was all right. You should probably practice more for when Ruth starts dating though."

Alfie grinned and pulled Ray closer. "Wanna help me practice?"

"Alfie!" Ray squealed as he nuzzled her neck.

"I'm going to leave you two to whatever you're doing," Bullet said uncomfortably as he pushed away from the wall. "Night."

"Night!" Alfie called. The two watched him walk around the corner before bursting out laughing.

"Okay, where the hell did that come from?" Ray gasped, holding her side.

"What?" Alfie tried to stop laughing but couldn't. "My smooth moves?"

"Yeah, sure."

"Hey, I'm smooth," Alfie argued playfully as they continued walking toward the parking garage where their cars were.

"No, you're not." Ray nudged him with her shoulder. "That's why I'm asking."

"All right, if you must know, I was channeling Matthew McConaughey – smooth, funny, charming. It totally worked. Admit it."

"It did," Ray conceded. She stopped at a black Mustang. "This is me."

"Awesome ride. I wanted a Mustang when I was younger."

"What do you have now?"

He pointed to the mint green car across from them. "That."

"A Prius? I never pegged you to drive a Prius," Ray laughed.

"Yeah, it's my moms. I don't have a car yet."

"Why not? Surely your first paycheck was enough to buy a car, or at least cover the down payment on one."

"Saving up to travel. Plus, I can walk pretty much anywhere I need to."

"Alfie, you are working for a company who not only sends you around the world, they are paying you to do it. Why not spend some of it?"

"Rainy-day fund?"

Ray laughed and pulled herself up to sit on the hood of her car. "So, earlier... It felt a little real."

"Yeah?" Alfie threw caution to the wind and leaned in close, aiming for a kiss.

"What are you doing?" Ray asked, leaning away.

"Getting shot down," Alfie laughed, embarrassed. "Sorry. Thought I'd give it a try."

"Were you going to kiss me?"

"I'll tell you something," Alfie stalled so he could move to lean coolly against the car next to her. "I was sure going to try and hope you didn't do any permanent damage to me afterward."

Ray stared at him for a long moment before moving so she had a leg on either side of him. "Do you want to try again?"

Alfie grinned and leaned forward. "So much for spontaneity."

Ray grabbed the front of his shirt and pulled. "Shut up."

******

Alfie groaned when he felt something hit his back. He was not a morning person, and he was a firm believer that Saturday mornings should be an observed holy time when nothing is done but sleeping. Waking him up during this most holy of times was the fastest way to make him grumpy... or just really groggy.

"How was your date last night?"

He rolled over to see his best friend standing in the middle of his room with her arms crossed and murder shooting from her normally brown eyes.

"Hey Tessa. What's up?" Alfie yawned and barely ducked in time to avoid getting hit by a shoe. "What the hell?"

"Forget something?" She didn't wait for his answer. She pulled out her phone and read "I'll be off at 6-ish. Want to hit the 7:30 show? I'm buying!"

"Oh shit. That's how I knew the show time. Dude, I'm sorry."

Tessa's jaw dropped. "You took your date to the movie we agreed to see together?!"

"Domestic troubles?" Robert asked, poking his head in the doorway.

"Just kiss and make up already!" Nathan called as he passed on his way to the stairs.

Tessa glared Alfie's brothers into submission as she marched to the door and slammed it. "Two questions, Alfred Louis Vihar."

Alfie cringed as Tessa used his entire name. He swung his feet over the side of the bed and reached for a pair of sweatpants.

"First: When did you start dating someone? Second: Are you going to be one of those guys who ditches his friends when he gets a girlfriend?"

"Tessa-"

"Answer the damn questions, Alfie."

"Trying," Alfie mumbled as he pulled on the pants and stood. He shuffled over and wrapped his friend in a hug, or attempted to. She wasn't in the hugging mood. "First: last night. It was more of an outing between two co-workers and ended up being a date. Second: I didn't with my last two girlfriends, what makes you think I'd ditch you for this one?"

"Gee, I wonder," Tessa snapped.

"Hey, it was once and unintentional. It will not happen again. Promise. Wanna go see the movie tonight? I'll

85

pay, plus ice cream after." Alfie gave Tessa his best puppy-dog eyes.

"I don't want your sympathy movie and guilt ice cream." Tessa tried to maintain her glare but a smile kept trying to break through. "Dammit, I hate you sometimes," she sighed.

"No, you don't," he grinned. "Okay. Want to do something else? Bowling? Putt-putt golf?"

"Naw. Brothers are home this weekend, so I have to do family stuff."

"Shit, I should probably hang with my brothers, too, since I bailed on them last night."

"Know the feeling." Tessa's grin was all teeth as she punched Alfie in the shoulder.

"I'm sorry, man!"

Tessa shook her head and chuckled, mad at herself for not being able to stay mad at Alfie. She looked down and noticed the red scar forming on his side. "Your side is healing really well. Any problems?"

"Only when somebody hits it, otherwise it's good. Hey, thanks for that, Tessa."

"What'd I do?"

"You helped me with it and kept it quiet."

"I wasn't exactly going to go tell Vivian that her son had been shot. Could you imagine the screams? We'd be deaf for a week."

Alfie laughed. "True. But thanks all the same."

"Well, seeing as things are getting all mushy, I'm going to go." Tessa said, grinning.

"All right. I'll see you later," Alfie chuckled.

Tessa opened the door and stepped back as Nathan fell into the room. She looked out and saw Robert and Ruth milling awkwardly in the hall. "Can I help you guys?"

"Nope. Just chilling," Robert grinned.

"Hey, Tessa." Ruth waved innocently.

"Hey, kiddo." Tessa ruffled Ruth's strawberry-blond curls and eyed the two oldest of the Vihar siblings. Both looked like Nordic gods with the light blond hair, blue eyes, and tall stature that they inherited from their father. "Good to see you guys. Robert, how's Lawrence?"

"Hey, Tessa!" Nathan grinned up at her from the flat of his back.

"Hey, honey." Robert pulled Tessa in for a bear hug. "He's good. You get more beautiful every time I see you." He brushed her dark brown curls back over her shoulder.

"If you keep saying things like that, I'm going to steal you from Lawrence."

"Aren't you precious?" Robert chucked Tessa under the chin.

"And I can cook better than my Italian grandmother," Tessa winked.

"Take me now!" Robert yelled dramatically.

"Keep it down up there!" George yelled from the bottom of the stairs. "Tessa, are you joining us for breakfast?"

"No, George! I've got to get home. We're running up north to see my grandma. Thanks though!" Tessa yelled back. She held out a hand to help Nathan to his feet. She wrapped an arm around him and her other around Robert. "I miss you guys! Come back more often!"

"Only if you promise to feed me next time," Robert laughed.

"Me too!" Nathan begged.

"Deal! See you guys. Bye, Ruth."

"Bye Tessa!" the Vihar kids said together.

"Dorks. All of you," Tessa laughed as she jogged down the stairs.

"We really are, you know," Ruth commented before turning back to her room to change out of her pajamas.

"So, little brother..." Nathan started, pushing his way back into Alfie's room.

"Well, this sounds ominous." Robert followed.

"Sometimes I hate you guys," Alfie sighed and closed the door behind him. He plopped back down on his bed and tucked a pillow under his head. "What?"

Robert settled in next to him and leaned against the headboard. Nathan pulled Alfie's desk chair out and plopped down before propping his feet up on the bed.

"Who's the chick?" Nathan said without preamble.

"Which one?" Alfie yawned.

"You got more than one?"

"There's a lot of chicks. You should be more specific," Alfie sassed.

"The girl you're dating, smartass," Nathan snapped.

"Ray," Robert supplied.

"What do you want to know?"

"What's she like?" Robert asked.

"Is she hot?" Nathan blurted.

"Seriously, guys?" Alfie laughed. "Yes, she's gorgeous. She's funny, sassy, and can kick my ass."

"What does she do at the gym? I'm assuming she doesn't work at the front desk?" Nathan winked.

"No." Alfie scrambled his brains for what Ray would do at the 'gym' he worked at. "She teaches the self-defense classes and Tae Bo."

"Ah, so she really could kick your ass."

"Yes."

"You kiss her?" Nathan asked.

"Yes. Well... kinda," Alfie mumbled.

"Kinda?"

"Wait, wait, wait," Robert broke in. "Did you kiss her or did she kiss you?"

"There's a difference?" Alfie stalled.

His brothers looked at him like he was a kid just back from his first boy-girl party. "Yes!" they both said.

Alfie chuckled. "I tried, caught her off guard, made a joke, and then she kissed me."

They both groaned. "You never let her make the first move!" Nathan exclaimed.

"Why not?" Alfie frowned at his brothers like they had lost their minds.

"Because now she has the upper hand in the relationship. You might as well grow out your hair and wear a skirt."

"Well... Not quite," Robert halted Nathan's rant with a raised hand.

Alfie shook his head and stood up. "Did you miss the part where she could kick my ass? That's not an exaggeration, guys. And I am 100 percent okay with the fact. Ray's awesome and the bad-assness is just a part of that."

"Bad-assness? Dude, she works at a gym. It's not like she's a super spy," Nathan snorted.

"Hmm, so more Million Dollar Baby than Black Widow," Robert contributed. Nathan nodded.

Alfie had to bite his tongue so he wouldn't tell his brothers just how wrong they were. "Guys, Ray isn't the first girl I've dated. It's not like I'm an inexperienced fifteen-year-old fumbling with a bra clasp in the back of mom's car." He turned a pointed look at Nathan, who actively avoided catching his eye.

"You're packing, right? You know, safe," Robert asked, flipping through a college catalog he found on Alfie's nightstand.

"And now we're changing subjects," Alfie blurted as he pulled a pair of jeans on and dug through his closet for a clean shirt. "What are we doing today?"

War Pigs by Black Sabbath blared from Alfie's cell phone, cutting off Robert's reply.

"Shit!" Alfie dove for his phone where it sat on the charger on his nightstand, afraid that work or Ray might be calling, but Nathan beat him to it.

"Alfred's answering service, this is Nathan. Alfred can't come to the phone right now. He's busy menstruating. May I take a message?"

"Nate, give me my phone!" Alfie hissed. He watched his brother's face turn from playful pain-in-the-ass smile to a confused frown.

"Yeah. Sorry. Hang on a sec." Nathan put his hand over the mouth piece. "Alfie, she sounds hot!"

Alfie growled in the back of his throat and reached for the phone again, but Nathan shouldered past him to perch on Alfie's desk. Robert dropped the catalog he was looking at and turned his attention to his brothers.

"You must be the infamous Ray we keep hearing about," Nathan said into the phone. "Now, you sound like a beautiful woman, why would you be dating my brother? No, more importantly, where in the world did 'Ray' come from?"

Robert snorted as he tried to choke back his laughter. Alfie growled again and grabbed Nathan by the front of his shirt. "Give me the damned phone!" he hissed.

"That's wonderful. I better give the phone to my brother before he strokes out. Nice meeting you, Ray!" Nathan yelled the last bit as Alfie ripped the phone from his hand and stormed out of the room.

Alfie ran down the stairs and locked himself in the first-floor bathroom. "I am so sorry about that, Ray," he apologized as he sat on the floor with his back against the door. "My brothers are assholes."

He heard Ray's breathy laugh come through the phone and smiled. "It's okay, Alfie. He seemed... nice?"

"You're too kind," Alfie laughed. "What's up?"

"I had fun last night, Alfie." Ray's voice turned from laughing to smoky in those few words.

"I did, too." Alfie's stomach suddenly had an entire flock of seagulls in it. In the past, he had been good with relationships, but he was always a nervous wreck during the 'dating' portion that led to the relationships. "We should do it again sometime."

"That's actually what I was calling about," Ray said.

Alfie wasn't sure, but he felt like she was almost as nervous as he was. "You want to go out again?"

"Yeah, I mean, if you want to," Ray stuttered. Then she laughed. "God, listen to me sounding all eloquent."

"It's nice to hear you sound human," Alfie laughed.

"What does that mean?"

Alfie breathed deep and took the plunge. "I don't know if you know this, but you're pretty much perfect. It's nice to find out otherwise."

"Wow. Uh, thanks." Ray's grin was evident in her voice. "How about tonight?"

"Yes, oh, wait. No, I can't tonight. We're celebrating my mom's birthday all weekend, which is why my idiot brothers are here. It's probably too soon to invite you to a family affair." Alfie joked, half hoping she would say yes, half hoping she would say no.

"You could say that," Ray giggled awkwardly.

"Right. How about Monday? There's an Irish band playing in the courtyard outside O'Rory's Pub. They have good food and Cameron has never brought in a bad band. She's getting known for it around San Luca."

"Cameron?"

"She owns O'Rory's. Her father opened it twenty-some-odd years ago, and she took it over two years ago. She and my brother, Robert, dated a little in high school."

"Oh, okay. Yeah, that sounds cool. We can head over there when we're done at work."

"It's a date."

"Yes, it is."

Alfie grinned at how sure Ray sounded. "All right, since you told my brother, you have to tell me now. Where did 'Ray' come from?"

Ray laughed. "I was wondering how long it would take you to ask. People usually ask within the first few days. I got it from one of the guys I trained with for the Olympics. My trainer introduced me as Evelyn Renae Green, and one of the guys thought he said Evelyn Ray Green. He teased me about it for a few weeks and the rest sort of adopted it as a nickname for me. It's stayed with me since. Where did Alfie come from?"

"A little kid who couldn't say his own name so started calling himself Alfie enough that his family picked it up."

Ray giggled. "That's adorable."

"Sixteen-year-old me didn't think so. I spent six months trying to convince people to call me Louis because I thought my middle name was cooler than Alfred."

"No!" Ray laughed again, making Alfie smile. "How did that go for you?"

"Well, I'm still being called Alfie, so you tell me."

Her breathy laugh washed over him, warming him to his toes. "I'll see you Monday, Alfie."

"Bye, Ray."

******

The Vihar family was just sitting down to the table at Vivian's favorite Italian restaurant on Sunday evening when *War Pigs* blasted out of Alfie's phone.

"Shit! Sorry, sorry!" Alfie apologized to his parents and pulled his phone out of his pocket to silence it when he saw Health Universe on the caller ID. "Oh. No. I have to take this. I'll be right back."

"Alfie! It can wait!" George called after Alfie as he headed for the door.

"Hello?" Alfie answered cautiously.

"Vihar," Gibson started. "We are having a meeting at HQ. Be here in 20 minutes."

"I can't, sir. I'm in the middle of a family thing."

93

"Vihar. You have 20 minutes to get here," Gibson gritted out. "You have no option in this."

"Shit!" Alfie looked over his shoulder through the window at his family. "Fine. I'll be there ASAP."

"20 minutes," Gibson repeated before the line went dead.

"They're going to kill me," Alfie muttered before heading back into the restaurant. He walked right over to his mom and kissed her cheek. "I am so sorry, but I have to go. There's been an emergency at work."

"An emergency at a gym?" Nathan scoffed. "Come on, Alf. Where are you running off to?"

"What kind of emergency?" George's concern was written across his face.

"Was that Ray again?" Robert grinned knowingly at his brother.

"No. It was my boss at work. He needs me to come in. I'm so sorry, mom." Alfie gave Vivian his most apologetic look and threw in his puppy-dog eyes for good measure.

"Oh, all right, Alfie. Just hurry home as quickly as you can for cake and ice cream." Vivian pulled Alfie down so she could kiss him on the cheek. "Shall we get some lasagna to go for you?"

"That would be great. Thank you, mom. Sorry about leaving."

"It's okay, dear." She pressed her keys into his hand. "We'll ride with your brothers. Oh, stop!" Vivan scolded her other three children for groaning. "Drive safely."

"I will. See you all later." Alfie walked away from his family with a sense of loss and dread. He hated leaving his family like this, but he had never been called into work before. He couldn't even think of something that Gibson would call him in for. Alfie didn't think it was for a job since he wasn't told to bring his go bag or to get to the den for briefing, and the unknown was making him nervous. He climbed into his mother's Prius and turned it toward HQ.

Alfie parked the car a half a block away from HQ and walked through the dark streets to the back door. He quickly scanned the area before swiping his ID badge to unlock the door. The hall was quiet when he entered. He found out why when he found the gym all but abandoned except for two women from Team 5 climbing the rock wall in the corner and a man from Team 14 running on the track above Alfie's head. He tucked his badge and car keys into his pocket and headed for Team 9's den.

"Vihar!"

Alfie skidded to a halt and backed up a few steps when he heard his name shouted from conference room Tango. "Sir?"

"Come in and have a seat." Gibson started piling up papers into a folder. He sat alone in the room and had his papers scattered across the table, reviewing them before his team showed up. "You made it faster than I expected. How did your family take the news?"

"Um... What?" Gibson had never talked about Alfie's family before, and his question caught Alfie off guard.

"Didn't you say you were at a family thing?"

"Yeah. We were out for my mom's birthday." Alfie finally recovered enough to sit down across from Gibson. "My brothers will be giving me crap for leaving for a few days, but my mom didn't seem too mad about it. Are the others coming?"

95

Gibson chuckled. "Yes. You can relax. This isn't a one-on-one."

"*Bonsoir le capitaine et le garçon!*" LeRoy said as he walked into the room right on cue.

"*Bonsoir!* But seriously, dude, we're not on a ship," Alfie laughed.

"*Que?*" LeRoy asked as he settled himself in a seat at the head of the table.

"*Le capitaine* is for a leader of a ship. I think *le meneur* would be more suitable for Gibson."

LeRoy glared at Alfie. "Who's the Frenchman here, *môme?*"

"Well, aren't you technically Cajun?"

"And that's a bucket of crayfish we don't want to open," Ray said with a horrible Louisiana accent as she walked in and plopped down next to Alfie.

"Comedians, both of you." LeRoy glared at the two, but he had a slight sparkle in his eye that told them his anger wasn't real.

"Found them, sir." Nikolai walked into the room followed by Bullet and Warp.

"No Crux? Dad let them out on their own, eh?" Alfie whispered to Ray, who giggled quietly. Bullet eyed Alfie and Ray together but didn't say anything.

"Dr. Monte-Piere, were you able to find anything else out about the problem in Canada?" Warp jumped right in without any preamble.

LeRoy flipped through his notes. "There seems to be a few guys raising hell up there."

"So much for Canadians being the nice ones."

"Vihar, shut it," Gibson ordered.

"Yes, sir."

"There are three I like for this particular job: Luther Gates, Gustav Farthing, and Andre Roux. All three have been making some purchases that are used in processing and using uranium. Here are their last known addresses and an accounting of their suspicious activity." LeRoy handed Warp a folder. "Also, a source of mine up north told me that a few scientists who are known for working on the shady side of their science have been missing for a few months. At last account, they were working together to develop a rudimentary way to process uranium on-site so the time from mining to finished product could be cut in half. I'm betting they have either been recruited or forced into helping one of these men."

"Does one of these three look better for it than the others?" Bullet asked.

"Not particularly. But both Farthing and Roux have sped up their rate of purchases and both have contacted various groups looking for assistance."

"Lab help or henchmen?" Warp asked.

"Both, although Farthing has spent more on henchmen than lab help."

"He's expecting a big fight, then," Bullet concluded.

Warp nodded her agreement. "All right. This all looks good. Is there anything else worth mentioning, Dr. Monte-Piere?"

"Well, Canada has a lot of resources that these guys could be going after. Uranium was just an educated guess, but there's oil lines, diamonds, water, forests-"

"Syrup."

"Vihar!" Gibson growled.

"Sorry, sir."

97

"Joke if you want, but maple syrup is a huge industry for them," LeRoy pointed out.

"Not really a high-risk industry, though," Warp said, mocking LeRoy.

"Seen stupider things," Nikolai said, warningly.

"All right. Enough," Gibson cut in. "Anything else need to be discussed?"

"I believe that is all I had. In my opinion, Roux and Farthing are greater threats than Gates. So if you were watching any of them, it should be those two," LeRoy finished.

"We will get this information to Crux and let you know what we decide. When do you think either of these two will make their move?" Warp asked.

"I would say within two weeks. They are both moving into position, so it won't be long now."

"What a tomcat says in a room full of rocking chairs," Alfie whispered to Ray.

Gibson closed his eyes. "Vihar, I swear, I will gag you."

"Yes, sir."

"Keep us informed," Gibson said, standing up. He held out his hand to shake with Warp and Bullet. "Thanks for coming out."

"Of course." Bullet's smile was friendly as he shook hands with the rest of Team 9. "We will see you guys soon to fight the bad guy."

"Child," Warp mumbled as she followed Bullet from the room.

"Bitch," Ray muttered.

"You could say that again." LeRoy dropped into his chair.

"Agreed," Gibson mumbled. "All right, guys. I'm sorry for calling you here for that. When they called me, they made it sound much more important. Go back to what you were doing and I'll see you in the morning. Let's make it a 10 a.m. to make up for this little mess."

"Thanks, sir." Ray playfully punched Gibson in the shoulder.

"Get out of here before I regret my decision," he growled.

"Good night, sir," they all said and headed out the door.

"Alfie," Ray put a hand on his arm to stop him. "Want to do something tonight since we're already together?"

"I'd love to, but my family's probably still at the restaurant. I can still catch them there." Alfie hesitantly took Ray's hand as they walked down the dim hallway for the door. Nikolai and LeRoy's silhouettes were just visible ahead of them. "We still on for tomorrow night?"

Ray squeezed his hand. "Of course!"

They held hands until they reached Alfie's car. "This is me."

Ray chuckled, "I remember."

"Good night, Ray." Alfie pulled her close for a kiss, which she deepened until she had him pressed up against the Prius.

"Good night, Alfie." Her voice was rough as she left him with a smile.

******

"Hey! You saved me some garlic bread! That was nice of you!" Alfie snagged the last piece off of Nathan's plate as he dropped into the empty seat next to his brother.

"Jerk," Nathan muttered with a fierce glare.

"Boys," George warned.

Alfie laughed as he dodged the punch Nathan aimed at his side. "Sorry about ditching you. The 'emergency' wasn't as catastrophic as we were led to believe."

"Well, I'm glad everything is okay." Vivian handed Alfie the box with his lasagna in it. "Do you want to eat it here while it's still warm?"

"Naw, you're all done. I can nuke it when we get home," Alfie said around the last bite of garlic bread.

"Okay, let's go then." George stood up and pulled Vivian's chair out for her.

"Thanks, dear." She smiled at her husband then put an arm around Alfie's shoulders. "What was the emergency that wasn't an emergency?"

"You know, I don't really know myself." Alfie laughed, his mind racing. "They had a late night meeting with a partner-"

"At 7 p.m. on a Sunday?" Robert cut him off.

"Uh, the partner was from Japan. It's Monday morning for them."

"But if they were meeting here, it's still Sunday night," Ruth pointed out.

"Video conference call. Isn't the internet great?" Alfie blurted. "So how was dinner?"

"It was good. Would have been better if all of my kids were there for it though." Vivian winked at Alfie to let him know she wasn't mad.

"So why did you have to be there if they were just video conferencing with a partner?" Ruth clung to the previous topic.

"My boss had the calls mixed up. He, uh... thought it was with the partner in Berlin, and he wants me there for that one since we will be discussing opening another branch to, uh, be our sister branch."

"Sister branch?" Ruth asked, a doubting look on her face.

"Yeah! All the new branches get partnered with an established branch so the management has someone to go to with questions. Plus, the higher ups of our branch will go over and train the employees at the new branch and help with opening." Alfie could not shut his mouth off and he could feel himself sink lower and lower into the lies he was spewing.

"So why did you have to be there?" Nathan asked.

"Oh! Well, they wanted me to see what it's like dealing with partners. And I speak German! They thought it could help. Here's the car." Alfie paused next to it, hoping everybody would get in and they could change the topic of conversation.

"So what happened when they realized that it was Japan and not Berlin?" Robert asked.

"Well, I had to run to the manager's office to get the right file and entertain them for a bit while he read over what we were supposed to be talking about. Then-"

"How did you entertain them?" Ruth asked.

"What? How did I entertain them?" Alfie felt his mind go blank. "Well, I attempted to introduce myself in Japanese and when that failed, I just told their translator about myself and why I was there and she relayed it."

101

"That's not really entertaining," Ruth frowned.

"I know," Alfie sighed. He felt drained. All he wanted was to go home, eat his lasagna, and sleep.

Robert nudged Alfie with his shoulder. "So what exactly do you do at this gym? We kind of heard but we didn't get the whole story."

Alfie collapsed against the car. "Can we talk when we get home? I'm hungry."

"Oh, my, yes! Let's take this home and you can keep talking." Vivian moved to the car but Robert's words stopped her.

"Nate and I aren't going back to the house, mom. We told you that we were heading north right after dinner. Nate has to work tomorrow and I have to keep Lawrence from killing his mother. Apparently, she is the worst patient."

"Oh, that's right! Well, continue Alfie."

Alfie groaned inwardly. "I'm kind of a 'jack of all trades, master of none' sort at Health Universe. They have me shadowing in the offices in the morning, then I'm out on the floor in the afternoon. I'm learning all about how the business runs – payroll, scheduling, management, membership stuff, in addition to the gym side – classes, equipment, working with members, you get the picture."

"That's a lot of stuff." Nathan was impressed.

"I would have never pictured you in a gym, little brother." Robert put an arm around Alfie's shoulders. "But it sounds like you're getting a handle on it. Plus, after how you tossed Nate, I'm guessing you're learning something, too."

"More than you can imagine," Alfie mumbled. "Oh! Mom, dad, my boss told me tonight that they are planning another trip to Albany this week and they want me to go with them."

"So soon?" Vivian asked.

"Yeah. Apparently I impressed somebody last time, so they want me along again."

"When are you leaving and getting back?" George asked, pulling out his phone so he could put it on his schedule. "You were going to go with me to that tradeshow on Sunday."

"Shit! I totally forgot." Alfie cringed. He loved going to tradeshows with his dad because everybody took him for a sucker. He helped his dad score some good deals on parts by pretending to know nothing about cars and then figuratively slamming the vendors up against the wall. George was usually the only mechanic shop owner who didn't get taken to the cleaners at the tradeshows. "I don't know. They don't have a date yet. They just know it'll be this week."

"Okay." George tried to not look disappointed. "We'll play this one by ear, eh?"

"I could go with you, dad," Ruth said hesitantly.

George looked down at his youngest in surprise. "You would? When did you start wanting to come with me to tradeshows?"

"I don't know," Ruth paused. "Now?"

George grinned and pulled her into a huge hug that had her feet leaving the ground. "That's great! We'll have fun! You already know more about cars than a lot of those idiots who are supposed to be experts. We'll have fun with them."

George finally set her back down and she frowned up at her father. "Dad, I'm not helping you swindle them."

"Alfie and I don't swindle them! We just get better deals, but that's fine. I just can't wait to see their jaws drop when you start talking about intake manifold gaskets and crankshaft oil seals."

"Well, anyway. It was good seeing you guys." Alfie started the goodbyes before the conversation could turn back to his job.

"Yes! Thank you boys for coming down to celebrate my birthday." Vivian gushed as she pulled Robert and Nathan into her arms. "Don't be such strangers. I miss you two."

"You're going to miss us more if you suffocate us." Robert choked out.

"Air!" Nathan gasped.

"Sorry!" Vivian finally let them go and kissed each of them on the cheek. "But seriously, come visit more. And Robert, you better bring Lawrence with you next time. I never get to see him."

Robert laughed. "I will, mom."

George was next to hug them, but he was less forceful about it than his wife. "What your mother said," he grinned.

"Bye squirt." Nathan ruffled Ruth's hair as Robert pulled her into a hug.

"Bye guys." Ruth let go of Robert and quickly hugged Nathan.

"Glad you're leaving, you pains in the ass." Alfie grinned and hugged his brothers, too.

"Keep me up to date about your job," Robert ordered. "I'm glad you found something you seem to enjoy."

"I do. Thanks, Rob."

"Call me when Ray dumps your ass. I wouldn't mind getting to know her." Nathan winked, then flinched when Alfie punched him in the shoulder, hard. He rubbed his arm. "Damn, man! You didn't used to be so strong."

"I work at a gym, remember?" Alfie laughed.

"Hey, can we get a discount?" Robert asked.

"You're going to drive to San Luca every day to go to the gym but you only come every few months to see our parents?" Alfie teased.

Ruth laughed. "Don't tell mom."

"Oh, stop!" Vivian laughed. "Boys, you better hit the road if you want to be home by midnight."

"All right. Happy birthday, mom." Robert kissed her cheek. "Love you."

Nathan kissed her other cheek. "Love you, too, mom."

"I love you, boys. Now go before I start crying." Vivian wiped at her eyes.

"Bye!" Robert and Nathan called as they got into Robert's car.

The rest of the Vihar family stood on the curb and waved as the car drove off.

"All right, back to casa de Vihar."

"Dad, did you just mix Spanish with Scandinavian?" Ruth laughed.

"Yeah, what of it? Get in the car," George growled playfully.

Alfie and Ruth climbed into the back of Vivian's Prius as she slid behind the wheel and George took shotgun.

Ruth leaned close to Alfie and whispered so their parents wouldn't hear. "Are you ever going to tell the truth about your job?"

Alfie stared at her a long second, trying to figure out what to say. "What are you talking about, Ruth? I am."

"Yeah, I'm not an idiot, Alf. I've been tested."

"Those results aren't official."

"Still doesn't make me an idiot."

Alfie stared at Ruth, who glared back at him. "You wouldn't believe me anyway so-"

"Try me."

"Ruth, I can't. Maybe someday, but not now." He put a gentle hand on her shoulder. "Please, don't ask me."

"Fine," Ruth sighed. "But you'll tell me eventually."

"I'll try."

"No." Ruth scooted closer and rested her head on Alfie's shoulder. "You will."

Alfie grinned into the darkness. "Okay."

******

"You are going to love this." Alfie was so excited he was almost bouncing.

Ray chuckled. "Why do you think that?"

"Oh, come on! You don't think you'll like it? Irish music, great little pub, amazing food, good beer – or so I hear. I've never had it since I'm still under age." Alfie emphasized the last bit with a grin and a wink.

Ray laughed and shook her head. The pair walked down the quiet residential street where they had parked a block away from the busy little downtown area of San Luca. The mile-long cobblestone main street was full of little shops, bars, galleries, and pitted with courtyards featuring beautiful wrought-iron fences. O'Rory's Irish Pub was two blocks into the area on the northern edge and was set back from the street by one of the courtyards. Its iron fence was done in intricate Celtic knots and clover leaf patterns and had been featured in many tourist and bar magazines across the country, as was their food, entertainment, and atmosphere.

"Is that Alfie Vihar I see?!" A tall, willowy woman dressed in an emerald green dress stood just outside the gate of O'Rory's courtyard as Alfie and Ray approached. Her riot of red curls poured down her back and fought against the hair tie she had used in an attempt to keep them reined in.

"Hey, Cameron!" Alfie hugged her briefly before turning to Ray. "Cameron, this is Ray Green. Ray, this is Cameron O'Rory, first generation American and owner of the finest Irish pub in southern California."

"Oh, stop!" Cameron laughed as she shook Ray's hand. "Good to meet you, Ray. Are you two here for the band?"

"Yep! And the food. Is it any good?" Alfie teased.

"The food or the band?" Cameron finished writing on the blackboard that sat on the sidewalk and motioned for them to follow her into the courtyard where the band was warming up.

"Either?"

"Alfred Vihar, you know better than to ask about my food." Cameron snapped a towel at him.

Alfie laughed. "I know! What about the band? Who are they?"

Cameron settled them at a good table and handed them menus. "Miles from Dublin is their name. They're from Nebraska or something. I actually don't know if they're good. I've never heard them, but they have some good reviews online."

"That's weird for you." Alfie rested his arms on his closed menu and looked up at her.

"I know. There's some Irish band convention in San Diego. I had no idea they did that, but most of them were booked at various places closer to the city. I called a buddy of mine to see if any of them were available for tonight when one of my regulars canceled. They were the only ones who were free, so I booked them sight unseen. You'll let me know if they're bad, right?"

"Of course. Right after I post it all over the internet that Cameron O'Rory has lost her touch."

"I'm going to personally spit in your food."

"Good! I was going to order extra spit."

Cameron was the first to break when she threw her head back and laughed heartily. "I've missed you, lad. You and Tessa haven't been here in a while, but I'm glad to see you brought someone new." She turned her attention to Ray. "Have you ever been here before?"

"I don't think I have," Ray answered.

"Well, welcome to O'Rory's!" Cameron said with a huge grin. "I'll leave you alone so you can check out the menus. Can I grab either of you drinks?"

"Biggest mug of Guinness you have!"Alfie nearly shouted.

Cameron's eye ticked. "Guinness is served in special pint glasses."

"Fine! A special pint glass of Guinness!"

"A Coke it is." Cameron laughed. "How about you, lass?"

"I'll take a Coke, too."

"Two Cokes. Let me know if you need anything else."

"She's pretty cool," Ray whispered to Alfie behind her menu.

"Yeah. She and Robert probably would have gotten married, which would have been awesome! I would have had a guaranteed job here in the summers and after graduation."

"Why'd they break up?"

"Robert joined the other team. They're still pretty close though. She'll probably be the god mother if Robert and Lawrence ever adopt."

"Oh! Robert and Lawrence? That's cool."

"Yeah, Lawrence is pretty awesome. His family is insane though. They're the crazy rich, disconnected from real people, Beverly Hills type. Plus, his mom kept trying to 'fix' him for years after he came out. She eventually backed off but kept prodding. My mom finally had a sit-down with her to make her leave Lawrence alone."

Ray laughed. "Are you serious?"

"Yeah. Now, I think she feels so guilty that she's just throwing stuff and affection at both Lawrence and Robert."

"Your family sounds so fun. What do your parents do?"

"Coke and Coke." Cameron set their drinks down on the table. "Do you guys know what you want?"

"Oh, umm…" Ray quickly flipped through the menu. "I'll take the fish and chips. Can I do cocktail sauce instead of tartar sauce?"

"Sure. Alfie, you still do bangers and mash?"

"Absolutely! Don't forget my extra spit!"

"Ass." Cameron blew him a kiss over her order pad and headed to the kitchen.

"My dad owns Rustic Motors and my mom is an appraiser at Franklin and McKeen Auction House."

"Rustic Motors? That's so awesome! I had to take my car to one of your dad's garages a few years ago because he was the only one with the part that I needed. They were super nice and the price didn't make me hate all mechanics like they usually do."

Alfie laughed. "Yeah, my dad tries to do his best to not gouge people, unless they're assholes. Then he has no problem charging double for labor."

"And your mom is an appraiser? I don't even know what that is."

"She examines the items people bring into the auction house and gives them an estimated value. She's the leading expert on Bronze and Iron Age Scandinavian artifacts in California in addition to a whole lot of other European stuff." Alfie shrugged with a laugh. "She knows so much that she's gotten a ton of offers from colleges and universities all over the country and a few in Europe to teach classes, but she always turns them down. She loves her job and doesn't want leave dad."

"Fish and chips with cocktail sauce for Ray." Cameron swooped in and deposited plates in front of each of them. "Bangers and mash with extra spit for Alfie."

"Thanks Cameron!" Alfie called as she headed for her next table. "What about your family, Ray?"

"Well, there's not much to tell," Ray started as she took a bite of fish. "Oh my god, this is amazing! Anyway, my family is a pretty standard American family. My dad took off when I was fourteen and my mom has been working her ass off to give me everything she can since. I have one brother who I haven't seen since he went to live with our dad when I was sixteen."

"Oh, Ray." Alfie reached over and took her hand.

"No, it's okay." Her smile wobbled a little. "My mom and I are a good team, and she gave me everything. I wouldn't change it. And now that I'm with R.I., I can afford to put her up and give her what she went without. Plus, I have Team 9. I have two brothers and an... uncle, since I can't think of Gibson as a dad." They laughed and Alfie agreed with her. "And now I have you dragging me to bad movies and Irish pubs, so my life is good."

Alfie leaned over and kissed her cheek. "I'm glad."

The courtyard had filled up with people by the time they had finished eating and the band started playing.

"They are better than I feared," Cameron said quietly as she stopped to pick up Alfie and Ray's empty plates.

"We were just talking about that," Ray told her.

"Are you dancing tonight?" Alfie asked.

Cameron sighed. "I don't know yet. One of the bartenders called in so I have to cover for her."

"Hey! I can cover the bar when you're dancing!" Alfie exclaimed.

Cameron frowned at him. "Right. You guys need refills?"

"Sure."

"Thanks." Ray handed Cameron their glasses.

"Be right back." Cameron turned and spotted a pretty brunette heading toward her. "Hey Tessa! I was wondering if you were coming tonight."

"Hey, Cam!" Tessa wrapped an arm around the bar owner in a quick hug. "I've been talking about O'Rory's for years and Rocco was finally able to come with me." Tessa motioned over her shoulder with her thumb, indicating the tall, dark, and handsome Italian otherwise known as her oldest brother.

"Tess, I didn't know you were coming out tonight." Alfie jumped to his feet and stood by Cameron.

"Hey, Alfie! You told me that Cam had a band tonight, remember?" Tessa laughed.

111

"I'm losing my mind. Must be too many shots to the head." He turned and winked at Ray, who laughed, knowing she was responsible for most of those.

"Oh, Ray. This is my best friend, Contessa Pellegrini. Tess, this is Ray."

Tessa laughed at Alfie's attempt at a formal introduction. "You can call me Tessa. This is my brother, Rocco." She motioned for him to join them at the table. "Cam, I don't think you've met him either, have you?"

"No, I haven't," she said with a sultry grin, putting her hand out. "I'm Cameron O'Rory."

His interest evident, Rocco glanced at Cameron before glancing briefly at Tessa, who nodded surreptitiously. "Good to meet you." He gently took her hand and stepped close.

"Have a seat." Alfie motioned to an empty chair at their table and sat back down next to Ray.

"Thanks." Tessa dropped down on Alfie's other side. "I don't mean to interrupt your date."

"That's fine," Ray said with a warm smile. "I'm glad to finally meet you. Alfie talks about you all the time."

"Then you have the advantage." Tessa laughed. "I've heard little about you, but I haven't seen Alfie much the last couple of weeks, so it's understandable."

Alfie grabbed Tessa's hand. "You need to help me convince Cameron to dance tonight."

"Yes!" Tessa spun in her chair and grabbed Cameron's arm, breaking off the conversation she was having with Rocco. "Cam! You have to dance tonight!"

Cameron laughed. "Dammit, Alfie. This is your doing. All right, I'll dance, but Tessa, you have to join me."

"Man!" Tessa looked down at her jeans and flip flops. "I'm going to have to change."

"Since when can you dance?" Alfie asked as Tessa stood up.

"Cam's been teaching me. Rocco, can I have the keys? I need to get my bag out of your car."

"Yeah." He handed her the keys and she took off.

"Any particular song, since you're the one requesting the dance?" Cameron asked Alfie with a pointed look.

"I don't know what they can play, so pick something you know." Alfie grinned. Cameron glared at him and punched him in the shoulder before walking over to the band's manager.

"Here!" Tessa tossed the keys on the table as she ran past, heading for the bathroom so she could change.

"Rocco, man. Have a seat." Alfie indicated the other chairs.

"Sure." He folded his tall frame onto an iron chair.

"Rocco is Tessa's oldest brother and was two grades above Robert and Cameron in school," Alfie explained to Ray. "Rocco, this is Ray. She and I work together and are..." he paused, looking at Ray for confirmation.

"Seeing each other," she finished with a grin.

"Company ink, Vihar." Rocco's voice rumbled with suppressed laughter.

"Shut up, Pellegrini," Alfie grinned.

The waitress who dropped off Alfie and Ray's Cokes nearly swooned when she took Rocco's drink order, much to the couple's amusement.

"Here's a pleasant surprise for us," the lead singer of the band said into the mic. "Our lovely hostess and owner of

O'Rory's would like to dance for us all! Please put your hands together for Cameron and Tessa!"

Everybody in the courtyard cheered and clapped as Cameron and Tessa moved to the small open area between the stage and the tables. Tessa had changed into a black skirt and soft-soled black shoes. The band struck up *Finnegan's Wake*, and Alfie quietly sang along as the two women began dancing. The crowd loved it and quickly started clapping and stomping in time with the music. By the time they finished, everybody was on their feet cheering.

"Yeah, Tessa!" Alfie whooped and hollered for his friend. When she got back to the table, he picked her up in a hug and spun her around before setting her back on her feet. "That was awesome! Why didn't you tell me you were learning step dancing?"

Tessa laughed. "It was kind of a joke in the beginning and then I realized how much I liked it." She picked up Alfie's Coke and took a big swig before dropping back into her chair.

"If you guys liked our dance, you're going to love the next surprise." Alfie turned when he heard Cameron's voice over the crowd. She was up on stage, staring at him with a small grin on her face.

"Shit," he muttered.

"I have another friend who would like to sing to you. Alfie, get up here!" Cameron motioned for him to join her as the crowd started cheering.

"Shit," he said again.

"What is she doing?" Ray whispered in his ear.

"Go!" Tessa laughed, pulling him out of his chair.

"Cameron!" Alfie yelled, shaking his fist at her as he made his way to the stage. "You going to join me?"

She about turned him down but the crowd started cheering, so she ruefully nodded. "What song?"

"Hmmm, do you guys need a break?" Alfie asked the band as he climbed onto the stage.

"Sure." They all agreed, settling back into their chairs and waiting to see what would happen.

"Well, Cam, do you know *Johnny Be Fair*?"

"Of course!"

Alfie winked at her and took the mic. "Well, since this was a surprise, I'm going to fall back on an old favorite of mine, although it's traditionally sang by a woman. *Johnny Be Fair*."

Alfie waited for the clapping to stop before hc started, counting on Cameron to jump in when she was ready. Alfie finished the fourth and final verse before turning to grin at Cameron where she stood as far from the mic as she could have gotten as the crowd laughed and clapped. "Thanks for the backup, Cameron."

"Always, Alfie." She laughed and bowed to the band, thanking them for letting her take over for a few minutes.

"I forgot that you sing that," Tessa said as she gave Alfie a hug.

"Me too, until I got up there." Alfie dropped back into his seat and put an arm around Ray. "Tessa and I did that for a talent show in, what? Tenth grade? We got one of the guys to act it out with her and I sang it. We were a hit!"

"Yeah, but then the jerks who destroyed a Beach Boys song beat us," Tessa grumbled as she finished Alfie's Coke.

Ray looked back and forth between the two friends. "How did they destroy it?"

"Ugh!" Tessa groaned.

115

"They reworked it so it sounded like a boy band song." Alfie laughed.

"That sounds horrible."

"It was. But they were the star football players singing and dancing. Of course they were going to win," Tessa explained with a shudder.

"How did you guys get interested in Irish music?" Ray asked, leaning her arms on the table.

"Her," Alfie and Tessa laughed as they answered and pointed at Cameron in unison.

"When Robert and Cameron started dating, they always hung out at my house, which is where Tessa usually was to avoid her five brothers. No offense, Rocco." Alfie grinned when Rocco shrugged with a chuckle.

Tessa continued, "We thought she was really cool with her red hair and accent, so we started bugging them every chance we had. She was super nice and tolerated it."

"Robert always beat me up for it later," Alfie laughed.

"Wow. You guys have been close for a long time," Ray said.

"Ten years." Tessa grinned and smacked Alfie's shoulder.

They all jumped as *War Pigs* blared out of Alfie's pocket. "Shit! I need to turn that down!" he exclaimed as he dug his phone out.

"You need to pick a different song. Something that won't frighten children," Tessa laughed.

"Shit," Alfie muttered and turned his phone so Ray could see the caller ID.

"Shit," she echoed. He jumped up and walked to a quiet corner so he could answer the call.

"What's wrong?" Tessa asked, watching Alfie.

"Work," Ray answered simply.

"Oh." Tessa stayed quiet, unsure if Alfie had told Ray that she knew what he did. They watched Alfie hang up his phone and head back to the table. Just as he reached them, Ray's phone rang in her purse.

"Did you tell them we were together?" she asked Alfie with a frown.

"No. They just gave a time and hung up."

She nodded and followed his lead by heading to the quiet corner to answer the call.

Tessa leaned close to where Alfie sat. "You have to head out again? To what you did that got you..." She surreptitiously touched her side, indicating where Alfie got shot.

"Yeah. This one shouldn't be too bad, though," he whispered back before he realized that Rocco had left them to corner Cameron at the bar.

"Good. Because if you come back with another gunshot wound, I will kill you," Tessa scolded.

"Yes, ma'am," Alfie grinned.

"Alfie?" Ray put a hand on his shoulder.

"Yeah, we have to go. Sorry for blowing you off again, Tess."

"Hey, I interrupted your date. It's perfectly fine." She reassured him. "Good luck at work."

Ray looked at her sharply, wondering how much she knew, but Alfie just smiled. "Thanks!" He tossed a couple of twenties on the table to cover supper and they headed back to the car.

"Your friends are nice," Ray commented.

"I'm glad you like them." Alfie took her hand. "Sorry if that got a little out of control. I was planning on a quiet dinner and the band. I wasn't expecting everybody to be there and then getting dragged up on stage."

"No. It's okay. It's a different side of you that I wasn't expecting," Ray chuckled. "You and Tessa are pretty tight, huh?"

"Yeah, we've been best friends since we were eight. There were some days where I refused to talk to my own siblings but I'd talk to her. I was a weird kid," Alfie laughed.

"You're still weird." Ray grinned. "But I like it. Tonight was unlike any other date I've been on, and I'm kind of surprised to say I had fun."

"Surprised, eh!" Alfie teased. "Fine. Next time, you pick what we do. I want to see what you do when you're not being super henchwoman."

******

Alfie called his parents on their way to HQ to let them know he was leaving for Albany for work, still feeling guilty for the necessary lie. They were surprised at how soon he was leaving, but George was hopeful that Alfie would be back by Sunday so he could take his two youngest kids to the tradeshow with him.

Ray and Alfie were just walking into the den as Gibson was picking up his phone. "Hey, captain!" Ray called as she dropped her bag on the floor and flopped onto the couch.

"Where they hell have you been?!"

"Calm yourself, sir. Traffic was a bitch downtown," Ray explained.

"And you, Vihar?" Gibson growled at Alfie as he dug his go bag out of his locker.

"Uh, what she said, sir." Alfie motioned at Ray before digging into his bag to make sure he had everything.

"Fine. I'll be right back. Finish getting ready. Your own combat clothes. No uniforms on this job." Gibson stormed out of the room.

"Yay! No shitty uniforms made for guys that don't fit me! So, what's the situation?" Ray asked.

"A douche on the Jersey Shore," Alfie answered quietly as he repacked his go bag. He didn't realize that he had said it out loud until LeRoy snorted. "Sorry."

"Naw, man. That was funny," LeRoy mumbled with a grin.

"We don't know. Gibson walked in here few minutes before you. He's been with the director since we got off," Nikolai finally answered her from his seat at the table.

"Awesome." Ray jumped up from the couch and headed for the door. "He'll probably be a few more minutes, so I have time to restock my chocolate stash from the galley. Anybody want anything?"

"Coke!" LeRoy called.

"Doritos," Alfie added as he dropped his bag on the couch and joined Nikolai at the table. "Are you doing a crossword puzzle?"

"Yes."

"Cool." Alfie raised slightly in his seat to see the clues. "22 down is Vesta."

Nikolai slowly raised his head to glare at Alfie, who wisely backed off. Nikolai went back to his puzzle. "Ah, you are right. I was stuck on that one." He quickly filled in the remaining words and tossed his pencil down victoriously.

"Glad I could help," Alfie muttered dryly.

"LeRoy, catch!" Ray called as she threw a plastic bottle at the Cajun. He snatched it out of the air with a nod of thanks in her direction as she dropped a handful of fun-sized candy bars into her go bag. "Alfie, they were out of original so I grabbed Cool Ranch. That okay?" She leaned against the table next to him.

"Works for me. Thanks!" Alfie smiled up at her as she slid into the seat next to him.

"Everybody take a seat!" Gibson ordered, walking into the den. He paused, then realized that they were already sitting. "Good. We are headed to Canada. Saskatchewan, to be precise."

"Who?" Ray asked simply.

"Ore."

"Or what?" Alfie joked, earning himself sighs and eye rolls from the others. "Sorry."

"Gustav Farthing, known as Ore-" Gibson started with a pointed look at Alfie, "ended up being the first to make his move."

"I knew it!" LeRoy cheered.

"He has taken control of uranium and diamond mines just outside of Prince Albert, Saskatchewan. He has also taken around 50 miners prisoner and is working on something in the mines."

"What are his demands?" Nikolai asked.

"Nothing yet. LeRoy, any ideas?"

"My theory is he took control of the uranium to make a weapon to ensure his hold on the diamond mine, but he could be working on something bigger. He has a lot of uranium at his disposal and a lot of people who could make it weapons ready."

Gibson shook his head slowly. "Well, let's hope he hasn't gotten that far yet, or this will be a short trip. As you already know, we are working with the AOJ on this. Earth Child and Force Field are still dealing with something in South America, so we will be assisting Crux, Warp, and Bullet.

While the others groaned, Alfie was worried about being around Bullet and Team 9 for so long simultaneously. He turned and caught Ray's eye. She looked just as concerned as he felt.

Alfie raised his hand. "I thought the AOJ worked with the UN. Why are they using us for this mission?"

"Finally, an intelligent question from Vihar. The UN is who called in the AOJ to deal with The Phantom because they couldn't handle him on their own. Ore has not made any international threats yet, so the UN has no jurisdiction. The Canadian government called in the AOJ for this. We were hired because the Canadians don't want anything to do with Ore more than they have to. Plus, while they have experienced troops, they don't really have anybody prepared for what we're about to do," Gibson explained.

"So the AOJ is essentially a 'for hire' group like we are."

"If it helps to think of them that way, yes. Anything else?" Gibson stood when Alfie shook his head. "All right. Finish up here and meet me at the van," Gibson said as he left the den.

Nikolai got up from the table to finish packing, leaving Ray and Alfie alone at the table. "How do you want to play this?" Alfie whispered.

Ray ran her hands through her hair. "Shit, I don't know. LeRoy already suspects something and I'm sure

Gibson has a theory, too. Let's try to avoid boyfriend/girlfriend stuff when we're just around them. When Bullet's around, we can do a little to keep it in his mind, but I'm sure he'll think we're just trying to be professional."

Alfie nodded. "Agreed." He glanced at their teammates, then leaned close to Ray with a grin. "Boyfriend/girlfriend, eh?"

She giggled quietly. "Yeah?"

"Yeah."

"Move it! Prince Albert awaits!" Gibson yelled as he strolled past the den door.

LeRoy suddenly dropped onto the table in front of them. "What are you two giggling about?" he asked suggestively.

"We... were wondering if Nikolai had Prince Albert in a can," Alfie lied with a grin.

"Yes." The large Russian reached into his bag and pulled out a red tin. He tossed it at Alfie.

"Well that failed," Ray laughed as she took the can from Alfie and sniffed it. "I didn't know you smoked, Nikolai."

"Not anymore, but tobacco has good pain relief," Nikolai answered. "Why you ask for Prince Albert in a can? Does it come in something else?"

"It's an old joke, friend," LeRoy laughed. "If you say yes, they follow it with 'You better let him out!' or 'How did you get him in there?!' It's mostly used by kids making prank calls."

"You Americans are easily entertained." Nikolai frowned as he caught the tin Ray threw back to him.

"Speaking of Prince Alberts!" LeRoy started excitedly, pulling out his phone. "Have you guys ever seen one?"

"NO!" Ray and Alfie both screamed.

"Apparently, I do not want to," Nikolai responded hesitantly, concerned with their reaction.

"Damn. I was hoping you guys would help me pick out barbell styles."

"You have one?!" Alfie asked with a cringe of discomfort. He crossed his legs at the thought.

"I'm thinking about getting one," LeRoy grinned.

"If you're done..." Gibson glared at them from the door. "The AOJ awaits."

"What? Are we flying north with them?"

"Yes."

The laughter died in Ray's throat at Gibson's answer. "Damn," she muttered.

"Move it! I'm not telling you four again!"

Team 9 slowly picked up their gear and headed out the door.

"Okay, I'm still new here, so answer me a question," Alfie started. "Why are we so hesitant to work with the AOJ – the 'good guys' – but we had no problem running out the door to help Huánxiáng, who was the 'bad guy.'"

"You've met the AOJ, Alf," LeRoy laughed.

"They're assholes," Nikolai contributed as he held the door open.

"Well, most of them, yeah. But they do save the world a lot. Don't they kind of deserve to be a little pretentious?"

"A little pretentious? Yes," Ray began before LeRoy interrupted her.

"A quintet of throbbing-"

"Douche canoes," Ray nearly shouted, cutting off whatever LeRoy was going to finish with. "No. They don't have the right. And we don't deserve to be treated the way they treat us. They have powers and that's awesome, but they can't do their job without backup, even if it is just us lowly henchmen."

"Enough of the lady-products-on-a-boat conversations. Get in the damn van!" Gibson growled as they approached. Alfie snorted loudly, earning himself a fast smack on the back of the head. "Shut up, Vihar."

"Yes, sir."

******

The plane ride to Saskatchewan was one of the most uncomfortable things that Alfie had ever done, and he grew up with two brothers who had enjoyed torturing him when they were younger. The animosity between Crux and Gibson was palatable, the hostility rolling off of Warp was directed at everybody in close proximity to her, and Bullet kept watching Alfie and Ray, looking for any signs that they were lying to him about their relationship.

Nikolai and LeRoy avoided everybody by starting a card game at the back of the plane that was quiet except for random outbursts of cussing in Russian or French. Alfie pulled up an e-book on his phone and settled in to read while Ray napped leaning against him. Gibson poured over maps and diagrams of the area that they were headed into. Crux stood at his shoulder, examining everything also. The two men worked in tense silence. Warp stared moodily out the window refusing to talk to anyone. Bullet sat at the front of the plane cleaning and checking his guns to make sure they were in perfect working order.

It didn't help that when they landed, Gibson held Alfie back while the others disembarked to have a nice little 'chat' about inter-workplace relationships. Alfie barely managed to appease Gibson by telling him he was only helping Ray avoid unwanted attention and advances from Bullet.

The eight of them packed into a van and were taken to a grove of trees a few miles from a hidden entrance to the mine where Ore had his operations set up. When they arrived at the rendezvous point, they unloaded, gathered their gear and weapons, and hoofed it to the entrance.

Bullet led the way into the mine, his M4 at the ready and his night vision goggles down. Ray stayed close to his right elbow in the tight tunnel, making sure her side was clear of possible enemies while trying to keep Bullet's constantly weaving gait away from the end of her barrel. Crux was directly behind them, concentrating on turning the moisture in the air into a wall of fog that would give them valuable seconds should they encounter any of Ore's lackeys.

Warp and Gibson followed, his M4A1 looking puny compared to the cannon she had strapped to her arm in her favorite fighting shape, which, to Alfie, looked like a scaled-down version of Optimus Prime after a gender-realignment surgery. Gibson was staring at a small green screen in his hand that mapped out their location in relationship to where the evidence pointed Ore's stronghold to be.

LeRoy had his throwing knives at the ready and was locked tight between Gibson in front and Alfie behind. Protecting LeRoy was their secondary objective since he was the only one who could shut down any nuclear devices that Ore might have developed.

Alfie held his AR in a relaxed grip with the muzzle pointing just in front of his left boot. He still was not combat comfortable with it (hence the semi-auto AR instead of the fully auto M4A1), and he was ready to drop it for the two M&P pistols at his waist and the 1911 tucked into the small of his back. Nikolai had the rear and kept his eyes pointed behind the group more than ahead, his AK-47 constantly moving, searching for something to shoot.

"If you can't walk a straight line for your own safety, can you do it for my peace of mind?!" Ray finally hissed into the darkness after Bullet's elbow caught her rifle and nearly knocked it from her hands.

"Green!" Gibson's hoarse whisper seemed to echo in the tight space.

"Sir. He keeps walking into my line of fire," Ray whispered back.

"Bullet, keep to your own line! You won't do us any good if she shoots you because you stepped in front of her," Gibson ordered quietly.

"You're giving orders now?" Crux whispered coolly.

"Seriously?! Now is not the time for your pissing contest!" Alfie was taken aback by his quiet outburst. The entire crew stopped in their tracks and turned to stare at him.

"What?" Alfie stood his ground. "We're kind of in the middle of something. Can't your shit wait until we are not trying to sneak up on a guy who may or may not have a nuclear weapon?"

"The boy is right. Mission first, then personal problems," Nikolai growled.

"Thank you!" Alfie whispered, turning to fist bump Nikolai. The Russian had not quite gotten the gist of it, so Alfie grabbed his wrist and bumped Nikolai's hand into his own.

"Carry on," Gibson ordered, motioning for everybody to start moving again.

"Alf, how are you doing with the enclosed space?" LeRoy whispered over his shoulder. "Thinking about the tons of earth above us, pressing down."

Alfie could feel the cold sweat drip between his shoulder blades. He had been concentrating on not thinking about it, and LeRoy's words brought it crashing down. "That was a bastard thing to say," Alfie gritted out from behind clenched teeth.

"LeRoy!" Gibson hissed over his shoulder, ordering silence. The team marched on for another half hour in the darkness before Gibson stopped them. "Ray, check that tunnel to your right."

"Roger," she whispered before disappearing down the dark tunnel. They all waited in tense silence until Bullet shifted away from the tunnel opening, signaling her return. "Sir, about 75 feet down the tunnel is a set of stairs that go straight down into the mine. There's light and noise coming up. I think we found the spot."

"All right. Ray, you and Bullet-"

"No. Warp will take point," Crux cut off Gibson.

The leader of Team 9 clenched his jaw but had enough class to keep his mouth shut.

"Warp, stealth mode," Crux ordered. Warp stepped past Ray into the tunnel and transformed back into her human form. Then, darkness rippled across her skin as she took the coloring and texture of the rock around her. "Good. Bullet, you next, cover her as we look for Ore. The rest of you-" Crux finally addressed the henchmen, "follow behind. And try to not get killed."

"Wait," Alfie whispered and raised his hand. "So we're just going in, grabbing Ore, and it's all over?"

"Yes," Crux gritted out, his frustration at being questioned by not only a henchman, but a new henchman, evident in his tone.

"What happens if his people keep fighting?"

"They won't," Warp's quiet answer was creepy coming from moving rock.

"Why? Why would they stop just because their leader was taken captive? Why not fight to try to get him back?" Alfie stubbornly clung to his question.

"They never do," Bullet answered gently with a smile. "Let's go."

Alfie waited a beat for the AOJ to move down the tunnel. "That sounds like a horrible plan."

"That's what the plan always is, Alf," LeRoy whispered. "Henchmen never keep fighting after the leader is taken."

"Why?"

"They have no reason to," Gibson quietly tossed over his shoulder.

"Keep eyes open, though," Nikolai whispered in Alfie's ear. Alfie glanced back at him and saw a smile glint in the darkness.

"Right." Alfie checked his pistols again and pulled his rifle tighter to his body, hoping he was ready for whatever was at the bottom of the stairs.

Team 9 watched in awe as Warp seemed to liquefy and melt down the stairs. She looked like jellied rock as she hugged the corners and slid from shadow to shadow down the spiral stairway. Crux motioned for them to follow as he stepped down the first step, making sure he didn't step on Warp.

They all followed Crux's lead and quickly descended the stone staircase. As the light got brighter, they flipped off their night vision goggles and packed them away. Suddenly, Crux's fist flew up, calling them all to a halt as a voice drifted up the stairwell.

"There was a small group of people spotted sneaking around the mine entrances to the west. You three, go check it out."

"Shit!" Gibson whispered. "Crux?"

"Pull back, Warp," Crux whispered just as they heard footsteps on the stairs below them. Crux raised his arms out to his sides and swiftly brought them together. The rocks from the sides of the stairwell broke away and tumbled down toward the bottom. He held out his hand to hold a pocket of air between the group and the dust cloud that rolled back toward them.

As the rocks settled and quieted, they could hear shouts and cursing filter through the gaps.

"Warp, go down and see what's happening," Bullet whispered. The gelatinous mass seemed to nod before seeping through the debris on the stairs.

Suddenly, there were sounds of flesh hitting flesh on the stairs above them. They turned to look up as Nikolai walked down to them, slinging his rifle back into place. "Would be bad if someone came up behind us," he said with a pointed look at Crux.

Crux nodded and shoved through so he could reach the top of the stairs. A grinding noise echoed in the stairwell as he moved rock into a wall, cutting off the entrance. "I believe that will suffice." He shoved his way back through to take up his place in front.

Ray snapped a few light sticks and tossed them on either end of the stairwell, lighting it enough for them to see. "Now what's the plan?"

"We wait for Warp to report back with intel," Crux snapped.

"Dude. You've got stuff on you," Alfie motioned at Nikolai's jaw, where blood spatter showed black in the neon-green light.

Nikolai nodded his thanks as he wiped at it with the back of his hand, smearing the spots into a long streak.

"That's better," Alfie said dryly.

"Sir." Warp had silently returned and took a humanoid form but still looked like the rock around her. "Your rockslide cut off their only direct path to the west entrances of the mine system. Right now they are working their way to the top of the staircase through other tunnels to investigate what happened. They know we're here, but they don't know exactly who or where we are yet."

"That's good," Crux nodded. "Is Ore there?"

"He is. His second-in-command is there also."

"What is the layout?" Bullet asked.

Warp crouched and drew in the dirt on the stair that Gibson stood on. Ray handed him a light stick to make the drawing easier to see. "The room is a big circle, most of the equipment is directly across from us coming out to about halfway across the room. The rest is mostly open with just a few desks and chairs. There are two other entrances. One is directly across from us on the other side of the equipment and the second is about halfway between on the right. There is a circle of pillars about here holding the ceiling up."

"What the hell?! I swore the door was right here!" a voice echoed down to them from above.

"They're here," Alfie said in a creepy voice. Ray punched him in the shoulder.

"Warp, how many people were left in the room when you came back?" Gibson asked quickly.

"Five in addition to Ore and his second."

"We can handle seven. Crux, move the rock. We'll go in before the others return."

"Who's in charge here?" Crux hissed.

"Seriously?" Alfie nearly shouted.

"He's right, boss. Later." Bullet stepped forward so he was nose to nose with Crux in the tight space. "Let's go in while we still have a little surprise and can quickly deal with the numbers."

Crux looked from Bullet to Warp, who nodded. "Fine. Warp, go through and stay in the entrance. Bullet, stand in front with your gun ready. When I move the rocks, be ready to run in. Warp, see if you can buy us a little time if we lose the surprise."

"Yes, sir," they answered together and moved to follow their leader's orders.

"We'll just stay back here, then," Alfie whispered. LeRoy snorted and Gibson turned to glare at them, motioning for them to stay silent.

Crux raised his arms again and pulled the rocks back into place. As soon as it was clear, Bullet ran down the stairs and rolled into the room, coming to a stop behind a desk that sat near the entrance. The others listened and didn't hear anything, so they quietly moved down the stairs. Gibson peeked into the room and saw that nobody had noticed their entrance.

"Move in," he whispered.

Ray slid to cover on the other side of the door and helped cover as Crux boldly walked into the room.

"Ore. I am Crux of the Alliance of Justice! We have you surrounded. Surrender now and nobody will be hurt!"

A blond man in a suit turned around to stare at Crux. He smiled coldly. "No."

With his one word, his men rose from their defensive positions around him and opened fire. Crux spun with an arm out, moving the air with such a force that the first wave of bullets turned and pitted the wall just over Ray's head.

"Dammit, Crux! I'm here!" Ray screamed as she curled into a ball with her arms over her head.

"Cover fire!" Gibson yelled. Bullet and Ray rose into crouched positions and opened fire at Ore's lackeys, giving Gibson and Nikolai enough time to join Bullet and Ray. All four dropped back to the ground as the enemy returned fire. Alfie crouched in the tunnel beside LeRoy, waiting for his chance to join the fight.

"Vihar! Distract!" Gibson yelled.

Alfie muttered a quick prayer and stuck his barrel out of the opening. He popped off a few rounds, trying to draw attention, which he did marvelously. He dropped to the floor but kept his eyes open as Gibson and Nikolai started shooting, giving Bullet and Ray the chance to move into better positions.

As Alfie watched, he saw one of Ore's men drop to the ground with a knife in his throat. LeRoy chuckled gleefully next to him. "Was that you?!"

"You bet your sweet ass it was! I'm *merde* with a gun, but look out when I have a knife!" LeRoy pulled another from his belt and threw it, dropping another man.

"I'll remember that." Alfie rose to a knee and popped off a couple more rounds. He saw another man fall and didn't think he had hit him. Then he saw what he assumed was Warp, but she had transformed into a black, shiny substance that was absorbing the bullets that hit her and instead of hands, she had sharp claws that were slashing at any who were unlucky enough to be within arms' distance.

Alfie harrumphed at Warp's form and turned to LeRoy. "Should I stay with you?"

"Vihar! Get out here!" Gibson yelled, answering his question.

"*Bonne chance!*" LeRoy yelled as Alfie half rolled, half tripped to Gibson's side.

"You called, sir?" Alfie asked, changing the mag in his AR.

"Give me that." Gibson pulled Alfie's rifle sling over his head and took the rifle. "You're a better shot with pistols. Use them."

"Yes, sir!" Alfie grinned and pulled an M&P from the holster. He turned and used the desk to steady his hand. On the first trigger pull, he put a man to the floor with a bullet in his knee. The second had a guy down with a blown shoulder.

"Ore!"

They heard Ray yell as the suited man crouched low and ran for the door. Alfie took aim. "Sir? I have him."

"Injure," Gibson whispered a second before Alfie pulled the trigger.

133

Ore's scream echoed in the room as his hip was shattered by Alfie's bullet. He fell to the ground, and Warp was quickly there to take him prisoner.

Crux walked out of the tunnel with his arms up. "Your leader is ours! Throw down your weapons and you will walk out of here!"

Ore's lackeys stopped firing and looked around in confusion. They stayed under cover, which gave Alfie a bad feeling. "Sir, I don't think this is over."

Gibson looked over the desk and took in the scene. "I think you're right. They should be standing." He caught Nikolai's eye and motioned for him to stay down. Alfie motioned to LeRoy to stay back. They both motioned for Ray to stay down, just as she was standing up from cover. She dropped and her movement caught Bullet's attention. He noticed that Team 9 was still hidden, and he crouched down, just in case.

"Nice try." Ore's second-in-command stepped out from behind a pillar and fired at Crux. The bullet caught the leader of the AOJ in the shoulder before anybody could react, then Ore's men opened fire again.

"Son of a-" Gibson grunted as he crawled to where Crux lay and drug the man back into the tunnel. "Wall yourself off until we finish this! LeRoy, stay here and protect him." Gibson pulled a pistol from his ankle holster and pressed it into LeRoy's reluctant hand. He crawled back out to where Alfie crouched as the stone closed up behind him.

"They'll stop when we get Ore, eh?" Alfie asked, his voice full of rancor.

"Shut up, Vihar," Gibson growled.

Ray and Bullet were doing a great job of picking off the lackeys, but they seemed to be multiplying. "Vihar, make your way to that doorway and keep more from coming in!" Gibson ordered, pointing at the door a quarter way around the circle.

"Sure, sir." Alfie dropped to sit on the floor and grinned up at Gibson. "Do you happen to have any explosives? Maybe another rock mover in your pocket?"

"Dammit, Vihar! Be creative," Gibson snapped. He pulled a small box from his belt pouch. "Use this."

"Roger roger." Alfie waited until Gibson had risen up to cover him then raced for the cover of a filing cabinet near the door.

"Hey, sugar britches, come here often?" Ray called from a nearby desk with a smile.

"Naw, my first time. Maybe you could... show me the ropes," Alfie called back with a wink. Her laughter was cut short as a wave of bullets passed just over her head. Alfie holstered his first pistol and drew his second in enough time to shoot the knees of the next two men unlucky enough to come in through the door.

"You're hell on knees, Alfie!" Ray called.

"That's forward of you!" Alfie called back with a suggestive grin. He opened the box and found a small packet of white substance with an electrical device stuck to it. "Well, if my movie demolition degree is worth anything, this is C4."

"Vihar! The door!" Gibson yelled.

Alfie took a deep breath, shot one more man coming through the door, then jumped up, slapped the C4 above the door and took cover. "Now what?!" he yelled to Gibson.

"Did you turn it on?" the captain yelled back.

"You didn't tell me to!" Alfie sighed when he heard Gibson growl. "Here goes nothing," Alfie muttered as he took aim and shot at the small white square.

"How the hell did you miss that?!" Gibson yelled from across the room.

"No pressure or anything!" Alfie yelled back. A man raced through the doorway and headed straight for Alfie. Ray managed to put a bullet in his knee, but he kept coming. Alfie jumped to his feet, dodged the attack, and fired, hitting the detonator. The explosive blew, blocking in the door and knocking everybody within twenty feet to the ground.

Nikolai and Gibson took it as their chance to rush Ore's second-in-command, who apparently was actually in command. They were slowed by the few lackeys who were still able to stand.

Alfie regained his feet and rushed to check on Ray. He had to move a rock that had her knee pinned to the wall, but aside from some cuts and bruises, she was fine. "Go help Warp. I'll help Gibson and Ivan."

Ray smiled through the pain of putting weight on her injured knee. "Nikolai."

"Right, right. I keep forgetting." He pressed a quick kiss to her cheek and ran toward the Russian and team captain. Ore's second-in-command also chose that time to try to run for the last available exit. Unfortunately for both of them, Alfie got in his way. The man tried to dive around Alfie, who tried to stop in order to miss him, making them collide.

"Out of my way!" the man yelled, throwing a wild punch.

Alfie dodged it and shouldered the guy, causing him to trip. "Are you the ass responsible for this?!"

"I am the genius responsible for this!" the man yelled. He once again tried to get around Alfie, who had had enough.

Alfie tackled the man, and they both fell to the floor with Alfie on top. He straddled the man and started punching and yelling at him. "You lunatic! You get somebody to pretend to be you so when we capture him, your people keep fighting! Those men could have been killed! WE could have been killed! Why are you trying to start shit in Canada! They are nice people! Why would you do this! Diamonds and uranium! Why?! You know what you can do with those diamonds and uranium?!"

"Vihar, you can stop anytime now," Gibson called after he and Nikolai neutralized the last of the lackeys. He walked over to where their entrance had been and knocked on the rock. "Crux, you can open up. It's over."

Alfie threw one last punch at the guy's face, knocking him out, and staggered to his feet. "You guys are batshit liars!"

"What does that even mean?" LeRoy asked as he picked up one of his knives and wiped the blood off of it.

"I have no idea!" Alfie stumbled to a chair and plopped down. "They don't keep fighting. They'll give up once we get Ore. This is the only plan we ever need," Alfie screamed. "I hate you all!"

"Done?" Nikolai sat down next to Alfie and nudged him with a shoulder.

Alfie took a deep breath and wiped away the blood that was dripping in his eye from a cut on his forehead. "Yeah. I'm done."

"All right. Let's get going," Gibson ordered. "Crux, get in contact with the Canadians. We took out the threat; it's their turn to clean it up."

137

"Oh, taking charge again I see," Crux sneered.

"For the love of everything that is holy! What is your problem?!" Alfie exclaimed. The room fell silent as Crux just glared at Alfie.

"All right," Gibson relieved the awkward silence. "LeRoy, get to work on what Ore was developing here. If something looks like it's on a timer, you stop it. Get everything out of his files you can, and we can check them out back at HQ. Nikolai, you and Vihar lock everything down here. Tie them up and take anybody else who comes strolling in."

As if on cue, one of Ore's lackeys walked through the door and was quickly rendered unconscious by the butt of Bullet's rifle.

"Good. Bullet and Warp, you're with me. We'll search the tunnels and see if there are any more hanging around. We also need to see if we can hunt down the miners Ore had taken captive. You've got an hour, then meet back here. Ray, you're on first aid. Wrap them up so they don't bleed to death, but don't waste too much time on them."

"Yes, sir," they all said.

"Let's get after it." Gibson slammed a fresh mag into his rifle and headed out the door.

******

By the time the Canadian officials showed up, Gibson, Warp, and Bullet had rounded up fifteen more people hiding in the mines. They also set the miners free and on their way to the surface. Crux was in poor condition to take charge of passing responsibility to the Canadians due to him being a motionless pile on the floor. Ray, who was more than tired of listening to him complain about the pain in his shoulder while she was hobbling around on an injured knee bandaging people up, had offered to give him a mild painkiller. One shot of morphine, and he was out like a light.

Gibson didn't say a word when he saw Crux passed out in the corner. He just nodded in Ray's direction and finished helping Alfie and Nikolai tie up the six men he had brought down.

"Who is in charge here?" A man in a black suit walked into the room just as Ore's second-in-command was starting to come around. Gibson motioned to Ray, who ended his tirade the same way she ended Crux's – with a needle stick.

Team 9 and the two remaining members of the AOJ turned to Gibson since Crux was busy drooling on his shirt.

"I guess that would be me. Jeremiah Gibson." He walked forward and held out his hand.

"Agent Garceau. You are... not Crux."

"Very observant, Agent Garceau," Gibson and pointed to the corner that Crux was propped up in. "He was injured and our field medic gave him something for the pain. With him out of commission, I am in charge. What do you need?"

Alfie watched his team captain smoothly take the control that should have been his from the beginning.

"I don't know if you knew this, but you're bleeding, pretty profusely." A young Mountie stopped by Alfie and pointed to a cut on Alfie's shoulder that had soaked through his shirt.

"Oh, yeah. Thanks." Alfie pulled some gauze out of his belt pouch and pressed it to the cut.

139

"So you were with the team that neutralized Ore's operation?"

"Yeah. This was my second mission and it was a little more exciting than the first... minus the gunshot wound. That was an experience."

The Mountie looked at Alfie in awe. "Cool. This is my fifth big job, but I've never been around anything this... bizarre."

"I hope I get used to it, because this is probably going to be the norm for me." Alfie chuckled and held out his hand. "I'm Alfie."

"Officer Conway."

"Hey! Can I get a picture in your hat?"

Conway laughed and shrugged. "Normally no, but why not? Nobody's going to believe this anyway. Superheroes and supervillians. What are we in, a comic book?" He took off his hat and handed it to Alfie.

Alfie laughed. "Right? I couldn't believe it when I took the job as a henchman. Ray!" Alfie motioned for her to join them.

"Henchman? Seriously? We are in a comic book!" Conway laughed.

Alfie nodded and handed his phone to Ray. "Take our picture!"

"Gibson is going to kill you." She grinned and took the phone.

"Yep!" Alfie and Conway posed for a few shots, making sure that Ray angled it enough to get the tied-up bad guys in the background.

"That's awesome. Here's my e-mail. Send those to me." Conway pulled out a notepad to jot down his address and handed the paper to Alfie.

"Absolutely. Now, I'm going to steal your hat!" Alfie turned and pretended to run away with it, only to run directly into Gibson, who was less than amused. "Apparently, I am not." Alfie took it off and handed it back to its owner, who was getting death glares from his own supervisor.

"Done?" Gibson asked quietly.

"Yes, sir. Ready when you are, sir."

"Good. Go help Nikolai with Crux."

"Yes, sir." Alfie turned and felt Gibson slap him on the back of the head. "I deserved that one," he muttered to himself, then grinned at Ray, who was walking with him to check on Crux's condition. "Totally worth it."

Three Times Unlucky

"What did we learn?"

Alfie dropped the letter on the table in Team 9's den with a groan. "Don't try to steal a Mountie's hat," he mumbled.

Gibson glared at him for a long moment. "Correct."

"In my defense, I wasn't actually going to steal it. Officer Conway willingly gave it to me for pictures." Alfie shrank back from the censure in the captain's eyes.

Since none of Team 9 had been seriously injured in Canada, they were given a two-day leave and were back to work on Friday. Gibson had met them all in the den for their reviews, and he had promptly pounced on Alfie first.

"Vihar, the fine will be docked from your next paycheck. Don't do it again."

"Yes, sir."

"And the pictures?"

"Will never see the light of day, sir."

"Just keep them off Facebook, Twitter, Instagram, and whatever else there is."

"Yes, sir."

"All right, other than that, you did fairly well. You still need to stop hiding when the fighting starts, but, once again, when you started, you performed well. Oh, and your little stunt with the C4 makes me think that we all need a review of explosives, so we all are scheduled at the Pit on Wednesday. Meet here and we'll go over in a van."

Alfie looked around in confusion as the others groaned. He thought learning about explosives would be fun, and he figured the others would feel the same. "What's the Pit?" Alfie asked.

"An old mine outside of the city. It's Resources, Inc.'s private test range for explosives and large weapons," Gibson explained.

"So what's with the groans?"

"Daniel Johnson," Ray groaned again.

"Who's Daniel Johnson?"

"I think he's the only human I've ever met who I'm sure is made completely of Saltines... And I'm not one hundred percent sure he's still alive." LeRoy flopped dramatically into a chair. "I think his dead body is just puttering around the Pit out of habit and desire to torture us with his 'lessons.'"

"He's not that bad. Stop complaining," Gibson scolded.

"If I remember correctly, you've fallen asleep at least once during his lessons," LeRoy pointed out.

"Enough." Gibson stopped their commentary with a wave of his hand and picked up his file. "Back to business. Ray, good job on not getting hit in the head. I appreciate the effort, although it was probably more luck, especially when we consider how close you were when Vihar blew the door. How's the knee?"

"A lot better, sir. The swelling's down and the bruising is turning a nasty yellow."

"Good. Make sure you check in with the doctor before you leave just to make sure everything is getting better."

"Yes, sir."

"Now," Gibson looked at her over the top of his paperwork. "Care to explain the incident with Bullet?"

143

Ray and Alfie exchanged a look before she answered. "What incident, sir?"

"The one in the cave that resulted in you yelling at him. Is there another one I should know about, Ray?"

"Uh, no, sir," Ray stammered. "There isn't. The thing in the cave, you pretty much know all of it. He can't walk a straight line and kept hitting me, so I started walking a pace behind him to give him more room. He shouldered my weapon hard enough I almost dropped it. That's when I yelled at him. It was unprofessional, I know, but I'd had enough and my temper snapped."

"Understandable. Just try to stay calmer in those situations. Oh, and Ray? It is never a good idea to drug or otherwise render a team leader unconscious. Consider this your official rebuke."

"Sorry, sir," Ray responded quietly.

"Now, unofficially, you have my thanks for handling Crux in a manner that made the cleanup a lot smoother." Gibson nodded when Ray looked up at him with a grin. "Even more unofficially, I have never seen Brutus laugh as hard as he did when I told him that you drugged Crux, so you have his thanks also."

"Crux ratted you out." Nikolai's tone indicated it wasn't a question.

"Crux's review of me was less than complimentary but, then again, it never is, so no harm done." Gibson shrugged. "LeRoy, good job with the knives. It looked like you're getting a larger range?"

LeRoy nodded. "I switched it up to some titanium knives. They're lighter so they fly farther without sacrificing size."

"Good. Keep it up." Gibson flipped a page and turned to the last on his team. "Nikolai, no complaints about your performance, as usual. You are doing great. And thank you for keeping your glee during the fighting to a minimum on this mission."

"Was difficult," the Russian mumbled, looking like a grumpy toddler.

LeRoy leaned over and threw an arm around Nikolai's shoulders. "Aww, we appreciate the effort, big guy. You'll get there eventually." LeRoy gently slapped Nikolai on the chest with his free arm and chuckled when the Russian turned an angry look at him.

"On the upside," Gibson cut in before a brawl could break out in the den, "Bullet gave us an exemplary review, and Brutus hasn't been this proud of Team 9... ever, I think. So, good news for you, Ray, he did not take offense at you yelling at him."

"Can Bullet take offense at anything?" Alfie asked with a laugh. "He seems like a pretty easygoing guy."

"True," Gibson agreed, "but we don't usually get good reviews from employers, so let's just take the win. Now, jobs for the week. LeRoy, I want you going through the information you pulled from Ore's computers. Find out what he was planning and if he had anything else in the works that we need to put an end to. The rest of us will take turns helping LeRoy and doing our standard training. Nikolai and Ray, you're both going to work with Vihar on hand-to-hand." He put up a hand as all three groaned. "Vihar, you need to get up to par or you will be more of a hindrance than a help. Nikolai, how is Vihar doing on rifle training?"

"Good. Is doing better than most beginners."

"Thanks, man!" Alfie leaned over for a high five but slowly moved back to his seat when the large Russian just stared at him.

"That was uncomfortable to watch," LeRoy drawled.

"Okay, checkups with the doctor for those who need them and back to work for the rest," Gibson instructed, ending their meeting abruptly.

They all stood and dispersed from the den to get to work, but Ray cornered Alfie in the hall. "Hey." She pressed a quick kiss to his lips.

"Hey back at you." Alfie wrinkled his nose at his lame line, making Ray laugh. "Sorry. What're you doing tomorrow?"

"No plans, why?"

"Wait, I've got plans with Ruth and Tessa tomorrow. How about Sunday?"

Ray laughed. "Still no plans."

"Want to go out?"

"Sure. What were you thinking?"

Alfie wrapped his arms around her waist and pulled her closer. "Well, since our last date was something I like, how about we do something you like this time?"

"Sure!" Ray grinned. "Can you dance?"

Alfie slowly shook his head. "Like I have two left feet and an inner ear problem."

Ray's laugh echoed down the hall. "Okay, no dancing. I'll think of something else and let you know. I'll keep it something calm since my knee isn't one hundred percent yet."

"Perfect." Alfie gave her a quick peck on the cheek and reluctantly let her go with a wink. "No rest for the wicked. Back to work."

******

"What the hell happened to you?" LeRoy eyed the ice pack Alfie had pressed to the side of his head.

"Tripped myself and ran into Nikolai's fist."

"*Quoi?*"

Alfie sat down next to LeRoy with a sigh and propped his elbow on the desk. "Nikolai and Ray were trying to teach me a new move. My foot caught in a seam of the mat and I fell right as Nikolai was coming at me with the expectation that I would be able to stop him. My head was where my arms were supposed to be blocking the punch, and Nikolai didn't have time to stop."

LeRoy chuckled and patted Alfie on the shoulder. "You really are more of a hindrance to yourself than a help, aren't you?"

"Absolutely." Alfie pulled the ice pack from his head and gingerly touched the goose egg that was forming on his left temple.

LeRoy whistled. "Wow. That had to hurt!"

"Yeah. Blacked out for a few seconds."

"Concussion?"

"Nah. Dr. Olafson cleared me. She said I'd have a headache for a while and to see a doctor immediately if I start seeing black spots or get dizzy."

"Oh yeah, those are always fun. Once, after I got a good knock on the head during a job, I spent twenty minutes trying to clean my monitor before I realized the spots I was seeing were from a concussion and not stuff on the screen."

"Great. I drove today." Alfie sadly shook his head before giving LeRoy a grin. "What're you working on?"

147

"Oh, I'm going through everything that Ore had on his computers." LeRoy turned back to the screen. "The man was obviously crazy to think his plans would work, but he did have a few good ideas. It looks like his second in command, the one who was the 'power behind the throne,' so to speak, was the mastermind and Ore was his puppet. They actually had plans to sell the refined uranium on the black market and use the money to create a giant diamond-powered 'death ray' to turn the moon into a Death Star."

"Okay, seriously. These people need to stop watching movies. Isn't that essentially the plan of both Moonraker and one of the Austin Powers movies?"

"Sure." LeRoy shrugged. "And while the moon part of the plan is rather ridiculous, the weapon they designed is actually pretty ingenious. With some mild tweaking, I could make it operational in very little time."

"Why would you want to create a death ray?"

LeRoy's eyes reluctantly moved to a plastic-covered form in the corner.

"You actually made it?" Alfie exclaimed. "Why?"

LeRoy shrugged. "I had two days off."

"Wait, you made something in two days that Ore's people had been working on for..."

"Probably six months." LeRoy's pride was evident in his tone.

Alfie sighed. "Why?"

"Why not?" LeRoy chuckled.

"Are you actually a supervillain in disguise as a henchman?"

"Yes, but let's keep that between us girls." LeRoy chucked Alfie under the chin and turned back to his computer.

"One of these days, I'm going to figure out when you're serious and when you're kidding." Alfie gently pressed the ice pack to the side of his head.

"Not likely, *garçon*," LeRoy laughed.

******

"Alfie, move your ass! We're going to miss the last show at the planetarium if you don't hurry!" Ruth yelled up the stairs. She and Tessa leaned against the door in the entryway of the Vihar home, waiting for Alfie to join them.

"Keep your shirts on! We have like half an hour!" Alfie yelled back.

"We still have to get there!" Ruth hollered, rolling her eyes at Tessa.

"It's a ten-minute drive," Alfie grumbled as he jumped down the last two steps and settled his backpack in place.

"What's with the bag?" Tessa asked, raising an eyebrow.

Alfie shrugged. "You never know when you'll need a Band-Aid or shuriken." Alfie opened the door and motioned for them to walk through. "Let's go, ladies, the planetarium awaits!"

"Sure, act like we're the ones making us late," Ruth muttered, shouldering her brother as she walked through the door.

"Love you, too, Ruthy!" Alfie said to her back. "Mom! Dad! We're headed out!" he yelled over his shoulder.

"Okay! Have fun, honey!" Vivian's voice floated to him from the living room.

"Bye, kids!" George yelled from the garage.

149

"You guys are the most passive-aggressive fighters on the planet." Tessa waited on the top step for Alfie to lock the door. "We just throw a few punches and we're over it."

Alfie chuckled. "That's because you take a hit better than Ruth does. I fight with Nathan and Robert like that."

"I've seen you take a hit. You don't handle it much better than Ruth."

"Hey! I am improving, or do I need to remind you of..." Alfie trailed off and touched his side where the bullet wound from his first job as a henchman was turning into a pink scar.

"How long are you going to keep milking that?"

"Until you have an injury that's way cooler."

"Alfie!" Tessa dropped her voice when Ruth turned to look at them from the car. "Getting shot is not something to be proud of."

"Dude, I know that." Alfie rolled his eyes. He had seen Tessa's brothers dealing with wounds for years and knew what it did to her every time she visited them in the hospital or helped them change their dressings. "I was just being a smart ass. Let's drop it."

"Agreed," Tessa growled before climbing behind the wheel of her Jeep.

It was an uncomfortable drive, but by the time they reached the San Luca History and Science Complex, Ruth's excitement about visiting the planetarium had infected Tessa and Alfie. Alfie was stoked to see the visiting Egyptian exhibit that had artifacts from King Tutankhamun's tomb and the mummy and sarcophagus of a mid-level priest. Tessa was just glad she had a weekend off from her internship at the hospital.

They made it to the museum with more than enough time to make the last planetarium show of the day and headed to the Egyptian exhibit after. It was the last weekend for the exhibit, and the display rooms were packed with people. Alfie and Tessa kept a close eye on Ruth in the crush, but they were able to enjoy seeing the shining gold jewelry and the dusty stone statues. Alfie ignored the nasty looks that were thrown his way as he gently shoved his way through the crowd around the glass mummy case. He had wanted to see a mummy since he was little and was transfixed by the linen-wrapped form lying in the stone coffin.

He was pulled from his trance by a raised voice behind him. He quickly worked his way out of the crowd around the mummy to see a well-dressed woman yelling at a man in a museum polo.

"The displays are wonderful, but you really should limit the number of people allowed in at a time! I couldn't really study anything and was running into people everywhere!"

"I apologize, ma'am, and I will let my supervisor know about your concerns."

"I don't think you're hearing me. It's too crowded! Nobody can see anything!"

Tessa nudged Alfie with her shoulder. "What a bitch," she whispered.

"Yeah, he doesn't deserve that." Alfie took a step toward them.

Tessa held him back with a hand on his arm. "What're you going to do, Alfie?"

Alfie grinned mischievously. "Just watch." Alfie wound his way over to where the woman was still yelling at the museum worker. "I'm sorry for being rude and interrupting," Alfie began, reaching a hand between them toward the employee. "I just want to let you know how much I enjoyed the exhibit, and seeing as it is the last weekend for it," Alfie paused long enough to give the woman a pointed stare, "I understand why there are so many people here visiting before it leaves San Luca."

They both stared at Alfie for a long moment, then the employee smiled slightly and shook Alfie's outstretched hand. "I'm glad you enjoyed the exhibit. It's one of my favorites that we've had here and I'm glad so many people are coming out to see it."

"Keep up the good work, young man!" Alfie slapped the employee on the shoulder and turned to rejoin his sister and friend. "Young man?" Tessa whispered as they all turned to leave the exhibit. "Alfie, he was easily five years older than us. I think that knock to the head you got at work yesterday rattled something loose." She looked back over her shoulder to see the woman glaring daggers at Alfie and the museum employee trying to control a grin.

Alfie smirked. "I know, but I was on a roll!"

"Who are you and what have you done with my brother?" Ruth laughed as the three left the main building.

"What?" Alfie chuckled.

"My brother would never, in a million years, confront anybody like that! Who are you?"

Alfie laughed again and turned to Tessa. She could only shrug, unsure herself. "I don't know. Maybe I'm just getting tired of people pushing around the little guy, you know?"

"Tired of being the little guy?" Tessa teased gently.

Alfie scoffed at the suggestion.

"Little guy? Tess, have you seen him? He's bulking up," Ruth crowed. She jumped in front of Alfie and grabbed the front of his shirt. "What are they doing to you at that gym? Are they forcing you to use steroids? You can tell us!"

"What?" Alfie asked, half laughing, half incredulous.

Ruth pulled Alfie closer so their noses almost touched. "You know the juice will make the jewels shrivel into sun-dried tomatoes."

Tessa smirked and eyed Ruth. "Aren't you a little young to be watching *Son-in-Law*? I mean, Pauly Shore is probably less mature than you, but the movie itself is a little old for you."

"Thanks for the concern, Crawl, but I'm not doing steroids. I work at a gym. What did you think would happen?" Alfie shrugged out of Ruth's grasp and pulled the complex map out of his back pocket. "Where to next, ladies?"

All three turned so they could look across the open space in the middle of the complex to the eight historic and modern buildings that housed San Luca's history and science collections.

"The meteorology building!" Ruth bounced on the balls of her feet, ready to take off at the first agreement from the other two.

They all flinched as thunder cracked overhead.

Tessa looked up and saw the clouds starting to swirl. "How about we go to the Mission first? The sky's getting nasty looking and it's closest."

"I thought you said it was supposed to be nice today!" Ruth yelled at Alfie as the wind started to howl.

"It was!" Alfie yelled back as the rain started coming down.

Katherine Wielechowski

They made it to the Mission just as the rain turned to hail. Alfie nudged Tessa gently as they stood just inside the doors watching it come down. "Your Jeep has hail insurance, right?

******

Alfie climbed up the steps, carefully shoving boards and debris aside until he reached the top. His breath caught in his throat as he turned in a circle and took in the destruction around him. The entire complex had been flattened except the main building, which had survived unscathed.

"Stay down there. I'm going to check to make sure it's safe," he called over his shoulder, knowing that Tessa and Ruth probably wouldn't listen to him anyway. He searched the floor quickly for a safe path to solid land, thankful he had decided to wear his heavy boots. All of his injuries from his missions were finally completely healed up, so the last thing he needed was a nail through the foot. He was glad that Dr. Olafson insisted on a tetanus booster when he started at Resources, Inc. Judging by the destruction around him, it was likely he'd need it.

The wood from the Mission was splintered all around them, but rough nails and bare wires were the parts of the mix that Alfie was most concerned about. He picked up a piece of a board and gently moved wires out of his path.

"Damn."

Alfie looked behind him when he heard Tessa's whispered curse. "I told you to stay down there until I checked it out." He sighed when he saw Ruth's head pop out of the rubble. She whistled. "Fine, just walk this way and watch out for wires."

"I doubt the power is still on, Alfie." Ruth, always practical, gently nudged the shattered remains of a picture frame away from the stairs with the toe of her shoe.

"I'd rather not find out the hard way, sis," he muttered, studying the rubble for another step toward earth. He slowly waded his way through the mess, mindful of wires and places that looked like the floor would collapse, his patience wearing thin with tension and fear. Finally, he found solid ground. He just wished he hadn't face planted into it when he tripped over the edge of the building's foundation.

"That was graceful," Tessa observed dryly, holding out a hand to pull Alfie to his feet. "Did you have a nice trip?"

"Ah, shut it," Alfie grumbled and stalked away, searching for any other signs of life.

"See ya next fall!" Tessa called after him as she and Ruth dissolved into giggles.

"Come on, guys. Let's see if there's anybody else buried," Alfie called.

The closest building already had a man trying to crawl out from under the collapsed roof. Alfie took charge and started ordering his sister and friend around. "Tessa, grab that two-by-four and put the end here." He pointed to a spot under the roof near where he knelt. "Hang on, guys, we're going to lift it up a little. You should be able to crawl out," he explained to the people struggling to escape the debris. "Ruth, help them out." Alfie and Tessa pulled down on the board and were able to move the roof enough for the first person to wiggle out.

"Look out!" Tessa yelled as the board slipped and the roof fell back into place. "Damn." She rubbed at the raw marks the rough board left on her hands.

"You all okay?" Ruth called.

"Yeah, just get us out!" a woman near panic yelled back.

Alfie repositioned the board and, with the help of Tessa and the man who had climbed out, they levered the roof up again. Ruth helped the last two people quickly scramble out.

"We need help over here!" A teenaged girl ran over to them with blood running down her arm and trickling out of her broken nose. Tessa quickly pulled Alfie's pack off his back and dug though it for first-aid supplies.

"Stay with Tessa. She'll get you bandaged up. Where do they need help?" Alfie asked, his eyes scanning the complex as people were gradually emerging from piles of rubble.

"Big building on the other side of the Mission," she gasped as Tessa dabbed at the cut on her arm. "My family is trapped. My dad is pinned under a beam and I think my brother broke his leg."

"Ruth, stay here and help Tessa with the injured and call 911. If any of you can help, come with me," Alfie ordered. "Wrong Side of Heaven" by Five Finger Death Punch blared from the phone in his pocket as he and two of the men jogged around fallen trees and boards to get to the building where the girl's family was trapped. Alfie pressed ignore without looking to see who it was. It immediately rang again and he reluctantly answered. "I can't talk right now," he said before hanging up again.

It rang a third time.

"Vihar, you hang up on me again, I'll hang you from your balls in the den."

Alfie froze in place when he heard Gibson's voice bark out of his phone.

"Captain?"

"You need to get to HQ. Now."

"I can't, sir. I'm helping people who got trapped by that freak storm."

"That freak storm is why you need to come in," Gibson said, his voice softened slightly.

"Give me an hour." Alfie pressed his phone to his ear with his shoulder so he could help lift part of the building frame.

"Now, Vihar."

"No, sir," Alfie growled. "I'll be in, in an hour." He quickly hung up and shoved the phone back into his pocket so he could help free the girl's family. He sent a quiet thanks to the universe when he heard sirens getting closer.

"Anybody else?" he called after they finally freed the father from under a beam and gently pulled out the boy with a broken leg.

"There's a couple trapped under here!" One of the first men they had helped was peering under a wall that had collapsed in the building across from the one they were at. Alfie quickly explained how to splint the boy's leg with boards and a belt before jogging over to help. They hastily got the wall pulled up and the couple freed.

The police and paramedics arrived and took over the scene. Alfie jogged back to where Tessa had set up a rudimentary first-aid station.

"Tess, I gotta go." He started pulling the rest of his first-aid stuff from his pack and setting it beside her.

"What?" She looked up from a wound she was bandaging.

157

"My boss called me in."

"I think this is a little more important!" she hissed, going back to her work.

"He said it has something to do with this." She gaped at him and he nodded. "Ruth!" he yelled, shouldering his pack. She came running over.

"Sup?"

"Tessa, can you make sure that Ruth gets home?"

"Of course, Alfie," she said, slightly insulted that he would even ask.

"Thanks." He wrapped an arm around her and squeezed. He hugged his sister for a long moment and dropped a kiss on her hair. "Help Tessa with this, will you?"

"Of course," Ruth answered, hugging him back.

Tessa reached up and pulled Ruth down beside her before taking Alfie's hand. "Stay safe."

"Always." He grinned and took off, tripping over a camera bag on his way out of the destroyed complex.

"Miss." A reporter sat down next to Tessa while a cameraman hovered a few feet away. "Who is that young man?"

******

Alfie barely had a foot in the door of Team 9's den when he felt himself being roughly pulled back by his pack. He attempted to pivot and elbow his assailant, but a large hand grabbed his arm and turned him so he smashed face-first into the opposite wall. He felt a hot breath on his face.

"Vihar. When I call you in, you come. No questions, no waiting, no saying 'no'."

"Captain, let go of me," Alfie gasped.

"Do you understand me?!"

"Captain, let go of me." Alfie emphasized his words by tapping his knife point against Gibson's abdomen.

"Are you going to use that?" Gibson pressed Alfie harder into the wall.

"I would really like not to."

"If you're going to pull a knife on me, you better use it. Or I will." Gibson grabbed Alfie's wrist, spun him around and had Alfie's knife to his throat in a blink.

Alfie dropped the knife and shoved off the wall with his foot, propelling himself and Gibson into the opposite wall, his years of pushing people around on the football field paying off. They hit the wall with a grunt. "Are you going to let me explain or just beat me up some more?"

Gibson grabbed Alfie's hand and bent his fingers back. When Alfie reared back in pain, the captain kicked his feet out from underneath him, dropping him flat on his back.

"Fine. Come talk to me when you can breathe again." Gibson picked up Alfie's knife from the floor and entered the den. Ray, Nikolai, and LeRoy scattered from the doorway where they had rushed to watch the fight.

LeRoy squatted down and slapped Alfie gently on the cheek. "Ya all right, youngin?"

"I'll let you know when I find my lungs," Alfie gasped as he struggled into a sitting position. He grimaced when he moved and found the exact spot where he had landed on the water bottle in his pack.

"You'll live," Ray observed coolly before returning to the den.

The men watched her go with matching looks of surprise.

"How'd you piss her off?" LeRoy asked.

159

"I'm as clueless as you guys are," Alfie mumbled. He slowly got to his feet and followed his teammates into the den. Ray had her legs up on the couch that she and Alfie normally shared and was blatantly ignoring him. He frowned in confusion but took a chair across from Nikolai at the table.

"Now that we're all finally here," Gibson said, pausing to turn a pointed look at Alfie before continuing, "we have a job, which Brutus was about to give to Team 10."

"Can I explain-" Alfie started.

"No," Gibson cut him off. "It looks like the Alliance of Justice is going after a new supervillain who declared herself today."

"Herself?" Ray leaned forward. "A woman? That's weird for a supervillain."

"Yes, but not unheard of. She is calling herself Trade Wind and can control the weather."

"WHAT?" Alfie exclaimed, jumping to his feet.

"Tech or powers?" Nikolai asked.

"Right now, we are not clear on that." Gibson flipped open a file and scanned it. "We do know that she is responsible for the tornado that ripped through downtown San Luca earlier."

"Oh my god," Alfie whispered, dropping back into his seat.

"We with the AOJ or Trade Wind on this?" LeRoy asked.

"The AOJ. Trade Wind contacted Brutus about getting a few henchmen of her own, but she was too late."

"I thought the AOJ was in Europe fighting Ringworm?" Nikolai asked.

"Earth Child, Warp, and Crux are in Europe. We will work with Bullet and Forcefield on this."

Alfie raised his hand. "Sir, I would like to volunteer to work for Trade Wind."

"That's not how this works, Vihar," Gibson said, not looking up from his folder.

"Wouldn't it be easier to defeat her with somebody in her camp?" Alfie argued.

"We're not vigilantes, Vihar. We go where the job is and right now, that job is with the AOJ."

"I would like the chance to try, Captain."

"No, Vihar."

"But-"

"No." Gibson's tone stopped all argument in Alfie's throat.

"Why do you care so much?" Ray asked, her tone indicating more to the question than simple curiosity.

"My friend Tessa, my sister, and I were at the History and Science Complex this afternoon. It was flattened by a tornado with us and fifteen other people inside of it. Thankfully nobody was killed, but people were hurt." Alfie stared at Ray in confusion when she scoffed.

"Vihar, do not make this personal," Gibson barked. "Hundreds of people were hurt in the tornado today. Three were killed. Our job is to assist the AOJ with stopping Trade Wind. That is what you can do." He stared hard at Alfie, daring him to argue. "All right, now, we don't know what Trade Wind is after or if she's after anything. Brutus has people working on it, but, LeRoy, I want you looking into it, too. Find out what you can on her and what she may be up to. Brutus sent you all they have so far, so you have somewhere to start. We don't think she's going to go hole up somewhere until we forget about her before lashing out again. She will probably attack again soon. Don't leave town and don't make any plans that you can't break."

"How do we fight the weather?" Nikolai asked.

"We... are still working on that also," Gibson said slowly. "As much as I hate to admit it, Crux would be a help here, but since he's unavailable, we will have to figure something else out."

"Forcefield can help contain the weather Trade Wind makes, right?" Ray offered.

"He should be able to, at least to an extent, but he'd really only be able to block it or redirect it. His powers won't be able to stop it completely," Gibson answered, but he wrote her suggestion down anyway.

"Well, I'll just go home and re-watch all the X-Men movies since my life is becoming a freaking comic book," Alfie mumbled. He caught movement out of the corner of his eye and had just enough time to duck out of the way of the stapler that was aimed at his head. "Hey!"

"*Tuat t'en grosse bueche*!" LeRoy whispered to Alfie, trying to get him to stop talking.

"I've had enough of you today, Vihar!" Gibson yelled. The group was shocked by his uncharacteristic outburst. "Everybody out. I'll contact you if we have anything new come in."

"What was that all about?" Alfie muttered to LeRoy as they all filed out of the den.

"*C'est sa couillon!* What is wrong with you?"

"Me?! What did I do?" Alfie exclaimed.

"When Gibson calls, you show up!" LeRoy yelled.

Alfie grabbed LeRoy's arm and pulled the short Cajun to a stop. "People needed help! Would you have just walked away because Gibson was calling?"

"Yes."

"Would you really?" Alfie got close enough that their noses were almost touching. "If there were fifteen people trapped in the rubble and you were the only one who could help them, you would really walk away because the job was calling?" he gritted out from behind clenched teeth.

"When Gibson calls, yes. I walk away from everything."

"I guess that's the difference between us." Alfie let go of LeRoy and turned to see Ray and Nikolai watching. "How about you two? Would you have walked away in my position?"

"They were strangers. Gibson is captain. Yes. I walk away," Nikolai answered quietly before walking out of the building.

"And you?"

"Well, I guess it would depend on who was there that needing saving," Ray snapped, her sarcasm and the fire in her eyes telling Alfie she was talking about something completely different than they were.

LeRoy whistled. "Time for me to leave." He grabbed Alfie's arm. "You better learn fast that this job is a priority in your life. Here, we don't just answer to the people around us, we answer to the world... or at least a small corner of it." LeRoy followed Nikolai out the door with Ray hot on his heels.

"And if I'm not okay with that?" Alfie called after them.

"Get okay with it!" LeRoy called over his shoulder.

"Not likely," Alfie muttered. He waited in the dim hallway for a long second before pushing out into the sunlight. Before he got two steps from the door, he felt a

Katherine Wielechowski

hand around his arm pulling him backwards. He slammed into the warehouse wall hard, the force driving the breath out of him.

"I saw you on the news, hero boy."

"Ray, what the hell?" Alfie wheezed.

"What do you have to say?"

"The news was covering the tornado hitting the complex? I didn't even see them there, but I was a little busy." Alfie couldn't help but adding a healthy dose of snark to his answer. He was getting tired of being thrown around by his co-workers, and having it come from his girlfriend was the last straw.

"I saw you snuggled up to some girl. Who was she?"

Alfie's jaw dropped open. "Are... Are you seriously jealous?"

"Who was she?"

"I was there with Tessa and Ruth. I don't know what girl you thought I was with but you're wrong." Alfie struggled to keep his tone even to try to calm Ray down to a point where they could have a reasonable conversation.

"She was blond. I saw you kiss her!"

Alfie frowned, his mind going through the events of the day, trying to figure out what Ray had seen. Suddenly the light bulb turned on. "Ah... Was she about this tall," he asked, holding up a hand to the height of his nose, "with long, strawberry blond hair, wearing a red sweater and probably Chucks?"

"Yes!" Ray's victory cheer died in her throat when Alfie started laughing. "What?"

"That blond is really cute, isn't she? She's very important to me. I love her, Ray." He held up a hand when she started to growl, unwilling to give up the fun he was having teasing her. "I've known her for about fifteen years and I'm unwilling to give her up. Ray, you'll just have to get used to her being in my life. I'd really like it if you two met someday."

Ray grabbed Alfie by the front of his shirt in both hands and slammed him back against the wall again.

"Okay, too far." Alfie struggled to laugh and breathe at the same time. "Ray, that girl is my sister, Ruth. I kissed her goodbye before coming here."

"Your sister?" Ray growled. Alfie nodded. "Your sister, Ruth?" Alfie nodded again but did the wise thing by not laughing. He stayed very still, barely breathing, waiting to see what Ray would do with that information.

Ray slowly smoothed out the wrinkles she put in the front of Alfie's shirt. She studied the fabric for a long moment, refusing to meet his eye.

"Do you want to... discuss this?" Alfie asked quietly.

"Yes... just not now," Ray whispered, still not meeting his eye.

"Wrong Side of Heaven" sounded from Alfie's phone in his pocket. "Saved by the bell," he whispered, laughing softly.

Alfie's joke finally cracked Ray's frozen demeanor, and she smiled slightly up at him. "Dinner, tomorrow night?"

"Pick you up at seven," Alfie agreed. Ray nodded and gave him a peck on the cheek before walking away. He pulled his phone out of his pocket as he headed for the bus stop. "Hello?"

"Alfie, are you okay?!" Alfie held his phone away as his mother's voice screamed at him.

"Where the hell are you?!" His father's voice joined the noise, telling Alfie that he was on speaker phone.

165

"I'm fine. I had to come to work. We had some damage from the storm but I'm on my way home now. Did Tessa get Ruth back okay?" he blurted out in an attempt to keep them from interrupting with more questions.

"Yes. They just got to the house and you weren't with them! Alfred Louis Vihar, you get home now!"

"Calm down, mama bear. I'm walking to the bus stop now. I'll be there in twenty minutes." Alfie cringed at the false humor that sounded forced even to him.

"Don't you dare start with me! We are having a long, painful talk when you get home!" Vivian snarled into the phone before hanging up.

Alfie sighed. "Best. Day. Ever."

******

"Who takes a girl out on a Sunday?" Ruth was sitting on Alfie's bed watching him struggle with a tie.

"People... I don't know. But I'm sure that, in the history of human beings, I am not the first man to take a woman out on a Sunday," Alfie growled as his tie knotted again, but not in the good way.

"Do you need help?" Ruth asked.

"What? You know how to tie ties now?"

"No, but I know somebody who does."

"MOM!" both Vihar children yelled out the open door at the same time.

"Jeeze, what?" Vivian rushed in a minute later.

"Alfie needs help with his tie," Ruth blurted out.

Alfie glared at his sister in the mirror. "Thanks."

Ruth grinned. "Any time."

"Alfie, you really need to learn how to do this." Vivian gently chided as she untangled his tie and smoothed the wrinkles with her fingers. She popped his collar and put the tie around his neck.

"Why? Dad doesn't know how to tie his tie." Ruth climbed off the bed so she could get a closer look at what Vivian was doing.

"Yes, but your father is helpless." Vivian winked at them.

"I'm totally telling," Alfie laughed. "Have you forgiven me for yesterday?"

"No, but I'm coming around," Vivian sighed. "I understand your job is important to you, Alfie, but your sister should be more important."

"She is, mom... even though she can be a big pain in the butt." Alfie laughed when Ruth stuck out her tongue at him. "Does it help to know that I put my boss off for over an hour while I helped at the complex?"

Vivian finished tying his tie and smoothed his collar. "It does."

"And I got in trouble for doing that when I got to work?"

"Better." Vivian kissed him on the cheek. "You look handsome." She smoothed his hair down, causing him to grimace.

"Thanks, Mom."

"Have fun with Ray tonight." Vivian pressed car keys into his hand and turned for the door. "And Alfie, your father and I would like to meet her sometime."

Alfie groaned internally but smiled at his mom. "I'll ask her tonight." He looked down at the keys in his hand.

"Mom! These aren't for your Prius! These are for the Charger!"

"I talked your father into letting you take it out. A Prius, while great for the environment, is not the car a young man takes a girl out in." Vivian winked and left the room.

"She's totally forgiven you for abandoning me in my time of need and in the middle of a natural disaster zone. I guess we know who her favorite is." Ruth flopped back on Alfie's bed.

"Don't be a drama queen, sis." He pulled on his jacket and tickled her bare feet as he walked by the bed.

"Mean!" Ruth yelled at him as he raced down the stairs.

It was very rare that the 1973 Charger even left the garage, and Alfie could perfectly recall the one time he got to drive it. He had begged his dad for several weeks to let him take it to prom and, for once, Alfie's luck let him get through the entire night without anything happening to it. His date did go home with somebody else and he ended up having to pay for a ruined tuxedo jacket, but the Charger was safe.

He smiled the whole way to Ray's house, the purr of 550 horses soothing away the insanity of the last few days.

Ray was waiting for him at the curb, looking beautiful in a sage green sundress and her brown curls cascading around her shoulders. Alfie threw the Charger in park and jumped out of the car to open the door before she could.

"Nice car." Ray grinned and kissed him gently.

"It is, isn't it?" Alfie laughed as he helped her in and closed the door behind her. He hurried around the car and got back in behind the wheel. "It's my dad's. He spent a better part of his high school and college years rebuilding her."

"It's amazing." Ray slid her hand across the white leather to take Alfie's hand. "So what's the plan for tonight?"

"Well, I promised we would do what you want, so I have some options in mind for you to choose from."

Ray laughed. "So I'm picking from what you've already picked?"

Alfie grinned over at her. "Kind of, but not quite. First things first. What are you craving for dinner?"

"Hmm, Italian or Chinese."

"Ok, I know great places for both. Do you want fancy sit down, cozy and intimate, or quirky and unique?"

"Quirky and unique." Ray giggled, having fun already.

"Perfect. I know two Italian places that fit the bill or one Chinese."

"Well, now, I can't make it easy for you. Let's do Italian."

"All right." Alfie stopped at a red light and studied Ray for a long moment. "Do you want the place with the amazing dessert in house or the place with good dessert but is across the street from the best ice cream in San Luca?"

"Oooh, ice cream sounds great."

"La Piastra it is, followed by Shay's Cooler."

"I have never been to either," Ray grinned.

"Perfect!" Alfie quickly changed lanes and went around the block to head in the other direction. "Now, they are on the southern edge of downtown. We can do some window shopping after ice cream, or we can do something else."

"Are you one hundred percent sure dancing is out?" Ray asked, holding up crossed fingers in hopes he would change his mind.

169

Alfie laughed. "I would seriously love to, but you've witnessed me giving myself a black eye. Do you want to be around that?"

"Yes," Ray said adamantly. "You said I could choose!"

Alfie groaned and glanced over at her hopeful grin. He chuckled and shook his head. "Okay, there's a little martini bar a few blocks from the restaurant that has a house jazz band."

"Yay!" Ray laughed and threw her arms around Alfie, giving him a huge kiss on the cheek. "Oops, sorry." She laughed and wiped the lip gloss off his cheek.

"I should make you sign a waiver that you won't hold me legally responsible for anything that happens while we're dancing."

"You'll be fine." Ray smiled and took his hand again. "How do you know about these places?"

"How do you not?" Alfie laughed. "When Robert was dating Cameron, I got stuck hanging around O'Rory's a lot after school. I'd take off and explore downtown while they did whatever it was they did."

Alfie pulled the Charger into a parking spot at the edge of the downtown area under a street lamp. He sent up a small prayer that nothing happened to it while they were gone as he walked around to the passenger side to open the door for Ray.

"When did you become such a gentleman?" Ray commented when Alfie pulled her hand through his arm as they walked to the restaurant.

"My mother would kill me if she found out that I took you out for a fancy date and didn't do it right," he grinned.

"Plus, wearing a tie makes me feel like Cary Grant or something, so the gentleman stuff just happens."

"Catch me if I swoon," Ray teased with a laugh.

"Catch me if I trip," Alfie answered, only slightly joking. He let go of Ray so he could open the door to the restaurant and motioned for her to go in first.

"This is fun." Ray looked around at the dim restaurant, taking in all of the old Italian memorabilia on the walls between faux grape vines and wine bottle candle sconces.

"Alfred Vihar! It has been too long!" An old man in a sharp pinstriped suit walked around the hostess stand to wrap Alfie in a bear hug.

"Massimo." Alfie wheezed as the old man squeezed the breath out of him.

"Ah, and who is the beautiful lady?" Massimo smoothly took Ray's hand and kissed the back of it, making her giggle.

"Massimo, this is my girlfriend, Ray. Ray, this is Massimo Corelli. He owns La Piastra."

Massimo slapped Alfie's shoulder. "Alfred, she is too beautiful for you."

"I know, but what I lack in looks, I make up for in charm and wit." Alfie's grin was as big and goofy as he could make it, causing the others to laugh. "Massimo, what are you doing hosting? I thought that was beneath a big restaurant owner like you!"

"All sass, this one," Massimo said in a stage whisper to Ray. He put an arm around Alfie and pulled him close. "I have decided that it is time for me to retire!"

"So, Vincent is running Massimo's and you are running La Piastra?" Alfie guessed as Massimo let go of him

171

and led them through the restaurant to a cozy table in a corner next to a large window that overlooked a quiet courtyard between La Piastra and the next building.

"Correct," Massimo laughed.

"What's Massimo's?" Ray whispered to Alfie.

"It's the really fancy Italian place on the west side of town next to the business district," Alfie whispered back.

"That makes no sense," Ray replied, frowning.

Alfie winked at her. "I know."

Massimo bowed slightly as he pulled a chair out for Ray. He handed them menus and motioned for a waiter to come take their orders. "Now, how is my grandniece? You need to tell her to come visit me! I have not seen her in too long."

Alfie chuckled awkwardly with a quick glance at Ray. "She's good, Massimo. She has that internship at the hospital and has been really busy."

"Ah, yes, our future doctor. We are very proud of her!" Massimo nearly bellowed with a loud laugh. Customers at nearby tables turned and smiled at the restaurant owner. "But you did not come here to talk to an old man! Back to your date with the beauty. Let me know if you need anything."

"Thanks, Massimo." Alfie stood to shake his hand once more while Ray waved goodbye.

"He is something else." Ray chuckled before sipping her sparkling water. "Did you meet him while you explored downtown?"

"No," Alfie paused, hoping Ray was back to herself and not the jealous woman he met the day before. "Massimo is Tessa's great uncle. I know him through the Pellegrini family."

"Oh, that makes sense. I didn't know Tessa had an internship." Ray reached across the table and took one of Alfie's hands.

"Yeah, she's been wanting to be a doctor since we were kids. They don't usually give internships to people just out of high school, but Massimo is good friends with the chief of medicine and pulled some strings. It didn't hurt that Tessa took a few AP Biology classes in high school and a pre-med bio class through the community college."

"You're proud of her," Ray quietly observed, watching Alfie closely.

"Of course. She's my best friend and is making huge strides toward achieving the goal she has wanted most of her life. It all started when her dad was shot on the job. According to her mom, Tessa was the best little nurse, making sure he had everything he needed."

"Shot?"

"Yeah, Leo was a cop at the time, but he's a detective now. The desire to become a doctor only got stronger when her brothers joined the police force or various military branches. She wanted to make sure she could take care of them if they ever got hurt."

"That's an amazing and selfless goal," Ray said softly.

"Yeah," Alfie mumbled as he stared into the candle in the center of their table. He could feel Ray watching him and waiting, but he had no idea what to say. "My parents want to meet you," he blurted.

Ray's spine stiffened slightly. "They... they do?"

"Yeah," Alfie sighed. "Do you hate the idea?"

Ray was silent for a moment. "No?"

"Not tonight, though."

"Oh, okay, good!" Ray relaxed a little with a nervous laugh.

"No, I wouldn't make you do that. We've only been dating for like two weeks. That's a little crazy."

"One week," Ray corrected.

"One week? Are you sure?" Alfie shook his head when Ray nodded. "Man, a lot has happened in that one week."

Ray laughed. "Yeah. Speaking of which... you got to see my crazy yesterday."

Alfie sobered. "I did."

Ray grimaced. "I'm sorry, Alfie. I usually try to save that for date five." Her attempt at making the conversation less awkward fell flat. "I really am sorry. I'm not usually the jealous type, it's just that I had a really bad relationship that ended in a really bad break up, and I guess I'm not as over it as I thought I was."

"How bad?"

"World War Three."

Alfie whistled and squeezed her hand. "If you want to talk about it, I'm here. If not, that's fine, too."

Ray sighed. "The long and the short of it is, he cheated on me. A lot. And I had my suspicions from the beginning, but I never had enough proof. Then, when I'd confront him about it, he'd deny it and get mad at me for accusing him."

"Red flag."

"I know. By the end, I was so paranoid and suspicious that I couldn't even trust my own decisions. It finally took LeRoy sitting me down to convince me that I wasn't the defective one in the relationship."

"LeRoy?" Alfie was surprised that Ray would turn to a co-worker with a situation like a cheating boyfriend.

"I was messing up so much at work because of the relationship stuff that he sat me down after training one day in the den, got me roaring drunk, and made me tell." Ray smiled slightly at the memory.

Alfie's jaw dropped. "You got drunk in the den?"

Ray laughed. "Yeah. Gibson wasn't too happy about it, but he covered it so Brutus wouldn't find out. I'm not completely sure that he doesn't know, but he's never reprimanded any of us for it, so nobody brings it up."

"Well, just so we have our bases covered..." Alfie moved his chair so he could sit closer to Ray. "I think cheaters are the lowest of the low. The only thing below them in hell are murderers, child abusers, and people who talk at the theater." He held up a hand when Ray started to speak. "Second, I know that you are fully capable of kicking my ass, so, to save my own skin, I would never consider cheating on you."

Ray threw back her head and laughed. "Thank you."

"Plus, if you don't, I know the rest of Team 9 loves you more than me. They'd make sure I disappeared if you didn't kill me first."

"Very true!"

Alfie pulled Ray closer and kissed her, sealing his promise with what was in his heart.

"Alfie! I didn't know you were planning on coming to La Piastra tonight."

"Vivian, hush! The boy's busy!"

Alfie grimaced and closed his eyes briefly before turning around in his chair. "Ray, let me introduce you to George and Vivian. My parents."

175

Katherine Wielechowski

******

"Hey! How's it-" LeRoy hit Alfie in the face with a poncho. "-going?"

"Get packed up, we're flying out in ten," Gibson called over his shoulder as he walked out the den door.

"Flying out?" Alfie asked, confused. He walked over to his locker and pulled out his go-bag. It had been just over a week since the job in Canada, and he wasn't sure how he would explain another work trip to his parents in such a short time.

"There's some weather anomalies north of San Francisco. They think it's Trade Wind. Forcefield and Bullet are meeting us at the airport," Ray explained as she zipped up her bag. She smiled when she saw the panicked look on his face. "It should be a short trip, so don't worry about your parents."

"And the poncho?"

"She controls the weather. It will probably be raining." LeRoy's tone was teasing as he threw a few more things into his bag.

"Rain doesn't hurt much. We'd do better to pack helmets for the hail she's going to throw at us," Alfie grumbled.

Nikolai picked up a helmet from the table and tossed it over to Alfie. "Here is your helmet."

"Thanks." Alfie rolled his eyes and examined the helmet. It was shaped like a helmet one would wear while riding a horse, but much thinner so it sat closer to the skull. "Is this going to protect the head at all? It's like the thin candy shell around an M&M."

"Worried about your noggin?" LeRoy teased.

"Yes. It doesn't do much and it's not much to look at, but it's the only one I have!" Alfie exclaimed, pulling on the helmet to check for fit.

"Special plastic. Works better than normal helmets." Nikolai rapped on Alfie's helmet with his knuckles.

"Great," Alfie mumbled as he pulled off the helmet and packed it in his bag. He threw the poncho back at LeRoy and pulled his rain coat out of his locker. "Any other special equipment or uniforms we need?"

Ray shook her head. "Just combat gear, bad weather gear, and weapons."

"Any intel saying Trade Wind has henchmen?"

"Not that I've heard," Ray said slowly, looking to Nikolai and LeRoy for confirmation. "She did try to hire from us, but the AOJ beat her to it after the tornado."

"We can probably assume she went to S&T when Brutus turned her down," LeRoy speculated.

"S&T?" Alfie asked.

"Stealth & Tactics. They're another henchmen agency based out of Los Angeles with satellite offices all over the world, including one here in San Luca. Their cover is aftermarket gun accessories and shooting gear," Ray explained.

"Bunch of douche bags," Nikolai growled as he pulled his bag closed and slung it over his shoulder. "Don't know what they're doing half the time and purposefully mess things up other half."

They watched him storm out of the room before Alfie turned to Ray and LeRoy for an explanation.

"Nikolai used to work for S&T. Then when one of the guys he was working with decided to go all hotshot and about got Nikolai killed, he changed agencies. He was one of the first members of Team 9. He and Gibson built this team, and they were one of the best teams at RI for a while. Then two of their members got killed in a freak accident and destroyed the team's rep." LeRoy told the story with a rare solemnness that went against his playful personality. "Gibson's been trying to bring it back from the brink for years now. Ray, your addition to the team was a huge win for Gibson. Team 5 was campaigning hard for you."

"LeRoy, you were probably a bigger win than I was." Ray dropped a kiss on the Cajun's cheek.

"*Chère,* aren't you so sweet." LeRoy grinned up at Ray as he finished packing and stood.

"I didn't know any of that," Alfie whispered as they watched LeRoy leave.

"I knew most of it. I didn't know that I was Gibson's hope to revive the team." Ray pulled her bag onto her back.

"Looks like I've got to buckle down. Try to help bring back some of Gibson's glory." Alfie zipped up his bag and picked it up.

"It's not all on you, Alf." Ray put an arm around Alfie's waist as they walked to the door. "To be honest, Gibson didn't really want you, but Brutus made him take you."

Alfie rolled his eyes as he wrapped an arm around Ray's shoulders. "Awesome."

"BUT you have far exceeded everybody's expectations. Just keep working on it and you will prove to everybody that you deserved your spot." She kissed Alfie briefly. "Thanks for last night. I had fun."

"Even with the whole 'meeting my parents' thing?" Alfie cringed at the thought.

"Even with," Ray chuckled. "They're really nice. I now know where you get your sense of humor."

"Yeah, my mom."

"And the red hair." Ray leaned close and pressed a gentle kiss against Alfie's neck. "You're a better dancer than you let on. Let's go."

"Right behind you." Alfie followed Ray out of the building to the van. His thoughts were racing with the story LeRoy told and ideas of how to try to prove to Gibson that his being on Team 9 was not such a horrible thing. He cleared his mind when a tiny annoying voice asked again if he truly wanted to be a henchman anymore.

******

"Please tell me we have a better plan than 'capture bad guy and go home.'" Sarcasm dripped from Alfie's question as they drove through the streets of San Francisco. It was just before noon, but the bizarre weather was keeping people indoors, leaving the streets mostly clear for the coming encounter with Trade Wind.

They had taken a small plane from San Luca to San Francisco and had just managed to land before the weather got really dicey. They took a van to the northern edge of the city where the weirdest things were happening. They drove through quarter-sized hail for three blocks, which stopped just to change to straight winds two blocks later.

"We've never encountered someone who can control the weather like this, so it's going to be a bit on the fly," Gibson started, almost sheepishly. "I don't know how reliable our firearms are going to be in this, so play it by ear. If you have the shot, take it. Don't worry about permission.

179

We haven't had a visual on Trade Wind, so we don't know who we're looking for. Just keep your eyes open and find somebody who is out of place. She probably won't be affected by the weather like we are. That will be your confirmation."

"Our radios are waterproof, so keep talking to each other," Bullet added. "We're going to split into two-man teams and sweep the area. Forcefield and I will take point on the middle block. You guys will spread out behind us. Nikolai and Vihar will be to the west, LeRoy and Ray will be to the east with Gibson right behind us. We are coming in from the south and will continue to move north until we find Trade Wind."

"Do we have intel on if she has hired any henchmen?" Ray asked as she pulled on a pair of gloves.

"I think it's safe to assume she will have a few around her." Gibson tightened the strap on his goggles so they stayed on his helmet and pulled it on his head. "They might not be close, so when we find her, keep your eyes on the surrounding buildings."

"I am going to try to contain as much of her weather as possible. When I do that, Bullet is going to try to take her out. If that doesn't work, we will have to improvise," Forcefield finally spoke. He pulled on a pair of blue goggles that, when combined with his blue-green skintight suit, made him look like a fish out of water.

"The van will get us as close as it can to what looks like the center of the weather disruptions. We will hoof it after that. Stay low and try to keep under cover as much as possible. While your helmet and flak jackets will protect you from hail, they won't do much if she sends a tornado that tosses a car at you. Keep your weapons as hidden as possible until you need them. There are people around and we don't need anybody causing mass hysteria by running down the street looking like a rogue shooter," Gibson finished. The van rocked violently in the wind and quickly pulled into a parking garage. "This is it."

They bailed out of the van and stood staring at the deluge that was coming down outside.

"I picked a hell of a week to quit smoking." Gibson popped three pieces of gum in his mouth and settled his goggles over his eyes.

"Hey, Forcefield. What are the chances you can put a ball around each of us so we don't get wet?" Alfie asked with a strangled laugh. The superhero glared at him and headed for the exit. Gibson gave Alfie a dirty look before turning to follow Forcefield. "What? I had to ask." He shrugged at the others. "Just trying to release the tension."

"Come." Nikolai roughly grabbed Alfie by the back of his collar and dragged him to the west exit.

"You can let go of me." Alfie roughly pulled away from Nikolai, though it did nothing for his ego knowing that the only reason he got away was because the Russian released him. He settled his pack on his back more comfortably and followed his teammate north along the street. They stayed close to the buildings, using the cover to keep from getting completely soaked or blown away.

"All teams move one block east," Bullet's voice crackled through their ear pieces.

"They must have found her," Alfie commented.

"Or think the center of weather has shifted," Nikolai responded.

They quickly moved to the end of their block and turned east; ducking low to combat the wind and sticking close to the walls, they made it the one block east and turned to head north again.

"We've got some severe hail here," Alfie heard Ray shout on the radio. Both he and Nikolai looked up at the rain falling on them and then looked east to where Ray and LeRoy were. There was definitely a green tinge to the clouds over those blocks.

"Hunker down and move as soon as you can," Gibson ordered. "Nikolai, Vihar, report.

"Just rain and wind, sir," Nikolai answered.

"Hey, hang on. I wonder if-" Alfie started as he ducked into a building on their right.

"Dammit, Vihar!" Nikolai called after him. With nothing else to do, Nikolai stood watch at the door and kept an eye on the street. Suddenly, there was a bright light and a loud crack of thunder. Alfie trotted back out shortly after.

"I knew it! The whole first floor of this building is a small mall with windows that run the length of the block. We can get out of the rain!" Alfie stopped when he realized that Nikolai was on the ground. He reached down and helped Nikolai to his feet. "What happened?!"

"WHAT?" Nikolai shouted.

Alfie's eyes widened when he noticed some blood coming from Nikolai's ears and smoke coming from the radio on his belt. He looked around and noticed a destroyed light pole three feet from where Nikolai had been standing. "Dammit," he muttered.

"WHAT?" Nikolai shouted again.

Alfie shook his head and put his index finger over his lips, indicating to Nikolai to be quiet. He dragged his teammate into the building and pulled a small marker board and a marker from his pack. He hastily wrote 'lightning strike don't yell' on the board and showed it to Nikolai.

The Russian quickly read it and nodded. "OKAY!" he shouted.

Alfie shook his head and put a finger to his lips again. Nikolai nodded again and wiggled a finger in his ear, trying to get it to work. Alfie tapped him on the shoulder and quickly wrote 'I'll radio Gibson' on the board. Nikolai nodded again and tried working his jaw in hopes to get his ears to pop.

"Captain, we have a situation," Alfie said into the mic.

"What's wrong, Vihar?" Gibson barked back.

"Nikolai was too close to a lightning strike. It fried his radio and deafened him." Alfie sighed and leaned against the wall in the entryway, watching Nikolai's vain attempts to get his ears working again.

"You okay?" Gibson asked.

"Yeah, I ducked into a building to find a better path. It happened when Nikolai was outside."

"I'll save my lecture about not leaving your partner for later, Vihar," Gibson snapped. "If Nikolai is still on his feet, carry on as usual. We'll figure this out after we deal with Trade Wind."

"Roger that, sir." Alfie sighed and quickly scribbled instructions on the board. He tapped Nikolai on the shoulder again and showed him what he had written. Nikolai nodded and Alfie made a gesture to indicate that he would lead and Nikolai would follow. Alfie was worried that he would argue, but, after a brief glare in Alfie's direction, Nikolai nodded his agreement. Alfie started walking north along the windows, glad to be out of the rain, no matter the dirty looks they were

183

getting from the shoppers who slipped in the puddles of water they were leaving behind.

Alfie stopped suddenly as a thought crossed his mind. He quickly wrote 'know sign language?' on the board and showed it to Nikolai, who shook his head. "Worth a shot," Alfie laughed. He wrote down what he had said when it looked like Nikolai was about to shout at him again.

Alfie and Nikolai reached the north side of the building and were about to step back outside when Bullet's voice came over the radio. "We have eyes on Trade Wind."

Alfie scribbled the news on the board and showed it to Nikolai, who grabbed the marker and wrote 'where?' Alfie shrugged and held up a hand telling him to wait.

"Trade Wind is on Carter Boulevard centered between 10th and 11th streets. All units converge," Bullet ordered.

Alfie raced to the window to see what street they were on. "Excuse me," he said, stopping a woman as she walked out of the shop closet to the door. "Can you tell me where Carter Boulevard is?"

"Yeah, it's two blocks north." She eyed Nikolai with obvious interest and held out her hand. "I'm Nina."

"He's gay and deaf," Alfie barked before shoving Nikolai toward the door. He ignored the woman's snort of disgust from behind him. They stopped under an awning a few doors down, and Alfie had the chance to explain the situation to Nikolai. He quickly wrote 'TW spotted Carter Blvd between 10 & 11 2 blocks N 1 block E.'

Nikolai nodded his understanding, and Alfie finally remembered to report back. "We're three blocks out, on our way."

"Good, and hurry. We're getting pinned down," Gibson quickly responded.

Alfie motioned to Nikolai to follow him, and they set off running for 10th Street. The closer they got, the deeper the water got, and it was well over mid-calf by the time they reached 10th. Alfie quickly turned north, and they were both flattened by the wind that was howling down the street. Nikolai tapped Alfie's shoulder and motioned for him to follow. Alfie nodded and watched Nikolai roll over onto his stomach and float in the water. The Russian started pulling himself along using his hands against the pavement and kicking his feet in the water. Alfie struggled to keep up as he followed Nikolai north along 10th. The wind got stronger the closer they got, but the water got shallower until there was nothing under them but wet concrete. They stayed on the ground and crawled along, staying as close to the buildings as they could.

Alfie glanced up at the next cross street and saw they had finally reached their goal. He hit Nikolai's foot until he stopped and turned to look at him. Alfie pointed up to the street sign and Nikolai nodded, understanding. They carefully got to their feet and pulled their weapons out of their packs. They slowly crept to the corner of the building and looked east down Carter. There was a woman in a flowing gray dress with dark blue hair standing with her arms outstretched in the middle of the street. There was a wall of lightning dancing in front of her and the wind seemed to pour off of her in waves.

"We're here, sir. We see her," Alfie whispered into his mic.

"Where?" Gibson barked.

"Southeast corner of 10th and Carter."

"I'm about twenty feet east of you with Bullet. Forcefield is directly across from Trade Wind. He's trying to get a field around her, but she keeps defeating it somehow. Ray and LeRoy are on the corner of 11th and Carter," Gibson reported.

"Roger. Do we have a plan?"

"Not... yet," Gibson answered slowly.

"Roger that."

Alfie tapped Nikolai and motioned for him to follow him back a few feet into a recessed doorway. He pulled out his marker board and told Nikolai where everybody else was. Nikolai nodded his understanding and wrote 'plan?' on the board.

Alfie shook his head with a shrug. Nikolai motioned for Alfie to stay there and headed back to the street. He came back a minute later and took the marker board from Alfie. He quickly scribbled a picture of the street with an arrow from where they stood to the building on the other side of Carter. Nikolai motioned that they should race across the street, go into the building and sneak up on Trade Wind from behind. Alfie looked from him to the board and back, trying to decide who was more insane, the Russian or himself for agreeing to the plan. He nodded and motioned for Nikolai to lead. Nikolai handed the board back to Alfie and headed for the corner.

Alfie quickly called to Gibson on the radio. "Sir, Nikolai and I have a plan. We're going to enter the building on the north side of Carter and try to get behind Trade Wind."

"That's the stupidest thing I've heard all day!" Ray yelled back.

"Good luck, Vihar. We'll distract her for a bit," Gibson answered.

"Roger," Alfie responded. He tapped Nikolai on the back and gave him the thumbs up. Nikolai grinned and looked around the corner again.

They heard gunfire and lightning crack as the rest of the team tried to distract Trade Wind, then they raced across the street. The locked doors didn't have a chance against Nikolai's shoulder, and he and Alfie ran through the empty office space trying to find a good vantage point. The walls were all brick with two-foot by four-foot windows near the ceiling.

"HERE!" Alfie yelled, estimating that they should be behind Trade Wind.

Nikolai nodded and jumped up on a desk to look out the windows. He shook his head and motioned further down the wall. Alfie ran down a few cubicles and climbed onto a desk. He could see Forcefield across the street a few yards further. He motioned for Nikolai to move on and jumped off the desk. He joined Nikolai in the cubical directly behind Trade Wind. Nikolai was writing on the desk pad calendar with a marker. Alfie moved so he could read 'go back to that cubical and break window be ready to shoot – if I fail up to you.'

Alfie felt his stomach drop to his boots. He grabbed the marker and wrote 'what're you going to do?'

Nikolai grinned and pulled a grenade out of his pack. He motioned for Alfie to move and jumped onto the desk.

Alfie raced back to the other cubicle and called over the mic. "We're in position. Nikolai's going to try to take her down with a grenade. I'm in position to fire if it doesn't work." Alfie pulled both of his pistols out of the conceal

187

holsters at the small of his back and jumped onto the desk. He shoved the window open and propped his arms up so he could take aim at the blue-haired cause of this week's hell.

"We're ready, Vihar!" Gibson responded.

Alfie tried to concentrate on his breathing as he waited for Nikolai to act. He barely caught the movement of the grenade as it flew from the window and landed a few feet from Trade Wind.

"Grenade!" a lackey in a dark blue jumpsuit and mask yelled from his position crouched behind a car a few feet directly in front of Alfie.

Alfie thought time slowed as Trade Wind turned to look at it. She flung out a hand and the grenade blew down the street toward Ray and LeRoy.

"Ray! Get down!" Alfie yelled into his mic as he opened fire. Trade Wind jerked his way when a bullet grazed her upper arm. She pointed at him, and he threw himself to the floor as lightning struck the brick wall under his window.

"The weather is mine! No one will control it but me!" Trade Wind screamed.

He heard the wind increase until it sounded like a train in the street, then there was silence. He lay on the floor for a long time thinking he was dead until Gibson's voice crackled in his ear.

"Everybody okay?"

"Ray and I are fine," LeRoy answered.

"Good," Bullet said.

"Fine," Forcefield grumbled.

"I'm alive. Let me check on Nikolai," Alfie groaned as he got to his feet. He slowly walked to the cubical where he had left Nikolai and found the Russian leaning against the desk digging a hole in the carpet with his knife. Alfie looked around and pulled a neon green clip from the cubical wall and tossed it at his teammate. Nikolai jumped when it hit him in the chest. Alfie waved and motioned for him to follow. Nikolai nodded and got to his feet. They walked out of the building and headed for where the rest of the team had already gathered in the center of the street.

"What about her people?" Alfie asked as he joined them.

"We only saw two and they got away in the vortex she called down," Forcefield sighed as he angrily pulled his goggles off his head.

"How is he?" Gibson asked, motioning to Nikolai with his head.

"Fine other than not being able to hear," Alfie answered as he put an arm around Ray.

"I'M FINE!" Nikolai yelled.

Gibson chuckled a bit and put a hand on Nikolai's shoulder with a nod.

They all stood there for a minute examining the damage around them.

Alfie harrumphed. "So this is what a loss feels like."

******

Ray laughed, then grimaced. She gently touched her bottom lip. "Still have a fat lip."

Alfie studied her for a second. "It happened yesterday, give it time. Plus, you're one step closer to being a Kardashian. You'll just have to dye your hair black and forget you have any talent."

Ray threw back her head and laughed. "You'd have to be black, too."

189

Alfie waved it off. "If Robert Downey, Jr. can do it, I can too." Alfie stopped suddenly and looked at Ray with wide eyes. "I'd have to learn how to play basketball." He vigorously shook his head. "Nope. Not going to work."

"Or you could learn how to sing."

"Girl, I know how to sing!" Alfie struck a pose. "Now. I am not saying she is a gold digger, but she is not messing with a broke... person."

"Person, eh?" Ray laughed. "Could you get any whiter?"

"Probably. Michael Jackson did. Hey, how are they going to deal with Nikolai's ears?" Alfie asked suddenly, changing the subject.

"I don't know. I did hear that they got them fixed, though," Ray giggled. "No pun intended. But seriously, it was probably some super-secret cure-all that Dr. Olafson and the RI medical team cooked up."

Alfie's jaw dropped. "It's been less than twenty-four hours. How the hell would they get them fixed already?"

"We deal with people with superhuman capabilities," Ray laughed. "Why is this a stretch for you?"

"*Team 9 to conference room Foxtrot. Team 9 to conference room Foxtrot,*" Esther's voice echoed in the den, causing Alfie and Ray to jump.

"Wonder what's going on," Alfie mumbled as he and Ray walked down the hall to conference room Foxtrot. They were the first ones there and sat down at the table to wait for the others.

"Everybody sit down and shut up!" Gibson barked as he marched into the room, followed by Nikolai, LeRoy, and a group of people Alfie didn't know.

"For those of you who don't know, this is Team 7." Gibson made a point of looking directly at Alfie for the introduction. "Brutus has assigned them to help us with the Trade Wind situation. Team leader Tina Wilkins will be taking charge from here on out. This is rest of her team: Erin Skarret, Jackson Pearitig, November Falls, and Olsen Michaels. And we will all be playing nice. Nikolai." Gibson's warning tone stopped the former spy's glare from melting the pretty woman with maroon and black hair from Team 7.

"Gibson and I will be leading together." A short woman in her early thirties with brown curly hair stepped forward. "I know there has been some animosity between our teams in the past, but with the departure of Pavel and the completion of anger management classes, I think we are all in a better place to team up."

"Who's Pavel?" Alfie whispered to Ray.

"Asshole who used to run Team 7. Tina's better at it and way nicer," Ray whispered back.

"What happened to him?"

Ray shrugged. "Killed by some falling debris from a building that Forcefield blew up."

"Seriously?" Alfie gasped.

"Green, Vihar," Gibson barked.

"Sorry, Captain, sir. I was just curious as to who Pavel was. Ray was kind enough to explain the change of leadership of Team 7 to me," Alfie explained in the most exaggerated contrite voice he could.

Gibson rolled his eyes. "Smartass."

"Ah, you must be the newbie who got shot." Tina walked forward with her hand out.

191

"Is that how people know me around here?" Alfie asked as he shook Tina's hand.

She chuckled. "Yeah, but it's quite a feat to get shot on your first mission and not even know it. And it's even more impressive that you came back afterward."

"Well, thanks." Alfie's embarrassment colored his face. "I'm horrible at hand-to-hand," he blurted.

Team 7 collectively smirked. "We've heard." The woman with streaked hair that Nikolai was glaring daggers at walked over to shake his hand, the movement revealing a full sleeve of tattoos down her right arm. "We're not holding it against you, though." Alfie noticed that she had close to a dozen piercings in her ears in addition to the ones in her lip, nose, and eyebrow. "I'm November."

"Alfie. Did those hurt?" He motioned to his own face indicating her piercings.

"Not as much as a gunshot." She grinned and stepped away so her teammates could introduce themselves to Alfie. Erin was a short, sturdy-looking blond with fire and intelligence in her eyes and a ready laugh. Jackson was a tall, soft-spoken Indian man with side-parted, short black hair and glasses who looked to be about fifty. Olsen was an unremarkable looking man in his late twenties with patchy stubble and a mop of brown curls that hung over his eyes.

"Now that the introductions are done, we need to get to work," Gibson started. "Tina?"

"Yes. LeRoy, I want you working with Erin. Jackson, you go with them, too. We need to figure out what is going on with Trade Wind. She has caught us off guard twice already, and I don't like getting caught with my pants around my ankles. Brutus's people haven't been able to get any good information on her. You three need to find something we can use. I also want to know where she will strike next."

"Nikolai, Ray, and November come up with some way we can fight her more effectively. I know we have no chance against a tornado, but see if you can modify our equipment to withstand high winds and hail. Also, figure out a way to tether us down so we don't blow away but can still move easily," Gibson ordered. "And if you can figure out some way to combat lightning, I'm all ears."

"I can help with that also," LeRoy volunteered.

Gibson nodded. "Fine. But getting all you can on Trade Wind comes first."

"Good idea," Tina agreed. "Olsen and Alfie, while neither of you are experts at anything yet, a fresh eye always helps. Float between the two groups and see if you can help them spot anything they've missed. When you're not doing that, Olsen, see if you can give Alfie some pointers on fighting." Tina pulled her phone out of one of the many pouches on her belt and tapped the screen. "Gibson, Brutus wants to see us. Looks like they might have a lead."

"What exactly will the AOJ be doing while we do all the work?" Ray asked, her sweet tone doing nothing to cover the rancor in her voice.

"They got called to another problem in Florida but should be back by the end of the week," Tina explained when Gibson stayed silent.

"Nice. We do the work, they get the glory," Ray mumbled.

"We're henchmen. That's our lot," Tina scolded. November winked at Ray, letting her know she was thinking the same thing.

Gibson stood. "We have a lot to do and little time to accomplish it all. To work, everybody!"

******

"Weather control." Alfie dropped the paper he was looking at and stared at Jackson with wide eyes. It had been a week since San Francisco. Teams 9 and 7 had been working day and night trying to figure out what Trade Wind's game was. "That's what she wants."

"Alfie," LeRoy leaned back in his chair and rubbed his face, exhausted from hours of staring at a computer screen. "Trade Wind controls the weather. That's kind of her thing. We know that already."

"No! Well, yes, but no! Where has she attacked?" Alfie rushed over to a map of California that was tacked to the wall.

LeRoy held up a hand and started counting off places on his fingers. "Well, it's unconfirmed, but we believe that she caused the lightning strike that fried the computers at the Los Pallos observatory. Then, we know she sent the tornado that flattened downtown San Luca. We also think she is why it rained so much that a landslide buried that tiny town-"

"Jeffersville," Erin interjected.

"Yes, Jeffersville, up in the mountains east of Bakersfield," LeRoy finished.

"And we couldn't stop her from wrecking the northern edge of San Francisco with those winds and hail." Alfie quickly grabbed the paper he dropped and a marker and started writing on the map.

"What do you have?" Erin slowly walked over to look over Alfie's shoulder. Jackson and LeRoy joined them.

"The Los Pallos observatory is also home of the Southern California University Meteorology lab. A former professor named-" Alfie paused to check the paper in his hand, "Dr. Meredith Jennings and her partner Dr. Val Stevenson were just visiting to give a presentation on their experiments on weather control."

LeRoy sighed. "Alf, people have been trying to control the weather since man discovered fire."

Jackson rocked back and forth a bit. "Well... rain dances, offerings to the gods, et cetera."

"I know, but Jennings and Stevenson were working on developing a machine that will actually control the weather."

"This sounds like an episode of Kim Possible," Erin scoffed and plopped back down at her computer.

Alfie frowned at her. "Dude. You're a henchman. But hear me out. They were at the observatory two days before the lightning strikes. They did some work with the students while they were there and lost the work they did on the observatory's computers in the storm."

"How do you know this?" LeRoy asked.

"Oh! I found that in a newspaper a couple of days ago," Jackson answered, digging through a pile of papers on his desk before finding the clipping he was looking for.

"I saw that yesterday when I was helping," Alfie added. He hit the map with the marker. "So we have Los Pollos. Then, we have the San Luca History and Science Complex. Jennings and Stevenson work in the meteorology building there but were in New York for some science awards thing when the tornado flattened it."

"How'd you know that?" Erin asked.

195

"My sister told me. We were at the complex when it was hit. Ruth doesn't have much interest in science, but the weather has always fascinated her, so she was looking forward to visiting the meteorology building and possibly seeing the doctors. She was bummed later when she found out that they weren't even there."

"What about Jeffersville?" Jackson asked, beginning to believe Alfie's theory.

"There's a small meteorology station in the mountains a few miles above Jeffersville." Alfie made a small mark on the map.

"The Medard station," Tina said from the door. Gibson stood just behind her. "It was destroyed in the mudslide, killing the three people who worked there. One of whom was Dr. Lee Walker."

"He was developing his own system for controlling the weather," Gibson added.

"And a huge rival of Dr. Jennings," Tina finished.

"The town was collateral damage," LeRoy whispered, realizing that Alfie's theory was right.

"San Francisco?" Jackson asked.

Alfie frowned and shook his head. "That I couldn't quite-"

"The government has a research lab there specializing in meteorology," Erin said suddenly. She jumped out of her chair and started digging through the piles on her desk. She found a paper and turned to them with wide eyes. "The United States National Weather Service is working on a joint project with the Department of Defense to develop weather affecting equipment that will aid and assist soldiers on the battlefield," she read.

Jackson waved his hand. "That's nothing new. The DOD was trying to seed clouds in Vietnam to muddy up trails."

Erin shook her head and continued. "This joint project is led by visiting experts in meteorology, Dr. Meredith Jennings and Dr. Val Stevenson."

"Did they survive Trade Wind's attack?" Alfie asked.

"Yes. They were back at the Los Pollos observatory working on the research they lost," LeRoy answered, looking up from his computer screen.

"What does this all add up to?" Gibson asked.

"Weather control." Alfie pointed at the map, explaining everything to the team leaders. "Trade Wind is trying to get rid of anybody who is working to develop true weather control. A part of my mind stuck on what she said before she disappeared in San Francisco and I just finally put the pieces together."

"She said something in San Francisco? What was it?" LeRoy asked.

"'The weather is mine. No one will control it but me,'" Alfie quoted.

"We've got it!" LeRoy nearly shouted.

"Gibson, go tell Brutus. Tell him we know what she's after and that we need to get Jennings and Stevenson into protective custody until we can stop Trade Wind," Tina ordered.

"Won't Trade Wind go to ground if she can't get to the doctors?" Erin asked.

"Would you rather use them as bait?" Tina snapped.

The room went silent as they all honestly considered how to go about doing just that.

197

"Stop," Gibson ordered. "We'll get her some other way. Good work, guys."

"Alfie figured it out," LeRoy corrected, throwing an arm around Alfie's shoulders.

"Really?"

"Don't sound so surprised, sir. I had to do something right sometime," Alfie grinned.

Gibson smiled and shook his head. "Well, good work. I guess you're not as detrimental to this unit as I thought you were."

"Right back at ya, Cap!" Alfie flinched back from Gibson's hard stare. "I mean, thank you, sir." Alfie continued to squirm under Gibson's glare. "I got this one." Alfie smacked himself on the back of the head to save Gibson the trouble.

Gibson shook his head again and left the room. After a long moment of silence, they could just hear his laughter echo down the hall.

******

LeRoy walked into the den with his face half hidden behind the paper he was reading. He found his way to his locker by muscle memory and started digging around in it without looking. He finally looked up when he sensed someone staring at him, only to find his entire team watching. "Whatshappenin?" he drawled.

"Aww, just hanging out. Being awesome." Alfie winked at him and leaned back against his locker with his hands behind his head.

"Nice of ya to join us," Ray mimicked LeRoy's accent.

"Who are you?" LeRoy frowned at Alfie as he pulled a folder from the shelf in his locker.

"It's just me being me." Alfie grinned and wiggled his eyebrows.

LeRoy turned to Ray where she sat in front of her locker on his left. "Is he drunk?"

"He's only eighteen!" Ray giggled.

LeRoy frowned at her. "That doesn't mean anything. Are *you* drunk?! Why aren't you sharing, *chére*?"

Nikolai wordlessly reached across Ray from where he sat in front of his locker and handed a black flask to LeRoy.

"Why wasn't I invited?!" LeRoy's fake indignation caused Ray and Alfie to giggle and even brought a smile to Nikolai's face.

"It's nine o'clock in the morning, LeRoy!" Ray laughed. "Plus, we have work to do... maybe."

"We wait for orders, friend." Nikolai nodded his head toward where Gibson sat at his desk on the phone.

"Oh, okay." LeRoy spun around and plopped down on the seat in front of his locker. He twisted the lid off the flask and took a hesitant sniff. "Ugh! You're not actually drinking this, are you?"

Ray laughed. "No. We're just bored. You all packed?"

"Yeah, have been for two days." LeRoy took a quick sip from the flask and put the cap back on with a shudder. He handed it back to Nikolai, who tucked it into one of the side pockets on his pants. "Think today is the day?"

"Yes, sir," Gibson said suddenly and slammed the phone down. "Everyone-"

"*Team 7 and Team 9 to the roof,*" Esther's voice echoed around the Henchmen Division headquarters.

199

"All right, grab your gear! Let's go!" Gibson ordered as he headed out of the den. Team 9 hustled to follow. They fell in line with Team 7 in the hall, and they all marched silently to the roof where a helicopter was waiting.

Erin nudged Alfie playfully when she noticed the blood drain from his face. "Never been on a chopper before?"

Alfie swallowed a few times but could not find his voice, so he simply shook his head.

Erin chuckled and put an arm around Alfie, guiding him to the front of the group. "Ma'am," Erin tapped Tina on the shoulder. "Newb's never been on a chopper. Permission to load him first?"

Tina nodded. "Go ahead."

"Sir?" Alfie's voice was strangled.

Gibson nodded his head toward the helicopter, indicating for Alfie to load. Alfie stared at Gibson with wide eyes, his feet rooted to the helipad. Erin rolled her eyes, grabbing Alfie's upper arm, and stubbornly pulled him toward the chopper. Alfie reluctantly followed while looking over his shoulder at his teammates, who were all struggling to contain their laughter.

"It's all right, newb. Most people struggle with their first chopper ride." Erin tried calming Alfie down as she got him fastened into the center seat of the U-shaped bench at the back of the helicopter. She gave the strap one final tug and turned to leave as the pilot started the engine. Alfie panicked and grabbed on to her, refusing to let go. Erin stared at his hand where he tightened his grip on her wrist and sighed. "Fine, I'll sit next to you."

Erin settled to Alfie's left as the rest of the team climbed in. Ray gave Erin a questioning look when she noticed Alfie's death grip on her. Erin shrugged and Ray shook her head as she settled into the seat to Alfie's right. As soon as she was done tightening her harness, he took her hand and refused to let go.

"Alfie, let go so I can put these on you!" Ray yelled over the noise of the rotors as she pulled a headset down from the hook behind them. Alfie stubbornly shook his head. Ray looked across the cabin at Gibson. "Captain?" she pleaded.

Gibson smiled slightly and nodded to LeRoy. The Cajun steadied himself as the chopper lifted off and carefully stepped over to put the headset on Alfie before helping Ray put hers on.

"Alfie, can you hear me?" Ray asked into the mic. Alfie nodded once while keeping his eyes glued to the windshield between Gibson and LeRoy's heads. "Alfie, you need to relax. Control your breathing. Nothing is going to happen. Shit!" Alfie had turned gray to green, and Ray started hunting blindly under the seat. She managed to find an air sickness bag and get it opened in front of Alfie before he lost his breakfast.

Everybody not in Alfie's death grip suddenly got as far away from him as they could in the small space.

"Really? It's not even a rough ride!" Jackson exclaimed as tried to scoot further away while keeping his seat.

Nikolai looked a little green himself as he hooked a strap from his belt to the rack above the door, pulled the door open, and stepped out onto the landing skid.

Olsen tapped Nikolai on the shoulder. "Can I join you out there?"

"Add 'air sick' to the list," LeRoy laughed.

201

Katherine Wielechowski

"Has he had any trouble on the planes?" Tina asked as she dug around in her gear bag, finally locating a bottle of water and tossing it to Erin.

"None," Gibson muttered, staring at Alfie's pallor, baffled and concerned at how sick he was.

"Sorry," Alfie wheezed before gulping the water Erin handed him.

Ray smiled and put an arm around him. "It's okay."

"If you throw up two more times, you'll beat my record, little man!" November laughed as she reached across Erin and patted Alfie's knee.

"Thanks," Alfie grimaced and wiped his mouth off with the back of his hand. Tina dug around in her bag some more and found a towel, which she tossed over to him.

"Alfie, do you think you're done or do you have more?" Tina asked, not looking up from her bag.

"Not... sure," Alfie gasped, trying to get his stomach under control.

Tina unhooked her harness and leaned forward to slap a patch on Alfie's neck. "Like Dramamine but stronger. Let me know if that doesn't help."

"Thanks."

Ray squeezed his hand. "Breathe, Alfie."

He nodded and closed his eyes, concentrating on his breathing.

Erin sighed and moved his mic away from his mouth so the rest of them wouldn't have to listen to him. "Just don't hyperventilate, man."

******

"So what's the plan, captain?" Olsen asked as they dropped their gear bags and settled in the desks that were scattered around the room.

The chopper had dropped Team 7 and 9 off at the Pit, the abandoned mine that Resources, Inc. used for a weapons and explosives test site. Gibson and Tina had hustled them all inside the main concrete bunker, hoping their arrival had gone unnoticed. Daniel Johnson had met them at the door, and they followed his slow shuffle as he guided them to the classroom at the back of the building.

"The plan is to do what I say," Forcefield announced from the doorway. Team 9 all rolled their eyes as he made his way to the front of the room.

"You're in charge?" Nikolai asked, glowering at the superhero.

"I am." Forcefield returned the glare before motioning at the door.

Everybody turned to see Bullet escorting a man and woman into the room. He turned them over to Forcefield and dropped into the desk next to Ray.

"Hi, Evelyn." He quickly gave her a once-over and a charming grin.

She nodded at him and slid her desk closer to Alfie's.

"This is Dr. Meredith Jennings and Dr. Val Stevenson, the people we believe Trade Wind is after."

Alfie snorted then cringed when he heard how loud it was. It was a minute before he realized that it was so loud because the others in the room had done the same thing at Forcefield's announcement.

Forcefield ignored their reaction, but not before he glared at all of them. "The doctors will be held safely within the bunker here. Dr. Monte-Piere and Ms. Skarret will 'leak'

203

the location of the doctors, and we will wait until Trade Wind shows up. When she arrives, I will work to set up a field around her so her weather won't affect us. Bullet, Maklakov, and Gibson will work together to capture her. Misses Green, Falls, and Skarret will defend the bunker. Michaels, Pearitig, and Vihar will deal with any henchmen Trade Wind brings with her. Ms. Wilkins will stay with the doctors inside of the bunker with the Pit guards and make sure they are safe. We-"

"Anybody else think that's a little sexist?" Erin interrupted. "I mean, November is a much better fighter than Jackson. No offense."

Jackson tried hiding his relief. "None taken."

"Erin," Tina silently scolded her for interrupting. She stood up and went to stand next to Forcefield at the front of the room. "As Forcefield meant to say, Bullet, Nikolai, and Gibson will deal with Trade Wind. Ray, November, and Olsen will deal with any henchmen. Erin, Alfie, and I will defend the bunker and Jackson will stay with the doctors."

"That's not what I-" Forcefield's face started turning red because of how the henchmen were arguing with him.

"Of course it was." Tina shushed him with a gentle hand on his arm. "Now what would you like us to do in the meantime?"

Forcefield sighed and turned to the back wall where a map of the Pit was taped to the marker board. "We set up a perimeter with people here." His finger followed a series of markings that made a double circle around the bunker. "The second circle is a step above the first and should have unlimited sight to the entire place and the sky above."

"Any chance of Crux showing up?" November said with a sweet grin. "As big of a pain in the ass he is, your brother would come in handy here."

"He is... otherwise engaged at the moment," Forcefield sputtered.

"Yeah, he and Warp are... 'dealing' with something in Paris." Bullet grinned and winked at November.

Nikolai growled dangerously, wiping the smile off of Bullet's face. November raised an eyebrow at the Russian before turning away with a small grin.

"So we *are* using them as bait," Jackson commented as he leaned back in his chair with his arms crossed.

"Yes," Forcefield barked.

Gibson quickly stood up and rubbed his hands together. "All right, LeRoy and Erin, you guys get to working on the leak. The rest of us will finish final preps and practice with this new equipment. Once you get done with that, join us." He turned to shake the hands of the two scientists who had stayed silent throughout their discussion. "Dr. Jennings. Dr. Stevenson. We will do what we can to keep you safe. Follow Jackson's orders and stay inside this bunker."

Tina shook their hands also before turning back to the henchmen. "Let's go, team."

Teams 7 and 9 spent the next hour acquainting themselves to the modified equipment that Nikolai, Ray, November, and LeRoy had developed. It consisted of weighted harnesses that each person would wear over their flak jackets that was full of rings, rope, carabiners, and pockets. Each vest also had an air pistol grappling gun attached to it with rope, so if any of them were in danger of blowing away, they could shoot the spike into the ground and keep themselves tethered.

LeRoy and November had spent two days closeted together to modify twelve sets of couplers that would work to anchor the wearer to the ground. Velcro straps wrapped around the ankle, calf, and knee, holding the unit in place on the outside of the foot; when they were activated, two anchors would extend out of the bottom of each, angled to the front and back, holding the foot in place until the anchors were retracted. They worked fairly quickly but not fast enough to allow somebody to move much faster than a slow walk.

"I swear, this rig weighs more than I do!" November joked as she tightened the straps of her harness over her bulletproof vest.

"Better than being blown away," Nikolai grumbled.

"Depends on what you're being blown away from," November sassed and stalked away.

"What the..." Alfie turned to Ray for answers, but she just shrugged, unsure herself.

"They used to be an item," LeRoy whispered from behind them. "It ended badly from what I hear."

"What happened?" Ray asked.

"Oh, you know. Office romances." LeRoy winked at them and stalked over to where Gibson and Tina were discussing final preparations with Forcefield and Bullet. "Captain, the leaks have been sent out. It's just a matter of time now."

"Good." Tina smacked LeRoy on the shoulder. "Guys, let's get into position. Those of you who are guarding the bunker with me, hunker down close to it. The rest of you, spread out. Just don't go far enough that you can't get back quickly under bad conditions. Remember, keep your helmets and goggles on. This will not be pleasant, so get ready."

"Any idea if Trade Wind is bringing company?" Erin asked, pulling on her helmet.

"We have some intel that she has hired heavily from S&T, so expect a number of well-trained henchmen to come with her."

Nikolai scoffed, "Well trained."

"You know what she means." Gibson frowned at his second in command. "Let's go."

Alfie and Ray walked to their positions together. "So the plan is... hope Forcefield can keep it up long enough for the others to tackle Trade Wind while the rest of us take care of her lackeys while trying to not die in the weather she will probably be throwing around?"

Ray laughed. "Apparently so."

Everybody got settled in their places, alert and waiting for Trade Wind to show up. After two hours of waiting, they all started to relax a bit and move around, striking up conversations with those around them.

Alfie joined Ray where she sat with her back against the stone wall, hidden behind a large plywood target. "So, I've been thinking about us and I think-"

Ray grimaced. "That maybe it was a mistake?"

"...that everybody knows." Alfie stared at Ray. "You think this is a mistake?"

"No. Yes. I don't know, Alfie," Ray mumbled as she sifted pebbles and sand through her fingers.

"Why?"

"We are two completely different people, Alf," Ray started.

"Which is part of the appeal, because I would never date me." Alfie attempted a joke that Ray barely cracked a smile at.

"We are at two completely different points of our lives. This is just a layover point before you move on. I'm

207

happy at RI. I can see myself doing this until I retire... or get killed. Whichever comes first." She smiled.

"Ray, you're only twenty-two. How do you know how you'll feel in fifteen years?"

"And you're only eighteen. How will you feel in fifteen years?" Ray responded calmly.

"I-" Alfie started.

"Weather's changing!" November's voice crackled through their ear pieces.

"Jackson, get into the bunker and lock it down!" Tina ordered.

Alfie and Ray both looked up to the sky to see it darkening with clouds and thunder was just audible in the distance. Alfie watched November jump from the Pit's edge eighty feet above his head onto the zip line that would take her to the bottom. "I'm heading back to my spot."

"Alfie! We'll talk about this later," Ray called after him.

He nodded without turning back to answer.

Alfie was just getting settled into a crouch behind a boulder when the wind picked up, swirling around the Pit, kicking up dirt and sand. He rested his left hand on the boulder, using his arm to protect his face as well as he could. His eyes were constantly searching the sky, waiting for the first sign of the villain whom he had been bested by two times before.

"There! Northeast rim!" Olsen's voice shouted over the radio.

Alfie turned slightly and saw a swarm of black specks heading toward the Pit. As they got closer, Alfie could pick out Trade Wind by the dress she wore, while her lackeys were dressed in dark blue, loose fitting jumpsuits and masks.

Fifteen in all descended over the rim of the Pit and down to the bottom, carried on the wind that their master controlled.

"When they land, I'm going to get a field around her. As soon as I do, get into position," Forcefield ordered.

"Get into position as soon as they touch down!" Tina counter commanded.

"Fine!" Forcefield barked, entirely hating that a woman kept changing his orders.

Alfie turned to check on Ray one last time only to find her watching him. He nodded at her and she gave him a little wave.

"Now!" Gibson barked as soon as the enemy's feet touched dirt.

Alfie ducked around the boulder and raced as fast as he could to the bunker, getting there just as Tina did. She pulled a rope from her harness and snapped the carabiner to the bar on the heavy door. Alfie followed suit and pulled his pistol from the holster on his belt. Erin quickly climbed to the top of the bunker and tied herself to the ladder and radio tower with three different ropes. She snapped a pair of binoculars down in front of her goggles and started shouting out positions to the others over the radio.

"You ready?" Tina shouted to Alfie above the wind. Alfie just nodded and watched as Forcefield put a dome over Trade Wind and her minions. The wind immediately stopped, and the Pit was filled with an eerie silence.

"That's it?" Alfie whispered.

Tina was watching Trade Wind carefully, and she pulled two long knives from under the back of her flak jacket and wrapped straps around her wrists to keep from losing them. "Oh no. She's just getting started."

They watched as Trade Wind threw her up hands and lightning crackled across the dome. Sweat beaded on Forcefield's forehead as he lost control. The dome collapsed.

Trade Wind's lackeys raced for the bunker. Olson, Ray, and November hurried to intercept them.

"Bullet, stop with the gun! You're going to kill one of us!" Erin shouted into the radio after a wind-tossed bullet pinged against the radio tower above her head.

Bullet put his gun away and tossed a lackey over his head on his way to Trade Wind. He, Gibson, and Nikolai came at her from three different directions, moving quickly and undetected.

Suddenly, a lackey saw them. "There!" He pointed at them and Trade Wind turned, swinging the wind with her, nearly knocking them all down. They quickly activated their anchors and crouched low so the wind wouldn't knock them down.

Alfie used the wind change to his advantage and opened fire. He took out the knees of two lackeys and nearly hit Trade Wind by the time she noticed. She flung a hand out at him and suddenly hail rained down on him and Tina. They plastered themselves to the edge of the bunker, letting the slight overhang take most of the beating.

"Take the bunker! Find the scientists who would take the weather from me!" Trade Wind screamed. She stopped the hail and set a line of lightning behind her as she and her minions moved toward the bunker. Nikolai, Gibson, and Bullet were stuck on the other side, unable to help their teammates.

Forcefield struggled to put up a wall between her and the bunker, but every time he did, she blew through it with a bolt of lightning. Ray, November, and Olsen joined Tina and

Alfie in front of the bunker, ready to fight to protect the doctors inside.

The lackeys moved quickly, trying to break up the line. Bullet climbed to the top of a rock outcropping and started sniping off Trade Wind's people. She took offense and turned a bolt of lightning on him. He managed to jump from the rock and catch the next ledge before he got fried. Alfie opened fire again, taking out one more lackey before they reached the henchmen.

Every cuss word he knew in five languages was flying through his head as one of Trade Wind's minions headed straight for him. Tina stepped in front of him at the last second and smacked the lackey in the head with the hilt of her knife, knocking him out.

"Thanks."

"Nut up, Vihar!" Tina shouted before going after the next one.

Alfie saw two lackeys attack Olsen; one of them kicked him hard in the knee, and he went down. Something shifted in his head as Alfie holstered his pistol, unclipped his rope, and raced over to help. Olsen was just struggling to his feet when one of Trade Wind's minions hit him hard in the face.

Alfie sped up and tackled the lackey, putting them both in the dirt. He quickly hit Alfie on the side of the head, knocking off his helmet, then rolled away and sprang to his feet in the blink of an eye. Alfie jumped up to face him. The lackey attacked, aiming a kick at Alfie's abdomen. Alfie stepped back, catching his opponent's foot and twisting, hoping to break his ankle. The lackey spun his whole body with Alfie's movement and jerked his foot from Alfie's grasp. He came at Alfie again, aiming an elbow at his face.

211

Alfie didn't see the elbow in time and felt pain explode across his right temple. Alfie managed to catch his opponent's arm before he could hit him again and used his own momentum to flip him over onto his back. The lackey kicked, catching Alfie in the chest, causing him to stumble back enough for him to regain his feet. Alfie's adversary was the first to move again. He ran full speed at Alfie. Alfie spun around and kicked him in the ribs. The force threw the lackey into a short retaining wall and he collapsed over it.

"Alfie, your six!"

Alfie turned when he heard Erin yell over the radio. He found another lackey trying to sneak up behind him. He sighed, pulled his pistol, and quickly obliterated his kneecap.

"Shit, man! You are hell on knees!" Erin laughed over the radio.

Alfie took a second to notice that there were only three lackeys left standing, not counting the one he had fought, who was leaning over the wall holding his ribs and staring at Alfie.

"Retreat!" Trade Wind yelled.

Alfie watched the lackey he had fought struggle to get back to Trade Wind. Olsen got in his way when he tried to keep him from getting to his master. The injured minion was barely able to raise an arm when he tried to hit Olsen. Olsen aimed a fist at his hurt ribs, and Alfie heard the lackey yell out in pain. He vaguely recognized the voice, and it was distinctly feminine.

"Olsen! Wait!" he shouted, but Olsen didn't hear him over the wind. Alfie started running toward them.

Trade Wind had also heard her lackey scream, and she threw out a hand, sending lightning bolts out of her fingertips. They slammed into Olsen in a loud clap of thunder. He dropped to the ground as Trade Wind grabbed her last four lackeys and called down a vortex to carry them to safety.

Alfie picked himself off the ground from where the vortex had tossed him and raced over to Olsen. He rolled him over and searched for a pulse. "Ray! Get over here!" he shouted, unable to find a heartbeat.

Ray dropped down next to him and put her fingers to Olsen's neck, also searching for a pulse. "Alfie, start chest compressions," Ray ordered as she started mouth-to-mouth. They worked hard for a few long minutes, trying to bring Olsen back.

Tina walked over and set a gentle hand on each of their shoulders. "It's too late." Her voice broke on the words. "Thank you for the attempt, but there are others injured."

Ray nodded as she wiped her eyes with the backs of her hands. "Alfie, get the first-aid kit from inside the bunker."

Alfie jumped up to do her bidding. He pounded on the door. "Jackson! It's over! Open up!" Jackson threw open the door, almost causing Alfie to fall down at his feet. "I need the first-aid kits!" Jackson wordlessly thrust them into his hands and followed him out onto the battlefield.

Ray grabbed some disinfectant and gauze and started wrapping a knife wound that Gibson had received on his throat. It had landed too close to the jugular for comfort, and she was working carefully to not cause any more trauma. Nikolai quickly forced Bullet's dislocated shoulder back into its socket, and Alfie dug around in the kit until he found some fabric to fashion a sling for him. LeRoy snagged some gauze to clean up his bloody nose before stuffing some up it to keep it from bleeding more.

213

Erin jumped down from the roof of the bunker, holding her wrist where an unusually large hailstone had hit it. She also had a few cuts and bruises all over her arms and face from the hail.

"Erin, you okay?" Tina asked. She patted Erin on the shoulder at her nod. "Good. Get on the radio. Call for the medevac for these guys and for the chopper to pick us up. Then have Ray wrap your wrist." Tina grabbed Alfie and Jackson to help her patch up the few bullet wounds that Alfie and Bullet had been able to inflict.

"Anybody else?" Gibson asked, looking around to make sure his team was still mostly intact. Everybody looked around and shook their heads. Most of the injuries they had sustained were superficial and needed no special attention.

Tina put a gentle hand on Alfie's shoulder. "It looks like you knew how to fight after all. Good job, Vihar." Alfie sputtered out a response, but Tina was already walking away from him.

"The choppers are on their way," Erin reported back. "The doctors are safe in the bunker and they'll stay with Daniel Johnson until it's time to leave."

"Good." Gibson paused a moment to light a cigarette before looking out over the bottom of the Pit where the fight had raged.

"Thought you were quitting," Tina scolded with a slight smile and unshed tears in her eyes.

Gibson shrugged and pulled up his sleeve so he could rip off the patch. "That was a battle hard fought. You all did well, and while we did not capture Trade Wind, we did keep the doctors safe. We lost a good man today. Tina, Team 7, I am sorry for your loss."

They all struggled to control their emotions at Gibson's words. November had tears flowing freely down her cheeks as she clung to Erin's uninjured hand on one side and Jackson's arm on the other.

Bullet silently shook Tina's hand, then moved to shake the hands of the others from Team 7. Forcefield sat alone, angry with himself for not being able to control Trade Wind.

Alfie found himself standing shoulder to shoulder with Ray, yet he did not touch her. Her worry that their relationship was a bad idea was still stinging in the back of his mind. He had never seen death before. He was sure men had died on his other missions, but he had not seen it or touched it like he had today. He did not know Olsen very well, but he had liked him. Alfie watched the rest of Team 7 and knew that Olsen would be missed. He glanced at his own teammates and could not imagine losing any of them. It hit home just how dangerous these missions were, and that little voice in the back of his head questioning his choice to stay a henchman got a little louder.

A loud noise overhead had them all looking to the sky. Three helicopters descended into the Pit and the henchmen scattered, giving them enough room to land. They got the injured lackeys loaded up, and under the watchful eyes of the medevac crew. They put the doctors in the second chopper with Bullet and Forcefield before placing the stretcher that held Olsen's body in the last chopper with them to head back to HQ.

"Alfie, do you need another patch?"

Alfie's head jerked as Tina's voice cut into his thoughts. "What? Oh, no. I don't think so. Thanks."

215

Ray exchanged a look with Tina and Gibson before turning to study Alfie, worried that what she had said earlier about their relationship had cut him deep. She quickly scrawled a note on a notebook she found in her pack and passed it to Alfie.

He read 'Do you want to go somewhere to talk tonight?' Alfie shook his head and took her pen. 'Not tonight. Maybe later in the week.'

Ray nodded, trying to not be hurt by Alfie pulling away from her, even though she knew it was her fault.

Alfie ignored the conversation going on around him as he stared at the floor in front of Gibson's toes. He had recognized his adversary's voice, but he couldn't quite place it. He went over the fight in his head, paying special attention to the lackey's build, height, how she moved, and her voice. Finally, he closed his eyes, picturing his opponent, starting at her feet and moving up. When he reached her masked face, his eyes snapped open as he gasped. He knew those eyes.

******

"Alfie! It has been too long!" Marie Pellegrini pulled Alfie into a warm hug like only an Italian mother can do. "What have you been up to?"

"Hi, Marie. I've just been working a lot since graduation."

"Oh, really? Tessa didn't tell us that you have a job. Where are you working? Are you hungry?" she asked as she ushered him into the kitchen.

"I'm working at Health Universe. It's a gym on the other side of town." Alfie took a cookie off the plate she offered him.

"You work at a gym?" Marie eyed him in a way that had blood rushing to his face. "I thought you looked a little bigger. I bet the girls are just throwing themselves at you now," she said with a wink.

Alfie choked a little on the cookie he was eating and coughed, embarrassed at Marie's comment.

"How are you and Leo? And the guys?" he asked, changing the subject.

"We are good and the boys are good. But you're not here for small talk. Tessa is out in her library."

"Thanks, Marie." Alfie smiled and snatched a couple more cookies off the plate before heading out the back door. He crossed the yard to the old garden shed that he had helped Tessa convert into a cozy library when they were fourteen. They had spent a lot of time doing homework and hanging out in there over the years. Then, when Tessa finally talked her parents into wiring it with electricity, they had epic video game battles and movie marathons that would last entire weekends.

As he approached, he heard heavy rock music thudding through the walls. He carefully opened the door and peeked in, looking for his best friend. He saw that she had moved everything to one side of the shed and covered the floor in mats like what they had at the gym. He finally spotted Tessa standing in front of a mirror propped against the far wall. She had the hem of her tank top pulled up slightly and was examining a bruise on her ribs that wrapped around her side. She poked at it gingerly with a grimace.

Alfie quietly walked in, closed the door behind him, and leaned against the wall. "It looks like somebody kicked you into a wall."

"Alfie!" Tessa gasped and whipped around. "Don't sneak up on me like that!" She smoothed her shirt back into place and tried to pretend Alfie didn't see what she knew he saw.

"Please, tell me I'm wrong, Tessa." Alfie pushed away from the wall and walked toward her. "Tell me you did not join S&T. I'm begging you, tell me you're not a henchman."

"I don't know what you're talking about," Tessa bluffed, avoiding Alfie's hard stare.

"Don't start lying to me, Tess," Alfie whispered as he stopped in front of her. He reached out and gently touched the bruise that was forming on her jaw and trailed his fingers down to the scrapes on her shoulder. Without warning, he pulled the hem of her shirt up, revealing the huge black and blue bruise on her ribs.

"What the hell, Alf!" Tessa screeched as she pushed her shirt back down.

"Dammit, Tessa! You're beat to hell and I'm the one who did it to you!" Alfie's anger simmered just below the surface as he struggled to control it.

"I fell down some steps at the hospital yesterday. I'm fine!"

"Did your parents buy that, because I sure as hell don't!" Alfie growled.

"Leave it alone, Alfie!" Tessa cried, shoving past him.

Alfie grabbed her wrist and spun her back toward him. "I will not! Tessa, you're supposed to become a doctor. You're better than this!"

"Oh, I'm too good for this? Or is it because I'm a girl and too delicate for this?"

Alfie scoffed. "Tess, I've seen you handle your brothers, you are not delicate using any definition for the word, and Ray is a henchman, so you know it's not because you're a girl! You're too good for this because you're too good for it!" Alfie sighed and pulled Tessa into a hug. "You deserve better than what this life will give you, which is probably an early grave if what I saw yesterday is any indication. You're too smart to be a henchman."

Tessa pulled away and glared up at him. "But it's okay for you to do it?"

"I never said I was smart."

"Alfred Vihar, you will not get out of this by making me laugh," Tessa growled. She shoved him back with two hands on his chest and turned once again for the door.

Alfie caught her wrist again, but she was ready when he spun her around. She used his momentum to add power to her right hook. Alfie was too surprised by the attack to defend himself, and he fell to the mat with his ears ringing and blood flowing from his nose.

"The hell, Tessa?!" He wiped at the blood with the collar of his T-shirt.

Tessa squatted next to him with her elbows on her knees and her hands clasped. "Don't tell me what to do, Alfie."

"I'm trying to protect you!"

Tessa eyed his bloody nose with a raised eyebrow. "Rich, coming from you."

Alfie glared at her and kicked his leg out, sweeping her feet out from under her. Tessa hit the mat with a thud, and Alfie was on her in a second, pinning her to the floor. Tessa bucked and rolled Alfie off of her so she could jump to her feet. She backed off a couple of steps as Alfie slowly got to his feet, eying her stance.

"Are we fighting, then?" Alfie asked quietly. He grinned at her adamant nod. "Fine." He shifted until his feet were shoulder-width apart and relaxed his upper body, waiting.

Tessa sneered at him and slowly paced forward. "You're letting me make the first move? Such a gentleman."

"My mom taught me manners." Alfie's grin widened.

Tessa shook her head and suddenly lashed out with her foot. Alfie calmly stepped to the side, avoiding the kick. Tessa kept advancing and threw another right hook. Alfie was ready for this one and blocked it with his left arm. He rolled his block and grabbed her upper arm, twisting so he tossed Tessa over his head and back onto the mats. She growled and jumped back to her feet. She spun, aiming a kick for his face. He threw himself to the floor to avoid her foot then rolled forward, tripping her. She fell to the floor once again. She scrambled over to him before he could stand and forced him to his back. She straddled him, punching with both fists as hard as she could. Alfie couldn't stop the first, feeling it hit him solidly in the right eye, but he blocked the second and finally grabbed her by the wrists.

"What the hell is wrong with you?!" he growled, lowering her so their noses nearly touched.

"I don't need somebody else planning out my life! And I don't need protecting!" Tessa cried, silently cursing herself for the tears she felt prick her eyes.

"I wasn't planning out your life! I thought becoming a doctor was what you wanted!" Alfie nearly shouted.

"You don't know what I want," Tessa whispered. She jerked her right hand from Alfie's grasp and grabbed his shirt, pulling him up to crush her lips against his.

Alfie was too surprised to stop it, and then he had no mental capacity to stop. A small part of him felt his hand release Tessa's wrist as he wrapped his arms around her, pulling her closer.

"Well, it's about damn time!"

The words were like cold water poured on them. Tessa jerked away to see a figure standing in the doorway. She glanced back down at Alfie with wide eyes before jumping to her feet and racing out of the building.

Alfie was mortified but could not move from the mat. He turned his head to see who had walked in on them and groaned. He slowly climbed to his feet and walked to the door. "Hi, Marie."

Katherine Wielechowski

<u>Four Horsemen</u>

Alfie was half surprised to not see a black rain cloud hovering near the ceiling when he walked into Team 9's den after his mandatory two-day-after-mission-but-uninjured leave. The cloudy Thursday outside matched Alfie's mood and, he was slightly disappointed that the weather had not followed him inside.

It had been a month and a day since graduation and two months since Alfie had sat in Mr. Kadish's office and told the CEO of Resources, Inc. that he reminded Alfie of James Bond. So much had happened in such a short amount of time.

Alfie stood in the doorway, watching his teammates. Nikolai sat in his usual spot at the table with pieces of his handgun spread out in front of him on a cloth, the barrel in one hand and a brush in the other. LeRoy sat across from the Russian with a laptop open and a small electric device in his hands that he kept turning over and over, twisting parts once in a while with a small screwdriver. Ray sat on the bench in front of her locker with her legs crossed and her eyes closed, making Alfie think she was meditating. Gibson was sitting at his desk typing on the computer while papers covered the normally neat surface.

Their last mission had left Resources, Inc.'s Henchmen Division Team 7 down one man and Alfie had no idea how to handle it. Day and night he saw Olsen's still form under his hands. High school had done nothing to prepare him for this.

"Vihar, are you going to lurk there all day or come in?" Gibson called without looking up from his computer screen.

Alfie sighed and finally crossed the threshold. He pulled off his backpack and tossed it into his locker, cringing at the loud sound it made.

"Problem, *garçon?*" LeRoy asked as he typed one-handed on the keyboard.

"No," Alfie mumbled. He glanced at Ray, who was still meditating, before settling down on the couch. He was ten minutes early for work and still found himself later than everybody else. He had long suspected that Gibson lived at HQ but he had a hard time picturing the others spending 24/7 in the building.

They all seemed so calm. Like the death was common-place for them, and maybe it was. He knew that henchmen were killed, not often, but fairly regularly. There had been an opening on Team 9 that Alfie had filled, but he had never bothered to ask about the person who had occupied it before him or why it had been vacant when he got the job.

Alfie shifted so he sat with his elbows on his knees and stared at the floor between his feet. He hadn't talked to Ray since they had gotten back from the Pit. He didn't know what to say to her. After her doubts about their relationship had put a wedge between them, he had no idea how to tell her about Tessa taking her and Alfie's friendship to a different level.

What hurt him the most about the situation was that he hadn't talked to Tessa since the kiss. He was cut off from his best friend. The person he had always talked to about all the problems in his life was gone. He thought about talking to Ruth, but she was busy for the summer helping with a local art program. Alfie had even started dialing his brothers to ask for advice before he thought better of it. They would, undoubtedly, offer great advice, and then proceed to tease

223

him about it for the rest of his life. Plus, he had no idea how to explain to his brothers about one of his co-workers dying in front of him. They thought he worked at a gym and gyms cause injuries, not deaths. Usually.

"Gibson?"

"Come on in, guys."

Alfie didn't look up when he heard people shuffle into the den, although he did take slight offense to somebody sitting right next to him on the couch. He stiffened when he felt an arm go around his shoulders.

"Hey."

Alfie looked up to find November Falls from Team 7 studying him closely.

"Hi, November," Alfie mumbled, noticing her normally green eyes were shaped like dark blue cat eyes. He looked around to find that the rest of Team 7 had joined them.

"Since it was a combined job, Tina is going to do reviews this time around," Gibson explained as he moved around his desk to lean against the front next to Tina.

"I think we'll just start with the biggest part," Tina started. She set the file down behind her and crossed her arms. "Olsen Michaels had been with Team 7 for just over five years. He was a 'Jack of all trades, master of none' sort, but he was a reliable member of our team. We had come to enjoy his quiet humor and dependability over the years and he will be missed. Vihar," Tina paused, then walked to where Alfie sat and crouched in front of him, resting a hand over his clasped hands. "I saw you try to stop him just before Trade Wind attacked him. You and Ray worked hard to try to bring him back. I, and the rest of Team 7, appreciate it."

Alfie nodded, unable to talk. He sniffed, surprised at how affected he was by Tina's gentle words. He could feel the knots ease out of his shoulders, and some of the guilt he had been feeling drained away. Tina squeezed his hands once before walking over to put an arm around Ray's shoulders. She whispered something in Ray's ear and Ray nodded, appreciation written across her face. Tina released Ray and walked over to resume her spot next to Gibson.

"His family has planned the funeral for Saturday morning at ten, and you are all welcome to attend if you would like. Gibson has the address. Now," Tina stopped to retrieve her file and flip it open. "Seeing as our main objective was to capture Trade Wind, we failed the mission, but we did keep the doctors safe, so the loss was not complete. Bullet has rated us well. Forcefield did not complete the evaluation as he has taken some time to 'refuel' his batteries." Tina awkwardly made air quotes while hanging on to her folder. "Gibson and my evaluations of all of you were high. You all operated as you should have, even going above and beyond. Gibson made special note that Vihar seems to have finally figured out hand-to-hand combat." Tina paused as the others congratulated Alfie.

Gibson waited for them to quiet down before continuing where Tina had left off. "Tina and I both wanted to recognize LeRoy and November for their ingenious design for the couplers that kept us anchored to the ground. Brutus has taken a look at them and agrees that they should be added to our arsenal. The R&D department will be working on improving and producing more of them, and you two are welcome to help them with it."

"Great. Two weeks stuck with the R&D nerds in the lab." November rolled her eyes at Alfie.

"You love those nerds, don't even try to make us think you don't," Erin teased.

November leaned close to whisper in Alfie's ear. "I really do. They're fun. And they're all closet freaks."

Alfie couldn't help but chuckle slightly as she winked.

"There you are." November gave him a peck on the cheek and sat back on the couch.

"You all did very well. It has actually been a long time since we have seen two separate units work so well together," Tina continued.

"So we're stuck together?" LeRoy complained with a grin at Team 7.

"We will probably be teamed up again, yes," Gibson confirmed.

"What will be done about Trade Wind?" Alfie asked quietly.

Gibson and Tina traded a glance.

"As far as we can tell, she's gone to ground," LeRoy answered without looking up from his computer. "We showed our hand at the Pit and she knows it. Now we wait to see if she shows back up."

Gibson nodded in agreement. "We are continuing the hunt for her and passing all of our information on to the Alliance of Justice. They are searching for her also."

"Will they send us after her again?" Ray finally broke her silence.

"I doubt it. We weren't much help at the Pit," Tina said with a shake of her head.

"Alfie shot her," Nikolai mumbled.

"What? When?" Tina asked, surprised at the information.

"In San Francisco, when Nikolai was trying to take her out with a grenade." Alfie shrugged. "It was just a graze."

"Well, graze or not, you got closer to stopping her than anybody else." Tina turned to Gibson. "Do the higher-ups know this?"

Gibson frowned. "It was in my report, but you know how many of those get read."

Tina nodded and turned back to Alfie. "Well, young Vihar, you are becoming a valuable asset to Resources, Inc."

Alfie shrugged, looking down at the floor. "More lucky than anything."

Gibson cleared his throat into the awkward silence that followed Alfie's quiet denial. "All right everybody, back to work. Team 9, we'll finish out the week with easy training. LeRoy, I want you to spend a few hours today and tomorrow with R&D working on those couplers. Vihar, you are to report to Dr. Olafson today at 1100 hours and Ray, you are to see her tomorrow at the same time. Her office is room 2319, second floor of the medical wing. Nikolai, you're with me. We have some paperwork to finish up."

"Team 7, we are being sent to Salt Lake, so pack a week's worth of comfortable clothes. They have laundry facilities if we are there longer. We leave tomorrow morning. Today, you can do what you will. November, I would like you to go with LeRoy to R&D to work on the couplers."

"You're not going to the funeral?" Ray asked quietly.

"We will visit Olsen's family before leaving town, but no, we won't be going to the funeral." Tina's expression tightened slightly, showing her sadness and frustration that they would not be able to attend. "If there's nothing else, everybody get to work."

227

Alfie waited for everybody to leave the room before standing up from the couch and walking over to where Gibson was back working on his computer.

"Sir, why am I to report to Dr. Olafson?" Alfie asked quietly. "I'm not injured."

Gibson continued typing for a moment before turning to give Alfie his full attention. "Vihar, Dr. Olafson is not just a medical doctor. She is responsible for deciding if people are fit for work both mentally and physically. With Olsen's death, it has to be decided if you and Ray are able to continue as henchmen."

"Why just us?"

"Anybody can to talk to her if they are struggling with something that would impede their job, but you two were the ones who tried to save him and you two are the most impacted by his death. As soon as Dr. Olafson clears you and Ray, Team 9 will be able to go back on jobs, but until then, we are grounded to HQ."

"What about Team 7? They're the ones who lost a teammate."

"Whenever there is a death, the whole team is sent to a facility just outside of Salt Lake City, Utah for counseling, team building, evaluation, and overall healing. They all stay there until they are all ready to go back to work.

"Why was there an opening in Team 9 when I was hired?" Alfie asked suddenly.

Gibson studied Alfie for a long second, unfazed, but unsure how much to tell. "The fifth member of Team 9 was killed during an altercation with the AOJ about a year before you were hired."

"The AOJ killed him?" Alfie was shocked that Team 9 would work with them after that.

"Her. And not necessarily." Gibson leaned back in his chair and crossed his arms. "Natalie Carter was the henchman who was killed. The first team member I've ever lost, so it hit hard. She was about 40 and had spent well over 20 years as a henchman. She made it longer than about 90 percent of people who do this job. We were working for The Wolf-"

"The guy who tried bombing the Golden Gate Bridge?" Alfie asked, remembering the name from his orientation.

"Yes. We were supposed to protect him while he planted the bombs. When the AOJ arrived, we went to work, trying to fend them off while The Wolf kept wiring up the bridge. Carter was too close to the edge when Crux simultaneously shook the bridge and used wind to knock us down. She went over the edge."

"Is that why you and Crux don't get along?" Alfie asked.

"One of the reasons, but we've never been friendly." Gibson scratched the back of his neck in thought. "Mainly because he's an ass."

Alfie smiled slightly and nodded.

"Olsen's death is hitting you hard," Gibson observed.

Alfie did not even attempt to deny it. "Yeah."

"First death?"

"Pretty much." Alfie pulled himself up onto the table facing Gibson's desk. "I mean, I've been to a couple of funerals, but they were for like old relatives I didn't know well. This was definitely the first one that I've..."

"Seen happen?" Gibson guessed with a small smile.

Alfie nodded noncommittally. "Contributed to?"

229

Gibson leaned forward and rested his elbows on his knees, his hands clasped. "Vihar, you did not have anything to do with Olsen's death. That is 100 percent on Trade Wind."

Alfie ran a hand through his hair. "I know that it wasn't my fault, but I was there. I yelled at him to stop. Tried to bring him back. Nothing I did saved him."

"There was nothing you could do, Vihar." Gibson answered quietly.

"I know, sir. It's just... I'm not explaining this well." Alfie gave a half laugh.

"That's why you're to see Dr. Olafson later." Gibson's not-so-subtle order brought Alfie to his feet.

"Yes, sir." Alfie turned to leave but stopped. "What am I to do until then?"

"Vihar, you can do pretty much what you want right now. Work on your fighting, work with LeRoy in the lab, run a few laps, whatever."

"Am I cleared for the range?"

Gibson looked up from his paperwork and studied Alfie for a long moment, then nodded. "I'll make sure it is all right. Give me fifteen minutes then head down there."

"Thank you, sir." Alfie gave Gibson a nod and headed out the door.

******

Alfie fired one more round then dropped the magazine and cleared the chamber. He pulled his phone out of his pocket and turned off the vibrating alarm warning him he had ten minutes before he had to meet Dr. Olafson.

"You heading up to talk to the doc?"

Alfie turned to see Ray leaning against the wall separating his lane from the one on his right. "Yeah." He picked up the brass casings sitting on the table in front of him and tossed them in the bin before grabbing the broom and cleaning up the brass on the floor.

"Are you ever going to talk to me again?" Ray asked quietly.

Alfie threw the rest of the brass in the bin and picked up the pistol and empty magazine before turning back to her. "Probably. I just want to get some stuff sorted before I do."

"It'd be faster if we talked about it."

"I'm not sure about that," Alfie said with a grimace. He nodded at her and turned in the handgun before heading up to the medical wing.

Alfie had only been in the examination rooms on the first floor that looked like a high-tech hospital. The second floor resembled the CEO floor of a Fortune 500 company. Lush carpet covered the floor, dark wood paneling covered the walls, and small tables that Alfie was sure cost more than he had made in his lifetime sat evenly spaced between doorways supporting huge bouquets of fresh flowers.

Normally, the expensive surroundings would intimidate Alfie, but he was distracted by the thoughts whirling through his mind. He trudged along until he reached the door marked 2319 with brass numbers. Alfie knocked gently on the frosted glass window in the middle of the door.

"Come in," a woman's voice called out.

Alfie walked in to see an elegant older woman sitting behind a heavy wooden desk.

"Oh! I'm sorry, I must be in the wrong office." Alfie backed out into the hall and rechecked the numbers above the window.

"Who are you looking for?" the woman quickly asked before he got the door completely closed.

Alfie stepped back into the office. "Um... Dr. Olafson."

"You must be Mr. Vihar." The woman stood and walked around the desk with her hand outstretched. "You are in the right place. I am Margaret, Dr. Olafson's assistant. Dr. Olafson got called to the medical floor but should be back in a minute or two. Can I get you anything to drink?" she asked, ushering Alfie to an interior office.

"Um... a glass of water?"

"Perfect! I will be right back." Margaret's friendly smile widened as she motioned for Alfie to take one of the chairs in front of the desk before she left the room.

Alfie stared out the window behind the desk. Whoever had planned the building managed to find one of the only good views of the neighborhood: a small park that had an even smaller pond in the middle that was surrounded by well-cared-for flowerbeds.

"Here is your water, Mr. Vihar." Margaret set the glass on the desk in front of him.

"Call me Alfie, please."

Margaret smiled and nodded. "Very well. I called down and let Dr. Olafson know you are here, so it won't be much longer. Can I get you anything else?"

"No. I'm fine. Thank you."

"You're welcome." Margaret patted Alfie on the shoulder and left the room, quietly closing the door behind her.

Alfie picked up the water and took a sip as he stood and wandered around Dr. Olafson's office. He recognized many of the art pieces scattered around the room as

Scandinavian in origin. There was even an ornate dagger that he was sure his mother had appraised for the auction house she worked at.

"You like my collection?" Dr. Olafson asked from the doorway. She pulled off her white lab coat, hung it on a hat rack next to the door, and walked over to join Alfie in front of the bookshelf where the dagger rested.

Alfie turned when he heard her voice. "It's really neat. This one is Norse Bronze Age, right?" he asked, pointing at the dagger. He frowned at himself when he realized that he had no problem talking to Dr. Olafson this time, when he could barely sputter out sentence fragments the last time he was alone with her.

Dr. Olafson smiled. "Yes, well, it would be if it was real. Sadly, it is a replica, a very good one, but still a replica. The real one is sitting in a museum in Stockholm. I like to stop and see it when I visit my family. How do you know about Scandinavian artifacts?"

"My mom works at Franklin and McKeen Auction House. She is an expert on Scandinavian art. I think she appraised this dagger, or something like it a few months ago."

"Your mother is Vivian Vihar?" Dr. Olafson asked motioning for Alfie to sit down on the couch against the far wall.

"Yeah, how'd you know?"

"I enjoy collecting Norse artifacts as you might have noticed. When I hear that Franklin and McKeen has something I might be interested in, I e-mail them. Your mother is usually the one who responds," Dr. Olafson explained as she picked up a leather notebook from her desk and settled in an armchair next to the couch. "Shall we get started? Now, have you ever seen a therapist or councilor of any kind?"

"No."

"All right. My rule is, you do not have to tell me anything that you are not comfortable sharing, but I cannot help you if you lie or withhold information. Everything said here is confidential; nothing will leave this room. However, I have an ethical obligation to alert anyone you have thoughts about, and report it if you have an urge to harm yourself or anyone else. My role in this relationship is to evaluate what you tell me. I will either recommend that you go back to work or are held back for more counseling."

"All right." Alfie rubbed his suddenly sweaty palms on his jeans.

"Tell me about your family."

"What do they have to do with Olsen?"

"Nothing, I just want to learn about them so I can get to know you better."

"Um, okay." Alfie shifted on the couch and crossed his legs. "Well, you have at least a passing knowledge of my mom. She's super smart and probably wasting her abilities and talents with Franklin and McKeen, but she is unwilling to move to a bigger city because my dad's business is here." Alfie paused with a frown. "You know, I don't know if that is quite right. Of course she doesn't want to leave my dad, who would never leave his business, but I think she's happy and content here in San Luca. She has the opportunity to do more, but she doesn't want to. As for her role in the family, she's the ball buster. We never wanted to make mom mad because she was the one to dole out punishment, but she wasn't a dictator, or anything. She did what she did to make us better people and none of us ever doubted that she loved us when she was yelling at us for doing something stupid."

Dr. Olafson smiled slightly. "She sounds like a good mother."

"She is. And we try to remind her of that every once in a while. Just in case she forgets," Alfie said with a grin.

"And your father?" Dr. Olafson prodded gently.

"He was the gentler of the two, at least when it came to us kids." Alfie spotted a string hanging from the edge of his shirt and started pulling on it. "He was busy building his business but he worked hard to make time for us. Most of that involved the garage. As soon as any of us asked, he had us working on cars and learning about the business. He never forced us. He also would take us hunting and taught us basic survival skills."

"How many siblings do you have?"

"I know you already know that," Alfie chuckled lightly when a brief smile flashed across Dr. Olafson's face. "Two older brothers and a younger sister."

"Want to tell me about them?"

"Sure, why not?" Alfie sighed and glanced out the window. "Robert is the oldest. He lives with his husband, Lawrence, in Bakersfield. They are weeks away from finally meeting the daughter they have spent over a year trying to adopt."

"Uncle Alfie?"

"Yeah," Alfie laughed. "Wow, I hadn't really thought of that. I knew I was getting a niece, but to think of myself as an uncle is insane. I'm super happy for them though. Lawrence hasn't had the greatest time growing up, and he's looking forward to having another person to love. Robert is equally as excited but I think for different reasons. To us, he

235

was always like another dad but without the rules, so I think he's happy to have a family of his own. Nathan is the second oldest and the rebel child, although I think we all have a little rebellion in us. He's a bachelor, still acts like he's in college, and teaches high school PE in Bakersfield. He's a goof ball and a big pain in the ass at times but he is loyal to a fault. Ruth is the youngest and hands down the smartest of us all. She is an artist and very talented, and although she's probably smart enough to join a brain trust for the government when she gets a little older, she has no real interest in science or math. She and I are a lot alike in that we are the quiet ones in the family, which is probably why I am closest to her. We're both nerdy and the older two don't quite understand that.

I think Nathan is closest to our dad and I'm probably the closest to my mom, but my parents went out of their way to make sure we all knew we were loved and special to them."

Dr. Olafson studied Alfie for a long moment in silence. "I noticed that you did not say 'I' much when you were telling me how your parents raised you."

Alfie chuckled awkwardly. "What'd I say?"

"We."

"Oh, well, with four kids, it was pretty much all or nothing."

"How did that make you feel growing up?"

Alfie shrugged. "I don't know. I mean, at times, I wanted a little more attention, but I was never neglected. Heck, there were times when I would have given anything for a little less attention. But, I think it helped us grow up a lot closer than if we had had more one-on-one time."

"So, you are really close to your family?" Dr. Olafson asked, making a note in her folder.

"Why do I feel like this is a trap?" Alfie laughed. "Yeah. A lot closer than most families I know."

"Have you talked to any of them about what happened?"

"You mean Olsen dying?"

"Hm." Dr. Olafson nodded.

"No." Alfie turned his attention back to the string on his shirt that was getting longer every time he tugged on it.

"Why not?"

"How do you tell your family that somebody got electrocuted by a supervillain at a gym?"

"They think you work at a gym?"

"Yeah, Health Universe. Our cover."

"You did not tell them that you are a henchman," Dr. Olafson stated more than asked.

Alfie laughed incredulously. "No. They wouldn't believe me, and if they did, they'd make me quit. They'd think it's too dangerous."

"Your job is dangerous," Dr. Olafson agreed. "Share about why you think they would make you quit."

"You mean other than that people try to kill me regularly and I actually got shot on my first job?" Alfie's rueful laugh was short and rough. "Because I lied. And because my parents want what's best for me."

"What do you think is best for you?"

"They think it's getting into business, going to college, getting a good job, and living happily ever after."

"I asked what you think is best for you."

Dr. Olafson's soothing voice took Alfie's mind to a place he barely admitted to himself that he had. "Writing. Traveling. Being alone but never being lonely."

"Does your family know this?"

"Kind of. They know about my writing and desire to travel."

Dr. Olafson studied him when he didn't go on. "What about being alone?"

"No."

"Ah. You do not want to hurt them."

"I-I guess not. I would hurt them if I told them I didn't want to be around them."

"The curse of the introvert."

"Thank you!" Alfie laughed. "It's nice to have that validated."

Dr. Olafson chuckled. "You're welcome. Now for the tough stuff. How are you feeling about Olsen's death?"

"Not good."

"Share a little more, please," Dr. Olafson urged gently at Alfie's hesitation.

Alfie stared at the carpet for a long moment, collecting his thoughts. "I didn't really know Olsen, so part of me is saying I shouldn't be too affected by his death. The rest of me is ashamed of the thought and then I feel worse about him dying. I feel guilty that I couldn't save him and I'm sad that he's dead. I feel for his family. I can't imagine losing one of my siblings or parents."

"Have you shared any of this with someone?" She glanced down at her folder. "Gibson has noted that you are close with a couple of your teammates."

"I would consider myself close with one teammate…" Alfie avoided eye contact and wrapped the string around his finger, tugging sharply, finally breaking it. He looked up when Dr. Olafson didn't prod him for more information to see her watching him. "Okay, Ray and I... kind of were dating. I know it's against the rules and it just sort of happened."

"Were?"

"Yeah. We went on a few dates, thought of each other as boyfriend/girlfriend, and then it ended." Alfie felt himself blush. "Well, kind of ended. I guess it was never an official ending."

"Sounds confusing."

"Yep." Alfie nodded absentmindedly as he shifted on the couch. "When we were at the Pit, LeRoy made a comment that Nikolai and November used to be an item and it ended horribly. Now they can hardly work together anymore. I didn't think much of it but apparently Ray did. She suggested that we were making a mistake by dating. I took it as she wanted to break up. We haven't really talked since."

"What about-" Dr. Olafson paused to check her folder. "Contessa Pellegrini?"

Alfie about came off the couch. "How the hell do you know about Tessa?"

"Resources, Inc. knows about all close associates of its employees. They pay special attention when one of those associates joins a competing agency."

"Is Tessa in danger of this company?" Alfie asked, his tone dangerous.

Dr. Olafson laughed. "Of course not. We are not spies, Mr. Vihar. You are an employee of a company. She would be in the same amount of danger from Resources, Inc.

if you both worked for competing restaurants or clothing stores. Does that help?"

"A little." Alfie gradually relaxed into the couch.

"Have you talked to her about any of this? I think she might be a good support since she is a close friend and was there when Olsen was killed."

Alfie snorted. "Well, the day after Olsen was killed, she changed the parameters of our friendship. It was not really conducive to having a heart-to-heart about a dead co-worker."

"What happened?"

"I confronted her about working for S&T. We fought, she kissed me, her mom walked in on us, she bailed, and I left her house."

"Wow that is a lot to take in." Dr. Olafson shifted slightly in her chair. "Share how you think the three events are affecting you mentally?"

"Well-" Alfie started ticking them off his fingers. "My girlfriend tells me that she thinks our relationship is a mistake, one of my co-workers dies in front of my eyes and I can't save him, and I find out my best friend is basically throwing away her chance at being a doctor so she can be a henchman moments before she kisses me and changes our relationship forever."

Dr. Olafson raised an eyebrow when he paused. "You just summarized the three events; you did not tell me how they're affecting you."

"Shit, okay." Alfie leaned forward on the couch and rested his elbows on his knees. "I'm kind of freaked out about Olsen dying. I mean, I could be next. And I'm sad because he was a pretty decent guy and it sucks that he's dead. I'm sad and pissed off that I got dumped by a woman I really liked just because we work together. While I know workplace relationships are not always a good idea, I thought we could make this work, at least for a while. I'm hurt and feel betrayed because Tessa has been lying to me, both about her job and her feelings for me. I'm also confused because I don't know where that leaves us. Or if I should tell Ray that Tessa kissed me because I don't know if we were officially over when it happened or if it's something she is going to think counts as cheating. That also freaks me out because I am not a cheater. I'm lost because the people I would usually talk shit over with either can't know about my job or is Tessa." Alfie leaned back and sighed. "Shit, I sound like a 15 year-old girl."

Alfie's self-evaluation startled a small laugh out of Dr. Olafson. "I apologize. That was unprofessional and uncalled for. Most people who sit in here are not so honest with themselves. I appreciate brutal honesty, especially when someone has experienced so much in such a short amount of time."

Alfie grinned. "My mom has always told me to be less self-deprecating. I never really figured out how."

"Well, Mr. Vihar, it sounds like you have a good understanding of how you feel about what is happening around you."

"Yeah, I understand it. I have no idea how to fix it."

"I think you know where to start and what to do." Dr. Olafson made one last note in her folder and closed it. "Your family and friends have been a very strong support system for you in the past. You are feeling lost right now because you do not think you can turn to them now. I believe you can. They do not need to know all of the details of the situation in order to help you. It does not sound like you are ready to tell them about being a henchman. Tessa is the only one who knows what you do and what happened at the Pit. In regards to her, your choices are to accept the change in your relationship and confide in her or pull away from her. Either way, your relationship will change because you are both going to be exposed to many adult experiences in your line of work and neither of you will be the same."

"What do I do about Ray?"

"I cannot answer that, Mr. Vihar. You need to figure it out on your own; I would suggest talking to her and letting her help you decide. A broken love affair is not a good enough reason to remove one of you from Team 9, so you will be working together for the near future. Smoothing this out quickly will help the team get back to working order."

Alfie smiled ruefully. "Wow, doc. Your recommendation is that I fix myself? Isn't that supposed to be your job?"

"Mr. Vihar, my job is not to fix you. It is to evaluate and decide if you are able to go back to work."

"Ball buster."

Dr. Olafson raised an eyebrow and cocked her head to the side. "It's shit or get off the pot time."

Alfie threw his head back and laughed before standing up. "Thank you, Dr. Olafson." He held out his hand to shake hers. "I appreciate the advice and I will work on it."

"You are welcome, Mr. Vihar. I want to meet with you again on Monday and hear about your progress on everything we have discussed."

"You're giving me homework? That sucks." Alfie grinned and headed for the door.

"This might be some of the toughest homework you have ever been assigned. Now get some rest and I will see you Monday. Any idea where you might start?"

"Saturday is the 14th, right? Well, looks like I'm in for an early-morning trip to the video store, a funeral, and then I'm off to see a girl about a superhero."

******

Alfie rushed into Tessa's shed without knocking. "I've got the new Marvel movie! That's new." Alfie stopped to examine the punching bag Tessa had set up in the corner.

Tessa stopped punching and fiddled with her wrist wraps, actively avoiding looking at Alfie. "Yeah. I just got it."

"Cool. Want to do this?" Alfie held up the DVD with a grin.

"Umm." Tessa finally looked at him.

Alfie quickly turned away from the uncomfortable look in her eyes. "Grab the beanbags. I'll get it going." Alfie headed to the entertainment center on the opposite wall and busied himself with getting the movie set up, expecting Tessa to play along. He relaxed when he heard her dragging the two large beanbags across the floor. He quickly grabbed the remote and plopped down in the closest beanbag. "I brought sustenance, too." He wriggled around enough so he could pull his backpack off his back and opened it with more glee than the situation required. "Here." He pulled out a bag of Doritos and tossed it at Tessa. A large bottle of Mountain Dew and a bag of M&Ms followed before he pulled out a bag of Doritos and a Coke for himself.

Tessa stared down at the junk food he had tossed at her for a long moment before looking at him. "Alfie-"

"Shush! It's starting!" Alfie wiggled deeper into his chair and turned up the volume.

Tessa's eyes narrowed at his dismissal but the opening credit music had her turning to the screen.

Neither of them said a word during the movie, but years spent watching movies together ensured they knew just when to pass the M&Ms.

"That was amazing!" Alfie pressed stop on the remote after the signature Marvel short clip at the end of the credits. "Probably my favorite Marvel movie to date!"

Tessa chuckled as she brushed crumbs off her shirt. "You said that after we saw it in the theater."

"Well, it's still true." Alfie threw his empty bottle at Tessa, which she ducked with a screech.

"Ass!" Tessa yelled as she threw the bottle back at him, catching him in the face. "Want to fight?" Tessa asked suddenly, a huge grin on her face.

"You. Want to fight me?" Alfie asked, puffing out his chest. "That is a poor decision, young grasshopper. You cannot beat me."

"Do I need to find a pin to pop that giant head?" Tessa teased as she climbed out of the beanbag chair and kicked it out of her way. "Besides, I think I can."

Alfie studied her in mock seriousness. "I accept your challenge," He answered stoically. He attempted to climb out of the beanbag as solemnly as possible, but it shifted just right and he fell on his face. He jumped to his feet and straightened his shirt, pretending the last few seconds had not happened. "All right, let's do this!"

Tessa doubled over with laughter. "Take off your shoes, Mr. Miyagi."

Alfie struck a ridiculous pose and waved his hands in the air. "Wax on! Wax off!"

"A kick in the jewels will make you cough!" Tessa spouted as she aimed a kick at Alfie's midsection.

Alfie jumped back and balanced on the balls of his feet. "Now that was rude and a terrible attempt at rhyming."

"What're you going to do about it?" Tessa lowered into Neo's pose from The Matrix and beckoned with her out-stretched hand.

"You have to let it all go, Neo. Fear, doubt, disbelief. Free your mind." Alfie quoted Morpheus as he followed Tessa's suit and mimicked Morpheus's fighting stance. "We are a little too nerdy to be normal."

"Meh, what's normal... besides me kicking your ass!" Tessa launched herself at Alfie, landing a fast punch to his jaw just as she aimed her left fist for his side.

Alfie managed to grab her left wrist before her hit landed. He twisted to the side, bending her arm into a painful position and kicked her ankle from underneath her. Tessa kept her feet and spun so she could get her left arm free. She jabbed upward with her knee, catching Alfie's thigh. He grunted in pain and grabbed her arm so he could toss her over his shoulder to the mat. Tessa jumped back to her feet before Alfie could recover and kicked at his face. He caught her ankle and stepped forward to land an open-handed blow on her chest. Tessa stumbled back, took a moment to catch her breath, then attacked with renewed ferocity.

The fight continued, both of them gaining and losing the upper hand until they both collapsed to the floor, gasping for air.

"Draw?" Alfie asked, holding out his hand to where Tessa laid a few inches from him, her head pointing in the opposite direction.

Tessa groaned, then finally took his hand. "Yeah, draw. You're pretty good, Vihar."

"You're not bad yourself, Pellegrini." Alfie laughed, then groaned when his bruised ribs protested. "You know, before you and I fought in the Pit, I could barely block a punch."

"How'd you get so good?"

"No idea. It was all in my head, but I couldn't make my body follow instructions." Alfie nudged her shoulder with his knee. "Must be fighting you."

Tessa rubbed her chest. "I'm honored."

"Hey," Alfie sat up with a groan. "Can we talk?"

Tessa closed her eyes. "About the kiss," she whispered.

Alfie beat a nervous rhythm on the mats with his fingers. "Actually, can we hold off on that talk for a few days?"

"Um, sure." Tessa slowly sat up and crossed her legs. "What did you want to talk about instead?"

"I went to a work-ordered psychologist this week."

"Okay."

"She has to approve me going back to work."

"Is that normal? We don't do that after jobs at Stealth & Tactics."

"How many jobs have you been on?" Alfie asked suddenly, taking off on a tangent.

"The Pit was my second job, but the first one was an easy guard and capture."

"Guard and capture?"

"Yeah, basically we used somebody as bait to capture the people who wanted to either kill them or kidnap them. Guard the bait, capture the enemy."

"Oh, I don't think we call it that at RI, but I've never been on a job like that. Well, now that I think about it, the Pit was that kind of job, wasn't it?"

Tessa nodded. "Basically. What kind of jobs have you been on?"

Alfie shrugged. "Pretty much save-the-world kind."

"Sure," Tessa laughed, not believing him.

Alfie nodded enthusiastically. "Like two weeks ago, a guy was captured in Canada after working to produce weaponized uranium in a diamond mine."

"Shit! You had the Ore job? My commander wanted that job so bad! He was a fan of Ore's and was so pissed when he heard it went to RI."

"No, we beat Ore. We were with the AOJ."

"Oh…"

"What?"

"It's nothing, just… they don't like working with the AOJ at S&T."

"We don't really either, but we take the jobs we're given. I've worked with the AOJ three times and against them once. They kicked our asses on my first job." Alfie laughed, remembering the look of shock on Earth Child's face when he pointed his gun at her cheetah.

"Did you see the psychologist after each job?" Tessa asked, gently bringing them back to the original topic.

"What? Oh, no. It's normal to see her when there is a death on a job," Alfie explained slowly, watching Tessa's reaction. Her shoulders stiffened and her head shot up.

"Somebody died at the Pit?"

247

"Yeah, a member of the other team. Guy named Olsen."

"Oh my God, Alfie! I am so sorry!" Tessa took Alfie's hand and squeezed.

"It's not your fault, Tess. It's no one's fault besides Trade Wind. She electrocuted him right before she took off with the few lackeys she still had standing."

"The one who hit me when I was trying to get back to Trade Wind," Tessa whispered.

Alfie nodded slightly as pain flashed across his face.

"It is my fault!"

Alfie shook his head and pulled her into his arms. "It is not your fault, Tessa. Believe me. Olsen's death is solely on Trade Wind."

"How can you say that? She killed him because he was going after me!"

Alfie pulled away and shook Tessa gently. "No, she killed him because he was threatening her retreat. You were a nameless, faceless henchman to Trade Wind. She would not kill to save your life. She would only kill to help herself."

"Are you sure?" Tessa asked, eager to believe his words.

"Absolutely. Besides, I would not have spent the last week blaming myself if it was your fault." Alfie gave Tessa a lopsided grin and she choked out a laugh. "Okay, pull yourself together because this is about me, not you."

"Jerk," Tessa snapped but Alfie's comment had the intended effect when she laughed. "Okay, what's going on?"

Alfie let go of Tessa's shoulders and leaned back on the mat, resting his weight on his elbows. "I've had shit happen in my life and the doc is concerned because I'm not talking to anybody about it."

"Isn't that her job?"

"Right?! That's what I said, but she wants me to fix myself by talking to friends or family. Since there is zero chance that I am going to tell my family about my job, and I really don't have any other friends I'd trust with this, you're the lucky winner!"

"Hey, I didn't even enter this raffle," Tessa teased as she leaned back on her hands and crossed her legs at the ankles. "What's going on?" Tessa repeated her question but without the teasing tone she used before.

"Well, you know about Olsen dying, but you don't know that I tried saving him after Trade Wind left." Alfie sat up, pulled his knees up, and rested his elbows on them. "Before Trade Wind hit him, I shouted for him to stop because there was something familiar about the way you screamed. That's when Trade Wind shot him with lightening and took you guys out of the Pit. Ray and I were the first ones to Olsen and we tried saving him, but we couldn't. I don't blame myself for his death anymore, but I do blame myself for not being able to save him. I don't think that feeling will ever go away."

Tessa rested a hand on his arm. "Alfie, you did what you could. You said that."

"Yeah, but I'm always going to wonder if there was more I could do."

"You're not a doctor, Alf. What else could you have done?"

"True." Alfie's eyes narrowed at a thought. "You are supposed to be the doctor."

"Hey." Tessa held up a hand at his accusation. "We are not talking about me."

Alfie pursed his lips together. "Fine, but we are having that conversation soon."

Tessa rolled her eyes. "What else is on your mind?"

"The Pit was kind of a trifecta of shittiness for me."

"What do you mean?"

"Well, before the action started, I think Ray dumped me."

"You…think?" Tessa asked slowly.

Alfie stared at Tessa with a suspicious expression. "Okay, I need my best friend for a bit, not the girl who looks like her."

Tessa took a deep breath and rolled her shoulders. "Okay, best friend here, not girl. What happened?"

"Apparently one of the guys on my team, Nikolai, the big Russian dude."

"Scary guy? Looks like Ivan Drago?"

"That's him. Well, I guess he and one of the girls from Team 7 used to be a couple. Sounds like it went bad and they broke up. Then it went worse when they had to keep working together. I think it spooked Ray, and she told me she thought our relationship was a bad idea. Well, we never got the chance to talk it out because you guys showed up right after and then Olsen."

"You haven't talked to her about it yet?" Tessa was surprised that Alfie would put off something so important.

"I didn't know how to talk to her. I told her then that I thought she and I could work, at least for a while."

"You need to talk to her, Alfie."

"I know." Alfie took a deep breath and looked up from the mats, meeting Tessa's eye. "I told you we weren't going to talk about the kiss yet, but I think we need to."

250

Tessa groaned and rolled to her feet. Alfie watched her walk away from him and pace in front of the TV.

"Why did you kiss me, Tess?"

"Why did you kiss me back, Alf?" Tessa snapped.

Alfie watched her in silence, waiting for her to answer him. She swung her arms and jumped up and down a couple of times like a boxer getting ready for a fight.

"I like you, Alfie. I have for a long time," Tessa started, her voice quiet but forceful. "I never knew how to tell you, or even if I should. You're my best friend and all that crap."

"I'm crap now?" Alfie laughed and climbed to his feet. "But I smell what you stepped in. Feelings change things."

"Exactly." Tessa threw a sharp jab at her punching bag but stopped just short of it so she wouldn't hurt her unwrapped wrist. "Where do we go from here, Alfie?"

Alfie leaned against the wall next to her. "I don't know, Tessa. I can't go anywhere until I figure out what is going on with Ray."

"And after?" Tessa avoided eye contact.

"I honestly don't know."

"Oh." Tessa wrapped an arm around the punching bag and finally looked at Alfie. "What was the third thing?"

"You."

"Now I'm shit?"

Alfie nabbed Tessa's arm as she tried storming away from him. "No, Tessa. What I mean is I didn't have my best friend to go to because I didn't know where we stood. Here I was trying to get through a possible break up, the death of a co-worker, and finding out that my best friend was putting herself in danger by being a henchman. All I wanted to do was talk to you about it and I couldn't. Throw in you kissing me and changing our relationship, and I didn't know which way was up!"

"Sorry, Alfie."

"You don't have anything to be sorry about." Alfie sighed and let go of her arm. "You just moved us to a place where we have never been before and we both forgot to leave breadcrumbs, but we'll figure it out. We always do."

Tessa gave him a small smile before her expression turned serious again. "You going to tell Ray about the kiss?"

"Yeah, I think so. I'm not a liar."

"Only to your family about a job that can kill you," Tessa muttered as she walked away from him.

"Oh, and I'm sure you've told your family that you have given up on your internship and are now a henchman at S&T," Alfie said sarcastically.

Tessa sighed as she dropped down on the bench that sat against the wall. "No, you're right. I haven't. I have no idea how to."

"What did you tell the hospital?" Alfie sat down next to her, close but not touching.

"I told them that I was overwhelmed and needed to take some time off to work on my mental health. They couldn't hold the internship, so it's gone unless I apply again and get accepted."

"Did Massimo's friend tell him about your break?"

"No, thank God." Tessa sighed and leaned her head against the wall. "Uncle Massimo would have run to tell my father. What am I going to do, Alfie? I can't tell them I threw away my future as a doctor so I could play commando."

Alfie put his arm around her shoulders when he heard the tears in her voice. "I don't know, but we'll do it together, okay? And I don't think you threw away your future as a doctor. You just graduated from high school. You have four years of college, three years of medical school, and however many years as an intern to throw it away yet."

Tessa made a sound half-way between a laugh and a sob. She wiped away the tears with the back of her hand and gave Alfie a hug. "Thank you."

"Anytime," Alfie whispered before sitting back. "So why did you decide to play commando?"

Tessa groaned. "Didn't we talk about this already?"

"I think I would remember that conversation."

"You have gotten a few good knocks to the head lately."

"Not that good." Alfie turned on the bench and rested his bent leg on the seat between them. "Why?"

"I have cops, soldiers, marines, sailors, and detectives in my family. They all play an active part in keeping the world safer for everybody. I guess I wanted a piece of that."

"And saving people's lives isn't helping to keep the word safe?"

"It's cleaning up the mess after the world is saved."

Alfie was surprised at the bitterness that crept into Tessa's voice. "Ever since we were kids and your dad got shot, all you wanted to do was patch people up. I remember you saying that you wanted to be a doctor so you could save the heroes. When did you change your mind?"

"When you got shot." Tessa slapped a hand over her mouth in surprise.

"Excuse me?"

"Alf, no offense, but you are about as far from a person people picture as saving the world but you went in there, did the job, got shot, and walked out like it was nothing."

"My first job wasn't exactly saving the world. We were supposed to keep a guy safe who was attempting to melt Beijing for a really stupid reason that I don't even remember. We were working for the bad guy."

"Yeah, but you were still injured. You got shot like my dad and you weren't even a cop or a soldier."

"Tessa, I hate to break it to you, but while a henchman has very similar job requirements as an infantryman, it is definitely a less noble profession. If you want to save the world, join the military! At least there, they'd pay for your schooling so if you decided to become a doctor later, you would have it paid for."

"They still don't let women in combat."

"So be a pilot. They get close to the front all the time. Wait, why do you want to be in combat?"

Tessa shrugged. "Everybody else is."

Alfie stared at her for a solid minute, trying to figure out if Tessa was being serious or if she had been taken over by a pod person. "I think you are the one who should be talking to a psychologist."

"Probably."

Alfie turned to lean his head back against the wall and stared across the shed in thought, trying to process what his best friend had just told him.

"Hey, you know my brother, Rocco?" Tessa asked suddenly.

"No, can you tell me about him?" Alfie rolled his eyes.

"Shut it," Tessa laughed. "Well, he and Cameron O'Rory have been seeing each other since they met that night when we ran into you and Ray."

"Seriously." Alfie nodded slightly as he processed the news. "I'll have to tell Robert when I talk to him next. Well, Rocco better treat her right or he is going to have two Vihars coming after him… And we know how to kick Pellegrini ass."

******

Alfie knocked as he opened the door to Dr. Olafson's outer office.

"Alfie, come in!" Margaret waved for him to enter from her desk.

"Morning, Margaret." Alfie propped a hip against her desk and gave her the sultriest smile he had. "How was your weekend? Get into any trouble?"

Margaret laughed and swatted at him with a file when he winked at her. "No. I had my grandkids this weekend so the worst trouble I got in was when my daughter-in-law found out the kids and I had an all-night movie marathon complete with junk food and footie pajamas."

"World War III?"

"End of days."

"Ooo…" Alfie cringed and clasped his hands to his chest.

"How was yours?"

"Well, I didn't get shot at, so I'm counting it as a win."

255

Margaret laughed and nodded her agreement. "Good to hear. Now you get in there. Dr. Olafson is waiting for you."

"See you." Alfie waved at the receptionist as he headed for the inner office. "Good morning, Dr. Olafson."

"Good morning Alfie. Have a seat." She pointed at the chair in front of her desk as she shuffled a few files around until she found the correct one.

"No couch this time?" Alfie joked. "Doesn't that violate some shrink code?"

"The American Psychologist Association abolished that rule five years ago."

"Did- did you just make a joke?" Alfie dropped into the chair in amazement.

"You'll never know," Dr. Olafson said with a small smile. "Now, I remember giving you homework for the weekend. How did it go?"

"Well, not as good as you probably wanted, but I am talking to Tessa again."

"Good. Want to tell me about it?"

"We didn't really resolve anything, but we did talk." Alfie paused but when Dr. Olafson did not interject, he continued. "I guess we got the 'Tessa as a henchman' thing resolved, although I'm still baffled."

"Why?"

"She comes from a long line of fighters-her dad, brothers, uncles, grandfather, et cetera all are or were either cops or in the military. She is one of the few females in the Pellegrini family and, unlike her female cousins, she is not satisfied to let someone else rescue her if she needs it. She is a fighter too, and while she's wanted to be a doctor forever so she could help if they get hurt, she now wants to see more action. And apparently, it's my fault."

Dr. Olafson frowned. "What is your fault?"

"Tessa decided to do something more active when I got shot. Apparently, I am not the 'hero' type, and since I could handle the job, she figured she could, too. Oh, hey, maybe she decided to become a henchman instead of joining the military because she saw that I could do it and figured she could do it, too… and she doubts that I would be able to survive military service. Hey!"

"Does that offend you?"

"Kind of." Alfie laughed. "I very much doubt I could survive boot camp or basic training, but having Tessa doubt me kind of stings." Alfie shifted in his chair and crossed his legs. "Huh, anyway, moving on, I told her about Olsen. Then, I spent a few minutes convincing her that it's not her fault that he's dead. She then spent a few minutes convincing me that there was nothing I could do to save him considering my lack of medical training."

"So you're over Olsen's death?"

"Whoa, doc! I'm not heartless. I still feel bad because he was a good guy, I just know that it wasn't my fault, nor was there anything more I could have done. I'm not over it, but I'm in a better place about it, if that makes sense."

"It does, actually." Dr. Olafson made a note in her folder before looking back at Alfie. "Do you have your best friend back?"

Alfie stared at the carpet for a long second, thinking about his afternoon with Tessa. "I think I do, for the most part. We haven't really talked about what her kissing me means to our friendship."

"Why not?"

"I want to talk to Ray first."

"So, you're leaving Tessa's feelings on pause until you resolve your relationship with Miss Green?"

"Now, that makes me sound heartless." Alfie sighed heavily. "I love Tessa. She has been my best friend forever. The last thing I want to do is hurt her or handle her feelings callously, but I don't feel like I am in any place to address her feelings for me when I am still in limbo with Ray."

"And when do you plan on talking to Miss Green?"

"Probably today, if I can drag her away from training."

"Do you think work is the best place for this discussion?"

"Oh, shit. No. No, it's not. Okay, so probably tonight after work." Alfie crossed his arms and leaned back in the chair. "It probably looks like I'm avoiding talking to Ray… which I am, but I know how important it is that I talk to her."

"Good." Dr. Olafson made one more note in her folder and closed it. She put the cap back on her pen and laid it precisely on the middle of the folder. "I think you are fine to return to work, as long as the issue between yourself and Miss Green is resolved soon. Schedule a meeting with me after you talk with her. If you need a mediator, I will be glad to be of assistance."

"A mediator? Does that happen very often?"

"The henchmen here at Resources, Inc. are very unique in the business. People hire complete units who are used to working together and have a relationship built on trust. That is why our rates are higher than the industry standard. Other companies hire out individuals who might have never even spoken to each other, let alone worked together. If there is a situation within a unit, we work hard to get it resolved so the whole unit can get back to working order. Until that happens, the entire unit is broken. It would be very beneficial to you and the entirety of Team 9 that you resolve the issues between yourself and Miss Green quickly."

"Heard loud and clear." Alfie rubbed his hands down his legs. "I will talk to Ray tonight."

"Very good, Mr. Vihar. I will see you later in the week then."

"Yep." Alfie stood at his dismissal. "Bye." He paused in the outer office to wave at Margaret, who was on the phone, before heading down to the den, only to find LeRoy alone in the room. "Hey, LeRoy, have you seen Ray?"

"I have not," LeRoy answered without looking up from the notebook in front of him on the table.

"All right. Thanks." Alfie turned to leave but stopped in the doorway when LeRoy spoke again.

"What happened between you two?"

"I don't know what-"

LeRoy slammed his hand onto the table. *"C'est des conneries!"*

Alfie put up a hand to ward off the anger rolling off the small Cajun. "Whoa. Where did that come from?"

"You have been avoiding each other since the Pit."

"Yeah, well a lot of shit happened at the Pit, none of which is your business."

Alfie's uncharacteristic bluntness gave LeRoy pause. He studied Alfie for a long minute, then nodded slowly. "You are right, *garçon*. But Ray is my friend, remember that."

Alfie felt the hair stand up on the back of his neck at LeRoy's subtle reminder that, to Team 9, Alfie was the

259

disposable one when it came to his relationship with Ray. Alfie nodded once and left the den.

"Hey, November!" Alfie called as he broke out into a jog. He caught up with her just as the hallway opened into the gym. "When did you get back from Utah? I thought Team 7 was supposed to be gone for a week."

"We just got in like an hour ago. We were supposed to be there a week, but Brutus called us back early after he got the okay from the head therapist there. Apparently we were needed for something that couldn't wait."

"Cool. Well, welcome back. Nice streaks."

"Hey, thanks!" November ran a hand over the new blue streaks in her black hair. "I've had the red for a long time and wanted a change. What's up with you, Alfie?"

"Looking for Ray."

"Oh, I just saw her on the wall."

Alfie's gaze followed November's arm as she pointed across the gym to the climbing wall in the corner. "Thanks." Alfie tossed over his shoulder as he started jogging away.

"Any time," November called after him.

"Slack!" Ray yelled down to Nikolai, who was spotting her from the floor.

"Say slack one more time..." Nikolai muttered as he tightened the belay line attached to Ray.

"Hey." Alfie stopped next to Nikolai and looked up at where Ray was nearing the top of the wall.

Nikolai grunted in greeting and pulled a few more feet of rope through the harness around his waist. The two men watched as Ray bunched her feet under her on a small ledge and sprang upward, reaching for the next handhold.

"Shit!" Alfie's yell echoed around the gym as Ray's hand slipped and she fell, just to be brought up short when she hit the end of the rope. The force yanked Nikolai forward a few feet before he got control.

"Again?" the Russian yelled up at Ray where she dangled thirty feet off the floor.

Ray propped her feet against an outcropping and leaned back so she was perpendicular to the wall, head toward the floor so she could see Nikolai. "Sorry! I thought I could get it this time!" She rotated back up until she was sitting in the harness and walked down the wall as Nikolai slowly fed rope to the pulley at the top of the wall.

"Nyet. You go again?"

"No, I'm done. I think I pulled something on that." Ray swung her arm around as her feet touched the ground. Nikolai nodded and walked over to the wall to begin coiling the rope up on the rack. "Hey, Alfie," Ray said after a brief hesitation.

"Want to go for coffee after work?" Alfie asked quietly, glancing at Nikolai to see if he had heard.

"Yeah," Ray whispered back. "You wanting to talk?"

"Yeah."

"Good." Ray nodded and started unbuckling her harness. "Mugshot and Muffintop on Hemlock Avenue has good coffee."

"Sounds good. See you there."

"Alfie," Ray chuckled as Alfie turned back toward her, "we still have like three hours of work left. I'm sure we'll run into each other again."

"You three! Over here!" Gibson barked.

"Exhibit A," Alfie muttered as he, Ray, and Nikolai hurried over to where the captain stood on the mats.

"Vihar, now that you've figured out how to fight, let's see if you can fend off two attackers at once."

Katherine Wielechowski

"Fan-freaking-tastic," Alfie sighed. He settled into a fighting stance facing Ray and Nikolai. They looked at each other and slowly advanced on Alfie. "Uh, I surrender?"

Gibson's smile was cold enough to freeze a man to the core. "No."

******

Alfie slid into the booth across from Ray with a groan.

Ray laughed lightly. "How're you feeling?"

"Like I got hit by a train."

"Don't worry. It'll be worse tomorrow."

Alfie grunted as he leaned forward so he could stuff an icepack between his back and the booth. Then he settled another on his shoulder before finally trying his coffee. "You're right, it is good." He closed his eyes and leaned his head against the backrest, praying for the pain pills Dr. Olafson gave him to kick in. After a long silence, Alfie opened his eyes to the sound of a paper coffee cup scraping the table. "Hi."

"You wanted to talk."

Alfie nodded but remained silent. He took a minute to look around the coffee shop/bakery and gather his thoughts.

It had a small front entrance, but it extended the full width of the building and actually had two storefronts, one on each side of the block. The kitchen was open and occupied almost the entire length of the shop, while the coffee counter took up the rest. The décor was a combination of grandma's garage sale and grunge-rock band tour bus while the music was a strange mix of alternative rock, old-school country, and Irish folk.

"Well?"

Alfie studied her as he took a long drink from his cup. "What did you mean at the Pit when you said you thought our relationship was a mistake?"

Ray sighed and she slumped back in the booth. "I don't think our relationship was a mistake. I think continuing it would be."

Alfie gaped at her. "Why?"

"You're eighteen-"

"And you're twenty-two. What does that have to do with the price of tea in China?"

Ray shook her head. "Alfie, it might only be four years in your mind, but its decades apart in experience."

"If the experience is henchman stuff, I'm sure I'll get there eventually."

Ray dropped her eyes to the cup cradled in her hands. "I've seen and done things that you can't even imagine."

"Like what?"

"Like I was homeless and lived on the street for almost nine months when I was fifteen."

Alfie's jaw dropped open. He suddenly realized that he didn't know much about her past, and he had no idea what to say. He reached across the table and took her hand.

Ray shrugged uncomfortably and took a sip of her coffee. "It's over. My mom and I are in a great place now and it's just a bad thing that helped teach me to survive. The thing is, Alfie, I think that you are meant for different things outside of San Luca. RI is not what you are going to be doing for the rest of your life. You are going to move on soon. I am not. I like it here and I like my job. I'm settling down. I'm looking at buying a house in the next few years. Your life is just starting. Mine is... well, mine is what it is."

263

"You make it sound like you're seventy years old on the edge of retirement."

Ray laughed. "I might as well be. Being a henchman is the best thing that could've happened to me and I love it. I can't see myself leaving except in retirement or in a body bag."

Alfie leaned back in the booth. "So this really is all about the job, isn't it?"

"To a point. Dating a co-worker is a terrible idea anyway," Ray said with a smile. "It's not like we've been together for years. A few weeks is hardly a relationship."

Alfie nodded as he stared at the table between them. "Tessa kissed me."

Ray blinked. "What?"

Alfie finally met her eye. "Tessa kissed me. The day after the Pit."

"What happened? Did you kiss her back?"

"I went over to confront her about being a henchman. We fought, she kissed me... I guess I did kiss her back. Her mom walked in on us and it ended."

"So the only thing that stopped you was her mom walking in?"

Alfie shifted uncomfortably in his seat. "Well, it's not like we were going at it. It lasted probably less than a minute."

"You lying piece of shit!" Ray hissed.

"What?! What did I lie about? I didn't tell you right away but we weren't exactly talking!"

"You told me you would never cheat! You said you hated cheaters!" Ray quickly gathered up her purse and coffee cup and slid from the booth.

"You wanted to break up the day before this all happened! How is Tessa kissing me cheating?!" Alfie exclaimed, oblivious to the attention they were getting from the other patrons of the shop.

Ray put a hand on the table and leaned close enough that their noses almost touched. "You kissed her back."

Alfie watched Ray storm from the shop. "Maybe I should have gotten Dr. Olafson involved," Alfie muttered into his coffee.

"Ass." A woman glared at him as she walked by his table.

"She practically dumped me before!" Alfie called after her. "Not that it makes a difference. I'm still going to get my ass handed to me at work tomorrow," Alfie mumbled.

"Women. Can't live with them, can't get the hell away from them." The bearded waiter in a fedora put the ticket and the bag of muffins Alfie had ordered on the table in front of him with a sympathetic smile and walked away. He stopped after a few steps and looked back at Alfie. "And that's not from me."

Confused, Alfie flipped the ticket over and found a phone number written under the total. He glanced around as he pulled out a few bills from his wallet and saw a cute blond girl wearing an apron behind the counter smiling at him. He sat back in the booth and pulled his phone out of his pocket. He hit the speed dial for his brother, Nathan.

"What's up, turd nugget."

"Always with the mushy, lovey stuff."

"Don't you know it?! What do you need, little bro? I've got practice in ten."

"Quick question: if a girl witnesses you getting dumped for being a cheater and then gives you her number, is

265

it safe to say she is crazy and to run in the opposite direction?"

"Oh yeah, she be hella crazy. Wait, you cheated on Ray?! What the hell, Alf! Why would you do that! The girl sounded hot! Is she hot? Who could you have cheated on her with? Would it be weird for you if I asked you for her number?"

"Bye, Nathan." Alfie ended the call while Nathan continued talking. He glanced back at the counter and saw the blond occupied with another customer. He grabbed his sweatshirt and muffins, left the cash and the ticket on the table, and sneaked out of the shop as stealthily as he could. "I guess I'm never going back there. Shitty though. They had awesome coffee."

******

Alfie was in the gym learning a few stretches from November to relieve the pain from his beating the day before when his phone wheezed and groaned in his pocket, indicating he got a text message. November gave him a strange look and he laughed. "Sorry, the T.A.R.D.I.S. sound is not the best choice for a ringtone. Thanks for the help. I'll talk to you later." Alfie headed to a corner where he would be out of the way of the other henchmen who were working out and flicked a finger across the screen. It was a text from his sister, Ruth.

What did you do to Ray? We just saw her downtown and while she was nice to mom and me, her glare nearly set me on fire when I asked about you.

Alfie groaned and set out to find a secluded spot to call his sister back. He ended up in the sniper's nest on the roof and pressed the call button.

"Dude, you messed up, didn't you?" Ruth said by way of a greeting.

"Hello to you, too," Alfie chuckled. "I haven't talked to you in like a week, so what makes you think I messed something up?"

"Ray was a nice one! What did you do?"

"How do you know she was nice? You never met her. Plus, why do you assume it was my fault? Wait, why was she out shopping? She's supposed to be here."

"A woman does not glare daggers at her boyfriend's mother and sister if she is the one who messed up."

"You are all of fourteen. What makes you an expert at relationships?"

"Alf, I'm serious. What happened?"

"Ray thought our relationship was a bad idea since we work together among other things. We didn't get a chance to talk about it. Then Tessa kissed me. I told Ray about it yesterday. It did not end well."

"What?! Tessa kissed you?!"

Alfie flinched at the volume and octave his sister was now screeching in. "Yeah."

"Are you two dating now?"

"What? Ruth, no. It all just happened. I don't know what is going on with either of them."

"You need to pick one."

"They're not flavors of pie, Ruth. You can't just pick one that sounds good at that moment."

"If you love two people at the same time, choose the second, because if you really loved the first one, you wouldn't have fallen for the second."

"Are you seriously quoting Johnny Depp at me right now?"

"The man knows things, Alfie!"

"I don't doubt that, Ruth, but I don't think Jack Sparrow is really at the Gandhi level of quotable advice yet."

"That's Captain Jack Sparrow to you. So do you want me to find a Gandhi quote that works for this situation?"

"That's not what I meant, Ruth."

"Well, that's what I heard. Gotta go. I only have an hour to find this quote before my next session. Bye, bro!"

"Ruth, seriously?" Alfie started, but he knew his sister hung up on him when he saw his phone light up out of the corner of his eye. "Damn."

"*Alfred Vihar report to Dr. Olafson's office. Alfred Vihar to Dr. Olafson's office.*"

Alfie jumped when he heard his name come over the loud speaker. "Well, that's unsettling." He quickly descended to the second floor and headed for room 2319. Margaret motioned for him to go right into Dr. Olafson's office. "Hey, doc."

"Sit down, Mr. Vihar." Dr. Olafson typed a few more things into her computer before turning her attention to Alfie. "You may have noticed that Miss Green is not here today."

"I didn't until my sister told me that she saw Ray downtown," Alfie said slowly.

"She and I talked this morning before I recommend she take the rest of the day off."

Alfie squirmed uncomfortably in his chair. "Should you be telling me this?"

"I'm not going to be giving you any details. She told me what you and she talked about yesterday. It did not end well, did it?"

Alfie exhaled noisily. "Not even close."

Dr. Olafson nodded. "For the sake of Team 9, you need to mend this. Ms. Green has agreed to talk to you again when she is ready. Think long and hard about what you want to discuss with her. I advised her to do the same."

"Thanks, doc." Alfie stood and shuffled out of the room.

"What happened, hun?" Margaret asked when she saw Alfie's dark expression.

"Women."

Margaret chuckled heartily. "I'm going to give you the amazing advice that my father gave my husband on my wedding day."

"Okay." Alfie walked over and leaned against her desk, waiting to have his mind blown.

"Apologize. Apologize until you are blue in the face and then apologize one more time for good measure."

"And if the woman in question is not my wife?"

"Throw in a few more 'I'm sorrys,' and you can't go wrong with a little groveling."

Alfie chuckled and shook his head. "I'll give it a go. Thanks, Margaret."

"Anytime, sweetie."

Alfie left Dr. Olafson's office and raced up the stairs to the sniper's nest on the roof. He thumbed through his contacts until he found Ray's number and pressed call. It rang twice then went to voicemail. Alfie groaned and ended the call before immediately redialing her number. He called her twice more before giving up the hope she would answer.

269

He pressed call one last time and waited for the beep. "Ray, its Alfie. Listen, I know I'm the last person you want to talk to right now. I just want to say I'm sorry. I didn't mean to hurt you, but I did, and I can't go back to change it, no matter how much I would like to. You don't have to call me back, I just... I just wanted to let you know how very sorry I am." Alfie ended the call and pressed his forehead to the cinderblock wall. "Oh yeah, she is never going to forgive me."

Alfie looked down at his phone when it groaned and wheezed to see another text from Ruth.

"Love is the strongest force the world possesses, yet it is the humblest imaginable" is the best one I could find from Ghandi

"Thanks, sis," Alfie mumbled as his text alert sounded again.

But I think this one from Mother Theresa works better: "Do not think that love in order to be genuine has to be extraordinary. What we need is to love without getting tired. Be faithful in small things because it is in them that your strength lies."

"Salt in the wound." Alfie quickly hit reply. *You sure know how to kick a guy when he's down.*

He laughed ruefully when Ruth answered immediately. *Pick yourself up, buttercup. It could be worse. They could destroy the earth tomorrow to make way for a hyperspace bypass.*

Alfie chuckled at his sister's use of *The Hitchhiker's Guide to the Galaxy* to make him put his life in perspective. He stood up and headed for the stairs as he sent her one last text. *I'd be lost without you, nerd. 42.*

1-800-Henchmen

"Team 9 to conference room Whiskey."

"Not now, Esther!" Alfie growled under his breath when the receptionist's voice came over the loud speaker. He slammed another magazine into the M4 and shouldered the rifle.

It had been a week since Ray had dumped Alfie in the coffee shop and she still wasn't talking to him except to pick a fight. She was no longer staring daggers at him whenever they were in the same room, but Alfie was still frustrated by her unwillingness to hash out their problems. Thankfully, Dr. Olafson had cleared Team 9 for work pending no break-up related issues arising between Ray and Alfie at work.

"Come, Vihar." Nikolai stopped behind Alfie on his way to check in his handgun.

"Give me-" Alfie squeezed the trigger and emptied half the mag in a long burst, "one more minute."

Nikolai rolled his eyes and walked away as Alfie finished the magazine. He dropped the magazine, flipped on the safety, and quickly cleaned up the pile of brass. He checked in his rifle as he left the range and raced across the gym to the conference room.

"You have a problem with punctuality, Vihar," Gibson commented without looking up.

"Yes, sir," Alfie muttered just because he knew the captain was not looking for an answer. Alfie took an empty chair and felt Ray's eyes glide over him as if he wasn't even there.

"I just got word from Brutus," Gibson hit a button on the remote in front of him and the flat screen TV on the wall lit up showing a woman with blue hair in handcuffs being loaded into the back of an armored van. "Trade Wind has been captured." Gibson held up a hand as everybody started cheering. "Apparently, the AOJ went after her when she poked her head out of a hole in Utah. Crux made short work of her weather control and they got her restrained long enough for the cops to take her into custody."

"Will the police be able to contain her?" Ray asked.

"Crux is keeping a close eye on her and a few secret tech agencies around the world are working together to find a way to contain her powers."

"Are we one of them?" Alfie asked, curious about the company he worked for.

"You really haven't figured anything out about RI yet, have you?" Ray snapped.

"What does secret mean again? Oh yeah, nobody talks about it!" Alfie glared at her, tired of the petty arguments they had been getting into since they broke up.

"Children." Nikolai ended their argument with his warning tone.

"Now for what I called you here for," Gibson started as he stood up from his chair. "We have found ourselves in a unique situation. The man hiring us for our next job is here to brief us."

Alfie assumed this was unheard of, judging by the looks of confusion and outrage on Ray and Nikolai's faces

"Where is LeRoy?" Ray asked suddenly.

"*La Grenouille Bouché* has arrived!" LeRoy sauntered into the conference room wearing a shiny purple and green jumpsuit, complete with a gold cape and mask.

"Is it Halloween?" Nikolai asked, taking in LeRoy's outfit.

"What is going on?" Ray looked back and forth between LeRoy and Gibson.

"You're going with 'the stupid frog'? Seriously?" Alfie translated with a laugh.

"*La Grenouille Bouché* means 'the killer frog,' you *imbécile,*" LeRoy snarled.

"Ah, no-"

"*La Grenouille Bouché* has hired Team 9 for a job," Gibson said, trying to pull them back on task.

"LeRoy is hiring us for a job?" Alfie asked slowly, disbelief written across his face. "Dude! You're not going to use that thing from the Ore-"

"Bip, bip, bip, bip." LeRoy stopped the question with a gold lamé glove on Alfie's mouth. "You fine folks are going to help me with a little project of mine."

"What?" Nikolai asked, his eyes narrowing.

LeRoy raised a fist above his head and struck a pose. "We are going to take over New Orleans! Tomorrow!"

Team 9 collectively blinked at their teammate, unsure how to respond to that announcement.

"Why?" Alfie was the first to break the silence.

"Because I fancy myself a king and every king needs a kingdom."

"So, pick a nice piece of the desert nobody wants and set up-"

"Vihar," Gibson said, warningly, "we do not question the motives of our employers."

"Even when the employer is a teammate who-"

"We're a man down," Ray objected, pointing at the bedazzled Cajun.

"We will be borrowing Skarret from Team 7 to round out our numbers."

273

"Well, I know how to make an entrance," Erin said dryly as Team 9 all turned to look at her in the doorway. "You guys hear about Trade Wind? Freaking awesome!" Team 9 murmured their agreement.

Alfie raised his hand. "How exactly do you plan on taking over New Orleans?" He didn't even try to contain the doubt in his voice.

"Oh, I have a plan." LeRoy grinned and rubbed his hands together. "A most excellent plan."

******

"Worst plan ever!" Alfie collapsed on the floor in the private jet that would take the henchmen back to San Luca. He had bandages around his thigh and from his elbow to his wrist, a splint holding his ring and middle fingers together on his left hand, and an icepack pressed to his head. The rest of Team 9 fared the same or worse.

"Who let him drive?" Erin croaked as she sank into the seat near where Alfie lay on the floor. Her eyes were still red and puffy from the tear gas, and the coughing had made her voice hoarse. Her left arm was in a sling and she had bandages wrapped around her right bicep and most of her right leg.

"He paid like every other employer." Gibson shrugged apologetically as he dug through his gear bag. He had a gauze pad taped to a cut on his forehead, gauze wrapped around his neck, and a broken nose with matching black eyes. He tossed Erin a small aerosol can of an anti-agent developed by RI to stop the effects of tear gas. She sprayed her face and passed it off to Alfie.

"We really need to screen employers better," Ray groaned as she lowered herself to the floor next to Alfie. She had an icepack bandaged to her ankle, a couple bruised ribs, a deep cut on her calf, and numerous other scrapes and bruises.

Nikolai climbed slowly into the plane muttering under his breath in Russian. He had a cut under his right eye and walked stiffly with a bandaged hand pressed to his side.

"You okay, man?" Alfie asked when he saw Nikolai grimace when Gibson accidently bumped him.

"*Nyet.*" Nikolai gently pulled his shirt over his head and turned, giving his teammates a view of his black and blue back.

"Jesus, Nikolai!" Ray carefully climbed to her feet as fast as she could to examine the extent of his injuries. "Gibson, I think he has some internal bleeding."

"*Nyet.*" Nikolai slowly moved around Ray and sat down at the end of one of the benches that lined the plane's interior. "Bag." He pointed at his black bag near the door. Ray hobbled over to it and handed it to him. He pulled a bottle out of it, dumped two green pills into his hand and quickly swallowed them. He barely got the cap back on the bottle before he fell backward onto the bench, unconscious.

Erin raised an eyebrow. "Those legal?"

Gibson shrugged. "Better to not ask." He took a seat near the door and Ray reclaimed her spot on the floor.

"What's going to happen to LeRoy?" Alfie asked into the silence that had descended on the plane as lifted it off from the small airport outside of New Orleans.

"That, Vihar, is a very good question." Gibson stood stiffly and ducked into the small room in the back of the plane.

275

Alfie frowned and rolled his head so he could look at Ray. "Did he just take a bathroom break so he wouldn't have to answer me?"

Ray chuckled then gasped in pain. "No, that's the intel room."

"The what?"

"It's essentially a bunch of computer equipment that lets us do a whole lot of stuff that the government doesn't know about."

Alfie pursed his lips and nodded. "Cool."

"He's probably on the com with Brutus right now working to get LeRoy released from police custody somehow."

"You seriously think he can get off? He just tried to take over New Orleans and got a bunch of people hurt!" Alfie exclaimed.

"Eh, weirder things have happened," Erin said as she slowly got to her feet. Alfie rolled slightly to the side so Erin could walk by him to the small kitchenette at the back of the plane.

"Hey, Alf," Ray whispered, "Thank you for pretty much saving my life back there."

Alfie grinned at her. "Now don't go falling in love with me after finding out I'm a full-on knight- in- shining-armor. You just dumped me and broke my heart."

Ray laughed again and cursed at her ribs. "You're more like an idiot in tinfoil."

"My mom thinks I'm special."

"You're a special something." Ray took his hand and squeezed it briefly before letting go. "But seriously, thank you."

Alfie nodded. "You're welcome, Ray."

Ray squinted at him. "You know that doesn't mean we're getting back together."

"WHAT?!" Alfie feigned shock as he clasped both of his hands over his heart. "There you go again, messing with my emotions!"

"Make me laugh again and I will stab you," Ray gritted through the pain of her bruised ribs.

Alfie laughed and held out a hand to her. "Less-than-mortal enemies?"

Ray nodded and shook his hand. "It's a good place to start."

******

"How is everybody feeling this morning?" Gibson asked as he walked into Team 9's den. Ray, Nikolai, Alfie, and Erin had all gathered after their five days off for the post-job debriefing. His black eyes had faded to a yellow tinge and the cut on his forehead was almost completely healed up.

"I'm beginning to worry about our healing abilities." Alfie looked down at his arm that had been nearly flayed open and was now just an ugly web of red marks. "Are they injecting us with Wolverine's DNA or something?"

"What'd Dr. Olafson tell you?" Erin leaned over and checked out Alfie's arm.

"She gave me a bottle of pills and told me to soak my arm in hot water and Epson salts and it would be healed up in a few days. I asked her if a few days would be enough with just hot water and salts. She was not impressed when I asked if I also needed to throw herbs in a fire and chant in Latin or sacrifice a virgin."

Erin laughed. "No Wolverine DNA and no sacrificing virgins, but they are working on fast-healing drugs. We are their guinea pigs."

"Don't they need our permission for that?"

Ray grinned at him. "You gave that permission when you started working for RI."

"Damn, I have got to start reading the fine print."

"Any word on LeRoy, sir?" Nikolai asked.

Gibson nodded. "He should be arriving back to HQ within the hour."

"Make that seconds!" LeRoy exclaimed as he burst into the room.

"Our justice system sucks these days," Alfie said dryly as he stood to shake LeRoy's hand. "Welcome back."

"You are so sweet!" LeRoy pulled Alfie into a hug that lasted longer than necessary.

Alfie wriggled out of LeRoy's grasp. "Yeah. Sure."

The rest of Team 9 and Erin gathered around to welcome LeRoy back from incarceration.

"How did you guys manage it this time?" Ray asked Gibson once they all settled back into their seats.

"Brutus had to do a lot of dancing to keep the police from actually charging LeRoy. He convinced them that the real *La Grenouille Bouché* had forced LeRoy to dress as him so the attention would be on LeRoy and he could escape when his plans started to fall apart. Brutus assured the police that we are concentrating on finding the real *La Grenouille Bouché* and that we will turn him over to them when we locate him."

"And what will they do when we never actually find *La Grenouille Bouché*?" Alfie asked.

Gibson shrugged. "Brutus will handle it. It's what he's here for. Now, usually we interview the employer for reviews, but since our employer is sitting right here, LeRoy, would you like to review the team's performance?"

"I would love to." LeRoy stood and slowly walked to stand next to Gibson. "I don't know what you all were thinking but my plan was perfection! You all ruined it! It-"

"Okay." Gibson cut LeRoy off and pointed the Cajun back to his seat. "LeRoy, one of the things that caused your plan to fall apart, in addition to it being a terrible plan, was the presence of another criminal team."

LeRoy jumped out of his chair. "WHO?!"

"Sit down," Gibson ordered quietly. LeRoy immediately complied. "It was the Four Horsemen."

"Who are the Four Horsemen?" LeRoy frowned, unfamiliar with the group.

"They have sporadically been popping up for the last six to nine months with small attacks. Mostly banking and business centers. They have not done any property damage and have only gotten away with about $50,000 total since they started. RI has been keeping an eye on them, but they have not been made a priority... until New Orleans. They got away with nearly a quarter million dollars from Global Exchange."

Alfie raised his hand. "What's Global Exchange?"

"Basically, it's the world's piggy bank that happens to also deal with international stocks," Gibson explained briefly.

"That's not a lot of money for a group who is trying to prove themselves on a big scale," Erin pointed out. "Especially from a multi-billion dollar business like Global Exchange."

"If Global Exchange is as important as you say, how'd they even get the money? Wouldn't Global Exchange have layers upon layers of protection?" Alfie asked.

Gibson shrugged. "Not sure yet. Intel believes that they would have taken more but it seems that *La Grenouille Bouché*'s attack ruined their plans."

"At least some good came from that disaster," Nikolai muttered.

"Sure." Gibson shook his head. "Brutus wants us to go over our time in New Orleans and see if we can find anything on the Four Horsemen. Ray, Nikolai, and Vihar, I want you watching all of the film from those body cameras *La Grenouille Bouché* had us wearing on the job. Watch them frame-by-frame if you have to. Find something. LeRoy, I want you helping me analyze their last jobs. The AOJ wants to know where they will strike next. It's our job to narrow down the possible targets."

Erin raised her hand. "What am I supposed to do, or am I not in on this?"

"Ah, no." Gibson looked almost surprised to see Erin still in the room. "Your job with Team 9 is done. Thank you for your assistance."

"Anytime. Later guys." Erin spun her chair around and headed out of the room with a wave.

Gibson clapped his hands. "Let's get to work."

******

"I can't watch any more of this," Alfie groaned as he pushed back from the computer. "I am literally watching my ass being handed to myself and it is not pretty."

"Was not a good fight," Nikolai agreed. He leaned over and offered Alfie a bowl of popcorn.

"You're eating popcorn while watching the crap get kicked out of us?"

Nikolai shrugged. "Yes. Love this part."

Alfie's jaw dropped when he glanced at the Russian's screen and saw that it was the part of the job that involved Team 9 getting hit with tear gas. Alfie shook his head and stood up to stretch as he wandered over to see what LeRoy was working on. "What're you doing?"

"Meh, this, that, and the other thing." LeRoy threw an arm around Alfie. "I hear you have a genius little sister. How does she feel about world domination?"

Alfie's eyes narrowed. "How do you know Ruth might be a genius?

"I have a program that watches online IQ tests. She had some pretty amazing scores."

"Why?"

"Looking for the next big supervillain. Imagine being the person who grooms the person who finally takes over the world!"

"You're kidding."

LeRoy stared at Alfie for a solid minute. "So… would she be interested in-"

"NO!" Alfie blurted, throwing off LeRoy's arm.

"How do you know? You didn't even ask her," LeRoy pouted.

"Ruth is not evil!"

LeRoy scoffed. "You don't have to be evil to be a supervillain. Look at me!"

Alfie looked at LeRoy skeptically.

"Will you just ask her?"

"NO!" Alfie screeched, throwing his hands in the air. "Drop it!"

"LeRoy recruiting a protégé again?" Ray asked, dropping into the seat on the other side of Nikolai.

"His sister is a genius," LeRoy said in defense.

"No recruiting at work," Gibson called from the other side of the room. He sat at a bank of computers and worked furiously on the keyboard while watching four different screens.

"Fine." LeRoy ungraciously dropped the topic and returned to his own computer.

"Who is that?" Ray asked suddenly. She stopped the video she was watching and slowly rewound it. She paused it when a compact woman with red streaks in her hair came on the screen. The woman was dressed in black cargo pants, combat boots, a black tank top, and had a backpack slunk over one shoulder. "When I first saw her, I thought she was November, then I remembered Team 7 wasn't in New Orleans with us."

Nikolai and Alfie gathered around Ray's computer to see who she was looking at.

"Not November," Nikolai mumbled.

"I know that. It doesn't look anything like her aside from the streaks in her hair."

"November's streaks are blue now. Have been since she got back from Salt Lake," Alfie said distractedly. "I think I remember seeing her on my footage. Why are we concerned with her?"

"She's dressed in combat gear. And that bump right there in her lower back," Ray tapped on the screen, "that looks like a handgun. If I'm not mistaken, that is the Global Exchange building she's going into."

"You're right," Gibson said from behind them. "It's a start. Nikolai, Vihar, start scrubbing your footage. Find her and see if you can find anybody she might be with. LeRoy, go through the traffic cam footage and find where she came from. I'll put her in the facial recognition software and see if we can get any hits there. Good work, Ray."

An hour and another bowl of popcorn later, Nikolai was the first to speak. "Found her."

The others rushed to join him around his computer screen. "Where?" Gibson asked.

"Here." Nikolai tapped his screen where they could just make out a woman with red streaks in her hair crouched behind a newspaper stand.

"When was this?" Ray asked.

"Right after first tear gas," Nikolai answered around a mouthful of popcorn.

"Could you tell where she came from?" Gibson slowly spun the dial that controlled the direction of the film, hoping to see where the woman was before she took cover.

"*Nyet.*"

"All right," Gibson sighed. "Keep looking."

"Cap," Alfie raised his hand, "I've got to take a break."

Gibson glanced at his watch, then rubbed a hand over his eyes. "All right. Everybody take fifteen, then back to work. We've got a lot of work to do yet today."

Alfie stopped in the kitchen and grabbed a Coke before heading up to the roof. It was after five and most of the henchmen had left the building for the day, but a few were still grappling in the gym. He needed somewhere quiet to call his parents to tell them he would be working late and figured the sniper's nest would be empty.

"Hey," he said awkwardly when he spotted Ray standing at the roof's edge with her back to him.

She turned around, her body language reflecting Alfie's awkwardness. "Hey."

"Sorry, I didn't know you were up here. I was looking for a quiet place to call my parents."

"Don't let me stop you," Ray snapped. Then, she closed her eyes and took a deep breath. "Sorry, still getting used to the peace."

Alfie shrugged. "It's all right." He sat down and texted his mom instead of calling her. "How're you doing?"

"Why do you care?"

"Ray," Alfie said very deliberately, "we just got back from a job where most of us got hurt pretty badly. I was referring to that."

"Oh." Ray rolled her head to loosen up her shoulders. "I'm doing much better. Almost back at 100 percent. You?"

"About the same." Alfie rubbed his hand down his injured arm, still surprised to find the skin whole again. "Ray, I'm going to bring it up. Just warning you."

Ray sighed and sat down on the bench facing Alfie.

Alfie kept his eyes on his phone as he turned it over and over in his hands. "I'm sorry."

"I'm sorry, too."

"You're- what?"

"I've been treating you like shit and you don't deserve that." Ray crossed her legs at the ankles and leaned back against the wall behind her. "Sure, we weren't completely broken up yet, but we hadn't had a chance to make it official. That was probably my fault for bringing it up when we didn't really have time to talk it over. You kissed somebody else. That was your fault, but you did tell me.

Most guys wouldn't have done that, especially after getting dumped. Or they would have brought it up to hurt the person dumping them. But do you even understand why I was so mad and hurt?"

Alfie nodded. "I promised I'd never cheat after finding out you were hurt by a cheater."

"Yeah."

"I never meant to hurt you, Ray."

"I know."

"I've never done something so shitty to a girlfriend."

Ray smiled slightly. "I believe that."

"I'm sorry."

Ray sighed. "I know. It doesn't make everything all right between us, but it does make it better."

"I'll take better." Alfie grinned.

Ray chuckled reluctantly.

"I know it'll be a while before you can trust me as a guy again, but can you trust me as a teammate?"

Ray frowned. "Alf, that was never in question."

Alfie sighed in relief. "Good. Because I have your back, no matter what the job."

"I think you proved that in New Orleans."

"Just double checking." Alfie laughed and glanced down at the clock on his phone. "We better head back."

"You go down, I'll be there in a minute."

Alfie nodded and ran down the stairs. He headed straight for the lab and got back to work on his camera footage. The sense of urgency pouring off of Gibson spiked Alfie's panic. He plugged his earbuds into his phone and blasted his music to help him concentrate on the screen in front of him. He got lost in the scene playing out in front of him and suddenly he was back in New Orleans, getting thrown to the pavement by a seasoned SWAT officer and being blinded by tear gas all while Five Finger Death Punch and Metallica played in the background. A glimpse of red snapped him to the present. He slammed his hand on the pause button, not completely believing what he was seeing.

Alfie jumped to his feet. "I got her!"

His sudden shout startled his teammates. They all rushed over and crowded around his computer.

"You can just see her right here." Alfie pointed at the screen. Everybody tilted their heads to the side so they could see the image correctly.

"Were you lying down?" LeRoy asked, frowning.

"Yeah, I had just got kicked to the concrete." Alfie waved his hands, brushing off the incident. "But here, you can see her talking to somebody."

Gibson reached over Alfie's shoulder and pressed a few buttons on the keyboard. The image turned upright and zoomed in on the woman they were looking for.

"You're right. She's talking to that blond woman," Ray whispered. She pushed Alfie out of his chair and slowly moved the footage forward and paused it just as the blond woman turned toward the camera. "Gibson, is that clear enough to use?"

"Yep! Send it to me and I'll get it out."

"Who's that?" Nikolai asked suddenly. He pointed at a figure just visible behind the blond woman.

"Let me see..." Ray advanced the footage more until the third person was clear. "We have a third face."

Alfie frowned. "Does that person look like the chick with red in her hair?"

LeRoy nodded. "Male, though."

"You think?" Gibson asked, leaning in for a closer look.

LeRoy grinned. "Yep, definitely male."

"All right, so maybe a brother of the red woman. We have three of them. I'll get their images out and see if we get any hits." Gibson rubbed the back of his neck. "Good work, everybody. Let's call it a night. It'll be hours before facial recognition software gets anything. Be back here at 0800."

******

"London," Gibson said as soon as Team 9 had settled into seats in the lab they had been using to research the Four Horsemen.

"What is… a place I've always wanted to visit?" Alfie guessed.

Gibson slapped Alfie on the back of the head but otherwise ignored the comment. "As best as we can tell, the Four Horsemen will be attempting another job in London this weekend."

"Have you found out anything else about them?" Ray asked.

"Yes." Gibson hit a few keys on his keyboard and four pictures filled the large screen on the wall. "Meet the Four Horsemen: War, Pestilence, Famine, and Death."

"Do they have real names?" LeRoy frowned.

"I'd imagine they do, but we could not find anything anywhere on the planet that reveals them."

"What do we know?" Ray asked, studying the pictures.

The first one was a picture of War, -the woman Ray had found on the footage that had started their search. She

287

was short and stocky with chin-length black and red hair. She had a tattoo on her neck that curled from just under her jaw down into her shirt. The picture looked like it was a mug shot from a prison in a third-world country and War was not happy to be there.

The second, Pestilence, was a man who greatly resembled War except he had white streaks in his long black hair and multiple facial piercings. The picture was from a security camera taken in a train station somewhere and showed Pestilence glancing covertly over his shoulder, a laptop case clutched tight to his chest.

The third picture showed a handsome blond man in a black-on-black-on-black power suit. Famine had been photographed stepping out of a black Maybach sedan in front of what looked like a country club somewhere tropical.

The fourth was of a beautiful blond woman with her hair pulled back severely from her face. Death was in a sharp charcoal suit, heels, and had large jade jewelry on that should have ruined the professional outfit but somehow enhanced it. She was standing in front of a steel-and-glass office building with a phone pressed to her ear and a briefcase in her other hand.

"Very little, actually." Gibson sat down and gave his team a rueful smile. "This picture was from when War was captured in Russia after leading an attack on a government building in Moscow. She is a combat expert and a fairly popular mercenary. Very few people have been able to best her, and the only reason she was captured in Moscow was because she was drugged by a person on her own team. Even then, it took three Russian soldiers to take her in."

Nikolai bristled at the thought that a small woman could get the better of his countrymen. "I will show her."

Gibson chuckled. "Pestilence is War's brother. As far as we can tell, they were born in Eastern Europe somewhere but spent a significant amount of their lives in the US. He is a ghost in the system and one of the best computer hackers I have ever seen or heard of. He is probably the reason the Four Horsemen don't seem to exist. It's tough to completely erase somebody from every computer system in the world, but a good enough hacker could do it, given enough time."

"He better than you, cap?" Alfie asked with an impish grin.

"Yep." Gibson's eyes glittered dangerously. "But that's not going to stop me from trying to bring him down."

"Those are some crazy eyes, you got there." Alfie leaned back with an exaggerated leery expression on his face.

Gibson shook his head and turned back to the pictures. "Famine is the idea man. He is the one who makes the plans and oversees execution. He creates relationships with powerful people in banks to get information about computer systems, layout, et cetera and then uses that information to make his plans infallible."

LeRoy scoffed. "No plan is infallible."

"*La Grenouille Bouché* would know," Ray teased.

"Last, but not least, is Death." Gibson cut them off before LeRoy could retort. "She is the one who gets the impossible information. No one seems to know how she does it. Even the people she has worked over can't explain it. They just know they gave her the information but they can't remember what kind of coercion she used. She works closely with Famine on the planning process."

"What's the plan?" Nikolai asked.

"What the plan normally is: direct confrontation, divert catastrophe, capture the bad guys."

"Make the AOJ look good," Ray muttered.

"We leave for London on Thursday morning. Let's get prepped."

******

"Hey, I need to find a phone booth," Alfie said as he glanced around. He was finding it increasingly more difficult to remember that he was in London for a job and not as a tourist. All he wanted to do was race off and explore the pubs and find the locations of his favorite movies and TV shows.

"Don't you have a phone in your pocket?" LeRoy asked.

"Yeah, but... Oh. My. God!" Alfie raced away from the group down a narrow side street. He had caught a flash of blue out of the corner of his eye and knew he had finally found one of the phone booths in question. He pulled out his phone and took a few pictures then turned around and took a few pictures of himself with the blue box behind him. "Tessa is going to be so jealous!" He could barely contain his excitement as he tried the door and found it unlocked. He took a few more pictures and rushed out of it to catch up with his team. He didn't see the blond woman until it was too late. He plowed right into her and knocked both of them to the cobblestones.

"What the hell are you doing, you idiot!" The blond woman's tone was frosty as she tried untangling herself from Alfie.

"I'm so sorry! I wasn't paying attention." Alfie accidently hooked his arm in the strap of her bag and pulled it from her shoulder as she stood.

"Give that back to me!" She yanked the bag away from him, breaking the strap and pulling his phone out of his grasp in the process.

"I am so sorry!" Alfie struggled to stand and attempted to locate his phone.

"Watch where you are going!" the woman scolded as she rushed off, awkwardly holding the bag tucked under her arm.

"Yes, ma'am. Sorry!" Alfie yelled after her. He finally found his phone in a pile of rubbish near the wall of the alley. He turned it on to make sure it still worked, and his jaw dropped. In the scuffle, he had managed to take a picture of the woman he had run into.

It was Death.

"Shit!" Alfie ran back to the main street and dodged people, looking for his team while keeping an eye on the woman.

"Vihar!"

Alfie felt himself fall backward as Gibson grabbed the back of his shirt and pulled him into the entryway of a nondescript building.

"Where they hell were you?!"

"I found a phone booth but that doesn't matter! I-"

"You leaving your team while on a job doesn't matter?!" Gibson's voice raised and Alfie flinched.

"Cap! I found Death!"

"You're about to!"

"No!" Alfie held up his phone to show Gibson the picture.

Gibson's jaw dropped and he roughly let go of Alfie. "Where?"

"I was following her until you grabbed me." Alfie stepped back out into the street and pointed. "I saw her turn right at that café."

"All right, Ray, LeRoy. Search her out. Nikolai and Vihar, you're with me. We need to meet up with the AOJ."

"Sir, the London office of Global Exchange is two blocks down that street," Ray whispered as she stepped out into the street next to Alfie.

"Damn! Ray, LeRoy, go! Coms on!" Gibson pulled out his phone and angrily dialed as Ray and LeRoy took off down the street. "It's Gibson. Death was spotted two blocks from the Exchange. They're closing in." Gibson ended his call and headed down the street, motioning for Nikolai and Alfie to follow him. They stuffed their coms in their ears and headed after the captain.

"Phone box?" Nikolai asked as they hurried to catch up.

"Oh, on one of my favorite shows, they travel in a spaceship/time machine that looks like a phone box."

"You're a weird guy."

Alfie shrugged. "I'm not arguing with you."

"Captain, we have eyes on Death. She just met with War in front of the Exchange. It looks like they're waiting on something," Ray's voice came over the coms.

"Good, keep eyes on them," Gibson ordered.

"Gibson, we need you at HQ," a voice crackled in Alfie's earpiece.

"Who was that?" Alfie called to Gibson.

"Warp," Gibson answered over his shoulder as he turned into an alley two buildings away from the Exchange and climbed a rickety staircase to a dilapidated door. "What?"

Warp and Crux turned at their entrance. "We have Pestilence's coordinates narrowed down but we can't pinpoint him. He keeps messing up our system." Warp stood up from the computer, freeing the chair for Gibson.

He sat down and got to work. "Nikolai, Vihar, you are with them. I'll smoke out Pestilence from here."

Crux nodded and headed out the door, Warp on his heels. "Let's go."

Alfie and Nikolai exchanged a look and quickly followed the AOJ from the small apartment. They hit the pavement and sprinted after Crux and Warp who were running full tilt for the Global Exchange building.

"Henchmen, do you have eyes on the target?" Crux barked.

"We have names, you know." LeRoy's droll tone startled a chuckle out of Alfie.

The AOJ members were less than impressed. "Target!" Crux nearly shouted.

Alfie saw a few people look their way. "Walmart! K-Mart! Bloody American capitalism!" He said loudly as he passed. "Crux, keep it down!" he hissed. The leader of the Alliance of Justice shot him a scathing look over his shoulder.

"One and two are in the building," Ray answered quickly, her voice a whisper in their earpieces. "We followed and have eyes on them. They are just standing in the center of the lobby talking quietly. I think they're waiting for something."

"Do not engage," Crux ordered. He and Warp stopped running almost at the same time and paused a few yards from the entrance to check the area. Alfie and Nikolai stopped a few feet behind them.

293

"Famine?" Nikolai said quietly to the group. He gave an almost imperceptible nod in the direction of a blond man in a black track suit leaning against a column in front of Global Exchange reading a newspaper.

"Can't tell," Alfie whispered back.

"I'm getting close to Pestilence. He is going to know I'm hunting him in about a minute. Act quickly." Gibson said over their coms.

"Stay here and watch," Crux ordered Alfie and Nikolai. Nikolai growled but he walked over to a newsstand and started flipping through the selection. Alfie plopped down on a bench at the bottom of the marble stairs that lead up to the Exchange.

"We think we found Famine. He's watching the entrance of the Exchange," Warp said quietly into her mic as she and Crux casually walked up the stairs.

"Something's happening," LeRoy whispered.

Ray cut out LeRoy. "Guys, I think we've been made."

"GOT HIM!" Gibson yelled over the radio.

"Shit!" Ray shouted as a loud explosion shook the building. People started pouring from the double doors just as Crux and Warp reached them. They quickly dodged to the side to keep from being trampled.

"They're heading out!" Ray yelled.

"Stop them!" Crux ordered.

"Oh yeah! While the building collapses on us!" LeRoy snapped.

Alfie and Nikolai ran to the bottom of the stairs as the people parted around them, searching for their quarry. Alfie glanced to the side where the man in black had been leaning.

"I lost sight of Famine!" Alfie shouted as he tried to wade through the people to where the leader of the Four

Horsemen had been standing. He fell to the stairs as another loud explosion rang out. He put a hand to his head where it had slammed into the step. "Whatever that is can stop anytime!"

"They had bombs rigged if their plan failed. Pestilence blew them when I got him," Gibson explained. "Everybody okay?"

The team all answered back that they were alive, and Alfie breathed a sigh of relief as he picked himself up. As he turned back up the stairs, a tall blond woman ran straight into him.

"You!" she yelled in surprise as she recognized him.

"Death?!" Alfie felt his jaw drop open. Without thinking he reached out and grabbed her arms to hold her in place. "I've got Death!" he radioed to his team.

Death took hold of his arms and tried to dislodge his grip. When his hold tightened, she pulled him close. "You will release me," she whispered.

Alfie's mind went blank. "Yeah, okay," he mumbled and let her go.

She quickly sidestepped him and rushed down the stairs.

"Vihar! What the hell are you doing?! Get her!" Warp shouted.

Alfie shook his head in confusion and turned around to watch Death reach the bottom of the steps. "Shit!" Alfie yelled and sprinted after her. As soon as he reached the sidewalk, he lowered his shoulder, picked up speed, and tackled her. They hit the pavement hard and Death was stunned enough that she didn't immediately try to get away. It was long enough for Alfie to pull her hands behind her back and pin her down. "I need some help here!"

"Release me!" Death screamed as she began to struggle.

Alfie felt his mind get fuzzy but not completely empty. "Umm…" He slowly lessened his hold but snapped out of it when he heard Warp's voice in his ear.

"On it," Warp answered. She morphed into a solid mass and barreled through the crowd, taking out quite a few people in her hurry to reach Alfie. She changed back to her normal form and handed Alfie a pair of handcuffs, then helped him lift Death to her feet.

"Where's War?" Nikolai asked.

"She just kicked my ass and headed out!" Ray shouted, her voice breaking in pain.

"She's mine," Nikolai growled.

"Does anybody see Famine?" Crux asked, searching the crowd from the top of the stairs.

Alfie spun around, looking for the man in black. He saw the blond man they were watching earlier staring at them. The man started when he noticed Alfie looking at him. He bared his teeth and looked like he was going to attack Alfie, but he changed his mind and ducked between a truck and a van parked on the side of the street.

"Keep her." Alfie shoved Death into Warp's hands and sprinted down the street to where he saw the man disappear. He slowed as he approached the gap. He cautiously checked to see if the man was waiting for him, but the space was empty. Alfie darted across the street, barely missing being hit by a taxi, and searched both directions down the sidewalk. He saw a blond man a dozen yards in front of him and ran after him. "Famine!" He grabbed the man's shoulder and spun him around.

"Release me!" the man shouted as he pulled out of Alfie's grasp.

Alfie took in the man's beard, business suit, and briefcase. "Sorry!" Alfie spun around, hunting for Famine. "Guys, I lost him," Alfie reluctantly admitted into his mic.

"Get back to the Exchange!" Ray ordered.

Alfie ran the two blocks back to Global Exchange to see a crowd had gathered at the foot of the steps. He found Ray halfway up the stairs staring into the crowd. "What's going on?"

Ray nodded to the center of the crowd as an answer.

Alfie's jaw dropped yet again when he saw Nikolai grappling with War. Even though War was nearly a foot shorter and probably sixty pounds lighter than Nikolai, she was more than holding her own against the Russian.

"Where's the AOJ and LeRoy?" Alfie asked, his eyes glued to the fight.

"They took Death to get locked up and retrieve Pestilence. Somehow, Gibson got him locked in the empty office building where he was working from about five blocks south of here. I was left behind to help Nikolai clean up the last Horseman."

"You're doing a great job helping," Alfie commented with a straight face.

"Well, she did kick my ass inside, so I'm enjoying Nikolai giving her a taste of that."

Alfie finally tore his eyes away from the fight and took in Ray's appearance. She had a large bump on her forehead that was already turning black and blue, a split lip, blood coming from a cut on her cheekbone, and from the way she was holding her arm across her abdomen, either a dislocated shoulder or her newly healed ribs were hurt again.

297

"Dr. Olafson is going to be so pissed about your head."

Ray sighed. "I know."

They held it together for about a half a minute before they both started laughing hysterically. Many people from the crowd turned to glare at them, which only made them laugh harder.

"Stop! We should be professional." Ray backhanded Alfie and tried to sober up, but she took one look at him and the laughing started again.

"Ouch!" Alfie flinched when War somehow managed to flip Nikolai over her shoulder and he landed hard on the pavement. The sound of their teammate hitting the sidewalk sobered them immediately.

"He's totally got her," Ray observed as she started down the stairs, but Alfie's hand on her shoulder stopped her.

"What do you mean?"

"That's what he does. Just watch."

Alfie watched as Nikolai kept hold of War's arm and pulled her to the ground. Fast as lightening, he had her face-down on the concrete, straddled her legs, and pulled her arms painfully behind her. As much as she struggled, she could not dislodge the Russian.

There was a spattering of applause as the crowd dispersed.

"We've got to get out of here." Ray quickly cuffed War and helped Nikolai to his feet. "The police are on their way and we need to get her contained before they try to take her."

"We got Pestilence in custody," Gibson reported. "How is capturing War coming?"

"Just tied her up, captain," Ray answered. She glanced up at Nikolai and grinned at the satisfied look on his face.

"What about Famine?" Alfie asked.

Ray shrugged. "They'll get him eventually. Let's go home and enjoy the weekend."

******

"Ruth! Ruth answer me!" Alfie shouted as he dug through the rubble where their father's mechanic shop had been. He choked on smoke and dust but his panic kept him going. "RUTH!"

"Alfie!"

His heart nearly stopped when he heard her quiet voice say his name. "Keep talking to me!"

"Over here!" she called.

Alfie saw her leg sticking out from underneath the remnants of the front desk. "Thank God!" He rushed over as quickly as he could while tripping over boards and hood-sliding over the poor Cutlass Supreme that had the bad luck of being in the garage when it was bombed. He dug his sister out from under the splintered wood, paying no attention to the cuts and slivers he received in the process. "Are you okay?" he cried as he pulled her into his arms.

"For the most part. My head hurts, though," she wheezed.

Alfie let go of her long enough to see that she had a long gash across her forehead. He pulled off his t-shirt and pressed the wadded-up cloth to the cut. "Hold this here." He scooped her up and carried her from the wreckage. He looked around, trying to figure out their next move when he noticed

299

their dad's old truck in the lot behind the shop. He raced around the lone wall that was still standing and gently set Ruth down next to the truck.

"What happened, Alfie?" Ruth's gaze took in what was left of George Vihar's business. "Where are mom and dad?"

"I don't know, Ruth." Alfie hesitated, unsure how much of what he suspected to tell her. "I think they were kidnapped by the same people who blew up the shop."

"WHAT?!" Ruth screamed. Her panic swamped her and she grabbed hold of Alfie as tight as she could. "What is going on?"

"Calm down." Alfie untangled himself from his sister and leaned down so he could look her in the eye. "Ruth, I am not going to let anything happen to you. I'm going to take you to the only place I know that is safe, but you have to promise me you will never go there again. You can't even tell anybody about it. Actually, forget you have ever seen it."

"What the hell, Alfie? Where are you taking me? Area 51? That's kind of a drive." Ruth's joke softened the demand for information.

Alfie quickly loaded her into the passenger seat. "Like I said, somewhere safe." Alfie slammed the door shut and ran around the front to the driver's side. He quickly jumped in and prayed that their dad didn't forget to leave the spare key under the gear stick. "Dad, you are awesome!" he shouted as his fingers touched metal. He shoved the key into the ignition, quickly threw the truck into drive, and peeled out of the parking lot, tires squealing as he raced for henchmen HQ.

He blew more than one red light as he sped through town, but the early morning traffic was light in the manufacturing district of San Luca. He wound his way through the streets, hoping to lose any tails if somebody happened to be following them, and parked in a crowded alley two blocks away from HQ.

He jumped out of the truck and hurried around to help Ruth out. "How are you doing, sis?"

"Well, my head still hurts," she joked weakly.

"Good. Pain tells you you're still alive." Alfie's chuckle was strained and short. He wrapped an arm around her and helped her walk out onto the sidewalk. He walked as fast as he dared, worry plaguing him every step of the way about attracting attention and Ruth keeping up.

They finally reached the back door of Henchmen HQ. Alfie glanced around surreptitiously before pulling the door open and dragging Ruth inside. They paused in the dim hall, and Alfie breathed a sigh of relief just before he felt Ruth go limp. "Dammit," he muttered as he pulled her into his arms and rushed down the hall and into the gym. Alfie raced across the mats and was just about to enter the medical wing when he heard his name echo around the room.

Alfie glanced over his shoulder to see Brutus standing in a doorway across the gym with his arms crossed and a dangerous look on his face. "Vihar! What the hell do you think you are doing?!"

"We were hit! She needs a doctor!" Alfie yelled back before hurrying into the medical hallway. He stopped the first nurse he came across. "I need Dr. Olafson, now!"

The nurse nodded and hit a button on her shirt. "Dr. Olafson to room four," she said into the microphone clipped to her collar. "Follow me."

"Vihar! Don't you ever walk away from me again!" Brutus bellowed just as the nurse was leading Alfie into an exam room.

"Sir, yell at me all you want, but later. My sister needs help," Alfie responded quietly. He gently laid Ruth on the examination table and stepped back so the nurse could get to work.

"What is all the yelling?" Gibson walked in carrying Alfie's bloody shirt. He took in Ruth and Alfie's injuries and Alfie's naked torso. "Found this in the hallway. I'm guessing it's yours." He tossed it on the counter.

Brutus turned on Gibson. "Your rookie brought his sister here!"

"You did what?" Gibson turned on Alfie.

"Everybody who is not the patient, get out," Dr. Olafson ordered as she walked into the room.

Brutus started to object. "Tindra-"

Dr. Olafson stared at the henchmen director silently until he started to squirm.

"Fine." He gestured impatiently.

The doctor glanced at Ruth's still form then looked Alfie over. "You look bad. I'll deal with you after I take care of her. Name, age, allergies, existing medical conditions, and relation." Dr. Olafson's tone demanded answers as quickly as possible as she picked up a clipboard from the counter.

"Ruth, 15, no allergies or conditions that I know of, my sister."

"Good." Dr. Olafson marked a few things on the clipboard. "Now out."

The nurse ushered the three men out into the hall and closed the door in their faces.

"Vihar, when the doctor finishes with you two, you're gone. You're done with Resources, Inc.," Brutus growled.

"Fine!" Alfie got in Brutus's face. "My dad's business is destroyed, my sister is hurt, and only God knows what's happening to my parents! This would've never happened if I hadn't become a henchman! When my parents are found and the men responsible are dead, I'm gone!"

"Brutus, shut up. Vihar, calm down. You're not going anywhere."

Alfie felt his anger drain away as shock replaced it. Gibson did not talk back to the director like that. Brutus was so stunned he couldn't speak.

"What the hell happened? Why would you bring her here instead of to a hospital? And why do you think you were attacked because you work here?"

"My parents, Ruth, and I were at my dad's garage when all hell broke loose. Somebody had left a voicemail on the house phone that there was a break in at the garage. We stopped to check it out on our way out of town to see my brothers. Two masked men rushed in, grabbed my parents and got out before I could react. A third tried to grab Ruth, but I managed to fight him off long enough for him to rethink it and for Ruth to get away. He took off, then some kind of explosive or grenade came flying in the window and blew. The guys who did it are trained, either military or henchmen. I doubt my parents are into anything that would lead to commandos blowing up the garage and Ruth sure as hell isn't."

"Who's trying to kill you?" Gibson asked.

"I don't think they were. It came in the furthest window from Ruth and me. If they wanted me dead, it would have been easier for one of the men to put a bullet in me or to throw the grenade at my feet rather than across the building."

"Good deduction." Gibson nodded. "You were right coming here. If they want you or Ruth, they'll be checking hospitals now. You're safer here."

"She can't be here!" Brutus finally burst in.

"Where would you like us to send her? Put her in the street with a target on her forehead? Take out a full-page ad that says 'Ruth Vihar is at home, come and get her'? Would that work for you?" Gibson growled. "They stay while we figure out who did this. Vihar, you're bleeding all over the floor."

Alfie looked down at a cut on his arm that had started dripping down his fingers. "Awesome." He ducked into the next exam room and grabbed a stack of gauze pads before stepping back into the hall.

"Brutus, is there no chatter about an attack on a henchman's family?" Gibson was asking.

"None that we've heard. I'll get somebody on sorting through it all looking specifically for that. Are you sure this was an attack and not just a... gas leak or something?" Brutus asked, grasping at straws.

The death glare Gibson gave him spoke volumes of what he thought of the director's theory. "We both know that's bullshit. Vihar, we will get working on this and get your parents back. Sit down in there and wait for the doctor."

"We don't have the job so I'll have to clear it with upstairs," Brutus argued.

"When did you become such a bureaucrat, Brutus? You will tell upstairs that we are getting the boy's parents back and protecting his family," Gibson ordered. Brutus glared at him but finally headed for his office to do as he was told.

"Can somebody pick up my brothers, too?" Alfie called after him.

Brutus nodded without turning around. "Yeah, I'll tell my boss we are breaking the rules, then I will pick up some brothers, possibly a brother-in-law, too. Anybody else? Maybe the dog walker? I have nothing more important to work on today." His muttering trailed off as he left the hallway.

Twenty minutes later, Alfie was on an exam table while Dr. Olafson bandaged up his wounds and he reviewed the morning's event with Gibson.

Brutus walked into the examination room and cut into their conversation. "Vihar, I've talked to upstairs. We will protect your family, but they do not support an official operation to rescue your parents." Brutus turned a sharp eye on Gibson. "No official action can be taken. Whatever you idiots do in your own time, I don't care."

"Sir, what about Tessa?" Alfie asked. "If my family is being targeted, she might get caught in the crosshairs, too."

Brutus flipped through some papers on the clipboard he carried. "Contessa Pellegrini? She works for S&T. Let them protect her." He handed Gibson a small stack of papers. "This is all we could uncover. Good luck."

"Thanks," Gibson said dryly as Brutus left. He flipped through it quickly. "It's not much, Vihar. We'll go see what LeRoy and my spyware can uncover."

"Good timing. I am done." Dr. Olafson snipped the last thread and wrapped some gauze around Alfie's forearm. She held up a small prescription bottle. "Pain killers. They're low dosage, but don't take them if you're planning on doing something stupid." She stabbed a syringe into Alfie's shoulder. "Antibiotics, just in case." She stripped off her rubber gloves and exited the room.

"Sir, I'm still worried about Tessa. I don't get the feeling that S&T cares much about their henchmen."

"I agree. I'll send somebody to pick her up."

"Thanks." Alfie sighed in relief as he hopped off the table and pulled the t-shirt Gibson had brought him from his locker over his head. "Sir, I can't ask you to help me-"

"You already did." Gibson smiled slightly. "We'll get them back."

******

"Thank you all for coming in on your day off." Gibson leaned heavily against his desk and looked over the henchmen gathered in Team 9's den. All of Team 9 had come running when they heard about the attack on Alfie's family. Tina, Erin, and November of Team 7 had also come in to help when Gibson sent Tina an S.O.S.

Alfie sat on the couch with a bandaged Ruth tucked close to his side. Tina sat on her other side, waiting to help should either of the injured Vihar siblings need it. A ruckus at the door turned attention from Gibson.

"Tessa! What're you doing here?!" Ruth nearly screamed as she jumped unsteadily to her feet. Alfie and Tina both reached out to steady her.

Tessa violently pulled away from the escort who had a hold on her arm and rushed through the bodies standing between them to pull Ruth into a crushing hug. "I'm so glad you're okay!" Tessa had tears in her eyes when she pulled back so she could look Ruth over. "Alfie?"

"I'm okay, too." Alfie stood and gave her a small smile.

She made a choking sound and pulled him into the hug with Ruth. "I couldn't believe my eyes when I saw the garage! I'm so glad you are both alive! What happened? Do you know how your parents are?"

Alfie pulled out of his friend's death hold and motioned for her and Ruth to sit down on the couch. He nodded his thanks when Nikolai handed him a chair from the table. "You saw the garage? I didn't get a good look, I just wanted to get Ruth away. Is it completely totaled?"

"We drove by it. There's not much left." Tessa shook her head sadly. "It will have to be leveled and rebuilt from scratch. Your parents?"

"Gibson was just going to brief us." Alfie turned and nodded at the team captain.

"Thanks, Vihar." Gibson walked over to shake Tessa's hand. "Welcome to Resources, Inc. Henchmen HQ, Miss Pellegrini. For everybody who doesn't know, this is Contessa Pellegrini, on loan to us from S&T because of her ties to the Vihar family."

"Tessa, please." Tessa waved awkwardly at the other henchmen.

"This is what we have theorized about this morning's attack from the little information we have been able to dig up." Gibson jumped into the issue at hand. "We believe that it was executed by private contractors working for the Four Horsemen."

"What?" Ray sat up. "We have three of them in custody. How would they pull that off?"

307

"Why did they attack us and take my parents?" Alfie asked quietly. He leaned forward and rested his elbows on his knees.

"We won't know for sure until they contact us." Gibson sighed heavily and crossed his arms. "My theory is that this is Famine's play to get his team back."

"Warp said he looked pretty pissed when we captured Death." LeRoy crossed his legs and settled back in his chair. "I can't imagine hearing we had Pestilence and War made him feel any better."

"Could he be taking revenge for that?" Tina asked.

Gibson shook his head. "I don't see why he would go after Vihar's family when LeRoy should have been their primary attack if revenge was what they were after. After all, it was his plan that ruined what they were doing in New Orleans and their failure in New Orleans is how we found them in London."

"Thanks, captain," LeRoy commented dryly. "But they would be pretty hard- pressed to find me or my family. I have us so far buried, it's amazing we even see daylight."

"Should the rest of us be concerned for our families?" Ray asked suddenly.

"When I told upstairs that we believed the attack was orchestrated by Famine, Brutus sent people out to collect the families of Team 9. Tina, November, Erin, they are also collecting your families. Brutus just wanted to be cautious since we have worked together recently."

"Thanks," Tina sighed in relief.

"So we have upstairs' approval?" Alfie asked eagerly.

Gibson nodded. "We do."

"Is the AOJ coming in on this?" November asked.

"Not officially." Gibson shrugged his shoulders. "I have heard rumblings that one or two might help us out as private citizens rather than it being an official AOJ project."

"It's just me," Bullet said from where he was leaning against the doorframe.

Gibson nodded and motioned for Bullet to join them. "Well, we welcome the help."

"I'm glad the AOJ isn't working on this. They'll just mess it up," Alfie spat venomously. He paused in thought and turned toward Bullet. "No offense, man."

Bullet smiled kindly. "None taken."

Alfie stood to shake Bullet's hand. "Gibson, can I say something real quick?" The team captain nodded his consent. Alfie turned and looked at each of them. "I want to let you know how grateful I am that you are giving up your time and energy, and potentially your safety, to help get my parents back. I know I speak for my sister, my brothers, and myself when I say that we will forever be thankful."

Ruth echoed Alfie's thanks as he sat back down.

"We have plan?" Nikolai spoke for the first time.

"Not yet. Brutus has most of the intelligence unit working on this but they haven't found much yet. LeRoy, I want you to work on it with me, also."

"Yes, sir."

"I'll help you, too," Erin volunteered. Gibson nodded his thanks.

"As for the rest of you, if you have any contacts who might know anything about the Four Horsemen, get a hold of them. We haven't known so little about an adversary in a very long time and it is making Brutus cranky. Let's get as much information as we can and take these bastards down."

"Yes, sir!" the henchmen said in unison.

"They've made contact." Brutus walked into the den holding a sheet of paper above his head. The henchmen all settled back into their seats to hear what the director found.

Alfie jumped to his feet. "Who are they? Is it for sure the Four Horsemen? What do they want?"

Brutus stood next to Gibson and crossed his arms. "It's confirmed. It's the so-called Famine from the Four Horsemen. He is demanding that we release Death in exchange for the Vihars."

"Just Death, not the other two?" Gibson asked.

"He didn't mention them. Just that he wanted Death."

Tina looked up from the notepad she was scribbling away on. "What about demands for money?"

"Didn't mention money either." Brutus shook his head.

"Do you think it's her powers?" Gibson asked.

"Powers?" Brutus looked to Gibson in confusion.

Gibson nodded. "She has a supernatural way of persuading people to do what she wants. It works better on men, but women are affected also. That's how she almost escaped last night. Ray and LeRoy figured it out when she talked her way out of her cell but couldn't get past them."

Good work," Brutus commended them. "Famine seemed to legitimately care about Death's treatment. It could be her powers influencing him, or he cares about her personally."

Alfie frowned. "Powers? Is that how she almost got away from me twice in London?"

"I didn't know she did." Gibson studied Alfie. "What happened?"

"I don't know." Alfie shrugged. "She told me to let her go and my mind just sort of blanked. Next thing I knew, Warp was yelling at me to get her."

"The guards said pretty much the same thing." Ray looked to LeRoy for confirmation.

LeRoy nodded. "The one couldn't figure out how he was handcuffed to the cell bars. Video showed him cuffing himself."

"We think it's either something in her touch or eyes. All of the guards were within arm's reach of her when she was working her magic. Her voice doesn't seem to be extra persuasive since the people who questioned her were unaffected," Ray continued.

"My theory is it's more of a pheromone, but I'd have to do a few tests to confirm that. Erin, would you be able to help me with that?" LeRoy grinned.

Erin made a face at him. "You've got the mad scientist look."

"Oh stop, LeRoy," Ray scolded. "Brutus, I don't think it's her powers. They seem to only work in close proximity, which fortifies the theory of control by touch."

"Married," Nikolai announced suddenly.

"What?" Gibson asked.

Nikolai crossed his legs. "They're married. When I threw War in van with her, Death said husband would kill us all."

"That could be why he went after the Vihars. Alfie was the one to take down Death," LeRoy suggested.

"And you didn't think that was important?" Brutus asked, his tone quiet and deadly.

Nikolai shrugged. "In my report."

Tina's shrill whistle cut through the ruckus between Brutus, Gibson, and Nikolai. "Pissing contest later. Did Famine give a location and time for the swap?"

Brutus grumbled under his breath then looked down at the sheet he had crumpled in his hand. "Yes. He wants to make the swap at the Sunny Dale Mall on the north side of San Luca at 1200 hours today. He said he has eyes on the mall and if we try to clear it out, he will…" Brutus trailed off as he glanced at Alfie and Ruth.

"He will what?" Alfie demanded.

"Kill the Vihars," Brutus reluctantly finished.

Alfie collapsed back in his chair as Ruth cried out. Tessa wrapped her arms around Ruth, trying to comfort her.

"That's a lot of bystanders." November leaned back on the couch.

LeRoy nodded in agreement. "He doesn't think we'll try anything with that much potential collateral damage."

"And only-" Erin paused as she looked down at her watch, "two hours and 36 minutes to come up with a plan."

"Did he say where in the mall?" Alfie asked with a frown, his mind racing, trying to come up with a plan to save his parents.

"No, he didn't." Brutus crossed his arms and leaned back against Gibson's desk. "But he is going to contact us at 1100 for more instructions."

Alfie glanced over at Tessa, who was playing with her phone and whispering to Ruth. He nudged her foot with his toe. "Dude," he whispered.

"What? Oh, sorry." Tessa swiped her fingers across the screen one last time and looked up at Brutus and Gibson. "How many people do you have available right now?"

"What? Who is this?" Brutus looked at Gibson in confusion.

"Tessa Pellegrini." Tessa stood and held out her hand for Brutus to shake. "On loan from S&T."

Brutus's eyes narrowed. "Oh, you're that one."

"Yeah, I'm that one. How many people do you have available right now?" Tessa repeated her question.

"You got an idea?" Alfie asked, standing and looking over her shoulder at the phone still in her hand.

"Half of an idea, and most of it came from Ruth."

Everybody in the room turned their attention to Ruth, who suddenly tried to melt into the couch.

"Do you have a 3-D imager or a projection table?" Tessa asked.

"Oh, honey." LeRoy smirked at her as he pulled his phone out of one pocket and a small device out of the other. He snapped them together then tapped the screen a few times and set it in the middle of the table. Suddenly, a three-foot-tall holographic model of San Luca appeared on the table.

Tessa whistled. "That is cool."

"When did we get that?" Alfie asked, walking over to examine the model. He found the skyscraper that housed Resources, Inc.'s headquarters and tried to poke at it, but his finger went right through the model.

"It's a hologram genius." LeRoy rolled his eyes. "What did you want to see?" he asked Tessa.

"This." She held up her phone.

"Let me see." LeRoy took her phone, touched the screen a few times to send the image to his phone, then the hologram of San Luca morphed into the blueprints of the Sunny Dale Mall.

"Okay, what's your idea?"

Tessa turned to Alfie's sister. "Ruth?"

"Why can't you just tell?" Ruth mumbled as she stood up from the couch. She stalled by scratching under the bandage that wrapped around her head. "I just commented that if you could section off a part of the mall to keep civilians out, you could fill it with your people to reduce the chance of somebody getting hurt, but Famine would still think there were shoppers around and not be tipped off."

LeRoy nudged Alfie with his elbow. "Are you sure she wouldn't be interested in being a supervillain?"

"No!" Alfie snapped.

"It's not a bad idea, Brutus." Gibson walked around the model, his arms crossed, studying the layout. He pointed at an area on the south side of the mall. "This wing here only has two entrances and is pretty isolated from the rest of the mall. I think it would be a good place to do it."

Tina joined Gibson and Brutus at the table. "How are we going to evacuate without tipping off Famine?"

"I'll call Isha." Erin pulled out her phone. "She can get a dozen plain-clothes there in ten minutes. They can start a casual evac and do it quietly enough that it won't tip off Famine."

"Who's Isha?" Alfie asked.

"San Luca's chief of police and Erin's wife," November explained quietly as Erin walked away to make her call.

"Wait..." Alfie frowned. "A henchman is married to the chief of police? Does she know what Erin does for a living?"

November wagged her head back and forth. "Isha knows, but nobody lets on that Isha knows. It's safer for her that way. To the world, Erin sells insurance."

"What a sucky job."

November laughed. "It's just a cover, Alfie." She snapped around to eye Bullet where he stood a few feet behind them. "That doesn't leave this room."

His eyes widened slightly at the dangerous edge in her voice. "Of course. I'm just another henchman. No AOJ member here."

November nodded once before turning back around.

"Water main break," Nikolai said suddenly.

All conversation stopped as everybody turned to look at him where he sat in the corner.

November sidled up to Nikolai and wrapped an arm around his shoulders. "Care to explain, Ruski?"

"Clear people out of building." Nikolai explained simply.

Tessa shook her head. "If you get rid of everybody, we won't have the backup and Famine will know."

"What about a power outage in that wing?" LeRoy suggested.

"Still won't explain the backup. Shoppers would leave the area," Tina pointed out.

"Replace the employees," Ruth mumbled.

Alfie turned to look at her with wide eyes. "*Are* you an evil genius?!"

Ruth grinned. "Just a genius."

Alfie laughed and pulled Ruth into his arms. "My sister is a genius! We can clear the area with a power outage or a water main break, but before that happens, we just clear out the store employees and put our people in their place! They'd be expected to stay if there was an issue like that, even if there were no customers."

Erin walked back into the den. "Isha will have her people there by ten."

Brutus nodded and headed for the door. "Let's roll with it. I have two units here right now that we can use. Gibson, Wilkins, catch Skarret up and have her call the chief back with the update. Gibson, can you cut power to that wing from here?"

"I should be able to remote into the power grid, yes."

"Good. Do it. I'll have a dummy accident set up at the transformer to sell the outage. Gibson, let me know when you're ready to pull the plug and it'll happen. You and Wilkins clear up the details. We leave here at 1115," Brutus yelled the last over his shoulder as he walked out of the room.

Gibson quickly filled Erin in on the plan to replace the employees with henchmen and to cut the power to help the evacuation along. Then he joined Tina at the table where she studied the model while Erin called Isha back with the update.

"LeRoy, pull up a closer view of just that wing," Tina ordered.

LeRoy tapped the screen on Tessa's phone a few times and the hologram changed to show them just the wing Gibson had picked out for the operation.

"Can you put markers in?" Tina asked.

"Of course. What would you like?"

"I want Bullet here." Tina pointed to the overhang above the large department store's entrance. "He will have a clear view of the entire wing and he will be well hidden behind the marquee."

LeRoy tapped away on the phone and a small silhouette of a prone figure complete with rifle showed up on the model where Tina was pointing.

"Scatter ten henchmen in the stores on both sides," Gibson added as he circled the table.

LeRoy had ten figures inserted in the model in a few seconds.

"I think this will be the best place for us to set up for the trade-off." Gibson pointed at an open square in the middle of the wing. "Tina and I will have hands on Death. November, Erin, and Nikolai will be close by. Ray, LeRoy, and Vihar will be the furthest out."

"What about me?" Tessa asked.

"I don't know what you're capable of and frankly, I don't trust you, so I don't want you there," Gibson said bluntly.

"What?!" Tessa burst out.

"Captain, I can vouch for her," Alfie jumped to his friend's defense.

"That's great, Vihar. Doesn't change my mind." Gibson's tone was bland as he studied the hologram.

"From S&T," Nikolai growled as he stalked past Tessa and joined Gibson and Tina at the table.

"I may work for S&T but that doesn't mean I'm incapable of helping!"

"Sir, she's my best friend. She loves my parents almost as much as I do. Please let her help," Alfie begged, trying to appeal to Gibson's softer side, which he hoped actually existed.

Gibson finally looked up from the model and stared at Alfie and Tessa for a long minute as if trying to bore into their minds and read their every thought. Tina walked over to him and whispered into his ear. He shook his head sharply once. She whispered something else and he finally turned his eyes to her. He whispered something to her before turning his attention back to the hologram.

"Ms. Pelegrini can join us, but she will be stationed in one of the stores. She will not be involved in the exchange."

"But-"

Alfie clamped a hand over his friend's mouth. "She'll take it."

Ruth glanced around the room. "What about me? Can I-"

"NO!" ten voices shouted at once.

******

Gibson hung up his phone. "All right, team. It's time."

There was a flurry of activity as everybody jumped to their feet, gathered their gear and followed Gibson from the den. He stopped in front of a set of elevator doors that Alfie had never noticed before.

"When did we get an elevator?"

"When they remodeled the building in 1999," Ray whispered.

LeRoy glanced at Alfie. "Seriously, how have you never noticed it before? It's not exactly hidden."

Alfie shrugged. "Does it just go to the upper levels or is there some secret subterranean base I don't know about?"

Just then, the doors opened and they all came face to face with a figure in an expensive, fitted black suit with a black bag over her head and her hands gloved and cuffed behind her back. The two guards nodded at Gibson and passed the person to him without a word.

"Come along, Death." Gibson grabbed a hold of her upper arm and walked her away from the elevator. Tina took her other arm and the team fell in behind them.

"The elevators don't go up. They just go down to a few different labs, testing areas, and the detention block on the lowest level," November finally answered Alfie's question in a hushed voice.

"And they're not really a secret to people who work here," Erin added from behind Alfie.

"You guys really need to work on your orientation process," Alfie grumbled.

Gibson stopped in the hall just inside the door. "Nikolai and Ray you're in the car with us. LeRoy, Bullet, and November in the lead car. Erin, Vihar, and Pellegrini in the trail car. Stay together, but keep some distance. Everybody keep your eyes open. Full coms. If one of you sneezes, I want to be able to hear it."

"Gross."

"Shut it, Vihar. Let's go."

Nikolai and Bullet moved to walk in front of the team captains and the prisoner, and the group quickly pushed through the door out into the street.

"Stop right there!"

The henchmen froze as the voice echoed around them, unsure as to where it came from. Suddenly, the street in front of them was filled with dozens of people, all with guns pointed at the henchmen.

"Captain?" Ray whispered, surreptitiously reaching for the pistol holstered on her hip.

"Stay," Gibson quietly ordered his team. He left Death in Tina's grasp and took a few steps forward with his hands out to his sides.

"I said stop!" A tall, good-looking man in an all black power suit stepped through the line of people directly across from the henchmen and dropped a bullhorn on the ground. "Don't move another inch, or my men will kill you all." His voice oozed control and ego.

"Good to finally meet you, Famine," Gibson called calmly. "This doesn't look like the Sunny Dale Mall."

Famine smiled coldly. "Oh, a little surprise never hurt anyone."

"Where are my parents, you bastard?!" Alfie yelled. Tessa and LeRoy grabbed him by the arms to keep him from rushing forward.

Famine took a few steps to the side so he could see where Alfie stood behind the other henchmen. "Ah, young Alfred Vihar. So good to meet you. Your parents are lovely people. It's such a shame they raised a son who would lie to them like you have."

"Where are they?!" Alfie screamed again as he tugged against the restraining hands of his friends. November stepped behind him and wrapped her arms around his midsection to help when it looked like he was going to get away from Tessa and LeRoy.

"How's your sister doing?" Famine swaggered forward until he was a few feet from the henchmen. "She was the real target, you know. What I could have done with a young genius mind like that..." Famine tisked. "I guess I'll never know... unless you're willing to throw her in the pot? I have two prisoners, you only have one, it would seem like I am getting shorted."

"You son of a bitch!" Alfie struggled to get free until Nikolai calmly elbowed him in the gut. Alfie would have dropped to his knees if it weren't for his teammates holding him up.

"You asked for Death in exchange for the Vihars." Gibson slowly moved between Alfie and Famine to draw the villain's attention. "Your wife is right here. We can make this exchange right now. Where are the Vihars?"

"Oh, they're safe." Famine picked a bit of lint off of his sleeve like he had not a care in the world. "You hand over Death and as soon as we are away, I will call you with the location of where I am keeping the Vihars."

"No!" Alfie exclaimed.

Gibson held up a hand indicating for Alfie to stop talking. "I'll need proof of life."

Famine sighed. "Why are people so untrusting?" he mumbled as he lazily pulled out his phone.

"Maybe because you kidnapped innocent bystanders," Tessa growled. Gibson threw her a molten glare over his shoulder.

"Is anybody really innocent, Contessa Pellegrini?" Famine asked as he tapped his phone's screen.

Gibson's eyes narrowed when Famine called Tessa by her name. "So you've done your homework on us."

"Why yes, Jeremiah Gibson, I have." Famine grinned and raised his hand to point at each one of them individually. "Nikolai Maklakov, Evelyn Green known as Ray to her friends, LeRoy Monte-Piere who was recently known as *La Grenouille* Bouché. You really couldn't have come up with a better alter ego than 'the stupid frog'?"

"It is better than some, Famine," LeRoy gritted out from behind clenched teeth.

Famine smirked and continued with his role call. "Erin Skarret, Tina Wilkins, November Falls, and finally Daniel Zenkle otherwise known as Bullet from the Alliance of Justice." Famine's smug smile slid from his face and his eyes turned cold. "I am very well aware of who you are, who your families are, and where to find them. I only took two of them when I could have taken them all. I can be kind."

Erin grabbed Tessa's arm when she took a step toward Famine. "Calm down," she whispered.

Famine held the phone up to his ear as he turned to retrieve the bullhorn he had discarded. He said a few things into the phone and then held it up to the bullhorn.

Vivian Vihar's voice filled the street. "I don't understand what-"

"MOM!" Alfie screamed, dropping to his knees. Gibson whipped around to face Alfie and knelt in front of him. He pulled out his phone and started furiously tapping on the screen.

"Alfie?" Vivian's voice took on a panicked note. "Alfie, are you okay? Where's Ruth?"

"Mom! I'm fine! Ruth is safe! How are you? Is dad with you?" Alfie yelled.

"We are alive, Alfie. What's going on?"

"Where are you, Mom? Can you see anything?"

"Now, you know you can't answer that, Vivian," Famine said before she could answer.

"Keep her talking," Gibson whispered to Alfie.

"Mom, are you hurt?" Alfie called.

"I-" Vivian's voice cracked. "I'm okay. Your father is badly hurt, but he's alive."

"Was it the explosion, Mom?" Alfie asked, scrambling for more things to keep her on the line.

Vivian hesitated. "Mostly."

"You bastard," Alfie whispered, glaring at Famine.

Gibson put a hand on Alfie's shoulder, keeping the younger man on the ground. "Keep talking," he whispered again.

"Mom, Ruth is okay. She got a good knock on her head, but she's safe. She's being watched by one of the best doctors in California."

"Good!" Vivian's relief was audible. "What about... Have you let your brothers know she's okay?"

"Yes! I called them about an hour ago. They were- relieved to know we're okay." Alfie glanced at Gibson, pleading with his team captain to hurry with whatever he was doing.

Gibson suddenly glanced at Alfie for the briefest of seconds and nodded slightly, letting him know that whatever Gibson had been working on was a success.

"Mom?"

"Yes, honey."

"I'm going to get you and Dad back!" Alfie yelled. "I love you!"

"We love-"

Famine ended the phone call. "Well, that was too sappy for my taste." He tossed the bullhorn to one of his men and turned back to the henchmen. "Satisfied?"

Alfie wiped tears from his cheeks with the backs of his hands. "Captain?" he whispered.

Gibson wiped the sweat off of his forehead and slowly stood, pulling Alfie to his feet as he did. November wrapped her arms around Alfie, just in case he decided to go off halfcocked again. Tessa and LeRoy retook their holds on Alfie's arms.

Gibson turned to Famine after carefully tucking away his cell phone. "For the most part. I would have been happier to hear from both of the Vihars."

Famine shrugged. "I'm not really in the mood to make you happy. Release Death now and the Vihars will come to no more harm."

"Why didn't you bring them with you? That is normally how hostage exchanges work," Tina said, breaking her silence.

"Seeing as I don't have to explain my actions to you, I won't," Famine sneered. "Release Death!"

Gibson threw out his arm, blocking Death as she took a step forward. "Release the Vihars. Once I get word they are free, your wife goes free."

"Hmm, I like my way better."

"There is nowhere we can go. We are no threat to you. Let them go, and I will let your wife go."

The sound of a scuffle had everybody turning toward where the circle of gunmen met the side of the building. One lackey was helping another to his feet and waved when he noticed attention turned to them. "Sorry, he locked his knees and fainted for a second. I've never seen a grown man drop like that!"

"Dalton," November breathed. She surreptitiously pulled Alfie's pistol from his holster and pressed it into his hand. "Get ready."

Alfie was suddenly aware that his teammates were all covertly arming themselves with their weapons of choice. He kept his attention on the two lackeys who had ruined Famine's moment. His eyes widened when he recognized one of them as a henchman from Team 1. Emotions rolled through him, first betrayal that his company would rent henchmen to the people who kidnapped his parents. That was replaced when logic told him that RI worked hard to keep their people from working opposing sides of the same mission. Finally, he realized that Gibson had somehow called back the units that were chosen to go ahead of Team 9 to the mall and they were slowly infiltrating Famine's ranks.

Alfie watched as two men crept out from behind a car and silently took down two of the gunmen and tucked them away before taking their spots in the line. He had never seen anybody move that silently, let alone render two armed men unconscious without alerting the people standing within ten feet of them.

"I grow weary. Release Death and I won't kill you all."

"Alfie, now," November whispered as she slowly released him. LeRoy and Tessa had heard her quiet direction and loosed their grips.

Alfie ripped away from them with a scream and tackled Death. The pair stumbled out from the protection of the henchmen into the open space before Famine.

"Wise boy," Famine complimented Alfie's action, but spoke too soon.

Alfie raised his pistol and pressed the barrel against Death's temple. "Release my parents or I blow her head off."

"Vihar! What the hell are you doing?" Gibson barked.

"I grew weary of the talking," Alfie's sneer rivaled Famine's. "Stay out of this, captain!"

Fear flashed on Famine's face before he covered it up with a calming smile. He held his hands out and took a step toward Alfie.

"Stay where you are!" Alfie ordered.

Famine froze. "No need to be hasty, son. Let's talk, you and I."

Alfie glanced behind Famine and saw henchmen replace three more gunmen. By his estimation, all ten were now in place, evening the odds enough that the henchmen had a good chance of winning should fighting break out.

"Don't you dare call me son! I have only one father, and he is twice the man that you are!"

"Really?" Famine scoffed. "Then why do I have him chained up and at my mercy?"

Alfie narrowed his eyes as he felt a profound calm roll through him. He heard somebody's foot scrape concrete behind him and knew his team was moving. Time slowed as he flicked the safety off his gun, swung it around, and fired.

******

"Am I the only one who can't believe that Alfie actually shot Famine?" November popped open a beer and dropped onto the couch next to Nikolai. She swung around to lay her legs across his lap. She handed him the second beer that she had snagged from the cooler on the table.

"Only the shoulder. He will live." Nikolai opened the beer and took a swig.

"I'm kind of pissed that I didn't get to after what he said about George." Tessa hopped up on the table with a Coke and a slice of pizza.

"How the hell did the other units get there so quickly?" Ray opened a beer and joined Tessa on the table. "They had to have been half way across town when Famine cornered us."

"Aren't you guys working on teleportation or something ridiculous like that?" Bullet teased as he sat on the table next to Ray. He held his can out to Ray and, after a long pause, she silently tapped her beer against it, agreeing to his silent request for peace.

"That's still a few years away," LeRoy mumbled around a bite of pizza.

"Seriously?" Everybody turned to the door at the unknown voice. Erin walked in with her arm around a beautiful Indian woman in a dark pinstriped pantsuit. Her black hair was pulled back in a bun, and the slightest glint of a gold shield could be seen on her belt under her jacket.

"You didn't hear that," Erin whispered loudly to her wife then waved at the henchmen. "Everybody, this is Isha. Isha, this is everybody." The henchmen casually welcomed their teammate's wife into their group as if a stranger in the building was normal.

"Beer in the cooler, pizza on the table," November offered.

"I'm good, thanks." Erin settled into a chair she pulled from around the table. Isha followed her lead and sat down next to her. "Any word on Alfie's parents yet?"

"Brutus came in about ten minutes ago and said that they were safe. The helicopter was sent out to retrieve them and bring them back here for emergency medical care. Alfie flew out on the helicopter so he could be there when they were rescued," Ray answered.

"And Alfie's sister?"

"Dr. Olafson came to get her just before you came in to run some more tests. They want to make sure she doesn't have a concussion or any other issues from the explosion this morning," November responded.

Katherine Wielechowski

"And Famine?"

"The good doc patched him up and he and his team are now in federal custody," Gibson said, walking into the room. He stopped and eyed the refreshments the henchmen were enjoying. "Just don't let Brutus catch you with the alcohol."

"Brutus doesn't really care what the hell you all do right now." The large man walked into the den behind Gibson and collapsed into the armchair. "New rule: no more standoffs or gunfights on the back step of this place."

"Here, here!" LeRoy raised his beer in the air to cheers the new rule. The others agreed and followed suit.

"The Vihars have landed and are being rushed to the hospital as we speak." Tina finally joined them and brought good news with her.

The henchmen once again raised their drinks in celebration.

"Don't celebrate too soon. Vivian is banged up but doing pretty well. She has a few broken ribs, a shattered femur, and lots of cuts and bruises. A lot of them were defensive wounds so we know where Alfie got his scrappiness. George is in bad shape. He has been unconscious since shortly after we got to them. He's got a pretty bad head wound and internal bleeding, a broken nose, two or three broken bones in his left leg, and a dislocated shoulder. Dr. Olafson wanted him in surgery as soon as possible."

"What the hell did they do to him?!" Tessa cried.

Ray awkwardly wrapped an arm around her as she burst into tears.

Tina walked over and put a hand on Tessa's shoulder. "Alfie and Ruth are waiting in the medical wing. Would you like to join them?"

Tessa nodded and slid from the table. Tina wrapped an arm around her and escorted her from the room.

"Brutus, I think our system needs to be revamped a bit when it comes to protecting henchmen's families from backlash." Ray's tone was cold.

Brutus ran a hand over his shaved scalp and nodded. "Upstairs is already working on it. They are also working on increasing our computer system's security. Famine should not have been able to find out who you all are."

"Do they have any leads as to how he found out?" Gibson asked.

Brutus nodded slowly. "It took us about a half an hour to get to Pestilence after we took down Death and War. We think he somehow blasted through our firewalls, got the information, and sent it to Famine before we took him into custody."

They all sat in silence, absorbing what Brutus said. Bullet reached into the cooler and tossed a beer to Brutus. The director of RI's Henchmen Division stared at it for a long moment before cracking it open and draining it. He crushed the can and tossed it back to Bullet.

"The AOJ is going to be mad they missed this one." Bullet grinned into his beer.

Brutus started as if he had just realized that Isha was in the room. "This goes without saying, Chief…"

"My lips are sealed, Director." Isha's Indian accent had an English lilt and was soothing to the caustic mood of the room.

329

"Back to work." Brutus stood with a sigh and left without another word.

"All right, everybody." Gibson stood from his desk. "You don't have to hang around here any longer. Brutus has approved five days off for all of you and we will debrief when you get back."

The henchmen refused to move. If anything, they settled deeper into their seats and stared at Gibson. He nodded and gave them a half smile. "I'll let Vihar know that you are here for him."

******

Gibson raised his hand to get everybody's attention. Their five days were over and Teams 7 and 9 were back at work. All the henchmen who had worked to get the Vihars back from Famine were gathered in Team 9's den. "I have good news. Due to Brutus approving the use of some of our less-risky experimental healing techniques, the Vihars were released yesterday and are at home resting."

The collective cheers were loud enough to make passing henchmen stop in the doorway to see what was going on.

"Brutus decided to do the review that an employer would do and he ranked you all very high. Once the fighting started, you all worked well as a team and you did a very good job not killing the henchmen who were disguised as Famine's lackeys. Vihar, once again you were proven right about the hired guns not backing off when the leader was taken out. Apparently, our villains are getting better trained employees. And while I appreciate your quick thinking, your stunt with Death could have gotten you killed immediately.

Thankfully, it didn't and the time you bought the other units to get into place made all the difference."

"Woo Alfie!" November cheered. The others quickly congratulated him also.

Alfie shrank back from their adulation. "November told me to act."

"Well then, good job November!"

"Go me!" November laughed and hugged Alfie.

Tina took over for Gibson. "This operation really proved what a group of henchmen can do given the right circumstances. We have never had such cooperation between two teams before, and we have definitely never allowed a henchman from Stealth & Tactics to join us on a job. The plan was very well executed and the job was a success. You all should be very proud of yourselves."

Alfie stood suddenly and strode to his locker. He ripped open his duffle bag and started stuffing his belongings into it. The other henchmen watched in baffled silence. When the last of it was packed, Alfie zipped up his bag and slung it onto his shoulder. He headed to the door but stopped just before he exited the room. He pulled an envelope out of his back pocket and tossed it toward the coffee table. "My mom sent you all a thank you card for saving her and my dad. Since the henchmen business is the reason they needed saving in the first place, maybe we all should send her an apology card." He pulled a folded piece of paper out of his front pocket and dropped it on the floor at his feet. "My resignation. I'm glad I met you all and I really like you as people, but please don't be offended if I never talk to you again." Alfie left without another word.

"Alfie! Your family is safe! What are you doing?" Ray chased after him, trying to get him to come back to the den. "Stop, Alfie!" She caught up to him in the hallway leading to the back door. She grabbed his arm and pulled him to a stop.

Alfie spun around. The look in his eyes made Ray release him immediately. She had never seen him look so cold, or so dangerous.

"I am done. I am the reason my dad almost died and my mom was beat to hell. I'm the reason my genius little sister is on their list. I am the reason my best friend threw away her future as a doctor. I don't know what I ever thought I was doing being a henchman!" Alfie suddenly growled and lashed out, punching the cinderblock wall.

Ray gasped when she saw blood start running out of the cuts on his hand. "Alfie-"

"No. I'm not coming back, Ray. I'm done with this place and everybody in it. Goodbye." Alfie slung his bag back onto his shoulder and slammed out of Henchmen HQ into the sunlight.

1-800-Henchmen

Katherine Wielechowski

Half-Past Misadventure

When I originally released 1-800-Henchmen: Four Horsemen, I didn't include LeRoy's short adventure as the super villain, La Grenouille Bouché, *because the focus was on Alfie's life falling apart and of course, the Four Horsemen. I always planned on sharing the story and releasing the series in print is the perfect opportunity. This would fit into Four Horsemen on page 268.*

"I'm so glad you henchmen could finally join us." *La Grenouille Bouché* sauntered down the stairs from the warehouse's upper level, flourishing his cape behind him.

"We literally left the airport right behind him," Alfie muttered to Erin. "There's no way he got here fast enough to do more than run up the stairs."

"He does love his entrances," Erin chuckled.

Alfie rolled his eyes. "You have no idea."

The pair stifled their laughter as Gibson glared at them over his shoulder.

LeRoy clapped his gloved hands sharply. "I have uniforms for you in these boxes. You may wear your current gear belts. Your uniforms won't be as aesthetically pleasing with them, but I understand that you will need your equipment. There are rooms back there where you can change." LeRoy waved lazily to a doorway under the stairs, then turned his attention to a bank of computers set up in the middle of the empty warehouse.

Gibson motioned the henchmen forward. "You heard him. Get changed and get back out here." He picked up a small cardboard box that had his name on it and led the way through the doorway.

Alfie cautiously picked up the one with his name on it and his eyebrows shot up at how light it was. He hefted it a couple of times and gave Erin a meaningful look. She shook hers and shrugged.

The henchmen followed their leader into the dim back rooms, the men taking the room on the left and the women taking the one on the right. Alfie dropped his gear bag into a corner and started unbuckling his leg holster and belt.

"Cap, is this a usual thing, where a henchman becomes an employer?" Alfie asked as he flicked open his pocket knife and cut into the tape holding the uniform box closed.

Gibson paused with one boot in his hand, a thoughtful look on his face. "Not that I can think of, but LeRoy isn't exactly a normal henchman."

"I've noticed." Alfie laughed. "The world is probably safer with him as a henchman, though."

Gibson snorted. "I'm not going to confirm or deny that." He gave Alfie the ghost of a smile before returning to undressing.

"Stay on toes, Vihar. LeRoy likes surprises and won't stop because we are co-workers," Nikolai warned.

"Yeah, thanks. What the hell is this?" Alfie pulled a metallic jumpsuit in a gold, purple, and green harlequin pattern out of the box, and a gold mask fluttered to the floor as he shook out the thin fabric. There was also a belt with long wide strips of fabric on it to cover his gear and weapons. A quick glance around told him that they all had similar

335

pieces. A pair of gloves, one purple, one green, were at the bottom of the box along with a pair of gold sequined bits of cloth with an elastic cuff at one end and elastic strap at the other. "And what are these?" he asked, holding up the pieces in question.

Gibson glanced up. "They're spats, Vihar. They go over your boots."

"Spats?"

"Be grateful LeRoy did this instead of providing us with footwear to go with our uniforms. They never fit right and are usually difficult to run in."

Alfie looked to Gibson and Nikolai as they shook out their own uniforms. Gibson was going to be head-to-toe purple with a green cape and gold mask, gloves, and sequined spats. Nikolai's jumpsuit was a hooded black number with a knee-length green, gold, and purple harlequin-patterned tunic. His spats were covered in green sequins and he had a small container of black face paint in his box.

Alfie stared in concern as Gibson and Nikolai took in their own uniforms in disbelief. "LeRoy knows Mardi Gras was over a few months ago, right?"

Gibson took a deep breath as he studied the jumpsuit. "Boss's orders. Get dressed." He plunged his foot into the neck of the shiny green outfit, leading by example.

Nikolai and Alfie glanced at each other and followed suit. Alfie was glad to discover his jumpsuit wasn't skin tight like the one on his first job. The pants billowed from the hips but gathered at the ankles, very MC Hammer-esque, while the top was more fitted from the waist to the shoulder. The sleeves were like a second skin and had a pair of small loops at the cuff for his thumbs and middle fingers, which held the sleeves in place when he put on his gloves.

Nikolai wasn't as lucky. His black suit, complete with feet, was fitted head to toe. The tunic was a slightly heavier fabric that hung loose from his shoulders. He hooked his gear belt around his waist to hold the tunic in place, then sloppily smeared the black paint on his face.

Gibson's purple jumpsuit was loose everywhere except the wrists and ankles. The fabric puffed upward when he buckled on his belt and clipped the straps holding his leg holster in place. He put on the mask and spats, tucked the gloves into his belt, and plucked out one last piece from the box.

Alfie couldn't stop the laugh that escaped him as Gibson dropped a gold and purple turban on his head. It had strings of beads that draped off it and looked ridiculous on the hardened henchman.

One glare from the captain of Team 9 had Alfie kneeling on the floor, suddenly very interested in sliding his spats into place and picking up his mask. He glanced around, making sure he wasn't forgetting anything important, then stuffed his civies into his gear bag and hurried to follow Gibson and Nikolai out of the room.

They had beat Erin and Ray back to the main area and had to wait twenty minutes for the women to join them.

Erin's uniform was a one-sleeved black jumpsuit with a green, gold, and purple sarong tied around her waist and knee-high purple sequined spats. Her short hair had been styled into a fauxhawk that hung over her left eye.

Ray was wearing a gold top with puffy elbow-length sleeves, gold leggings, and a skirt made out of gold, purple, and green strips of sequined fabric. She was wearing thigh-high black leather spats over her leggings. Her dark hair had been straightened and pulled back into a slick ponytail that hung down her back.

They both wore ornate masks that sparkled with rhinestones and glitter.

Alfie tilted his head and looked at Erin and Ray questioningly. Ray rolled her eyes and walked past him without comment. Erin stopped and shook her head. "Dude, he had a whole stylist team in there for us. I'm wearing full makeup under this mask. So dumb." She eyed Alfie's outfit. "No stylist team for you guys, I see."

Alfie cringed and shook his head. "Nope, sorry."

Erin made a sound that was half snarl, half hairball and followed the rest of the henchmen to where LeRoy was working on the computers. Alfie was a pace behind her when he noticed other people were filling up the warehouse. Some were dressed in similarly ridiculous gold, purple, and green outfits, some were dressed in standard street gear, and some were dressed like they were going clubbing in the city.

Gibson stopped a pace behind LeRoy, and the Cajun turned as the rest of the team joined their leader. LeRoy clapped his hands in delight as he studied Team 9.

"You all look fabuleux!" He moved closer, examining each henchman individually. He adjusted Erin's sarong and kissed his fingers in approval of Ray.

Alfie cringed when LeRoy stopped in front of him. LeRoy motioned for Alfie to take off his mask, then pulled off his gloves and held out a hand to the stylist at his elbow. The woman squeezed something into LeRoy's hand, which he then smeared all over Alfie's face. Alfie sputtered and tried to dodge the attack, but the damage was already done.

Ray and Erin snickered. "You look like a disco ball!" Ray squealed. She pulled out her phone and took a picture before turning it around so Alfie could see his glitter-covered face.

Alfie made a face that was part disgust, part puppy-dog. "I look like the floor of a strip club dressing room." He put his mask on, wishing he could wear the black balaclava that was in his bag instead of the shiny gold mask that just made the glitter gleam brighter. He looked at his team helplessly as Ray snapped another picture.

LeRoy chucked Alfie under the chin before moving on to Gibson, who stared icily at him. "You try, I walk."

LeRoy hesitated the briefest of moments, the settled for reaching up to adjust Gibson's turban before moving on to Nikolai. The large Russian glared wordlessly at the small Cajun, who backed up a step. He motioned his stylist forward.

"Set it."

The stylist nodded before swiftly brushing a translucent powder over the black paint and spraying it with something in a small aerosol can. Nikolai growled at her administrations, but she just frowned up at him and gave him one more spritz.

LeRoy nodded and turned, leading the way to a parade float at the back of the warehouse. It was huge, animated, and sparkled under the lights that covered nearly every inch of it. It was a float fit for Mardi Gras royalty and looked very out of place in the dingy warehouse housing only it and the large bank of computers. One of the strangers who was dressed like Team 9 unfolded a set of stairs and helped LeRoy climb onto the float. *La Grenouille Bouché* turned dramatically to address the gathered masses, his cape flying out behind him.

339

"Welcome, everybody! We are here to make a life-long dream of mine come true. You will be handsomely rewarded if you help me succeed. You will be shamed within an inch of your life if you fail."

Alfie made a face at LeRoy and turned to see matching expressions of confusion on Ray and Erin's faces. Gibson and Nikolai looked bored. Too many years of listening to insane criminal masterminds spouting off about their genius would do that to a person, Alfie guessed.

"As you may have surmised from your très magnifiques tenues, we are going to a festival."

Ray leaned close to Alfie. "You know French, right? How did we know that we were going to a festival?"

"He said our 'very magnificent outfits,' or what apparently passes for magnificent in *La Grenouille Bouché* world," Alfie translated dryly. He was still miffed that he was the only one slathered in glitter. It would take a week to get it all off. He just hoped he didn't see his brothers or sister – or anybody else he knew – before he managed to remove the herpes of craft supplies from his face.

"I love LeRoy like a creepy second cousin, but I've seen better outfits at a bargain costume shop."

Alfie tried to hold back his laugh and loudly snorted instead. LeRoy, after a slight pause in his speech, pretended to not notice the disturbance, while Gibson gave Alfie a warning look.

Alfie and Ray exchanged conspiring grins, but the smile slowly slid from Ray's face and she took a couple steps away from Alfie. Apparently time hadn't healed that particular wound just yet.

La Grenouille Bouché threw his hands over his head. "Tonight, we celebrate the new mayor of New Orleans."

"LeRoy is mayor?" Alfie whispered in shock.

Nikolai frowned in thought, then shook his head. "I don't think so. He would have said."

"Anton Fortier was elected when they recalled the last mayor for corruption," Gibson said in answer to Alfie's question.

"Why do we–"

"Try listening, Vihar. You might learn something."

Alfie turned his attention back to LeRoy's speech, which was far more about his great attributes than about the evening's plans or what the mayor had to do with any of it.

Finally, LeRoy wrapped it up and the gathered minions clapped dutifully.

"Yeah, that didn't answer any of my questions," Alfie complained to Gibson as they climbed onto the float.

"*La Grenouille Bouché* has been playing the long game for a while. He set the last mayor up and planted evidence that he was in bed with some of the worst organized crime syndicates in the country. When he was recalled, *La Grenouille Bouché* worked on getting his puppet, Fortier, elected so he could take over."

"Ah, so why the theatrics? He could just pull Fortier's strings and control the mayor's office."

"*La Grenouille Bouché* needs the recognition and audience," Erin interjected. "You can't get that by playing puppet master."

"Exactly," Gibson agreed, nodding. "Fortier was the key to set LeRoy's plans in motion. Once he had control of the mayor's office, they would comply when he declared himself king."

Alfie stumbled a bit when the float jerked into motion but quickly steadied himself. "So what is the actual plan?"

Gibson shrugged. "LeRoy never actually explained. All he said was this float was the weapon and we were the support."

"We're bodyguards?" Ray asked, her eyebrows raising enough to be seen above the mask.

"That's what it sounds like. Nikolai." Gibson nodded his head toward the back of the float and the two walked away from the rest of Team 9.

"Why would LeRoy pay RI's prices to have a team of expert henchmen when we're just on bodyguard duty?" Alfie wondered as the float rolled through the streets of New Orleans. Alfie couldn't help but notice how much attention their appearance was garnering, and he wanted to find a hole to hide in.

Erin tilted her head in thought, seeming unsure of the answer herself.

"Because I wanted my friends here to witness ultimate success, garcon." LeRoy put an arm around Alfie. "Plus, RI henchmen add a bit of respectability to an endeavor such as this."

Alfie frowned at his former teammate and new boss. "How do you afford all of this?"

LeRoy shrugged. "I dabble a bit here and a bit there. Freelance for some organizations. It's amazing how much some people will pay for good tech."

"Bad people?"

"All sorts of people," LeRoy drawled, winking at Alfie.

"When do you sleep?"

"Sleeping is what you do when you are not motivated enough to do something more productive." LeRoy slapped Alfie's ass and headed for his place on the back of the float.

"No, sleeping is what you do so you don't die," Erin muttered at LeRoy's retreating form.

Alfie snorted. "Sleeping is what I do so other people don't die."

Erin gave him a patronizing look. "Aren't you precious?"

Alfie shrugged. "Who were all the other people in the warehouse? I didn't recognize anyone else."

"Just your standard mercs." Ray settled herself on the floor of the float and leaned back against the railing with her legs crossed at the ankles.

"Merc? Like a mercenary? LeRoy hired mercenaries?" Alfie sat down facing Ray. "There were a bunch of them, practically an army. He really is going to take over New Orleans."

Erin rolled her eyes and dropped to a knee next to Alfie. "Not likely. Unless he has some sort of powerful tech on this float, he's not going to get very far, no matter how many mercs and henchmen he hires."

"Why do you say that?"

"Alfie, how many jobs have you been on?"

"Five or so."

"Yeah, and in how many of those jobs has the bad guy actually succeeded?"

"None," Alfie replied, drawing the word out. He thought he knew where Erin was going with this line of questioning but wasn't quite sure.

"Exactly. The people who hire us never win because they go too big, too outrageous. If they kept it small and simple, quiet and behind the scenes, they'd succeed more, but they don't. That's how I know your boy isn't going to become king of New Orleans." Erin stood and walked to the front of the float, bracing a hand on an upright to steady herself when the float hit a bump.

"If that's true, we might be in trouble."

Ray frowned at Alfie. "We don't get prosecuted for things our employers do, Alfie. You know that."

Alfie shook his head and turned to study the large structure in the middle of the float that was at least ten feet tall. "That's not what I meant. I think LeRoy does have some serious tech on this float."

"We're nearing the start of the parade route," Gibson cut in, silencing Ray's response. "When we get there, we all disembark and walk along the float. Put these on and don't forget to hit record when we start." Gibson tossed each of them a small body camera. "Coms on," he ordered as he returned to the back of the float.

Alfie dug around in a pouch on his gear belt for his earpiece. He turned it on and put it in his ear as he looked between his uniform and the camera. "Just where am I supposed to attach this?"

Ray chewed her lip as she studied her own outfit before sliding the camera's clip onto the low-cut V of her shirt.

"I'm starting to hate your teammate," Erin declared as she rejoined Alfie and Ray.

"Get in line," Ray said, grinning up at her.

Erin growled as she struggled to clip the camera to the angled neckline of her jumpsuit. "The picture is going to be crooked, but that's the best they're going to get."

Alfie sat helplessly with the camera in his hand, trying to decide what to do with it, when a strip of green sequined fabric hit him in the face. He looked up to see Ray tucking a knife back into her boot.

"Tie that around your chest and hook the camera to it." She stood and went to check in with Gibson and Nikolai.

Alfie noticed a significantly shorter green strip on the side of her skirt, but did as instructed. He climbed to his feet as the float jerked to a stop. Then, he got to his feet for a second time and joined the group descending to the street.

"Here comes Fortier. He must be riding the float with *La Grenouille Bouché.*" Gibson indicated a remarkably unremarkable man walking toward them, flanked by a flurry of men and women in suits who dodged around mercs, henchmen, and regular parade participants.

LeRoy met Fortier at the stairs of the float and welcomed him aboard, pointing out all the interesting features of the float and gesturing exuberantly. Fortier's entourage was blocked from joining them and banished to the sidelines.

"Do you think he realizes he's throwing away his life by agreeing to be LeRoy's puppet?" Alfie asked nobody in particular.

Erin shrugged. "He probably doesn't even realize he's being played. Political puppets are picked for a skeleton-free closet, not their brains."

"Sad for him," Ray said. "Come on, guys. Gibson said the three of us are supposed to stay on the right side of the float near LeRoy. Gibson and Nikolai have the left. We protect *La Grenouille Bouché.*"

"I hope LeRoy doesn't think I'm taking a bullet for him. I like the guy, but not that much," Alfie grumbled.

"Nobody expects a henchman to take a bullet for their employer—"

"Except the madmen who employ us," Ray interrupted.

Erin nodded. "Sure, it does happen from time to time, but more often than not, it's an accident." She begrudgingly waved at the gathered crowd at the urging from the float's occupants. "It's like these people have never elected a mayor before. Do they do these parades every time?"

"No, but after the last mayor, they thought the city could use a celebration as a way to clear out the old, corrupt office and ring in a new, greater one," a man dressed as a jester, complete with bells on his hat and curled-toe shoes, explained as he walked by. He worked the crowd, getting them riled up by yelling and doing flips.

Team 9 stared after him. "I can't do that," Alfie whispered.

Erin shrugged. "Who can?"

Ray grinned at them, settled her mask in place, and took a few running steps, launching herself into a roundoff that led into a series of back handsprings and finished with a backflip.

The crowd went wild.

Ray bowed a few times, giving Erin and Alfie enough time to catch up with her. She rejoined them without a word.

"Really? We're not going to talk about that?" Erin asked after a minute of silence.

Ray shrugged and turned her attention to the crowd, waving and watching for any suspicious actions.

"We're nearing the stage," Gibson said through the coms. "It is on the steps of the Global Exchange building, big marble structure with the columns coming up on the north side of the street. The float will stop in front of it and Fortier will go to the podium to give his speech. That's when *La Grenouille Bouché* will burst in to make his demands. Be ready when that happens."

"I suddenly feel very vulnerable in this outfit," Erin whispered as she went on high alert for attacks.

Alfie's heart started beating faster and he began to breathe heavily. What was he doing going into a fight wearing nothing but a giant shiny onesie the approximate thickness of pantyhose? He tensed up and his stomach rolled. He barely trusted LeRoy as a teammate, and now he was following his orders. He was in a city he'd never been to, surrounded by a crowd of people that could turn into a mob in an instant, protecting a man who may or may not have a giant death ray hidden inside a parade float that would make RuPaul say, "Tone it down."

He jumped when he felt somebody touch his arm.

"Alfie? Are you ok?" Ray was holding his elbow. She and Erin had closed in around him in concern.

"What? Of course!" Alfie tried to bluff his way out, but he didn't even sound convincing to himself.

"You're close to hyperventilating and you're whiter than normal, which is pretty impressive for a ginger."

Alfie nodded. This was the nicest Ray had been to him since they broke up and he wasn't about to say anything to mess it up. He forced himself to inhale through his nose and exhale though his mouth, concentrating on slowing his heartbeat. "Sorry, guys. Just realized that I'm out here in basically a lycra condom and have no idea what's about to happen. Freaked myself out a bit."

Ray released him when she could tell he had calmed down.

"Happens to us all." Erin patted his shoulder and returned to watching the crowd.

"We're here, get into place," Gibson ordered through the coms as the float came to a halt.

Ray, Alfie, and Erin were on the opposite side of the float from the stage, and their job was to watch the far side of the street for anybody who might make a move on Fortier or *La Grenouille Bouché*. They spread out to cover as much of the street as they could. Alfie couldn't stop his hand from tucking under the fabric that hung down his right leg to touch the handgun holstered underneath.

The crowd erupted in cheers when Anton Fortier took the stage, and it took a few minutes for them to settle down enough for him to start his speech. It was the basic "Thanks for electing me, we're going to clean up the city, we can do anything if we work together, we'll turn NOLA back into the jewel we know it is" stuff that politicians always spout.

Alfie stopped listening after the first few sentences. He was busy keeping himself calm while looking for any suspicious activity in the crowd.

Then, all the lights on the entire block went out, and Alfie froze. It was nerve-racking to know he was surrounded by thousands of people but was unable to see any of them. Disoriented and unsure about what was going on, the crowd didn't move. Many people took out their cell phones and tried turning on the flashlights, but none of them worked.

Alfie could sense the panic rising, both in the crowd and in himself. He wrapped a hand around his gun and touched the safety with his thumb, leaving it activated but ready to flip it off at the first sign of trouble.

"*La Grenouille Bouché* is on the move." Gibson's whisper both startled and comforted Alfie. "The lights are about to come back on, so if you put on any night vision equipment, take it off now."

"I want night vision equipment," Alfie mumbled to himself, trying to remain calm.

"Alf, you alright?" Ray asked quietly from somewhere to his right.

"Define alright," Alfie grumbled.

Ray chuckled lightly. "You're doing just fine, smartass."

Gibson's voice came through the coms. "Lights on in three… two…"

Alfie squeezed his eyes shut so he wouldn't be blinded and held his gun tighter.

"One."

The lights came back on. Less than two minutes had passed since darkness fell, but it had felt like an eternity to the henchmen who knew to expect something but didn't know exactly what.

"Citizens of New Orleans, welcome to a new age!"

Alfie flinched as LeRoy's voice boomed from the speakers.

"This is going to be good." Erin's droll comment made Alfie snort.

"I am *La Grenouille Bouché* and I am your new king!"

Alfie rolled his eyes as confusion and humor rolled through the crowd. Someone nearby jeered, "It's not even Mardi Gras yet, so what's with the king stunt?"

The one response that wasn't evident was fear. Alfie relaxed slightly. Maybe this whole thing would end without any problems and the crowd would just think it was a prank.

A faint sound in the distance made Alfie turn north, straining to decipher what it was. "Does anybody else hear sirens?" Alfie asked over the coms.

"Yeah," Erin confirmed. "They're a ways out. Must be something going on somewhere else in the district."

"I'll check the police scanner," Gibson responded.

"Ah, I see some of you do not believe me." LeRoy's tone turned from mocking to victorious. "Well, let me give you proof."

Alfie, Erin, and Ray turned as one when a loud mechanical sound came from the float behind them. The women gasped and Alfie groaned when the tall center portion of the float folded down, revealing the large death ray LeRoy had been working on in the lab after the Ore job.

"What the actual f— Gibson, what is the plan here?" Erin yelled into her microphone. Revealing the huge machine had riled up the crowd and people were beginning to panic.

"Yes, New Orleans! That is a death ray! Powerful enough to wipe out an entire city block with just one push of a button. Declare me your king and all will be spared!" LeRoy's gleeful giggle was jarring against his maniacal declaration.

"Cops are headed this way," Gibson said over the coms. "You won't believe why."

"Really, cap?! I think we'd believe it!" Ray gestured dramatically at the death ray towering above them.

"Nope, I'll fill you in later. *La Grenouille Bouché*'s announcement has increased their numbers. Regular police and SWAT are headed this way in force. Get ready."

Alfie backed toward the float as a pair of uniforms ran through the crowd in front of him. "They're here!" he yelled into the mic as he turned and ran for the float, Ray and Erin on his tail. They climbed onto the gaudy creation of a disturbed mind and crouched behind whatever cover they could find.

"What's the plan here, Gibson?" Erin asked again, her voice a bit shrill.

"We do what we were hired for. Protect *La Grenouille Bouché*. The mercs will deal with the rest."

The float jerked as police officers climbed aboard. Erin, Alfie, and Ray headed for the opposite side, drawing their weapons and keeping behind cover as much as they could.

Alfie didn't see the officer until it was too late. A man popped up, cutting off Alfie's retreat to the other side of the float. He veered away from the cop and headed for the back, the movement of so many people making footing unsteady. He came to a dead end with a set of stairs that led to the platform at the back that LeRoy and Fortier had occupied the whole way there. Alfie glanced behind him and decided the platform was the only place he could go.

The horror movies he had watched growing up had taught him that it was the last place he wanted to be, but it was his only option. He just hoped there was a way to climb back down to the street on the other side.

Alfie rolled onto the platform, trying to stay as low as possible. He pulled off his mask, holstered his gun, and ripped off the fabric that was hiding his gear belt. He didn't need the added material coming between him and his extra mags or tangling in his legs. He crawled to the other side of the platform, not expecting a ladder, but what he found made him less than hopeful. There was a scaffolding of sorts that held the suspended strings of lights, but it looked like it was made of thin strips of wood and wire. Footsteps on the stairs made his decision for him. He holstered his gun and rolled so he went feet-first over the side. The first few wooden slats held, but Alfie could feel them give and creak as he made his way down.

"Stop!"

351

Katherine Wielechowski

Alfie looked up to see a gun barrel pointed right at him, an angry officer behind it. His foot slipped and hit the next slat, causing it to break and starting a domino effect of broken wood. Alfie struggled to find purchase anyway he could, but gravity was too fast. He jerked to a sudden stop as pain shot through his left arm; a string of lights had wrapped around his arm, keeping him from hitting the street in a pile, but it cut through the fabric of his sleeve and into his skin. He looked down to see he was just a few inches off the street. Enough for his toes to brush the pavement. He tried to pull himself up on the slats to make enough slack to untangle his arm, but the wood kept collapsing under his weight. He tugged at the wire, praying for it to give way from the scaffolding or for it to release from his arm.

Pain was making him lightheaded.

Warmth on his arm told him that the wire had broken the skin and he was bleeding.

The numbness in his fingers was a warning that if he didn't get free soon, he was in real trouble.

"Vihar!"

Nikolai's gruff voice almost made Alfie collapse in relief. "Nikolai, I can't get free!"

Nikolai joined him at the back of the float, staying close to the scaffolding to give a smaller target to the police on the platform. He felt around Alfie's arm, trying to unwind the wire. He stopped when Alfie groaned in pain. Nikolai studied the rigging for a moment, then grabbed the wire just above Alfie's hand and yanked down with all his might.

The platform collapsed, taking down three cops with it. Nikolai managed to pull Alfie back far enough to dodge most of the falling debris. He unwrapped the wire from Alfie's arm and surveyed the damage.

352

"Missed the important stuff." Nikolai grabbed Alfie's bicep and pulled him to where the henchmen had hunkered down behind the trailing float. It had somehow gotten tipped onto its side and was half on the sidewalk, half on the street.

"Where did you disappear to?" Ray asked as Nikolai and Alfie dropped down next to her and Erin.

"Got hung up." Alfie grinned slightly and held up his arm.

"Holy shit," Ray cursed. She pulled a roll of gauze from her belt and started wrapping Alfie's arm tight enough to control the bleeding.

"Gonna lose the arm, Vihar?" Gibson asked, looking back at him from where he crouched at the edge of the float, keeping an eye out for police.

"Yep, but I've got another one. It was just there for balance, anyway."

"Good to hear," Gibson said, nodding as he rose up just a bit to get a better view of the madness unfolding in the street.

The police and SWAT had swarmed the area, throwing smoke bombs and corralling parade goers. People were screaming and running in fear, trying to escape the chaos. Some people had even started fighting the mercs and holding them until the police could round them up.

There was no sign of *La Grenouille Bouché*.

"We need to find LeRoy," Gibson said. "The last place I had eyes on him was at the podium right before the first smoke bombs went off. Nikolai and Erin, you two swing around the far side of the stage. Ray, get Vihar fixed up, then you two take this side. I'll go down the middle. We need to find him and keep him safe. See if we can get him out of here in one piece. I've got some bad news: there's another

353

criminal team in play. The cops don't know if we're with them or in the wrong place at the wrong time, which means the normal rules don't apply."

"So we're fair game?" Erin asked, cracking her neck.

Nikolai shook his head. "They're fair game."

Gibson's eyes narrowed slightly. "Avoid getting shot. Don't rampage the cops, they're doing their job. Ray?"

Ray tied off the gauze at Alfie's elbow. "All set."

Gibson nodded. "Alright, everybody head out."

Alfie stayed seated as everybody rushed out from behind the float. Ray hung back. "You okay?"

Alfie nodded, trying to control his stomach and ignore the pain throbbing through his arm. He inhaled deeply and pulled his handgun from its holster. "Let's go."

They ran in a crouch toward the stage, keeping an eye out for their employer and any nearby police. Alfie risked standing so he could see on the stage platform while Ray dropped to her stomach and half crawled under it. She pulled a flashlight from her belt and shone it around, hoping to see LeRoy hiding in the darkness. She wriggled back out, unsuccessful. Alfie shook his head and pointed around the corner. Ray nodded and followed as he led her around the corner of the stage to the front.

Alfie heard something scrape against the street behind him seconds before he heard Ray cry out. He turned in time to see a uniformed officer grab her and start dragging her away from the stage. Alfie dropped his shoulder and tackled the man, taking all three of them to the ground. He managed to flip the cop over and slip some zipcuffs around his hands before the man could get his bearings. Alfie crawled over to where Ray was slowly getting to her knees, a hand pressed to her cheek.

"You're bleeding."

Ray waved off his administrations. "It's not bad. We need to find LeRoy." She stumbled to her feet and turned right into another cop who had his gun pointed at her head.

"Freeze!"

Alfie threw himself at the officer's feet, knocking him to the ground, then scrambled over the man to pull the gun from his hand and threw it with enough force that it slid under the stage. Ray was ready with another pair of zipcuffs and between them, they got the second officer on his stomach with his hands tied behind his back.

"Stop. Doing. That," Alfie huffed. Ray smiled at him from across the cop's prone form and nodded her chin toward the stage.

"Yeah. After you." Alfie could feel his strength waning. He just hoped he could make it until they found LeRoy and got somewhere safe.

Ray was just a few steps ahead of him when she went around the front of the stage, but a swell of people cut him off and he lost her in the crowd. An errant elbow connected with the side of his head and he went down hard. He caught some kicks to the ribs and what felt like a knife or a very sharp heel punctured his thigh. Alfie managed to roll free of the mob and found safety under the stage; the cacophony was muffled somewhat and the darkness was comforting. He struggled to stay conscious. "Somebody tell me what's going on," he said into his mic.

"We got LeRoy!" Erin shouted through the coms. "But we're pinned down on the float ahead of ours."

"Alfie, I lost you in the crowd. Where are you?" Ray asked.

"I'm either under the stage or I've gone blind."

"Stay there, I'm coming back for you."

"No, I'm safe for now. Get to Erin and Nikolai. I'll work my way there when I can."

"All converge on Erin's location," Gibson ordered.

He groaned but managed to roll over onto his stomach and crawl to the side of the stage closest to his target. Alfie paused, timing his emergence from safety when a crowd was close enough to block him from the cops but not so close that they would trample him again. He merged with the crowd, moving toward the float where Team 9 was meeting. He saw Ray climb onto it and race toward the back.

Alfie froze as a cop in riot gear came out from behind cover and aimed their rifle at Ray's back.

"RAY!" he shouted, unable to do anything else.

Ray turned and spotted the threat in an instant. She knocked the gun away and the two grappled. Ray hit the officer hard enough to stun them, giving her valuable seconds to turn and run, but it wasn't enough. The cop tackled her from behind and as floor gave way under them, they disappeared from sight.

Alfie gritted his teeth against the pain in his arm and leg and forced himself into a jog toward the float his team was on. He didn't know how much help he would be to them in his condition, but he had to try.

Out of the corner of his eye, he caught sight of another form in riot gear, this one sporting a gas mask. Seconds later, his lungs and eyes started burning. He doubled over, coughing, his face exploding with fire.

As he hit the pavement, Alfie heard Gibson croak, "Tear gas." He watched helplessly as Team 9 was pulled off the float in cuffs and led away by the police.

"Here's another one."

Alfie looked up at the muffled words to see another gas mask floating above him. Rough hands rolled him over and cuffed him before pulling him to his feet.

Everything hurt.

Everything except his left hand. He was pretty sure that was just gone.

He was escorted to an ambulance that was set up behind police barricades, separate from the first aid station that was set up for injured members of the public, and uncuffed so a medic could look him over.

The woman was all business until she saw the condition of his arm and visually flinched when she got to his hand. "Did you know you broke a finger?"

Katherine Wielechowski

Author's Note:

I know some of you might be let down or disappointed with how the Henchmen series ended. I read somewhere that an author should never defend their work, but I thought I might explain the ending. Hopefully, it will give you a little closure if you need it.

1-800-Henchmen was about Alfie's adventures at Resources, Inc. With the threat to his family, Alfie had no choice but to leave RI, thus ending the series. The events of the last two books forced Alfie to face things he never thought he would ever experience in his life, and he was unprepared to deal with them. He felt that the first step to try to repair his life was to leave the organization that put his loved ones in danger. Alfie grew up a lot in his months as a henchman and he showed wisdom and self-sacrifice in leaving RI for the sake of his family.

I had so much fun writing the Henchmen series. I love the characters and enjoyed going on their adventures with them. I may check up on them in the coming months or years to see what they've been up to. If they have kept up their shenanigans, I'll share their stories with you.

About the Author

Katherine Wielechowski is a Nebraska native who currently lives and works in Lincoln, NE. She started writing seriously while attending the University of South Dakota where she double majored in English and History. Her self-diagnosed ADD is blamed for her inability to stick to one genre and she has dabbled in historical romance, fantasy, horror, action, humor, dystopian fiction, and non-fiction. Her action-comedy novella series, *1-800-Henchmen,* is available on amazon.com as are her romantic-comedy novellas, *Love Drunk & Dragon Tears* and *Shenanigans & Jello Shots.*

You will also find her short stories "The Banshee Ciana" in *Portable Magic*, a collection of stories published by The Story Plant, "The Vaults" in *Below the Stairs: Tales from the Cellar*, a collection of horror stories published by OzHorror.com, and an excerpt from her novel *The Whiskey Widow* in the first Nebraska Writers Guild Anthology, *Voices from the Plains*.

She is surrounded by friends and family who act as cheerleaders and are constantly giving her welcomed advice and inspiration for her stories. She could not do this without them.

Follow Katherine on Facebook at www.facebook.com/Kwielech or read her blog *The Blank Page* at kwielech.blogspot.com.

Made in the USA
Monee, IL
30 July 2023

40114359R00203